POWER PLAY

MIKE NICOL

First published in the United Kingdom in 2015 by Old Street Publishing Ltd,
Yowlestone House, Tiverton, Devon EX16 8LN
www.oldstreetpublishing.co.uk

Published in South Africa by Umuzi, an imprint of Penguin Random House

ISBN 978 1 910400 21 0

10 9 8 7 6 5 4 3 2

A CIP catalogue record for this title is available from the British Library.

Printed and bound by CPI Group (UK) Ltd, Croydon, CR0 4YY

ABOUT THE AUTHOR

Mike Nicol was born in Cape Town, where he lives and writes. He is the author of several prize-winning works of fiction and non-fiction.

Of Cops & Robbers
The Revenge Trilogy:
Payback
Killer Country
Black Heart

'Here is a place of disaffection'
– T.S. ELIOT, *Four Quartets*

He sat in a chair beside the swimming pool. A big man with a shaven head watching her. The man she'd been hunting.

Mkhulu Gumede.

Sitting there with statue stillness, wearing a black jacket, open-necked shirt, black slacks. The shirt untucked. The jacket's sleeve pulled back at his left wrist, a trace of silver exposed. As if he'd arranged himself, carefully, purposefully.

The hunted come to the hunter.

Krista Bishop in her kitchen making coffee. Just returned from the pursuit, her backpack slung down on the countertop. Her gun in the bag.

Across the mountain the dawn light was hardening, darkness drawing back into the trees.

Mkhulu Gumede sat there watching her, unperturbed.

At the sight of him, Krista felt the adrenaline kick in. A sudden clarity. Her heart faster, a pulse in her neck, heat on the palms of her hands.

Remembered she'd been warned. He's a killer. That's what he's been trained to do. To kill.

Yes, well, she thought, me too.

Here the man she'd waited for all night in the quiet suburban street. That man, here, now, in her garden, waiting for her.

She slid a hand along the marble countertop, grasped her backpack, drew it slowly towards her.

Enough light now to see the man's face. The black eyes watching her. Confident. Relaxed. His hands loosely in his lap.

Had to be concealing a gun. Thing was, why sit there waiting for her? Like they were going to talk about it over coffee. Calmly. Reach some sort of understanding? Shake on it? They both go back into their lives. Game over.

After what he'd done?

No, boykie. No ways. No ways ever.

Her father saying to her, 'There comes a payback time, C. Probably it's a law of the universe. You know, an energy or something.'

The wisdom of Papa Mace. Not a girl's best role model.

'You always get a chance at justice. Just not often legal justice.'

Mace Bishop saying to her, 'Take it when it comes. Only comes round once. Be ready. You miss you can kiss your arse goodbye.' Always the sage. The two of them on the shooting range, killing targets of cardboard men.

She remembered these things he'd told her. Years ago. Seemed like years ago.

Her focus in this moment. The light sharper. The city below still in shadow. Sun coming onto the high cliffs, sliding down the mountain, reaching into the gorges. The glint of it off the cableway lines, the cable cars starting out of their stations.

She took the gun from her bag, found the silencer. Raised the pistol so he could see it. So he could see her fitting the can.

He kept watching. Didn't move. Didn't shake his head, hold up a hand to say, No need. We don't have to go there. Doesn't have to be like that. Didn't even show his weapon. So sure of himself.

He's a killer.

She knew that. No argument there, the reason she was chasing him.

The Bialetti came to the boil, spitting. She kept her eyes on him. Put the gun down, switched off the gas. Without looking found the handle to the coffee pot, lifted the pot from the hob. Watched him watching her. No movement in his face, no twitch, no grimace, no tightening of the skin around his mouth. Just the languid gaze. Alright, my brother, we play this game.

Krista took her eyes off him, poured herself a demitasse. Flicked back at him – he hadn't moved. Sat there relaxed, feet square on the floor. The only tension about him, the placement of his feet. Ready to stand, ready for anything.

She noticed his shoes then. Not trainers – she expected trainers – but long pointed-toe dress shoes. City-slicker pointers. What was it with guys and these shoes? They fancied them. Some hip image they craved.

She blew lightly across the coffee's surface. Wet her lips in anticipation, brought up the cup, tasted a hot mouthful. The French roast full on her tongue. Swallowed, felt the tension ease in her neck.

Nothing for it. Get out there, get it done.

Krista took another quick sip, put down the cup. With the pistol in her right hand, walked to the sliding door. Unlocked it, pushed it open. Stepped onto the patio. Faced him. The bastard not moving, staring at her. About nine metres separating them.

She heard him say, 'What's it you want?'

Oh, my brother, what a question. If you don't know the answer to that, what kind of agent are you? What kind of game are you running?

'To kill you,' she said.

He nodded. The only movement he'd made, thoughtful.

She heard the mountain for the first time then. Bird twitter. The shrill of cicadas anticipating the day's heat. From below, in the City Bowl, the morning prayer rising, a low hum. Smelt the camphor of the vegetation, the tang of summer.

In this time and place they talked. To no end. Staccato sentences, a language of difference. Until the words ended.

'You can try talking,' she heard Mace telling her. 'Sometimes it works. Most times it doesn't. Most times, in the end, you have to act.'

You're right, Papa, she thought, listening to Mkhulu Gumede making excuses.

Seeing him stand, holding the gun against his thigh: the long barrel, the silencer. Don't want to disturb the neighbours. She raised her pistol, held it on him.

'This's not only about Tami,' she said. 'D'you know what they did to her, to Lavinia?'

Hearing him going on about Titus the gangster, the gang wars on the Cape Flats, abalone poaching, the coming of the Chinese. Hearing him, not hearing him.

Watching him take a step towards her. Asking her to lower the gun. 'Please. Please lower the gun.' So condescending.

She kept the gun up, unwavering. He stopped.

'In a situation,' Mace would say, 'you got to get in first. Take this scene: you're in a confrontation, you're standing there, you've both got guns. He's the invader. Law says you can use equal force. So what you going to do? You can wait till he shoots you. You can. Be a good girl, stick to the letter. Then retaliate, let him have it. Assuming he's not killed you by taking *the advantage. Or you drop him. Me, I'd drop him. Worry about the law afterwards.'*

Mace Bishop Rules. Mace always inclined to sort things out his way when he had to.

'Step back,' she said. 'Sit down.'

Or what? Or you'll take Mace's advice?

Mkhulu Gumede didn't move. Except she saw the grip on his gun tighten, his arm rising.

Part 1: Lagoon Beach

1

I

They ate supper in a steak and seafood joint at Lagoon Beach, Titus Anders not letting go of how their little brother Boetie died.

Trussed in weight belts, dropped over the side of a rubber ducky in six metres of dark water, he went down to talk to the abalone. RIP Boetie.

'Yesterday I watched him going off with his chommies. Going camping in the mountains. All happy boys. Good boys. Nice boys. Teenagers, you know, joking around, no problems in the world. This morning he's dead.'

Fishermen found his body chained to a plastic buoy, mistook it for an abalone drop just waiting for smugglers. *Property of Titus Anders* written on the buoy.

'Stop it, Daddy,' said Luc, Titus's eldest. 'Leave it now. Please. We all feeling this.'

'No, man, I can't believe it,' said Titus, looking at Luc. 'Boetie was my boy. Your mommy's precious because they thought he was dead inside her. She said to me, "Look after Boetie, Titus. You got to look after him for me. Give him a good life." That's what she said. I never told you that before. Now look what we got to do.' He made a gun of his fist, held it up. 'I thought all this was past times. Over. Finished.'

'Not your problem, Daddy,' said Luc. 'Me'n Quint'll handle it. Like I told you. We got it sorted already.'

'You know what it's like to drown?' said Titus. 'Going down there holding your breath till you can't anymore. Till you have to breathe. Only you know when you open your mouth there's going to be no air. Only water. You know the panic that'll cause? The fright? Oh no, man, is there a worse way to die? Your lungs filling up with water.'

'Daddy, stop it.' Lavinia, his daughter, sitting there toying with her food.

'Don't,' said Luc, reaching across to grab his father's hand, lower it to the table. He glanced round the restaurant. Big zooty restaurant with views over Table Bay, the harbour, the soccer stadium flopped like a puffer fish beneath Signal Hill. Family diners at most of the tables. A Neil Diamond loop on the sound system. 'Not here, Daddy.'

Quint said, 'What's the plan?'

Quint the youngest of the family now, a monster man of muscle, neck the size of his head. Quint worked out, daily, ate a lot of meat. Had on the plate before him a five-hundred-gram T-bone, well done. A pile of fries beside it that spilled onto the table. What Quint meant was what would happen to the boy they'd got chained to a chair in a Montague Gardens warehouse.

The boy they'd taken as tit for tat not even an hour after they'd seen Boetie's body. Quint liked to think he and Luc worked fast.

'We got to kill him,' said Luc, cutting into his steak. He forked a chunk, chewed it. Tough, well-done steak the way he liked it. The brothers of a similar mind on their steaks, though Luc was a thin guy, weedy. Said, 'We cut him into pieces. Send him back to his mommy by PostNet.'

Titus said, 'These boys are too young. You can't use boys like this.'

'Wasn't us that started it,' said Luc. 'But we got to finish it. You know that, Daddy. You know that's what we got to do. It's what you would of done in the old days before. Nothing's changed. Then and now it's all the same.'

'I can't eat this,' said Titus, pushing away his plate.

He'd brought them in here because a family like his had to be seen. Had to act normal in times of trouble. For the sake of Boetie. Show everyone that the Anders family couldn't be messed with. Titus Untouchable.

Which meant blood in, blood out. Just why'd it have to be Boetie? Why'd she go for him? Not going to be so nice for her now they had her boy.

Titus looked at his daughter. 'What d'you think, Lavinia?'

Lavinia, a stunner. Big brown eyes. Delicate nose. Pouty lips that didn't often smile. His princess. She talked fancy. She gave the Anders name class. Titus thought that except for her dead mother, she was the only other woman he loved. Anything happened to her … He couldn't hold the thought, couldn't do that sort of what-if scenario.

Lavinia shrugged, nibbled at her onion rings. 'You want to do that, you do that, I don't care.'

'She killed your brother.'

'We've gotta hurt her,' said Quint.

'To even the score?' Lavinia stared at him. 'You think that'll settle it?'

'No,' said Titus. 'But where's our option?'

Lavinia flicked hair out of her face; it fell back in fine strands. 'There is always another option.'

'Like what?' said Luc.

'You got a plan?' said Titus.

'She's got shit for brains.' Luc sneering at his sister.

Lavinia raised her fork, brought it close to Luc's face. No anger in her gesture, just the menace of the fork millimetres from his face.

'What you want to do, sis?'

'Stab out your other eye,' she said. Luc with a pirate patch over his eye. As kids she'd blinded him in the right. Used a stick she'd found on the beach to limit his vision. So much for fun times at the seaside.

Titus waited until Lavinia lowered her fork. 'What's your plan?'

'I haven't got a plan.'

'So what d'you think? Man, girl, don't get clever with words.'

Lavinia went back to her onion rings. Long, fine

fingers picking at the food. Bright gold bands on her fingers.

'Tamora's your problem, Daddy,' she said.

'Ja, I know,' said Titus. 'That's what Luc's telling me.'

'She's a big problem, Daddy,' said Lavinia.

'That's why we gotta chop her boy into pieces.' Luc sat back. 'Teach her a lesson. Like tooth for tooth.'

'Eye for eye, first,' said Lavinia, looking at him, un-smiling. Luc frowned at her.

'We got to do it for Boetie,' said Quint. 'Tonight. Quickly like they did it to him.'

Titus let this rest there, thinking he didn't want it. He didn't want more blood. But what other way out? They didn't do this, Tamora would piss in his face.

'Alright,' said Titus. 'You and Luc.'

'We can chop him up?'

'You want to do that?'

'Shit, Luc,' said Lavinia. 'Just shoot him. What's your problem?'

'No problem.'

'Just shoot him, okay? One of those slow bullets. No mess, okay? Take him into the sand dunes, okay.'

Quint glanced at her and away, his jaw working at the meat.

'Pretty little sis giving orders,' said Luc. Held up his hand, the one with the deformed finger, made it into a gun as Titus had done: 'Just shoot him, okay. One of those slow bullets, okay. Take him out into the sand dunes, okay.'

19

'Luc,' said Titus. 'Stop now. Enough.'

Wasn't Luc though, it was Lavinia, always on her brother's case. Like the two were born to irritate one another. Sometimes Lavinia coming out with stuff like she was a hardarse woman. Use one of those slow bullets! Jesus!

They ate in silence. Titus opposite Lavinia, facing the view. The sun setting, the ocean turned liquid gold. Grief in his heart. Grief for a drowned son. Anger too that he'd been disrespected. That a woman he'd given a break was biting his bum. He pulled his plate back, ate without taste. There would be heartache. There would be tears. He was Titus.

Titus set down his steak knife, his meal half-eaten. He signalled for the restaurant owner. The man hurrying to him, grinning.

'Mr Anders.'

'Calvados,' said Titus. Pointing a finger round his family.

'Only the best,' said the restaurateur. He picked up Titus's plate. 'Something wrong, Mr Anders? The meal was good?'

'Fine,' said Titus. 'The Calvados, alright? And the bill.'

'On the house, Mr Anders,' said the restaurateur. 'Always a pleasure for your family.'

'I'll pay.' Titus waved his palm over the table. 'Tax deductable.'

The owner smiled. 'Sure, no problem' – calling to have the table cleared.

'I'm not finished, Daddy,' said Quint.

'Get a doggy bag.' Lavinia shoved her plate at him. 'You can have mine too.'

'It's raw.'

'Rare.'

Quint forked her meat onto his plate. 'I'll nuke it at home.'

'You better,' said Luc. 'A vet gets that, he can make it moo.'

Shots of Calvados were set down, the waiter said, 'Mr Titus, that man' – indicating across the restaurant – 'says he's paying for your drinks. He sends condolences.'

'Thank him,' said Titus, raised his glass in the man's direction. The man palmed his hands in supplication, bowed over them.

'Who's that?' said Quint.

Titus tasted the brandy. Got the kick of it at the back of his throat. 'Someone we helped with a loan.'

Luc snorted. 'He pays for the drinks with our money.'

'No, man.' Titus stared at his son. 'Don't always think the worst, man, Luc. He paid up. He acknowledges us. Our grief.'

'With interest?'

Titus shook his head. 'Don't start, okay, don't start.'

Luc kept his gaze lowered, toyed with his drink. He looked up there was Lavinia smirking at him. He wagged a finger at her.

'Come,' said Titus to the waiter, 'clear the plates. And a doggy bag for Quint.'

Lavinia's BlackBerry buzzed.

'Lover boy's after you,' said Luc. The sneer on his face now, his tongue snaked at his top lip. 'Doesn't matter that our little Boetie's been killed. Wants to know if it's his lucky night.' Luc taking up the song with Neil, singing: 'Hands, touching hands. Good times …'

'Shut up.' Lavinia focused on the phone screen. 'Just shut up, alright?'

'Is that Rings?' said Titus. 'Tell him howzit.' Titus holding out his drink. 'Come, come, chink chink for your brother.' They touched glasses. 'Boetie.'

Drank the rest of the apple brandy in a single toss.

'We got to do this now,' said Quint.

'Ja.' Titus stood, smoothed the sleeves of his leather jacket. Looked round for the owner, saw him standing at the grills, a cellphone to his ear. The owner saluted, saying 'Ciao, ciao.' Titus giving him a thumbs up.

The family angled through the restaurant, people saying sorry for your loss as they passed. Reaching out to touch them. Men shaking their hands. Women wanting to stroke Lavinia's arms. Lavinia holding herself rigid.

Titus unsmiling, thinking bad news got around fast. Was the right thing to be here. Give everyone the message, don't mess with the Anders.

A waiter holding open the door, offering a bowl of mints. Luc pushed past, turned to Lavinia. 'Bring you back some pictures, hey, sis.'

Outside the evening warm, windless.

II

Two gents in a Beemer M5 waited down the street from the seafood and steakhouse. Tamora's men: the driver and the shooter.

The driver's cellphone rang. 'They're leaving,' he was told.

The driver heard restaurant buzz: 'Sweet Caroline', chit-chat, the clatter of plates. He heard a voice call out, 'Ciao, ciao.' The driver thumbed off the connection. He fired the car, pointed down the street. 'Spot on, my friend.'

The shooter said something in Russian the driver didn't understand.

'What you saying?'

'Go, go,' said the Russian.

For more than an hour they'd sat there waiting. The Russian not talking much, the driver playing his iPod through the sound system, a medley of R&B, jelly-baby warbling.

The Russian had said, 'Shit music.'

'You got something else?' The driver sitting up in his seat. 'Let's hear it.'

The Russian had mumbled in Russian.

'Speak English.'

'Your arse,' said the Russian.

The driver's name: Black Aron Chetty. As he'd told the Russian, pronounced A-ron. He didn't know the Russian's name. Wasn't interested to know. Couldn't understand why Tamora wanted the Russian on the job.

'He shoots straight,' she'd said.

'I don't, you're saying?' Black Aron came back. Black Aron squirming beneath Tamora, popped his load between her thighs. She pressed down on his groin, grinding against him. Had sighed out, 'Depends on the rod.'

The Russian had an Uzi pistol, semi-automatic.

'Go,' he said to Black Aron. 'Go.'

Black Aron let out the clutch, easing the car into the street. No traffic. 'You wait until they're in their car,' he said, 'we're civilised here. Not like Moscow.'

'Your arse,' said the Russian.

'Why d'you use a gun like that?' Black Aron tapped his index finger against his head. 'Stupid gun. Stupid.' Black Aron pointed at the Russian. 'You.'

The Russian grinned at him, a perfect set of gold teeth. Lifted the Uzi, rubbed the muzzle behind Black Aron's ear. 'You think, stupid?'

Black Aron knocked the gun away. 'Just do your job, Smirnoff.'

He could see the Anders family getting into their car, a Merc, late '80s-style 300-series. Prick Titus could buy new models every year, but he kept an antique. Some kind of man-of-the-people gesture. Big windows to shoot them through. Nice one, Titus.

'You kill them, you won't find the boy,' Black Aron had said to Tamora. Not his place to make comments but sometimes he risked it.

Like earlier with Tamora dressed up in slacks, a

jacket (no camisole, no bra underneath), killer heels for some maker-and-shaker dinner. You saw her like that with her short spiky hair, slim figure, you wouldn't say she ran the Mongols gang, smuggled abalone for a living. You wouldn't say tattooed men with no front teeth listened to her.

As they'd left her apartment, she'd said, 'The boy's dead.' Her teenage son she was talking about, like she didn't care. Which Aron reckoned she didn't. The boy'd been living with other people for years. Story was she'd dumped him in some foster home for a couple of grand a month subsidy.

'You worry about the Russian,' she'd said. 'No cock-ups.'

The other thing about Tamora Black Aron couldn't work out was why she screwed him. He was low rent. Her driver. Her skivvy. Her messenger. She was moving up. Meeting important people. She gave orders. Got consignments.

Once he'd asked why me? She'd smiled, stroked his cheek. 'Is my A-ron nervous?' she'd said, coming in close to whisper in his ear. Her tongue teasing. 'Nervous he'll get pushed?' Her breath hot against his skin. 'Why d'you think?' she'd said, slid her hand down into his crotch. 'You give good cock, Aron.'

Which was the deal.

Which Black Aron Chetty saw as a skill he had the way some men were good at carpentry. For the moment he could live with it. Ever ready, though, for the throwaway occasion. Like she'd discarded her son.

'The boy's dead.' Tamora realistic.

'You don't know.'

'I know.'

'For sure?'

'The soon as they found sharkbait Boetie all weighted down, they took my boy. I know Titus, he kills chop-chop.'

'You can't be certain.' Black Aron going out on a limb. Not that he knew the boy – he didn't. Had seen him once in six months. But felt he had to make some play for the boy's life.

'What'd I say, I know Titus. Just didn't think the old man was so fast anymore.'

'Maybe you shouldn't've killed Boetie.'

'None of your business, Aron.'

He'd backed off right there. Watched Tamora slide into her car, sleek Golf 7 GTI, brand new.

'No other way to go, Aron. You know. What d'you boys say, blood in, blood out? Titus loves that one. What's his other saying? No pain, no gain. Like he's a MBA graduate.'

Black Aron shook his head. Tamora was a crazy fem. Crazy to screw, crazy to work for. But the money was good. Better still, looked like the money would pile up. The way she was heading he'd do alright. Might lose his privileges but she needed him as first lieutenant. At least that's what Black Aron Chetty had in mind.

He fastened both hands on the steering wheel. Smirnoff alongside him slid down the window, all ready there with his Uzi.

Black Aron drove slowly down the street. Stopped next to the big Merc, about three metres between them. He looked past the Russian, saw the Anders all staring at them. That oh-shit look coming into their faces.

'Spot on, my chinas,' he said.

III

Cape Town International Airport.

'You are women,' said the fat Chinese man. The thin Chinese man nodding alongside.

'You've got a problem with that?' said Krista Bishop, glancing from one to the other.

'Last time we looked,' said Tami Mogale.

'No, that is beautiful,' said the fat man. 'You are beautiful.'

Krista thinking, Here we go. The chick thing. Haven't even exited the airport, they're at it.

People pushing past to get out of the terminal, the four of them mid-flow, baggage trolleys causing mayhem.

Krista and Tami ushered their clients to one side.

The two men going at one another in their own language, Krista and Tami standing patiently. Both women in jeans and t-shirts, black linen jackets, black tekkies.

The two men bowed, straightened, held out their hands.

'I am Mr Yan.'

'I am Mr Lijan.'

'We are businessmen in your beautiful country,' said Mr Yan.

Krista and Tami shook their hands.

'You are Complete Security?' said Mr Lijan.

Krista said yes.

'In Johannesburg we had big black men.'

'I'm black,' said Tami.

'We can see. You are very nice. You are better for us,' said Mr Yan.

The two businessmen laughed.

'But you are very beautiful. The men were like bulls.' He held his hands either side of his shoulders. 'Shoulders like bulls.'

'These men don't talk,' said Mr Lijan.

'They stand and watch,' said Mr Yan. 'We say good morning, goodbye. That is all. You will be more friendly. You are nice women. Show us the town.'

'We're your security, Mr Yan,' said Krista.

'You look after us.'

'We are your security.'

'Full stop,' said Tami.

'Full stop?' said Mr Yan.

'That's our service. That's what you hired us for.'

'Very good,' said Mr Lijan. 'Very good.'

'You will come to our meetings? You will come with us seeing the sights?'

'If that's what you want,' said Krista. 'Yes. It's what we undertake.'

'Such beautiful young women to be our bodyguards. This is wonderful,' said Mr Lijan. 'Where is the transportation?'

Krista caught Tami's eye, rolled hers. Tami's mouth tight, not like she was enjoying this.

In the car, a seven-seater VW Sharan, one of the men took the middle row, the other the back. Talked on their cellphones, talked to one another, never quiet. All the way into the city. No comment on the shacklands, the rise of Devil's Peak against the twilight, no comment on the wall of Table Mountain, nothing to say about the city as they cruised down the boulevard into the CBD. Not like the women Krista and Tami guarded: the celebrities, the businesswomen, the wives of rich men, they had something to say about it all. The men, they kept chatting, but didn't say anything Krista could understand.

'You got to realise,' she could hear Mace sermonising, 'in the guarding business most of the time you don't know what your clients are on about. Jabbering away in their languages. They could be major hellhounds for all you know. You could be ferrying around serious players. Putting your life on the line for rubbish.' Mace always ready with the 101 lecture.

Tami driving, said in Xhosa, 'This isn't going to work.'

'It will.' Krista not entirely sure, talking herself into it. She glanced at Tami, Tami shook her head. 'We had no choice.'

'We've always got a choice. We don't do men. We've

never done men.' Tami jerked her thumb at the two behind them. 'They think we're part of the deal. Escort gals.'

'They're going to learn otherwise,' said Krista.

'We should've said no.'

'We couldn't, Tami. I couldn't. You know that, I couldn't.'

They came off the elevated freeway into the Waterfront, going out the top of the roundabout to the Cape Grace.

'So soon we are here,' said Mr Yan. 'Good driving. This is an excellent hotel, yes?' He looked across the basin at the hulk of a ship, dark, deserted.

'It's good,' said Tami.

'You know the story of the man who had his honeymoon bride killed?' Krista angled herself to look at the men behind her. Krista wanting to put in a touch of local colour.

Mr Yan shook his head. Mr Lijan raised his glasses above his eyebrows.

'Two pretty people,' said Krista, 'came here for their honeymoon. Only thing is the husband arranges a hit on his wife. Using the taxi driver.'

'Oh no,' said Mr Yan, 'even in Beijing this arrangement is not possible.'

'This isn't Beijing,' said Krista. 'Anyhow, what I heard was probably the husband's father who set it up for his son. Turns out the father is that kind of control freak.'

The Chinese clients shook their heads. 'Impossible.'

'You think so?'

'Why would he do this?'

'That's the mystery,' said Tami.

'They stayed here? She was killed here?'

'They stayed here,' said Krista. 'She was killed in a township. A pretend hijacking.'

'And what about the husband? The husband is alive?'

'That was the deal.'

'A taxi driver can arrange this?'

The two women nodded.

'So easy?' said Mr Yan.

'For how much?'

'Fifteen thousand rand,' said Krista. 'We charge more than that.'

The two men staring at her until Mr Yan laughed. 'You are making a joke. Very funny joke.'

Krista didn't say if she was or she wasn't.

IV

There was Mart Velaze sitting at the Vida e in Cape Town International with a double espresso when the two young women pushed through the glass doors. Mart Velaze watched them cross the concourse towards Arrivals. Fierce chicks. Lovely. Two women on a mission. Not a smile on their faces. About as grim a look as you could get on a pretty. Made Mart Velaze smile.

Hot babes, both of them.

Beddable babes.

That Krista especially. Skin like a smooth latte. Like you could lick it and taste a caffè macchiato. Would give a Sunday-afternoon phata-phata on the bed to die for. The other one, too. Tami. Both of them would be good. Entertaining was a word that came to the mind of Mart Velaze. A threesome idea something to fantasise about.

Mart Velaze finished the remains of his coffee, peeled the wrapper off the small Lindt square, let it melt in his mouth. Coffee and chocolate. Krista and Tami. He stood up, walked towards where they talked with the Chinese men.

This was the part he always enjoyed. The anonymity of the spook. Standing there pretending to be waiting for someone. Rising on his toes to see over the heads. All the time listening.

The girls not at all happy with the arrangement.

Tough titty, as the English would say.

The Chinese trying it on. Krista and Tami laying down rules.

'We are your security.'

'Full stop.'

Nice one, Tami.

They had mouths on them, these sistas. Mr Yan and Mr Lijan would know all about it sooner or later. Probably sooner.

When Mart Velaze'd phoned her, Krista had been, You can't do this, you can't do that, called him an extortionist. More exactly, a fucking extortionist.

What could you do? It's a tough world, babe. Sometimes you just got to live with things you don't like.

She didn't like hearing that her lovely home, her red Alfa Spider would disappear in the puff of a tax audit.

That'd got Krista firing. She came on like a witch exorcising devils. Entertaining. Even over the phone.

'Just you try it,' she'd said.

'I don't want to, sisi,' he'd come back. 'Do me the favour, look after the Chinamen and we're sharp.'

'Until next time.'

'Maybe there isn't a next time.'

'There's always a next time, buti.'

Mart Velaze picking up the sarcasm on buti. My brother. He'd let it go, told her: 'Do the job.' Gave her the details. 'They pay good money.'

And they were on it as he'd expected. Krista knowing what was good for her.

He followed the two women and the Chinese men out of the terminal into the sunset glow. Warm summer late light. A windless evening. Very rare. Rare as the bums on the two babes. Pleasure to walk behind them.

He put his hands into the pockets of his chinos, keeping back where the women wouldn't notice him. Then in the queue at the pay booth, he was suddenly behind them. Krista looked round, but he flicked his eyes away. Felt her staring at him. He drew cash from his pocket, counted change from one hand to the other.

Going out of the parking garage he was behind them in a white Audi, white the best colour you could have for a tail job.

He followed them onto the highway, accelerating into the traffic flow. He knew where they were going, he knew how long it would take them to get there. He could drive ahead, keep them in the rear-view.

Mart Velaze did not expect anything to happen to Mr Yan or Mr Lijan on their way to the Cape Grace. As he passed the power station, his cellphone rang.

An unknown number.

Mart Velaze squinted at the screen in the hands-free clip, wondered if he should answer. He did. The voice said, 'Chief.'

Mart Velaze frowned, tightened his grip on the steering wheel. Never had the woman they called the Voice ever phoned him on an operation.

'Ma'am,' he said.

'Everything alright with our guests and their … er … escorts.' A hint of humour in the word escorts.

Mart Velaze smiled. 'Everything on schedule, ma'am.'

'The Bishop girl didn't misbehave?'

'No, ma'am. She wouldn't.'

'And Ms Mogale?'

'The same.'

'Wonderful, chief. Now listen …' Then silence. Mart Velaze waited. Silences had become part of the Voice's conversation technique as she put one person on hold to talk to another. After all these years he still didn't know her name. But she was a survivor. As the Scorpions became the Hawks and the secret services exploded and imploded and re-formed, as cop commissioners rose, were corrupted, chopped down, the Voice stayed the same. Slightly husky, always calm, always polite.

At first Mart Velaze had thought of her as a large woman, but that had changed in recent months. Now he thought of her as slim, a power dresser, a short-dread hairstyle, discreet jewellery, sometimes a silver chain necklace, sometimes a diamond ring. No wedding band. The Voice was single. A woman alone, talking to people she'd never meet. A woman handling her spooks.

'Chief,' she said. 'Leave the escorts and the Chinamen.'

Mart Velaze checked the rear-view mirror, the vw coming up in the fast lane.

'Understood?'

'Understood.'

She gave him the name of the restaurant in Lagoon Beach. 'You got that?'

He told her yes.

'There's been a shooting there, chief, with interesting people. Titus Anders, one of those I told you to read up about. Seems I've got my fingers on the pulse. Let me know, asap. Go with the ancestors.'

Mart Velaze eased off the accelerator, let the vw overtake, tracked them up Hospital Bend down the boulevard, came off before the highway skirted the Foreshore.

'Till later, my hot babes,' he said aloud.

V

Transcript from the case file of Hardlife MacDonald:

You pay me cash I can tell you what's happening there in Mitchells Plain, onna Cape Flats. I got no problems, me myself. Ja, that's my real name. That's how I was christened: Hardlife MacDonald. You can see it on my birth certificate. It's there in my ID book. You want to know my family? It's Mongols. Mongols is my brothers. One time I was Pretty Boyz but now I'm Mongols. My uncle is Mongols, he say to come over that there gonna be big shit and when there is big shit you wanna be with the strong bones. You know what I'm saying? The manne, the men, the manne with the strong bones gonna live to fight another day. My daddy was Mongols also. He was killed in that other place, not Pollsmoor Prison, that other place, Sun City they call it that prison in the north. The men are fierce there. For a man from the Cape, he was a man alone.

What I got to say now is about what I heard. In the Cape Flats there is the place we call the Valley of Plenty. We call it this way because tik is wild there. I seen lighties not even into two numbers smoking tik. For us Mongols this is the place we gotto do business. Drugs: dagga, what they call buttons for a white pipe, tik, mostly tik. Everybody wants tik. You taste that lolly yous don't wanna know anything else about the world. Tik is not for me. I stay away from that one. You wanna be alive in the future, you stay away from tik. I can tell you drugs isn't our only business. Sometimes we do other things: perlemoen, shark fins, ja, even tortoises. Guns, too.

Anyway this Valley of Plenty is prime property, as the larneys say. We got to take possession. Make it our land, Mongol land. That's why there's Pretty Boyz on the roofs watching every night, sunset to sunrise they's keeping guard against us. Because there's gonna be big changes on the Flats, big changes. You heard of Tamora Gool? She's a wild chick that one. We use the word kwaai. You know this word? Kwaai: sort of wild and mad and bedonnerd. You know this word, bedonnerd? Ja, you could say berserk. A crazy person. You gonna hear a lot about Tamora Gool. Tamora Gool is our boss, the Mongols boss. She gonna rule the Valley of Plenty. Take it away from the Pretty Boyz. I can tell you this trouble is coming. Big trouble. Moerse trouble. A war with us 'n the Pretty Boyz.

2

I

The Russian had the Uzi out the window in his left hand, running the clip, the Benz sparking bullets.

Major noise. Cordite stinging Black Aron Chetty's nostrils, making him sneeze.

The third sneeze, Black Aron dropped the clutch. Took off at max revs with tyre smoke. Whooping, 'Spot on, man, spot on, spot on.'

The shooter halfway out the window to finish the clip. Shouted at Black Aron in Russian to slow down, then spun on him: 'Why you do that? Why? You can see I am on the job. Stupid.' Holding up the gun.

Black Aron took a right, tyres squealing. Shot the lights on red into Marine Drive. The Russian hurled sideways, the Uzi knocked from his hand and flipping out of the window. The Russian looked back at the gun lying there, middle of the intersection.

'The gun is gone. We must get the gun. Stop.'

Black Aron stoked. 'No ways, my friend. Here we go' – putting foot over the bridge.

The last the Russian saw of his Uzi was a motorist stopping for it.

'Someone has the gun.' The Russian twisted in the seat. 'Someone in that car.' Pointing at the vehicle way behind them. Shouting at Black Aron. 'We must get the gun.' His mouth jabbering Russian.

Black Aron took the BM to one hundred and fifty, one hundred and sixty, down the long drive. The Russian not letting up about the gun.

'Forget the gun, alright. Forget it. The gun's gone. Someone else's toy now. Someone else can use it. Someone's always got a use for a gun.'

'Stupid,' said the Russian. 'The gun must be thrown away. Bits and pieces.'

'Doesn't matter, understand. Job's done.'

'We don't do it this way in Moscow,' said the Russian. 'We break the gun.'

Black Aron grinned at him. 'Here it's different. Here no one cares.' He dropped the speed to the limit, cruised up to the Neptune Street traffic lights. Went left, left again among the warehouses, factories, cold-storage depots, engineering works of Paarden Island.

In an empty factory parked the BM next to a white Corolla. Black Aron got out, raised his arms above his head, stretched. Rolled his shoulders, cricked his neck. Rocked heel to toe on his low-tops. Caught the Russian looking at him. Said, 'All that sitting. You need to stretch.'

The Russian fished out a packet of cigarettes. 'You want?'

'Big no,' said Black Aron. Popped the Corolla's boot,

from a small backpack took out a flask of coffee. 'This's my A1.' Holding up the flask. A brushed steel cylinder, a birthday present from his mother.

The Russian lit his cigarette, sucked, blew out smoke. 'My money?'

'Oh no, not my scene,' said Black Aron. 'I'm the driver.'

'I do the job, I want the money.'

'You'll get it. Chill, my friend. Just not my problem.'

The Russian stared at him. 'My money.'

'You'll get paid. Relax.'

'I am not relax without the money.'

Black Aron rubbed the flask under his chin, thoughtful. 'Look, the story goes this way. We get the call that the job's done. I take you where you want to go, that's where your payment's waiting.'

'The job is finished.'

Black Aron nodded. 'Sure. But we need a positive.'

'He is dead. Maybe all of them.'

'Sure, probably they're all dead. But we need a positive. We get that call you're a rich man.'

'I am not happy.'

'Nothing I can do. We're waiting for the call.'

The two men eyeing one another.

'You got vodka?' The cigarette bobbed on the Russian's lips.

Black Aron unscrewed the top. 'I got coffee. You want coffee?'

The Russian shook his head, blew out smoke.

'What is it with you guys and vodka? I don't get it.

If you uncap a bottle you throw the cap away. What's that about? Don't you know drink's a killer?' Black Aron poured coffee into the cup. Lifted a Tupperware of samoosas from the backpack. 'You know samoosas?' – offering the box to the Russian.

'I know.'

'So help yourself. There's snoek, mince, veg. My mother's. Very good samoosas. Better than Malay crap.' He took a swig of coffee. 'Spot on.' Bit into a snoek samoosa. 'Tasty.'

'We must go,' said the Russian.

Black Aron thinking, What's the rush, Smirnoff. Said, 'You got a date?' – grinning, tags of snoek on the fringe of his moustache. He wiped his mouth with the back of his hand. 'Those Russian fems, hey? Whoolala. At Mavericks. They come off the pole for a lap dance, you have to cream your chinos.'

'Spot on,' said the Russian.

Black Aron glanced at him. That Russian deadpan. Tight mouth, coal eyes staring back. You couldn't tell if the guy was taking the piss. Watch it, Smirnoff, he thought. Bit into another samoosa.

The two of them standing in the empty factory, a double-tube fluorescent humming overhead, listening to sirens on Marine Drive. Aroma of samoosas and coffee pervading.

'We must phone,' said the Russian, dropped his cigarette. Crushed it under the toe of his shoe.

Black Aron swallowed mom's home bake. 'Relax, my friend.' Sipped at the coffee. 'The call'll come soon.'

The Russian said something in Russian.

'What're you saying?'

He flashed gold teeth. 'You must learn Russian.'

'Bah,' said Black Aron. 'We must all learn Chinese.' He finished his coffee, screwed the top into the flask. Stowed it in the boot.

'When is call coming?'

'Any minute. I told you. Any minute.' Black Aron pointed at the car, reckoned better to be driving than standing around talking shit with the Russian. Frigging gold-tooth weirdo could get out of hand. Said, 'Alright. Let's go. Where to? Where can I drop you?'

No response.

'When the call comes I'll say where we are, where to bring the money. So now, where to?'

'The Fez.'

Black Aron whistled, closed the boot, gently. 'Spot on. Quite a joller for a Smirnoff, a nightclub like that. All the cool people.'

'You will have my money there?'

'Chill, my friend. We get the call, your money will be there.'

The Russian shook his head, unhappy. Got into the car. When Black Aron started the engine, said, 'What is this joller?'

Black Aron snorted. 'How long've you been here?'

'Five month.'

'You haven't heard the word joller?'

'No.'

'You mix with the wrong types, my friend.' He reversed the Corolla out of the warehouse, pressed the remote, waited while the roller door came down.

'What is this joller?'

'You ask them at The Fez.'

They drove back to Marine Drive, headed for the city, the Foreshore tower blocks white against the twilight.

Black Aron said, 'Pretty nice city.'

'For me it is all the same,' said the Russian. 'When I have my money, I try Buenos Aires. Or maybe Rio.'

'You're leaving?'

'Of course. Why not? Time to say goodbye. You know this song?'

'Sarah Brightman.'

'Of course.'

'The blind dude.'

'Spot on.'

Black Aron unsure if the Smirnoff was taking the piss.

II

'Hey,' said Luc. 'Who's this?'

Luc in the front passenger seat, Titus driving, as Titus always did. 'I'm not a pensioner,' he'd say. 'My car, I drive.'

Titus glanced right, saw the BMW, the man with the Uzi grinning at him. Shouted, 'No.' Reaching down for the gun beneath his seat.

'Christ,' said Luc, opening the door, dropping onto the pavement.

Lavinia and Quint in the back of the Benz fell sideways at the first shots. Ducked down as Titus had always told them to. 'A strange car comes next to us, you get on the floor,' he'd drilled them from kids. In those years drive-bys were a vote of no confidence. In the years before he became the main Untouchable.

The four of them helpless under the Uzi fire. Glass shattering, bullets punching into the Merc's steel panels. Ricochets. The run of the Uzi going through a long clip.

Titus bent double, scrabbling for the gun with both hands. Eyes closed. Feeling the grip. He pulled it free: a 9mm antique. Thing is it fired better than most off-the-shelf new models. The shooter tried for a second clip, he'd nail him.

Titus tasted reflux, monkey gland sauce. Hated being caught. Exposed. All of them. His family, sitting there as targets. Why? The grinning face wasn't some Pollsmoor Prison piece of shit, it was white. Could be old-style cops. Czech scum. Maybe even Russian.

The BM took off.

Titus came up with the Astra 400. Saw Luc on the pavement, shielded by the car. Looked in the rear-view at Lavinia and Quint gazing back at him. Glass in their hair, sparkling. Blood on Quint's face.

'You okay, Quint?' he said. 'There's blood.'

Quint put a hand up to his head, a jag there, bleeding. 'It's nothing.'

They got out of the car, joined Luc, gazing at the Benz pocked, sagged on flat tyres.

'A miracle,' said Quint.

Lavinia brushed glass off her T-shirt. 'Miracle, bullshit, Quint.'

'Steel plates,' said Titus. 'Just as well.' He stuck the Astra in his belt, covered it with his jacket.

'Black Aron,' said Luc.

Titus shook his head. 'Nah. A whitey. Someone from the syndicates probably.'

'Driving,' said Luc. 'That was Black Aron driving. No question.'

People coming out of the restaurant, the owner on his cellphone. No one approaching the Anders. Everyone looking at them, at the car, back at Titus, Lavinia, Luc, Quint, saying it's a miracle, no one should've survived.

The owner clipped his phone shut, said to Titus, 'I've called the cops.'

Titus nodded. 'You see it?'

'Nothing,' said the owner. 'All happened much too quickly.'

'Anyone, hey?' Titus eyeing the Sunday diners.

A voice said, 'Bless you, Mr Anders, bless you, the Untouchable.'

People applauded, came forward to shake their hands.

Titus said to Luc and Quint. 'Do the job, okay. Tonight. Now. Go.' He waved them off. 'Before the cops come. Go catch a taxi.'

'What they do won't sort anything,' said Lavinia. 'While that woman is around.'

III

'We want to eat your famous abalone,' said Mr Yan. 'You know about such a place?'

Krista thinking, Bloody clients, no, not on a Sunday night. Thinking, Bloody clients could eat the famous abalone in Beijing, no problem. Most of it smuggled there anyhow.

Tami said, 'Right here. At the hotel's restaurant. Nice view there across the marina. Pity, though, getting too dark to see the mountain.'

'No, in the city,' said Mr Lijan. 'For us we would like to see your city. The fairest Cape Town. Yes, this is what the website calls it.'

'The hotel is too, how you say it, international,' said Mr Yan. 'In Beijing, hotel food is not proper Beijing food. Everywhere in the world it is like this.'

The four of them in the foyer of the Cape Grace. The bellhop standing by with the men's luggage on a trolley.

'Come,' said Mr Yan. 'We are ready to go.'

'You don't want to see your rooms?' said Krista.

'Later,' said Mr Lijan. 'Now it is time for food, and beautiful conversations.'

Krista looked at Tami. Could read her thoughts: Screw this! Was thinking the same thing. No way out of it. Said to Tami, 'Maybe that place in Lagoon Beach?'

Tami nodded. About as much joy on her face as gratitude in c-Max prison. Thumbed through her cellphone contacts.

Mr Yan stepped closer to Krista. 'This place is for local people?'

'Of course.'

'They make good abalone?'

'Steak mostly, but also seafood. Expensive seafood.'

'You do not eat it?'

'No. Too expensive for me.'

'Tonight you will eat it, yes.' He said something to his companion, turned back to Krista. 'You will be our guests?'

What's with these guys, thought Krista, not letting it go? Said, 'We are your security.'

'Excuse me.' Mr Yan bowed his head, smiled at Krista. 'We are pleased with this. You must understand, this arrangement makes us happy. But what is the danger? I will tell you there is no danger. You can relax, we are Chinese businessmen, not Triads.' He laughed.

Krista smiled. 'We hope not.'

Mr Yan and Mr Lijan grinning at her. 'Then you will escort us.'

Krista thought, Dudes, don't get your wing-wangs up.

Tami joined them. 'Can't go there,' she said. 'They've got a problem. Sounds really hectic.'

'What is this problem?' said Mr Lijan.

Tami looked from Mr Lijan to Mr Yan. 'A shooting. Outside the restaurant in the street.' Tami playing it straight-faced as if nothing out of the ordinary, the odd shooting.

Mr Yan said something in Chinese.

Mr Lijan said, 'This place is safe?'

'Usually.' Tami smiling. 'I made a reservation for tomorrow night. Real Cape Town.'

Mr Yan and Mr Lijan inscrutable.

'How about we leave it till then?' said Krista. 'We'll be here at eleven for your first appointment.' She and Tami backing away, saying goodnight.

In the van Krista said, 'You were joking, right? About the shooting.'

'Uh uh.' Tami shook her head. 'It happened.'

IV

Mart Velaze drove through the Lagoon Beach intersection, ramp-parked on the pavement, walked back. Blue lights everywhere. Paramedics, vulture trucks, gawpers. The scene lit up like a film shoot. The road taped off. A cop told him he couldn't go in.

Mart Velaze whipped out ID: had him as a crime-scene investigator. Independent Police Directorate. The cop let him through.

Didn't take a forensic to work out what'd happened.

Mart Velaze marvelled. Saw no blood. Saw little markers on the tarmac for shells. Found a shell the cops hadn't noticed in the gutter, ten metres from the scene. Like the shooter was still on the job while the driver got them the hell out.

Not exactly professional.

Mart Velaze crouched, picked up the shell, pocketed it. Stayed crouched there puzzling. So many shells? You got a proper hitman, he came in, wap, did the job. Didn't spray 'n pray.

Something else going on here.

Mart Velaze stood, folded his arms, looked round. The cops talking to the old man and his daughter. Law of averages one of them should've gone down, who-ever was driving. But there they are: the old man still untouchable, a big man. You looked at file pictures of Anders going back ten, fifteen years, he didn't age. A big target. Long time since someone had placed a score on Titus Anders.

Anders now what? Early fifties. His wife dead from cancer three years after Boetie was born, Lavinia about twelve at the time. He'd raised the kids alone. Got them out of Hanover Park to Sunset Beach, got them through school, Lavinia even doing two years at varsity, accountancy, before she dropped out. By then Titus well established in the motor trade, second-hand dealerships, panel beaters, tyres and exhausts. Didn't give his sons the same opportunity as Lavinia, took them straight into his businesses. Might have seemed the model of suburban life but street talk had it that Titus was still trafficking. Still running the Pretty Boyz. Any goods that could be moved, he moved them. Titus part of a trinity of Untouchables.

Mart Velaze eyed the daughter, Lavinia. One sexy chickie that. Standing there in her tee and tight jeans, hands in her bum pockets. Flicking back her hair. Standing there like this's no big deal. Inconvenient but no big deal. Staring down at her feet. Bored even.

Interesting stories about her floated around. Mart Velaze heard tell she was engaged to one of the Untouchables, banging another. Old man Anders found out he'd kill her. Happy families.

Mart Velaze watched her. The girl had attitude. You'd have thought her a teenager the way she pouted. Standing there with her high tits, her stomach exposed, little whorl of a navel showing. The jeans so low cut, wasn't for the big buckle she'd have shown a fringe of curlies.

Delicious.

Then again chick like that'd be waxed clean: not a Mart Velaze fantasy.

He walked back to check the car once more. No real bullet pattern. No concentration on the driver. As if the shooter wasn't after one target. Which was why he'd used an automatic. Meant to take out the whole Anders family. Except where were the boys, Luc and Quint, the teenage Boetie? No sign of them.

His cell rang: the Voice.

'What you looking at, chief?' she said.

Mart Velaze cleared his throat. 'The old man Titus Anders and his daughter and a shot-up car. Someone used an automatic, maybe an Uzi or a Beretta.'

'They're not wounded?'

'Nobody's wounded.'

'Miraculous.' A pause. 'Deliberate miss?'

Mart Velaze took a couple of paces across the road, out of earshot. 'I reckon miraculous. Perhaps it was a bit rushed though.'

'The sons in it too?'

'No sign of them.'

'Ummm.'

Then silence.

Mart Velaze gazed at the scene, wondered if she'd disconnected.

'Chief,' she said. 'Thing is I've heard young Boetie Anders was fed to the fishies. His body was found earlier today. Now this. After no gang tensions for years this happens.' She went quiet again, Mart Velaze waiting.

Then: 'Anders and his friends, those two he's most pally with. What's their names?'

'Saturen and Basson.' Mart Velaze coming in quickly.

'Them, yes, them. Rings Saturen and Baasie Basson. Our Untouchables these days. All behaving themselves like good citizens, having braais together, being more normal than normal. Good fellas running their legal businesses, no problems at all it seems. No visible connections to the gang, the Pretty Boyz. So what's the case? What's happening?'

Mart Velaze didn't answer. The Voice asked a deep question she didn't want an answer. Not there and then. She wanted legwork.

'Thing is, chief,' she said, 'timing's the issue. You follow?'

Mart Velaze didn't, couldn't say so. Said, 'Uh huh.'

'I'm thinking aloud here: a drive-by on Titus Anders says something's wrong somewhere else. You shoot a man like that, there's a power problem. Doesn't matter what we think of Anders nowadays, you got to remember his past. Titus was Pretty Boyz one time, big time. Ditto Rings. Gangsters can't wipe off what's tattooed on their hearts. They got to still be the Pretty Boyz running the show: abalone, drugs, cigarettes, alcohol. You tell me what what, I tell you they're doing it through the Pretty Boyz gang. Got to be. Only now they're Untouchable. No obvious association. Know what I'm saying? Also what I'm saying, I don't want a gang war on the Cape Flats, chief. I don't want some wannabe taking on the Untouchables. Making war with the Pretty Boyz. Last thing we want. This goes viral with the Chinese visiting our glorious Mother City, I will be unhappy. Very unhappy. You follow?'

'You want me to watch them?'

'Ja. Give you something to do.'

'All three?'

'Hey, chief, for a man like you, no problem.'

Mart Velaze whistled.

'What I need, chief, is to know what's happening. Who doesn't like Mr Anders anymore. If we got a problem here that's bigger than one man. We got to know what we're looking at when we look at a drive-by targeting such an individual. Also, as I said, why now? You follow?'

Mart Velaze said he did.

'Also the Chinese and the escort ladies. Keep an eye.'

Mart Velaze said he would.

'Go with the ancestors,' said the Voice.

Mart Velaze thought it was sometimes difficult keeping up with himself.

V

Transcript from the case file of Hardlife MacDonald:

We's gonna make a move. Me, myself I know we gonna make a move. You can feel that sort of thing even if yous smoked a pipe. Something in the night says there is a problem, like I know in my stomach there's gonna be shit in the Valley of Plenty. I can tell you this for sure. We got a watchtower where you look down on the Valley. Last night you can see there's no one inna streets. Not even a dog. Nobody. You can't see nobody in the backyards as well. All closed up. People got this fear in their hearts.

They can feel just like me. They waiting. Sitting inside, watching TV, waiting. All over the Valley of Plenty there's Pretty Boyz on the rooftops, guarding. Waiting in case we make a move. They shitting themselves for the Mongols. They knows we want their Valley. They knows one night we'll come. They can feel it. They can taste it in their spit. You drink a Blackie, a Black Label, it doesn't go away that taste, metal and blood. That's fear, my larnie, fear.

3

I

Tami drove the vw into the garage, alongside Krista's red Alfa Spider. Her father Mace's old car. Now her pride and joy.

'You're what?' he'd said when Krista told him she was getting the engine rebored.

She came back: 'Don't freak. I like the car.'

It'd been sitting in the garage on blocks for years. Her father too attached to have it scrapped. At the time not into getting it on the road either. Too expensive. Times had changed. Everything had changed. It was her car now.

Tami switched off the vw, said, 'We're partners, right?'

'Sure.' Krista opened her door.

Tami reached across, put a hand on her arm. 'Tell me why we're doing this, with these Chinese? Not the bullshit version. The actual version.'

'I need a whisky,' said Krista.

They went in. Krista poured two whiskies, three cubes of ice each, no water.

Had Sigur Rós playing through the sound system, 'Fljótavik'. Jónsi's spaced-out voice lifting over the piano, high, thrilling. Krista paused, closed her eyes, let the music surround her. The strange language: sad, beautiful.

Thought of Mace in the Caymans. Her mother scattered in the garden. The melancholy of her life.

'Are you going to bring those drinks?' Tami outside at the table beside the swimming pool. 'You've got that music on again. You're obsessed with it. Tells me you're in one of those deep moods.'

Krista smiled. Kicked off her shoes, went barefoot across the tiles onto the flagstones, their coolness like water beneath her feet. 'For madam,' she said, handing Tami the glass.

'I'll madam you,' said Tami.

Krista raised her eyebrows. 'Awesome.'

Tami held out a hand, took hers. 'Sit.'

They sat above the city. Listened to its growl, looked over the bowl of lights, the buildings rising like teeth, to the black bay beyond with ships lit up in the roadstead. As if from somewhere high on the mountain behind them, Sigur Rós came ethereal.

'Those Chinese are bloody unreal,' said Krista, releasing her hand. 'They can eat all the abalone they want in China. That's where it goes.'

'Long life,' said Tami.

'You believe the fat one, randy arsehole. Like we're agency girls.' Krista raised her glass, they clinked. Let the music play into the next track.

'So? Tell me.' Tami focused on her.

'I told you,' said Krista.

Tami sighed. 'You told me we had to do it.'

'I got a call,' said Krista, 'from this guy Mart Velaze.'

'This's new. Who's he?'

'Wait. I'll tell you.' She took another sip of whisky. 'He says to me he knows about Mace's money in the Cayman Islands. He says he knows that some money was brought back to pay for the house.' She glanced at the house: the house her mother had wanted, all chrome and steel and glass and concrete, high on the mountain. The rooms lit up like a lifestyle spread in *House and Home*. 'He says he knows that money's from Mace's days smuggling arms. He says, that's cool. No problem, Mace is a struggle hero. He's told my papa no problem. But like now there's an issue, he needs us to do a security job. He tells me it's the Chinese men. I tell him we don't do men. He says he knows, and he wouldn't ask but it's important. Why'n't I phone Mace, ask him how important? Cos he wouldn't want the tax guys looking into my accounts, how Mace paid for the house. Wouldn't want me having to lose the house, having to sell the Alfa to pay a huge tax bill.'

'Shit,' said Tami.

'Right.'

'You phoned Mace?'

'I phoned Mace, told him the story. He's like sorry Krista you got to work with this guy. I say who is he? He says an agent. A bloody spy.'

'When's this?'

'This morning. I told you right after I talked to Mace.'

'Okay.'

'Mace says he's got history with this guy Mart Velaze. Sorry but what can he say. The guy's pulling in favours. What's the job? I tell him, he says up to me. I do this—'

'We do this.'

'We do this, we're in credit with Velaze, he'll leave us alone. Probably.'

'Probably?'

'You know Mace, everything's probably. He says for years there's been nothing from this guy. In that time Mace brought in money illegally, paid for the house, sorted everything with the business, no chirp from the tax guys or the Scorpions, the Hawks, whatever they're called these days. They knew but they played ball. Wink of a blind eye.'

'Until now.'

'It seems.'

'But it's got nothing to do with us.'

Krista pointed at the house. Down at the city. 'This house. The office. The business. His, ours, we lose it, we lose everything.'

'It's our operation,' said Tami. 'That was the deal. We bought Complete Security.'

'Buying it.' Krista grimaced. 'We still owe Mace and Pylon.' Pylon Buso the other half of Complete Security. She tucked up her legs. 'You want to talk to Pylon?

He's the money man. Always was. Ran their business financially. That sort of stuff went way over Mace's head.'

'No, I'm not going to talk to Pylon. What's the point?'

'No point.'

They sat staring over the city. The night close, humid. The way the city got in summer, gasping for breath. Krista felt sticky. Could smell the mountain, pungent and fetid. She needed to swim, to move slowly through the water, length after length: let the swimming take away the Chinese, the worry of Mart Velaze. Let the water ease the heat.

Swim. It's what her father had done, what he'd taught her to do.

'Take yourself somewhere else,' he'd said.

Another time on the shooting range had said, 'If you kill someone, doesn't matter why, afterwards go swimming. A long one in the sea's best. Helps a lot.'

It did.

As it had that night at the military road block. Stepping out in full gear to flag down a car, the headlights coming towards her, slowing. An Audi pulling up. The driver's window sliding down. The gun visible. The voice saying, 'Let me pass, sisi.' Her voice saying no. 'Switch off, please, sir.' The shot. Her return of fire, a single R5 round. Slick. In the moment such a distant sound.

No nearby ocean, but an Olympic-size pool back at base. She'd done length after length after length watched by her captain, a stringy Afrikaans woman, tough as kudu biltong.

Middle of the night, 01h40, Krista swimming. Unthinking, only a body, the fluid flow of her muscles. Her eyes following the black tiles, end to end. Gone, the image of the man's body slumped forward, blood on the windscreen. The small hole in his head. Gone the adrenaline that had ritzed her.

She swam until her muscles ached, until they stopped. Rested then on her arms on the pool edge. Quieting her lungs.

The captain bending down to her, holding a towel. 'You can swim, really. I run rather. Marathons. I know what you're doing: chasing away the devils.' She laughed. 'Ja, that's why I run too.'

There on the spectator benches, the captain had tried a debriefing, a makeshift counselling.

'He shot at you,' she'd said. 'You were the lucky one. He wasn't. You got your rights to do what you did. Okay, no problem there. Also remember he's a hijacker. No loss to society. Good riddance. Anything you want to tell me?'

Krista shook her head.

'How you feeling?'

'I'm fine. No problems.'

The captain squeezed her wrist. 'Okay. If you can't sleep, you get memories, what the shrinks call flashbacks, you come to me. Any time you want.'

Krista told her thanks. Never had sleeping problems. Had some flashbacks. Nothing serious, nothing she couldn't live with. Nothing a long swim wouldn't sort.

'You're a tough cookie,' were Papa Mace's words to her after an extreme swim. 'My girl's not only a pretty face.'

'Another one?' Tami drained her glass, stood.

'Why not?' Krista stripped off. 'A quick swim, to cool down.'

Tami watching her, shaking her head. 'Yeah, and an hour later you're still doing it.'

'Just want to lie on the bottom, not feel this heat,' said Krista. 'Join me.' Krista naked on the edge of the pool.

'Tempting,' said Tami. 'But, you know …'

'Not your thing.' Krista opened her arms. 'Don't know what you're missing.' Stepped backwards into the black water.

When she came up there was Tami holding out her cellphone.

'For you,' she said. 'Some dude called Anders.'

II

Black Aron Chetty, hyped-up, antsy, wanted sex. Sex with Tamora Gool.

Imagined walking into her apartment. Slamming her up against the wall beneath those weird pictures of fancy people dancing, his mouth jammed on hers, his hand groping. Faint smell of oranges on her skin.

She'd be wearing a long T-shirt, no bra, little boobies floating free. A clutch at them then down under the tee. She'd have on one of those red thong-things she paraded.

He'd be in there toot sweet.

Spot on.

Which was where Black Aron's thoughts were on the ride to The Fez. Until the Russian started about the money again.

'I do not like this.'

Black Aron went from an image of Tamora hoisted on his hips, that red thong dangling off her foot, to the Russian striking up a cigarette. 'No smoking. Not in the car. No smoking.' Fanning the air with a floppy hand.

The Russian ignored him. Flicked his lighter.

'This is my car. You cannot smoke.'

The Russian blew a long exhale at the windscreen. 'I do not like this. You must pay me.'

'Ah, come on, Smirnoff,' said Black Aron. 'You think I'm driving around with your payout. You see a brief-case in the boot? You see one on the back seat? You see a packet of cash lying anywhere?'

The Russian turned sideways in his seat to look.

'Nothing, right. I told you' – Black Aron patting the steering wheel with both hands – 'I told you, you'll get paid. I don't do it. I'm the driver.'

'You have been paid?'

'No, I have not. Jeez, man, what's with you? Get it into your head, I am not the paymaster.'

'In Russia when we do this work, the pay comes straight. Or problems.'

'Maybe. But I told you. This isn't Russia, my brother, this is Cape Town. Different strokes here, different folks here. You know this saying?'

The Russian tapped a head of ash onto the console, sent Black Aron into a conniption.

Black Aron spraying saliva trying to get out his anger, his tongue caught in a sound stutter: 'Dough, dough, dough, dough, dough—' Bending to blow the ash away.

The Russian streamed a blue cloud at his head. 'You are not watching the road.'

'Don't,' shouted Black Aron, yanked the wheel to stop the drift across the lanes. 'Don't frigging do that. This's not your car. What're you, some barbarian? Some frigging Mongol from Siberia.'

'I am not Mongol.'

'I don't care what you are, Smirnoff. You're a savage. Mongol Siberian savage. What you do that for, hey? Tell me? Explain to me, why d'you do that?'

The Russian said, 'Stupid currymuncher.'

Got Black Aron into another flutter. 'Stu, stu what? What'd you say? What? Stupid what?'

'That is what they call people like you. Curry-muncher.'

'Peep … people like me? Smirnoff, you're frigging close to a major issue here.'

'With you?' The Russian laughed. 'You are a little boy Indian currymuncher.'

Black Aron took the town exit underneath the freeway. The first left into an empty parking lot: car show-rooms one side, a tile-and-marble emporium the other. He left the engine running. Turned to the Russian. 'You want to say that to me outside?'

The Russian glanced at him, frowning.

'You want to say that to me outside?'

'What is your problem, currymuncher?'

'Out.'

The Russian didn't stir. Sat there.

'Out.'

'Stop.' Now the Russian moved fast, brought up a blade under Black Aron's chin. 'My money?'

Black Aron pinned back in the seat. 'I haven't got it.'

'My money.'

'I told you, we get a call and it's a positive. I tell them where to take the money.'

'You phone.' The Russian moved the knife to his right hand, slid it down, pressed the point in at Black Aron's kidneys. 'You feel that?'

Black Aron winced.

'Now phone.'

Black Aron eased the phone out of his pocket, held it up for the Russian to see. He keyed through to Tamora's number.

'You still with the Russian sausage?' she said.

Black Aron said he was.

'They're all alive. Tell him that. Not one of them even hurt. Tell him that.'

Something Black Aron was keen to do. But wanted to know, 'Now what?'

'Now what? Now what he does the job properly. Tell him. Now what he gets out there by himself and does it properly. Now what I don't want this Russian borscht.'

Black Aron said to the Russian. 'They're alive. It's a negative.'

The Russian smiled, 'You joke.'

'Not about this sort of thing, Smirnoff.'

'You are lying, no one is alive.' The Russian shifting sideways to face him. 'You do not want to pay me, you lie' – his language changing into a loud run of Russian.

Black Aron backed away, pressed the phone to loudspeaker, held it up. 'Listen to what she says.'

Tamora's voice stopped the Russian. 'They're all alive, Ruskie. You want me to send you pictures?'

'You lie.'

'You wish it. No money, Ruskie. No money till I know he's dead.'

'Blya,' said the Russian.

'I don't know what that means but I wouldn't say it,' said Tamora. 'I'd do the job. Get rid of the gun, get another one, do the job.'

'The gun is lost.'

'What? What's he saying, Aron?'

'We lost the gun,' said Black Aron. 'Fell out the car.'

'It what?' Tamora shouting. 'I don't believe it. You couldn't have cocked this up more. Sort it, Aron. Get him to sort it. Like now.'

Black Aron ended the call. 'You heard her, Smirnoff. Over to you.'

The Russian didn't respond.

'What's this blya?' said Black Aron.

'Whore.'

'Nice word,' he said. 'Still wanna go clubbing?'

III

Mart Velaze reckoned keeping tabs on three guys was a big ask. Other departments in the secret service they organised phone taps, bugs, hidden cameras, surveillance staff for the legwork, monitors listening, watching, filing reports. Other departments would deploy twenty people.

The Voice didn't give a flying fig. 'Hey, chief, for a man like you, no problem.'

Big problem, thought Mart Velaze. Big goddammed problem. Not one of the three in the same area. Going to be a lot of driving around.

A few months back the Voice had told Mart Velaze to check out the trinity. Known on the street as the Untouchables. To his why, she'd said, 'Just do it, chief. Read their files, Anders, Basson, Saturen, do a recce on their homes and hangouts. Looks all completely kosher. But you know … You look at what they did, specially Rings and Titus, Pretty Boyz both. You look at how they live, you got to wonder. Maybe there's a hidden income stream. Maybe it's not only buddy-

buddy. Have a look-see. No urgency. Back burner for now. You follow?'

He didn't but wasn't going to argue.

First thing Mart Velaze got from the files was the padding between Anders and Saturen and the action that'd once been their lives. No ways these two or Basson could be connected to wrongdoing. Wrongdoing being specifically: the Pretty Boyz, drugs, abalone poaching, extortion, cigarettes, liquor, money laundering. Titus, Rings might've been Pretty Boyz but no connect visible nowadays. You looked at the files of these three gents the only links to crime were historic. Basson being the exception. Nothing on him but a speeding ticket. Anders's sons not tied in either. Clean upstanding members of society, all. Sure lifestyle question marks, except clean audits from Revenue. Interesting that.

Second thing he got from the files was that these guys were tight. Legit business partners: Anders–Basson; Saturen–Basson. The two old gangsters using Basson as the common denominator. Nothing wrong with that. The businesses legit, not fronting anything obvious. The men really friendly. Everything braai and boerewors. Street talk might say they were an alliance, a crime syndicate, but all you could see in the files was business associations. No gripes. No cracks. No dark dealings.

So, now, Mart Velaze sat in his car wondering why the Voice thought someone was causing shit. Or if one of them was making a power play.

Didn't have to be one of them, of course. More likely to be a wild boy – or girl – muscling in: the Cape Flats gangsters as restless as the wind.

Second question: what would Titus do? Would he phone his friends, tell them what had happened? Maybe he'd phone Rings Saturen, because they went back, way back. Those times this violence was their world. But surely not Baasie Basson. No reason to phone a business associate.

Mart Velaze decided he'd check out Titus's pad in Sunset Beach last. The cops weren't going to let Titus go any time soon. So if the once-upon-a-time gangster was going to meet Rings it would be hours before that happened.

Meanwhile he could make the Voice happy. Check up on the other two. Mart Velaze headed out of Lagoon Beach for Athlone, home suburb of Baasie Basson.

Baasie the good man. Not even a search and seizure writ put on his property at any time. Baasie kept his stoep clean.

Baasie also the youngest of the three with the most to gain if Titus went down. For one, his legit shares would bloom. Titus and Baasie partners in restaurants, a chain of panel beaters, tyre and exhaust workshops, two florists, a tax consultancy. This last Baasie's day job. He was a suit man, a commerce graduate.

You looked at Baasie you saw Mr Respectable. On the golf course Mr Urbane. You could be charmed by Baasie, think him one of the best-read, wittiest of men you'd met. Women loved him. But Baasie kept his distance from them. No steady girlfriend. No fiancée, never married.

Baasie lived at home with the Basson seniors. Huge palatial place on three plots, just the three of them rattling around inside it with a couple of maids sorting the cooking, the laundry, the cleaning. A chauffeur for his parents. Baasie drove himself: a Lexus coupé, IS 250 C. A colour called silvery blue on the specs, black leather interior. Baasie had a thing about top-down driving. Liked to connect with the outside world. Top down he could talk to street vendors, car guards, share his music. Nobody ever touched Baasie for money. They joked with him, laughed with him, watched him pull away, thinking Baasie was alright, my bru.

Apart from the Athlone house, Baasie's property portfolio listed five others in Athlone, Mitchells Plain, Parklands. Two were blocks of flats, three were houses. A nice rent coming in from each one.

In the Parklands house was a model. A standby Baasie could call on when he needed to flash a pretty face, boobs and long legs at some occasion. Baasie liked occasions. Art exhibitions, book launches, concerts, golf club dos. Once a month liked to have his zooty mates round.

This evening was one of those. Perfect weather for it too.

So Baasie Basson was at home. Back of the palace, Baasie had an entertainment area: swimming pool, gazebo, a braai corner that he called a barbecue zone. Baasie'd gone off the word braai. Too northern suburbs

Afrikaans. Barbecue, Baasie reckoned, had some élan. He used that word too.

Baasie's entertainment area had access off the back street: a parking area there set aside for friends. Four BMS lined up now. Mart Velaze stopped well down the street, walked back. Could hear the voices of enjoyment, low music, people splashing in the pool.

Some kids were peering through the slats in the gate.

'This Baasie Basson's place?' he asked.

They said yes.

'Is he there?'

They said yes, braaiing meat.

Mart Velaze took a look through the slats: saw men in shorts, women in bikinis, two of them topless. Très chic. Stepped back, said, 'Don't let him catch you.'

The kids said, Baasie didn't mind, usually brought them a plate of chops and sausage.

'Nice man,' said Mart Velaze.

Interesting, thought Mart Velaze, walking back to his car. If Baasie knew about what had happened to Titus, he wasn't showing much concern.

Next drove to Rings Saturen's residence.

What he'd read about Rings was that Rings had political ambitions. Had his eye on MP status. The very reason he crossed over the highway from Athlone to Pinelands, garden suburb of the political elite. Rings wanted to move in the same streets as politicos, judges, diehard commie MPS, trade union officials, directors-general, company hotshots with black-empowerment credentials.

Rings donated money to the party. Rings got onto political committees. Rings was moving up. The party apparatchiks loved him: he was big on community involvement.

Rings dished out money to crèches, schools, mosques, churches, feeding schemes, literacy drives. Rings stood loans at way less than loan shark interest to those down on their luck. The people loved Rings. Rings could be relied on.

Rings gave food parcels at Christmas, presents at Eid.

In the streets Rings would always greet you, Rings would never look away. Like Baasie, Rings knew about street PR.

This was what the file said.

The file also said that Rings bought his Pinelands house in 1998. A double-storey under thatch with bay windows, cottage panes, ivy growing up the wall. Could've been transplanted from England. The house on a street named after somewhere in the Lake District. Quaint suburb of mostly whites but the shades were moving in. Rings had been in the vanguard.

No sooner in Pinelands than Rings was divorced after an eight-year marriage. Two children lived with their mother. Straightforward divorce, mutual incompatibility. Mrs couldn't take gang life any longer. Got out, even though Rings was heading for a quieter scene by then, foregrounding his political ambitions. Rings was generous with her, never defaulted on maintenance.

As a single man, his love life was active. One-night stands, couple of affairs, none of them of any length. Then six months back he started a scene with Lavinia Anders. Got to be eighteen years between them. Rings not as old as Titus but somewhere in the mid-forties zone. What was this about? Titus moving for a closer association? The old dog. A coloured putting a bride price on his daughter like that.

There was much in the file going back to the mid-1980s about Rings Saturen, the gangster. Got going as a teenager did Rings. Where he met up with Titus, both of them in the Junkie Boyz that morphed with the Pretty Kids to become the Pretty Boyz. In that period added to his cv a list of charges: assault, aggravated assault, rape, theft, drug-dealing, possession of stolen weapons. He'd done three years on one of the assaults, walked on all the others. By the time of the Pretty Boyz, Rings was putting some distance between himself and the rough end. You didn't know his history, you wouldn't guess it. He tidied up, took elocution lessons, went political. Got into bed with Baasie and Titus, all legit, signed-up taxpayers.

With his name on the letterhead of a couple of businesses: an airport shuttle service for tourists, a car hire company with only Mercs on its books. He'd been in some of the restaurants with Baasie and Titus but sold his shares. The shuttle service gave Baasie as another director, ditto the car hire company. Mostly though it was politics that kept Rings busy.

Mart Velaze did a pass down the street where Rings

lived. There was his house, about three, four metres back from the street: cute little gate, low garden wall, short path to the front door through rose bushes. Drive-bys not a consideration in the life of Rings Saturen.

Downstairs lights on in the house. Didn't mean the great man was at home.

Mart Velaze checked his watch. About ninety minutes, two hours since the shooting. If Anders and Saturen were going to meet up, it'd be around midnight. Mart Velaze sighed. What to do? Decided to get out the binocs and the camera, sit tight for a while. Or until Rings made a move. A street like this no one would notice a stake-out. No one on the street to notice anything. He squirmed down in the seat, got himself comfortable. Would rather have been sprawled on a couch in his flat with a box of pork chow mein, a beer, watching some movie. Maybe a rerun, Clooney in *Michael Clayton*.

Instead.

Instead here he was bored in his car in a suburb of thatched homes, no one even taking the dog for a walk. Two cars in half an hour.

Forty minutes later Mart Velaze watched headlights in his rear-view mirror, the car came past him, turned into Rings Saturen's driveway. Stopped. Out got a woman. Mart Velaze sat up, sharpened the focus on the binoculars. Short dark hair, her face turned away from him. From her movement, he reckoned she had to be mid-thirties maximum. Dressed in black slacks, a jacket, high heels. He snapped off a couple of digitals for the record. Probably indistinct but …

Would please the Voice. Kept focused on the woman through the lens. Thing about the woman was she had a front-door key. Let herself in like she was at home there.

Mart Velaze doubted Lavinia Anders or her daddy knew about this scene.

IV

Montague Gardens, quiet place of a night. Recession quiet. Lots of empty warehouse space. Black holes between the going concerns. Some security guards locked up on the occupied premises. Otherwise a very quiet place of a night. Ideal. The way Luc thought about it, where else? You read crime novels this's where they did it.

You wanted to do someone serious harm, you weren't gonna do it in the One&Only hotel. View out over the Waterfront, all the pretty lights. Room service, thirty-eight-channel TV, wi-fi, bar fridge, chocolates on the pillows.

Though he could see possibilities. So much DNA lying around a hotel room, forensics would go batshit. Hair in the shower, sperm drops on the carpets, flakes of skin, probably even blood, menstrual blood, blood from a shaving cut. Forensics matched all that, it'd read like a who's who of politics 'n business.

Luc amusing himself as they waited for the gate to slide back. He and Quint in a Terios. Luc thinking another advantage of hotel rooms was cleaning staff to sort out the mess. All you had to do was walk out afterwards, close the door. Quietly. Don't want to disturb the sleeping.

He drove through the gate down an alley to a loading bay. Parked the Terios.

Quint said, 'How we gonna do this?'

'Like Lavinia wants,' said Luc.

'Really?'

'Dunno, Quint. See how it happens.'

Quint touched the cut on his forehead. He'd covered it with a plaster. Winced at the tenderness. 'We gotta send his mommy something. A present for Tamora?'

'Sure. A rack of ribs. A vid clip? Cellphone pictures?'

They sat in the Terios looking at the door to the warehouse. Luc said, 'There's some zol in the cubbyhole.'

Quint opened it, took out Rizlas, a bankie of weed. He rolled a joint.

'We're lucky, man. Way up lucky. You know that? Wanker sprays us like that, and we walk away. Should've been dead, a couple of us, should've been dead. Daddy. You.'

Quint rubbed the dry leaves between his fingers, spread the crumblings along the paper. 'Like I said, a miracle.'

'Arsehole Chetty.'

'You saw him?'

'He was driving. Him. Charra Chetty. What's Chetty

doing in this sort of stuff? Chetty's nowhere – No. Where. – A driver. A delivery boy. You see Black Aron he's outside a school dropping parcels for the tik merchants. Charra Chetty would kak himself doing anything more serious. He's not the sort pulls a drive-by. Shit, bru, doesn't make sense.'

'The man's coming up, moving into management.' Quint licked along the edge of the paper.

'Someone's desperate to want him.'

Quint put the stop between his lips, lit it with the car lighter. Sucked the smoke in, held it. He passed the hit to Luc, let the smoke trickle out, said, 'Lavinia's got it right about Tamora.'

Luc took a pull. When he'd blown out said, 'Lavinia's full of crap.'

'Lavinia knows.'

'You think?'

'So do you.'

'Tamora's arsehole.'

Quint had another tote. 'Pretty arse.' Laughed. 'Sort of arse you want to …' he pumped the middle finger of his right hand. 'Nice and tight.'

Luc scratched at the itch behind his eyepatch with his short finger, the one with one knuckle. 'I told him before, I told Daddy back then, Tamora's bullshit. He doesn't listen to me. Lavinia spouts something about Tamora he changes his tune. Daddy was poes-struck for Tamora. When he met her that's all he saw.'

'Tamora the whora.'

'I told Daddy she's a snake. But Daddy knows best. I

was there she comes flashing her mamas at him for a concession. I was there. She's all hello Luc-ie, your daddy in? Standing in black tights, her crack smiling at me, they was so tight. She rubs up to Daddy, he creams. Gives her what she wants. Xmas time with Uncle Titus. Tamora full of smiles and perfume. Let me dive for pearlies, Uncle Titus, I can do it. For you, Uncle Titus. You see how she touches her hair. For you, Uncle Titus. Smiles at him with those lips. Glossy like her poes. Gives him a sight of her tongue. Leans so he can see her boobies in a red bra. Shit, man, Quint, in our house. There in the lounge. We're sitting on the sofas, she and Daddy's on the one, I'm watching them. I want to smack her. She's pulling his wire full on. Might as well have had his knob in her hand. I can see it. Daddy's far away. Daddy's scheming he can get some of this pussy, she can get a concession wide as the ocean. She gets abalone, he gets blowjobs. Fair exchange. In his eyes, it's there, that's what he's scheming. I could see it.'

'She put out?'

'You think I watched?'

'She musta done.'

'Course, she must have. Look what she got. Put out big time. In the lounge, probably. On the sofa. Disgusting. Daddy can't see this arsecreep's riding him. Doesn't ask me, is this a good idea we give her half the best places? Just pulls out a map, shows her a stretch of coast. Ah, thank you, Uncle Titus, I can do it. You'll be pleased. Like, hey, Tamora, he's pleased cos his dick's in your tricky box. I buggered off, cos I was getting sick and tired of watching Daddy give her his balls. I told him, she'll want everything. Everything we got.'

'I don't remember this.'

'Two years ago. I don't know where you were. Maybe that time you checked out the rhino jobs, it happened. Doesn't matter, it happened, bru. Now we got the consequences. Now Tamora's heavy with the Mongols. I heard even the queen bitch. Causing shit for us cos she wants a takeover. Make a war, take over the Valley, take over the Pretty Boyz, all we got.'

They went quiet, passed the joint back and forth. Quint said, 'She killed our Boetie. Just' – Quint snapped his fingers – 'like that.'

'Yeah.' Luc squashed the roach. 'I told Daddy, she'll cause us full-on pain and suffering. Daddy says, ag, no, Luc, she needs a break. You gotta give people a break, Luc, show some humanity. Give her a chance, Luc, see what she can do for us.'

'Like kill us.'

'Like try and kill us.'

'Even before we done her boy.'

'She wants everything we got, bru. That's what I'm saying. Only thing she didn't reckon was we'd come back at her so fast. That surprised Queen Tamora. Now she's got another surprise coming.'

They headed for the warehouse, sign above the door read: Peninsula Butchery and Cold Storage. Beneath that an auction notice. Three locks to the door, different keys for each one. Quint went at it slowly, Luc holding up his cellphone to give him light.

Quint got the door open, they went in, closed it, bolted it. Clicked on a central light. Small reception room, just as it'd been left the day the liquidators came. Behind a glass panel the admin office, the desk cleared bar a small PABX system. In the room two plastic chairs, small table between them with copies of *The Butcher*, flyers from the Red Meat Producers Association. Door right opened to the factory: cold-storage rooms, racks of meat hooks, butchering tables, meat bandsaws, bone bandsaws, sluice trays, mincers, sausage fillers, scales, offal bags. Everything to go under the hammer. Also a pile of blue striped aprons on a table at the door. Neat rows of choppers and knives.

The brothers stood there in the doorway, breathing in the residue smell of raw meat, cloying, cold.

Quint hit a light switch, brought up two rows of fluorescents, popping, juddering, getting their act together.

They had the youth in a storage room: plastic ties at wrists and ankles fastening him to a plastic chair.

'Howzit, my bru,' said Quint.

The youth, a teenager, fourteen, fifteen tops, lifted his head. Good-looking kid with black hair, cowlick over his forehead. Took a glance at Quint, started shaking, crying, pleading.

Quint said, 'It's a shit life, bru, anyhow.'

In the factory Luc put on an apron, tied it behind his back. Got a Kolbe K430 bandsaw humming. Plenty of height and width. Nice sliding table. Blade looked brand new.

V

Transcript from the case file of Hardlife MacDonald:

I can tell you what happened. I went from the watch-tower to the captain's house. I know what happened. I was there, strues. I can tell you how the captain did it to the lighties. What I'm saying, what I'm telling you, this happened. The captain's got his men, he takes three lighties, seventeen, eighteen years, I was there once, doing what they gotta do. They got tattoos, like mine, all over. They got to do their orders. They got to let the blood run. We drink some Blackies, smoke some pipes. We's sitting in the yard there not far from the Pretty Boyz Valley of Plenty. We's joking, smoking, the captain's inside with his wifey. Young wifey he's got. Very beautiful. They's sitting inside there watching TV. Me myself know it's gonna happen, I got the feeling except you wonder when's the captain gonna make the play. It's late, in the midnight hour, the captain comes out with two pipe bombs. He say to the three lighties, 'Yous do good.' They take the two pipe bombs, the captain gives keys to a red Opel Kadett. We go into the street to where's the car. Everybody is grinning, laughing it's mos a big joke. I told you this was war coming.

4

I

Tami held out the cellphone. Krista heaved herself from the swimming pool, took the towel Tami offered in her other hand. Said, 'Anders?'

'Asked for you by name, Krista Bishop.' Tami with her thumb over the cell's mic. 'It's not your company phone.'

'I don't know any Anders.'

'He's got your private number.' Tami looking at her, raised eyebrows, quizzical. Straight cut to her lips, no humour there.

Krista wrapped herself in the towel, not bothering to dry off. Held out her hand for the phone.

'Coloured voice,' said Tami. 'But soft, maybe Athlone accent.'

Krista went in confident, what-can-I-do-for-you style.

Titus Anders gave his full name, said, 'You Mace Bishop's girl?'

'Girl?'

'Girl. Daughter. You know what I mean.' A throat clearing.

'That important, that I'm his daughter?'

Titus Anders going at that throat irritation again. 'Cheeky, hey, like your old man. Mace Bishop always quick with backchat.'

'How'd you get this number?'

'From your daddy.'

'I must believe that?'

'Phone him. I just talked to him now-now.'

'You spoke to Mace?'

'Ja, Ms Bishop, I spoke to Mace. Now I want to speak to you. Top priority.'

'I'm listening.'

'This's your attitude to a client? Be nice.'

'I'm doing nice,' said Krista, 'considering.'

'Considering?'

'Considering I don't know you. Considering you have my private number. Considering it's after hours. Considering you call me a girl.'

'Ms Bishop, please.'

'You wait,' said Krista, 'till I've phoned my father' – took her company phone from Tami, keyed through to Mace.

He came on she said, 'Mace, who's Titus Anders?'

Heard her father laugh. Say, 'I'm fine. How's my princess?'

'Not that sort of call, Papa.'

'Yeah, I know.'

Krista caught the downturn in her father's tone. Ignored it. Waited.

'Titus,' said Mace. 'Nice guy. Used to be a major gangster. He's phoned you already? Fast operator.'

'You gave him my private number.'

'C ...' Mace pausing, Krista waiting him out, wondering if he'd ever accept the new spelling of her name. He hadn't liked at all her dropping the Ch for a K. 'Why're you going all harsh and ugly? Christa's soft. Christa's my girl. With a K, that's strange, somebody else. I don't know this person. Why'd you want to change it?' Never getting that she had a new life. That her mother would have understood.

'C ...'

'You gave him my private number.'

'I did.'

'Why?'

'A favour.'

Krista wanted to say, how many more favours must I pick up? The audacity of Mart Velaze still rankling. Didn't. Held her tongue. Closed her eyes. Breathed in. Went with: 'He's still in the business?'

'Depends what you mean by business.'

'Crime.'

'I'm sure. Probably. He's one of the so-called Untouchables. Him and two other guys, Rings Saturen, Baasie Basson. Run most of the abalone trade, have done for years, since before forever. Keep it all hidden behind legitimate companies. So, yes, far as I know they're still in the business, yes. But the last I

83

heard he was also protected, politically protected, one of those privileged men of the community. Titus used to lunch with the police commissioner as I remember it. Told me he had some work for you. What's it specifically?'

'Don't know yet.'

A silence. Krista could hear the Stones. 'Paint it Black'. Her father never going to get out of that jag: mourning his wife, her mother.

'Titus is okay. Except if this is dirty Cape Flats shit, stay away. Stay out of that.'

Krista said, 'I've got to go.'

'You've got him holding on another line?'

'I have.'

She heard her father laugh. 'There's my princess.' A pause. In it Mick singing about a line of cars and they're all painted black. Then Mace: 'Sorry, C. Sorry about dishing out the phone number.'

Krista thought, You don't know the half of it. Said, 'All I wanted to do was read a book. Have a quiet evening. Bye, Papa.' Pressed him off. Mace still a hurt and sadness in her chest. Daughters and fathers. The way he'd walked out. Headed for the Caymans like she was a big girl now. Over to you, kiddo, all yours. Mace never able to work out how to handle the parental thing. Unless it was about shooting, swimming, killing. Then he was mouth almighty with good advice.

She caught Tami's eye, smiled. Tami taking the cellphone, stroking her arm. Krista went back to Titus Anders: 'Okay, we can talk.'

A bark from Titus Anders. 'What? Okay, we can talk? Hell, girlie.'

Krista said, 'Mr Anders, I'm Krista or Ms Bishop, not your girlie.'

A long exhale on the f-sound from Titus but he didn't say the word. He said, 'I want you to protect my daughter.'

Krista looked at Tami, smothered the phone against the towel. 'A job. Guarding his daughter.'

Tami held up her phone screen. 'I googled him. He's a gangster. A Cape Flats gangster. We don't do gangsters. Tell him no.'

Krista nodding, said, 'That's what Mace said.' To Titus Anders, said, 'No.'

'Ja, I expected that,' said Titus. 'Double your rates, Ms Bishop.'

'Still no.'

Titus Anders sucking in his breath. A pause, Krista wondering if he'd thumbed her off. Until: 'For my daughter, Ms Bishop. I'm asking you. I'm going to beg you, please. Please look after her. That's what I'm asking. That's all I'm asking. Keep my daughter safe.'

Krista hesitated, said, 'Safe from who?'

She heard Titus Anders sigh. 'Yesterday my youngest was killed. Just now, Ms Bishop, someone tried to kill my family. I don't know who. Someone, okay. We come out of a restaurant, they shoot us. We are citizens, ordinary people. My daughter needs protection.'

'Ordinary citizens don't get shot at.'

A silence. Then, 'You offer protection, that's your business?'

'It is.'

'You protect celebrities, movie stars, models, businesspeople.'

'Businesswomen.'

'What?'

'Businesswomen. We protect women.'

'That's what I want to buy, protection for a woman. My daughter.'

This time Krista put in a pause. 'Mace said you're a gangster.'

A laugh. 'Mace is romantic. He likes to live in the past. You know, the good old days. Today I'm a businessman, Ms Bishop.'

'Whoever shot at you is a gangster?'

'Yes.'

'I like to know who I'm protecting women from.' Krista kept her eyes away from Tami, knew Tami wouldn't go with this. Said, 'How old is she, your daughter?'

'Twenty-five.'

'She agrees with this? Going into protection.'

'Where's her choice? Someone wants to kill her, where's her choice?'

Krista looked at Tami. Tami grimacing, giving her a chop sign, cut the conversation. 'You've got people could protect her, Mr Anders. Gangsters. You've got your own protection.'

'I want her out of this. Away. Somewhere safe. Please, okay. I am pleading, Ms Bishop. I am begging you. One week, keep her safe for one week. That's all I'm asking. Just one week. For her sake.'

'Let me talk to her. What's her name?'

'Lavinia.'

Lavinia came on, Krista said to her, 'I need to know you won't cause us trouble, Lavinia.'

'I won't.'

'You want protection?'

'You heard my daddy.'

'You want protection?'

'Yes.'

No hesitation, took Krista by surprise. 'Okay.'

Tami said, 'Fuck.'

Titus Anders back on the cell said, 'Come and fetch her now, please. It is urgent. Very very urgent.' Gave an address in Sunset Beach.

Krista keyed off the phone, started dressing. Tami standing, glaring at her. 'Sometimes ...'

Krista fastened her bra, slid it round, cupped her breasts. 'Sometimes?'

'Sometimes you're like Mace, full on.' She tapped her head. 'Mad.'

There was this about Krista and Tami.

Krista had hated Tami, believed she was screwing Mace. Believed that Mace screwed Tami just days after her mother Oumou was murdered. Krista seeing her mother stabbed, her throat slashed, lying there in a spreading leak of blood one lovely Sunday afternoon, everyone on the patio enjoying a braai lunch. Downstairs in her studio the dying Oumou being cradled by Mace. Maximum grief and pain. All the same, Krista believed that days later Mace screwed Tami in the bed he'd shared with Oumou.

She'd gone into a bad scene. Cutting herself. Wanting the pain so that she knew she could still feel something. Wanting the pain to get her out of the numbness of grief. Night after night alone in her room with a three-blade razor head. Zip. The hot electric thrill. The beading blood. On her inner thighs mostly, high up. Her arms too, over her wrists. A half-arsed thought of suicide tingling in her mind. That maybe she was guilty. Maybe she'd caused her mother's death.

On all these nights Mace off somewhere doing whatever it was Mace did. Gone on some mission, out of the house, away, anything to be somewhere else. Screwing Tami. That's what she thought. Mace running from reality big time. And Tami only too happy to lie down for one of the bosses. That's what Krista'd thought. Believed. Was convinced of.

Until the night Pylon came round, told her Mace had been shot, was in a bad way, a really bad way.

Afterwards, when Mace had healed, they'd made up, reached an understanding. Father and daughter bonding while target-shooting in the quarry. Mace sprouting his homilies about she who owns a gun must be prepared to kill. Krista assuring him she had no hesitation. After what had happened to Maman.

Years later she had it out with Tami.

Tami back at Complete Security, working again for Mace and Pylon after a long sojourn in Johannesburg.

In stomps Krista in full gear: combat boots, khaki uniform, hold-all, back from camp for a ten-day pass. Krista been doing her thing in the army, running around the bushveld, jumping from helicopters, shooting FNS, M16S, RPGS, training to fight, assigned to a special ops unit. This pretty young thing with an iron bod, some weird shit in her head. You checked her out skew, she'd want to know what your case was. Best not to give her lip, Krista likely to put you on the floor before you'd finished being a smartarse. This prior to and after the road-block situation.

Except army life wasn't working out. Krista had a thing about being told what to do. So on that ten-day pass she was thinking about her future. Wondering if maybe Mace and Pylon hadn't hit on a good thing. A business in high demand in a country not exactly at peace. A useful way of earning the moolah. Also you didn't have to get shot up in some foreign field, more specifically some steamy broken part of the Congo. The whole romance of special ops wearing decidedly thin these days. Thoughts of other careers riding high in Krista's consciousness. The whole tangle of her life pissing her off.

Such is her mood the morning she comes into the office on Dunkley Square, sees Tami.

'What the fuck're you doing here?'

Tami's, 'Hello, Krista.'

'Get out. Now.'

Mace's, 'Children.'

Which gets right up Krista's nose. 'Don't start,

Mace.' No Papa, but Mace. Krista shifting her gaze from Mace to Pylon. 'Why's she here?'

Mace and Pylon and Tami sitting there in what they call the boardroom in the mid-afternoon, drinking beer. Pizza remains still in their boxes on the table.

Mace says, 'I thought you were over this.'

Pylon says, 'She's working here.'

Krista goes up to Tami. 'Out. Now.'

Tami stands but that's her only move. 'Hello, Krista. Nice to see you too. You're all grown up.'

The patronising pushes Krista's button. She makes her play, the one that's landed smartarses on the floor.

Tami stops her. Puts a clutch on her arm that not even iron-bod Krista can break.

'Girls,' says Mace. 'You wanna play boys, how about going in the backyard.'

'You screwing her again, Mace?' Krista not moving her eyes from Tami.

'He never did,' says Tami.

'I'm supposed to believe that?'

'Believe what you want. I'm telling you what didn't happen.'

'Confirmed,' says Mace.

'Guys,' says Pylon, 'can't we move on? We're talking history. Have a beer, Krista.'

'And that makes it better?'

'I reckon.' He uncaps a bottle for her. 'Been my experience. Starts the healing.'

Maybe it does.

Krista takes the bottle, sits down at the table opposite Tami. Drains off half. A malevolent presence. The fun and laughter dispelled.

'The army teach you that?' says Mace. 'How to drink?'

'Yeah, that. And how to kill.' Krista leaving it there. Uncompromising.

'Useful,' says Pylon. 'They must've stepped up their game.'

Brings a chuckle from Mace. He switches the subject. Talks soccer. He and Pylon getting into their favourite pastime.

Krista and Tami out of it. The two of them sitting silent, no eye contact, focused on their Millers.

Tami finishes up, says, 'I'm outta here.'

'Ah, no, man,' says Mace. 'Have another beer.'

'Home time,' she says, waving from the door.

'Hope you're not going because of me,' says Krista, her tone gloating.

'I am,' Tami comes back. 'Actually.'

Krista doesn't respond. Finishes her beer, goes for a second. The three of them sitting, listening to Tami walk down the corridor, let herself out, the door click softly.

'You should give her some due,' says Pylon. 'Don't be so angry. The history's not what you think it is.'

Krista looks at him. Pylon keeping the contact. 'Really, hey.' Pure disdain.

'Really.'

Strange way to start the healing. Except Krista thinks about things.

Day six into her leave, Krista says to Mace, 'Swear to me you didn't screw her.'

The two of them sitting beside the swimming pool, eating lunch in the winter sun.

Krista sees Mace look up from his couscous salad, eyes hidden behind sunglasses. Waits for it.

'That day at the quarry,' Mace says, 'that day I took you to shoot the Hämmerli, that day the Spider died on us, you said it was okay if I was seeing Tami. As it happens I wasn't. I was mourning your mother. I thought, you're only saying things like this because you hurt. You were thirteen, for Chrissakes. You'd seen your maman murdered. Everything was horrible. Black, black, black. It was a bad time, C. A bad time for us both. Probably you thought I didn't care. I don't know what you thought. We were strangers. After she was killed you doing all that cutting at your arms, on your thighs. Everything seemed like it was falling to pieces. But that day at the quarry I thought maybe there was a change in you. You seemed ... accepting. Then you bring out this thing about Tami. But it didn't matter then because Tami had gone to Joburg already. And we didn't fuck. Never had, never likely to.'

Krista sucks prawn heads, licks her fingers. Says, 'Okay, Papa. I believe you.'

'Don't have to believe me, go'n talk to her. Believe her. Tami's straight, C. Couldn't lie if she wanted to.'

'Alright.' Krista frowning at him, quizzical. 'I get it.'

He pushes back his sunglasses. 'Krista?'

'Yeah.'

'Couple of days ago you said the army wasn't working for you. So here's the thing: Pylon and I want out. We're thinking you and Tami should buy Complete Security.'

Krista says, 'You're mad.'

Mace says, 'I've put it to you, I plan to put it to her. You 'n her could do it. Run a good show.'

Krista does some more thinking. Sits up at the house beside the pool staring over the city. Swims when her thoughts get locked down by memories of her mother. The emptiness. The absence of her. Of her quiet way of dealing with the world. Yet an insistent 'Christa, cherie, sometimes you must listen to your papa.' Her mother's voice so real she can hear it. Decides, enough.

Day eight into her leave Krista walks into Tami's office, closes the door. 'Mace and Pylon asked you to buy the company?'

'Something like that,' says Tami. 'Can't see it working, can you? The two of us.'

'Maybe yes, maybe no,' says Krista.

Tami gives her the level gaze. 'Why'd I want to go in with you? We have baggage.'

'So?'

Neither of them smiles.

'You're serious?' Tami unbelieving.

'Uh huh.'

'Why?'

'A little desperate.'

'Desperate's not good.'

'It's better than half-hearted.'

Tami says nothing.

'You?' Krista hearing Tami sigh, watching her look away through the window at the back of a building. Pigeons playing coy on the guttering.

Tami eventually. 'This's my job. I like it. I like it here. I like working for Mace and Pylon. You and me working together, I couldn't think of anything worse. With your attitude.'

'I'm over that.'

'Easy to say. Till the next time something comes up between us.'

'Won't happen. Look, I'm asking you, alright, we take it on. Equal partners.'

'Still don't get the change of heart.'

'Okay, it's Mace. Mace thinks it'll work. So does Pylon. So does my mother.'

'Your mother!'

'Voice of the ancestor.'

'You're weird.'

'So?'

So this is what they do, buy Complete Security on a never-never basis. Both of them not sure they're doing the right thing.

'Children,' says Mace, 'good luck.'

'Piss off,' the children respond without hesitation. Cute beginning.

Pylon pulls the cork on French champagne.

Now Krista yanked up her jeans, smiled at Tami. 'There's a girlie in distress, how can we not help her?

It's what we do.' She fastened the zip. 'We're getting a rep for it.'

Tami shook her head. 'Seriously. What's the story?'

Krista told her, in the retelling realised the bigger picture. 'Hey! That was them. At the Lagoon Beach restaurant, the one we were taking the customers to. That was them in the drive-by. Well, how's that? Really exciting.'

'Krista,' said Tami, 'Krista think about this. Think about what we're stepping into. This's a Cape Flats gangster. Those guys go to war, people die in the cross-fire.'

'I know.'

'Well?'

'Well, this's our job. This's what we do. A woman wants protection, we provide.'

Tami clucked her tongue. Cursed in Xhosa. 'I thought Mace was crazy. You're worse.'

Krista grinning. 'Like they say, you get the gene, that's your scene.'

ll

Titus Anders and Lavinia at the Sunset Beach house, Titus on the phone to Luc. Heard Luc say, 'We're done.'

Titus looking at the front lawn in floodlight, the lawn fraying into dune grass and salvia shrub where it met the beach. No protection. You walk off the beach onto the property. No gate, no fence, no wall. That was what he'd wanted. A house on the beach. Not just any beach, this beach.

Titus had a story about the beach that came out when he was tanked.

'Here,' he'd say, 'my people.' Pause to tap his chest. 'My people chased off the whiteys. Five hundred years ago. Chased them back into the sea. Chased them into their little boats, the whiteys really shitting themselves, really kakking themselves. My people did that. These Europeans think they can just come ashore and steal my people. Take their children. Kill their cattle, rape their women, kill them. Nuh uh, no, my friends. My people smashed them, one time. In the surf. Killed them man by man on this beach.' Titus pointing at his floodlit front lawn, the beach beyond. 'On my lawn. In the sand there's the blood of white men. Nobody'll make that mistake again, try'n attack me.'

What he'd wanted with the house was openness, freedom. A sense of the house being part of the beach, the bay. His only concession bulletproof glass. But what use bulletproof glass to someone on a mission?

Titus staring at the ships' lights on the dark water, thinking anyone could come off the ocean in a rubber ducky. Attack his house.

Let them try.

'Okay,' he said to Luc on the phone, 'come home. You've got half an hour. I told Rings and Baasie twelve midnight.' He disconnected Luc, said to Lavinia, 'Your phone?'

Lavinia tightened the grip on her BlackBerry. 'No, Daddy, please.'

'Give it to me.' Titus reaching out for it. 'Come, meisiekind, how many times d'you want me to ask?'

Hadn't called her meisiekind in a long time. He'd used it in her younger days when he was cross with her. Slipping out of English into Afrikaans. Meisiekind, wat die donner – when she backchatted him. Girl child, what the hell, didn't have the same ring in English. Too endearing. You could pack considerable anger into meisiekind. Or love. It had both possibilities.

As it had now.

'Come, meisiekind, how many times d'you want me to ask?' The blue in his eyes went bright, his face pinched. He wanted his daughter safe. Lavinia injured or worse a thought that brought darkness behind his eyes.

He took the BlackBerry from her hand. 'They can find you with this,' he said. 'If they've got your number, they'll find you.' Titus opened the casing, took out the battery.

'Who's they, Daddy?' Lavinia being cheeky, goading her father into a temper display.

'I don't know.' He threw down the phone pieces. 'I'm finding out. All I know is we were targets. They already got Boetie. They missed us this time round, they'll try again. True as God, that's what they will do. Try again. Short and simple, they'll try again. So we take precautions.'

'Like you and the boys wait here for them. Have a shoot-out?'

'Maybe.'

'Very macho.'

Titus stepped up to her. 'What's your case? You got another plan? Hey?'

She put a hand on his chest, pushed him back. Gently. The bluster going out of her father. 'This's Tamora. You've got to face it. She wants more than what you gave her. You let her in a little bit but she wants more.'

'I gave her plenty.' Titus headed out of the room, beckoning her to follow.

'It's what I heard.'

Titus coming round on her. 'From who?'

'Friends. Friends of friends.'

'I don't want you mixing with those sort of people.'

'What sort of people?'

'You know what I mean. Mitchells Plain people. It's why we live here. Far away from there.'

'I have friends, Daddy. Some of them live there. They can't help it.'

Titus took her hand. 'What'd you hear?'

Lavinia held out her other hand, palm up, slightly cupped. 'She's got the Mongols. Like that.'

Titus snorted. 'Her! A woman!'

'It's what I heard.' Lavinia extracting her hand from her father's, moving away. 'It was Chetty driving, Daddy. Chetty's with Tamora. Her driver. Also she's got this weird thing with him.'

'What?'

'Like she screws him.'

'Black Aron Chetty?'

Lavinia nodded.

'You know this for sure?'

'Uh ummm.'

'How?'

'I told you, friends of friends. They get seen around. Tamora's got this apartment in the city. I got friends in the same block.'

'Jesus,' said Titus. Titus thinking the Tamora he knew was a street girl. The reason he'd given her a break with the abalone concession. She'd been making good money for him but not that good. Unless ... Unless she was on the take. Defrauding him. Except Titus couldn't see her doing it alone. Had to be someone behind her, using her, ja, that could be a scenario. But who? Russians, Triads, Nigerians, the scene was open these days. Plenty of types wanted what he had, was getting from the Pretty Boyz. So could be anyone. Could be a new Cape Flats hard man riding her. Could be Mongols. Could be but he'd know. There'd be talk. Someone would come to him or Rings or Baasie and say something. Whisper in their ears. Just came as a helluva surprise after all these years of quiet.

'Not for you to worry about,' he said. Led Lavinia into the room with the walk-in safe. He pressed numbers into the safe keypad, opened the door. Inside bundles of money in rands, dollars, euros, sterling, computers, phones, two-way radios, guns – both handguns and rifles – boxes of ammunition, teargas canisters, scopes, night-vision glasses, binoculars, torches. The Titus Anders apocalypse arsenal. He took out a cellphone. 'This's prepaid. Got my number, your brothers', Rings, Baasie, that's it. Nobody else from this phone, you with me?'

'Daddy!'

'You with me?'

Lavinia took the phone. 'I've got a life.'

'For a week, Lavinia. That's all I'm asking. Maybe less. So I know you're safe in some place nobody knows about. Just until we sort this out. Please. I don't want to lose you. I can't lose you.' Coming up to her, cupping her face in his hands. 'For your daddy. Do this for your daddy.' Staring into her eyes, Lavinia staring right back at him. No give. But he knew she'd do what he wanted. She was his girl, his daughter, smart, sassy, yes, but smart above all. He opened his hands, released her. 'Go pack a bag.'

'Rings won't like it.'

'Rings isn't your fiancé yet. He'll be okay.' He pointed at the staircase. 'Please, be ready. Those security'll come here soon.'

On her way upstairs to pack, Lavinia got her new phone working. Sent an SMS to Baasie Basson: Baby, Daddy's sending me to a safehouse. Don't know where yet. Love you. No smileys on this phone for her to add.

Baasie came back: Good idea. Use my apartment.

Maybe. Want to see you.

Will be there soon.

Sent to Rings as well. A smiley with a downturned mouth would have gone with this on her BlackBerry.

By return: Be cool.

Baasie the ever calm dude. How she could shuck Rings for Baasie was her problem. Her father would kill her, if Rings didn't. But Rings wasn't her type, boring, all politics, no fun and laughter, so old. No braais around the pool with the chickies flashing their boobs. Nothing Lavinia liked more than letting her little sistas hang out. Catch men looking, desiring. Knowing they were Baasie's.

Titus saw Luc and Quint were stoned. Not just dagga, pills too, he reckoned. If it wasn't coke. These days kids couldn't do a job, just walk away afterwards. No, had to get revved up. He watched them stop on the gravel drive, skidding. Luc driving the Terios, laughing, hyped. Quint out of it too, but more controlled. Titus saw himself in Quint. The body shape, the attitude. Couldn't see that in Luc. Where the hell he'd come from, who knew? His one eye, his damaged finger, his thing with violence. Thin, mean kid. One of those – what'd they call them? – psychopaths. Sociopaths. Freaky boy. Frightening, even to him.

Titus held up his hands. 'I don't want to know.' Saw Luc's face shut down. The boy eager to show him video clips. 'I don't want to see anything.'

'It's okay, Daddy,' said Quint.

Right then headlights came into the close, slowly approached.

'Don't say anything,' said Titus. 'Rings and Baasie don't need to know yet.' He pointed at the phone in Luc's hand. 'You haven't sent pictures?'

Luc shook his head. 'We's holding it.'

'Okay, fine. Fine. I'll tell you when. Okay?' Luc jiggled from foot to foot. Titus said again, 'Okay?'

'Okay, Daddy, no problem. Chill with a pill.'

'Luc,' said Titus. 'No shit, hey? Just stay shut up.'

The black Fortuner stopped, Rings Saturen got out. Rings dressed in a Madiba floral shirt, cream chinos, grey sneakers, light jacket draped over his shoulders in the European style. Rings put on the concern. Hugs and back slaps.

'Call down Lavinia,' Titus said to Quint, watching another car come into the close: a Lexus coupé, top down. Baasie came over. Behind him the car's top closing automatically, the lock lights flashing twice.

He greeted everyone by name, the brother's handshake. Eye-to-eye contact expressing his support. They went inside, Baasie at the rear. There was Lavinia descending the stairs, all long legs and camisole, flicking back her hair. Eyes on Baasie.

She kissed Rings on the cheek, let him embrace her. Let him hold her hand while she gave Baasie a peck, quick, nothing special. Baasie reached out to rub her arm. The only contact between them. Rings and Titus paying no attention.

They sat in the lounge with the sliding doors open to the darkness and the sea. Quint fixed drinks, mostly straight whiskies except Baasie was on a lite beer.

'That a good idea?' said Rings, pointing at the open doors. 'All of us sitting here in plain sight.'

'No one's out there, Rings.' Titus sat down next to him.

'That's what you thought earlier. No one's out there. But someone was. Someone could be now. Lining up to whack the Untouchables quick-quick.'

'No, man, no ways. You got to be stupid trying it again.'

'You got to be stupid trying it once.' Rings crossed his legs. Raised his glass. 'Longlive.' They drank to it. 'Okay, my brother, now tell us what happened. You're at Lagoon Beach, alright, having supper. Showing how you handle your grief. The family in mourning for the murdered son and brother. Dignified. Defying those who hurt us. Challenging them. Letting everyone see that you are a family. A family that cannot be defeated. I am right?'

Titus nodded.

'Then you leave?'

Titus let the question drop, stood up to take back some authority for his own story. Paced the room.

He told them to the point where he saw the shooter, where the shooter grinned at him, raised the Uzi. Titus glanced at his associates, Rings, Baasie, watched their faces, both men listening hard, their eyes on him. Titus half into saying, 'You know how you can't hear anything ...' Paused.

In the pause they heard a car stop, the throb of its engine. Everyone got tense. Hands reached for weaponry. In the pause, the doorbell chimed.

'It's okay,' said Titus, 'only the security.' Motioned Quint to let them in.

Quint came back with Krista and Tami, Krista's short hair frizzed out from her swim.

Rings wolf-whistled. 'This's security,' he said. 'Girls are security these days? Hello, poppies.'

'Complete Security,' said Tami.

'Really,' said Rings. 'Impressive.'

Titus got up to shake their hands. Said to Krista, 'You Mace Bishop's daughter?'

'I am,' said Krista.

'I can see it. Same eyes.' He pointed at Lavinia, sitting on a chair to the side of the group, waved her over. 'She's my daughter, you look after her.'

'It's what we do.'

'Better do it damn fine.' He glanced from Krista to Tami, frowned, seeing in their faces what he'd seen in the faces of hard men off the Flats. A lack. A lack of response. Men about to stick a knife in had that face. He smiled. 'Okay.'

'Mace Bishop's girlie?' said Rings. 'Where's Mace these days?'

'Caymans,' said Krista.

Rings whistled again. 'Expensive place. He lives there?'

'Most of the time.'

'Made a lot of money selling guns, sounds like.'

'Guns. Perlemoen. Tik. Where's the difference?'

Baasie laughed. Rings didn't. Took a taste of his whisky, kept his stare on Krista. 'Mace had a mouth.'

'Ha. I told her that as well,' said Titus.

Rings put down the glass on a coaster. 'I heard stories about you, my sister. Bad stories. You got a reputation for a young lady. Some men worry about that. About a lady like you with a rep-u-ta-tion. The sort of men I'm talking about aren't men, my sister, they're animals. You know what I mean, they don't understand about feelings. Men I'm talking about've eaten other men's hearts while it's pumping. You get my point here? You better watch out, there's people who know about you, who've seen you.'

Krista said, 'You're Mr Rings Saturen, you're the politician.'

'I am, my sister.'

She smiled, stepped forward, slid a business card across the coffee table towards him. 'For any women you know.'

Baasie laughed again. 'One for me?'

'Sure.' Held out a card between her fingers, Baasie withdrawing it slowly, smiling at her. 'You don't guard men?'

'No,' came in Tami, 'too many issues.'

'That's my woman you've got,' said Rings. 'I'm trusting you.'

Krista saw the glance: Lavinia to Rings then on to Baasie. Baasie winked. Rings oblivious, swirling the whisky in his glass. Krista touched Lavinia on the elbow. 'You ready to go?'

III

The Russian wanted another gun.

Said to Black Aron Chetty, 'You must get me a gun.' Actually specified a Heckler & Koch MP5K, what he called the kurz. Actually said, 'With that weapon there is no problem. The best weapon for this situation.'

Black Aron and the Russian sitting in the Toyota in the parking lot, staring at the shiny Mercs on a dealership's showroom floor.

'You know this gun?'

Black Aron shook his head, couldn't care less what sort of gun the Russian wanted.

'In many countries the cops use it. In my country the army.'

'And you can get this gun?'

'Spot on.'

Black Aron glanced at the Russian, again unsure if he was taking the piss. Considered, too, what the Russian was saying. Drummed his index finger on the steering wheel, kept staring at the cars, said, 'You're saying the gun, the Uzi, was the problem?'

'I am telling you with this gun, the kurz, then no one is standing.'

'The gun was the problem at the restaurant?'

The Russian lifted a cigarette packet from his shirt pocket, knocked out a stick. 'It is possible.'

'No smoking,' said Black Aron.

The Russian opened his door, lit the cigarette, blew out smoke.

'No smoking,' said Black Aron.

'This is not in your car,' said the Russian.

Black Aron turned his head: the Russian had his legs out of the car, the long curve of his back sloping up to his small head. Really small head for such a big man.

'So now you want this gun?'

'Why not?'

'You know where to get it?'

'Of course.'

'Figures,' said Black Aron. 'Plenty of Smirnoffs all over this city with hardware.' He swung the ignition. 'Where to?'

The Russian gave him a Sea Point address. Turned out to be a double-storey behind a wall topped with electric wire. Wrought-iron gate between two columns, an intercom box glowing on the right. Low lights up the garden path to the front door. Neat lawn patches either side, edged with white river stones. The Russian pushed the bell button. He and Black Aron Chetty standing side by side framed by the columns: looked like pizza delivery guys.

A boy's voice came on the box. Tentative, accented. The Russian said he wanted to speak to Dr Smul.

Dr Smul was with the rabbi, the boy replied.

The Russian said it was urgent. Said something in Russian.

The boy said wait.

'He's a doctor?' said Black Aron. 'This Dr Smul.'

The Russian nodded. 'For something.'

'Like medicine?'

'Medicine maybe.'

The boy's voice on the box told them to come in, the gate clicked open. They walked up the garden path to the front door. Knocked. Dr Smul opened. An irritated Dr Smul. Dr Smul a compact man, big head, moon face, big gut, wearing shorts and sandals, a long-sleeved lounge shirt untucked, open at the neck. Went in Russian at the Russian, pushing them into a reception room. Huge samovar in one corner, escritoire in another, a trunk serving as a coffee table with a chessboard centre stage, leather armchairs either side, towering over one a wooden standing lamp with a shade wide as an umbrella.

To Black Aron Dr Smul said, 'Are you cop?'

Black Aron said he wasn't. The Russian confirmed it.

Dr Smul glared up at them through owl glasses, even Black Aron a head taller than the doctor. 'So what is urgent?'

The Russian said he needed an H&K MP5, the kurz, a box of bullets.

Dr Smul took off his glasses, cleaned them with the ends of his shirt. 'In my dining room is the rabbi. He is my supper guest for a nice supper, fish, salad, fresh fish I buy today. The salad from Woolworths, garden greens. We have some white wine. You come here, my friend, you say it is urgent you see me. Okay, there are emergencies sometimes. I tell the rabbi wait a minute.

I tell him excuse me from the meal, rabbi, I must help a countryman, he has some trouble. The rabbi says, please Smul help the man. But what does the man want?' Dr Smul put on his glasses. 'The man wants a gun. At nine o'clock the man wants a gun. A gun and bullets. I am in my house with the rabbi having supper, the man says he wants a gun. You think I can get these things for you? Why? Why you think this? How much money will you pay? You don't show me any money? You say, Dr Smul, one gun with ammunition. One MP5. This is a very expensive gun. You think I am a shop merchant, my friend? You think this? You think I can just take one off the shelf? You see shelves with guns? Pah.' Dr Smul lifted the chessboard from the coffee table. 'You must learn. Dr Smul is not a shop-keeper.' He opened the trunk, inside an assortment of weaponry: handguns, machine pistols. Stacked in a compartment: boxes of ammunition. Dr Smul took out two submachine guns, scratched, unoiled. 'Which one you want, my friend?' The Russian pointed at the one Dr Smul held in his right hand. Dr Smul said, 'For you, five thousand. You bring it back in two days I pay you three thousand back. Every day you are late it is five hundred more.'

The Russian took the gun, checked the breach, the barrel, slipped out the magazine. Said, 'Okay.'

Dr Smul held out his hand. 'The money?'

The Russian looked at Black Aron.

'No, no, no, I'm the driver. You pay.'

Dr Smul spoke in Russian to the Russian, thrust a

receipt book at him. The Russian saying something in return, wrote in the book, signed his name.

'Da.' Dr Smul smiled at Black Aron. 'The driver. This is a good occupation? Driving for my friend.' He fished in the ammunition compartment of the trunk, handed the Russian a box of bullets. 'You like driving?'

'It's okay,' said Black Aron. 'It's not all I do.'

'I am certain,' said Dr Smul. 'Goodnight, my friends. The rabbi is waiting for me.'

In the car Black Aron said to the Russian, 'Why'd he let you have it?'

'He is my countryman. He knows I will pay. I have signed for the gun. He has your phone number. It is all … how do you say … spot on.'

'He has my phone number? You gave him my phone number?'

'Of course. He want insurance.'

Black Aron gripped the steering wheel with both hands, heat prickling across his back, sweat beading in his armpits. 'You … you …' He was panting, tried to control his breathing.

The Russian sat there with the gun on his lap. 'Don't worry, my friend.'

'You … you …'

'No problems, my friend, Dr Smul is a good man, yes, very kindly man. Very religious. Often the rabbi is there eating with him to talk about God. You must not worry. No problems.'

Black Aron headed for Sunset Beach, thinking the Russian was a problem, Dr Smul was a problem, Titus

Anders was a problem. Tamora heard about this one she'd be a problem.

He came along Ocean Way, did a dog's leg through the suburb to a parking place on the beach. One other car there, no one visible.

'This is very nice place to live,' said the Russian. 'Very peaceful looking at the sea every day.' He broke open the box of bullets, fed them into the magazine, a long clip holding thirty. 'Where is the house?'

Black Aron pointed into the dark along the beach. 'That way. You wait here, I'll take a look, find the right house.'

The Russian considered this. Then nodded. 'Alright. You want we do it in this way.' He eased the clip into its housing, laid the gun at his feet. 'You go.' Taking his cigarettes from his pocket.

'No smoking in the car,' said Black Aron.

The Russian grinned. Waved him off. 'Go, go, find the house, Mr Driver.'

Black Aron walked a trail of soft sand, his sandals soon gritty, the grit chafing his feet. He cursed the Russian, he cursed the place, he cursed Titus Anders. A relief to be without the Russian but the night was long still.

Across the beach scrub he could see into the houses. No one concerned. Windows open. Patio doors open. People watching television. People sitting out having wine. People enjoying the night. Lovely summer night on Sunset Beach.

He doubted they could see him. No one seemed to

notice his passing. He was invisible against the night.

The Anders house was the same as the others, open. He stood watching Titus Anders talking on his cell. Lavinia feet up on a couch, absorbed in her phone. You looked at this scene, you wouldn't say earlier they'd been shot at. Racked with gunfire was how a reporter would put it. Calm dad-and-daughter scene like this. Stunner the daughter. Black Aron crouched. He liked being there watching. This big man, one of the Untouchables, unaware he was being watched. Black Aron made a gun of his fist. Pow. One shot. Kill shot. Easy as that. Saw Titus finish his phone call, turn to Lavinia. This would be easy for the Russian. He could shoot them. The boys'd come running, shoot them too.

He walked back, told the Russian his plan.

The Russian heard him out. 'Nyet.'

'Of course, man.'

'No.' The Russian shook his head, held up the gun. 'There is no silencer. I shoot them there will be noise. Pah, pah, pah, pah, pah, pah. Too much noise. And this job it is half done. If you do not see the sons then where are they?'

'Somewhere else in the house.'

'Maybe. But also maybe not. Maybe they are not home. When everybody is in the house, then I can do the job.'

Black Aron let it go.

They sat out two hours, staring at the ships' lights in the bay, checked on the house every thirty minutes. Black Aron drank coffee, ate samoosas. The Russian smoked his cigarettes, complained when they were finished, he needed to buy more.

'No ways,' said Black Aron. 'No ways, Smirnoff. We're sitting tight.'

When Luc and Quint got home, Black Aron was watching from the beach. A luck at last. The family united. He hurried back to tell the Russian, Go, go, go.

Forty-five minutes later the Russian returned, running. Dropped into the seat. Said, 'Fast. We must go. Fast.' Coughing out the words. 'The woman has gone with two others.'

'What?' Black Aron turned in the seat towards the Russian. 'What're you talking about? I didn't hear anything. No shots. What's going on? What others?'

The Russian getting it out: the arrival of other men, the arrival of other women, these women taking away the man's daughter.

Black Aron said, 'Oh, shit.'

'They are taking her to another place.'

Black Aron said, 'I can put that together.' Took the Corolla out of the parking lot with a rubber skid. Tamora wouldn't be happy if they lost part of the target.

They came up behind a vw Sharan on Ocean Way: three women in it.

'There we are,' said the Russian. 'No problem.'

Followed it towards the city, past Lagoon Beach, the cops gone, no sign there'd been a drive-by earlier. Onto Marine Drive. Black Aron thought, How many times do I have to do this stretch in one night? Backwards and forwards like some minibus taxi. Black Aron giving the Sharan a hundred-metre gap. This hour of night anyone headed for the city had to take this route. No other options.

Followed the Sharan onto the N1, closing the gap to fifty metres. Back past the Merc dealership, the tile emporium, next set of lights the Sharan took a left onto the highway. Black Aron followed, realised the fems in the Sharan might be spooked.

Some traffic on the highway, enough to hide one car back.

'They know you are following,' said the Russian.

Which Black Aron didn't admit.

The Russian clicked his tongue. 'Stupid.'

Black Aron said nothing, put a couple of cars between them. Changed lanes. No ways the fems could keep them tagged.

Until the Sharan headed off at the first exit into Woodstock. Caused Black Aron to pull a manoeuvre over three lanes, cars sliding around them. They came down the off-ramp, saw the Sharan go left into a side street.

Black Aron worked the gears. At the turning, the tail lights of the Sharan two hundred metres away. 'You want to shoot her now?' he said. Quiet part of Woodstock, row of low semis either side the street, the street running out in the dark beneath the highway.

The Russian brought up the gun. 'If you catch them.'

'I know this place,' said Black Aron. Took a right, then left into the main road, there was the Sharan. 'Ah ha, you see.'

'Spot on,' said the Russian, that tone in his voice Black Aron wasn't sure about.

The Sharan accelerated through red traffic lights, opening the gap, headed towards the city. Black Aron put foot, got the Corolla screaming, wished he had the BMW. Round the Castle corner, at the Parade up Buitenkant, after the cop shop the Sharan going right into Barrack.

'Police,' said the Russian.

'So what?' said Black Aron, taking the lights on red.

'We do not want police.'

'We're not gonna get them. They hear tyre squeal, they shake their heads.'

They got into Barrack, the Sharan was nowhere. An empty street. No parked cars. No vagrants in the doorways. No lights on in buildings.

Black Aron lost it, pounded the steering wheel with both fists. Screamed, 'No, no, no, no, no.' Still did a drive around: Plein, Spin, Parliament, along Adderley to the Slave Lodge. Sat there looking up Wale Street. Lots of cross-street intersections. Occasions before when this'd happened you drove around waiting for some magnetic force to reconnect you. So often it did. You waited on a central street. The force worked for you.

Not this time.

They sat five minutes, the engine running. The Russian said, 'You take me to The Fez now.'

'Really,' said Black Aron.

'Is no use tonight.'

'Tomorrow.'

'Oh yeah, tomorrow.' Black Aron wondering how he'd tell Tamora this one. Before they'd screwed? After they'd screwed? While they screwed? Tamora lying there with that softness on her face, side by side on the pillow, hardly moving, Tamora's thighs clamped. He'd have to say, Ah, babe, the job's not done. We lost the chickie. She'd eject him faster than pulling a plug. Wouldn't open those smooth thighs till he told her otherwise about the job.

The Russian was saying, 'I know the car number. You have people to trace it?'

Black Aron looked at him. Got rid of Tamora's thighs, laughed. 'Spot on, Smirnoff.'

IV

At 23.29 Mart Velaze watched Rings Saturen come out of his cute Pinelands house, alone. Remote up the second garage, drive away in a black Fortuner, a no-shit military-style vehicle. According to the file, the Fortuner on lease through his car-hire company, even though said company ran only Mercs. A Benz not quite how Rings saw himself, Mart Velaze supposed.

He hesitated. Should he wait, see if the woman left? Could always catch up with Rings et al at Sunset Beach. Was unlikely Rings would make any stops along the way.

Mart Velaze looked at the time on his cellphone: 23.32. He'd give her five minutes. Picked up his camera.

23.35. There she was in the light of the porch.

Mart Velaze pressed off some digitals. Fine shots, the light on her face. Whatta babe. Grinned to himself at his instincts. You learnt one thing being a spook, it was to wait. The one who waiteth is rewarded. Something the Voice was always going on about.

He sat tight while the woman opened her car, drove away. Once she'd turned the corner at the end of the street, he put down the camera, started his car.

Twenty minutes later he was at Sunset Beach, fifty metres down from the entrance to the close where Titus Anders had his mansion. Angle of vision allowed him plain sight of the Anders property. There was a Terios in the driveway, Rings's Fortuner, Baasie Basson's Lexus, a nice bit of metal that, Baasie had taste. Baasie the stylista.

Mart Velaze'd been there ten minutes, in rolled a Sharan he recognised. Raised his eyebrows. Hello Complete Security. The pretties working overtime. Mart brought up his night-vision binocs. There was Krista and Tami alighting. My, my. Another thing you learnt at the spookery, never be surprised. Not only did shit happen, sometimes amazing shit happened.

Fifteen minutes later, out came Krista and Tami with Lavinia in tow.

'Ah, sweet,' said Mart Velaze aloud. 'Titus looking after his little girl.' Watched Krista close the Sharan's door after Lavinia, take a glance round the street. That Krista was sharp. A waste of talent, Mart Velaze believed. The sort of talent the Voice could put to good use.

He watched them reverse out of the close, drive away. All quiet, the minutes ticking by. Until his cell-phone rang: no less an entity than the Voice.

'Chief?'

'Ma'am,' said Mart Velaze, sitting up from his low-down slouch in the seat.

'You're outside the Anders place?'

He confirmed he was.

'You might want to listen to this, chief. Something to help pass the time.'

He heard Rings Saturen say, 'We can't chop and change. We, you got to meet with the Chinese.'

Titus: 'No, Rings, I'm not saying we don't meet, I'm saying we change the place.'

Baasie: 'He's got a point, Rings.'

Rings: 'To where?'

Titus: 'I go to the hotel.'

Rings: 'The Cape Grace. Hell, man, Titus. Where's your sense, man? Tomorrow's, today's front page the headline'll read: Titus Anders in drive-by shooting. They gonna have your picture right there, front page. You walk into the Grace, everyone looks up from their breakfast, sees the man they're reading about. How's the Chinaman going to feel? Seen there in the hotel with a gangster.'

Titus: 'Crap, man, Rings.'

Rings: 'That's what they'll write, Titus. Pull me and Baasie into the story, call us the Untouchables, pull in abalone poaching, drugs, our businesses, me on the politics, playboy Baasie. All over page one. Nice, hey?'

Mart Velaze smiled. Thought, How long'd the Voice had a bug in there? Typical. Never tell anyone anything. Only tell on a need-to-know. The Voice more paranoid than a sangoma throwing the bones.

Baasie: 'My other place, in Clifton. No problems there.'

A silence.

The Voice said, 'You're hearing this, chief?'

'Very interesting,' said Mart Velaze.

Titus came in: 'Okay, that's a plan. But maybe the hotel is fine. We can organise a room. Ja, we'll do that.'

A pause, then Baasie: 'I'm thinking this isn't random, tonight.'

Rings: 'Why not? It's Mongols causing shit. Wanting back on the abalone scene. It was Pretty Boyz took it from them. Remember. Our Pretty Boyz. That was a war. A big war. Lots of bodies. What I've heard, there's trouble on the streets.'

Baasie: 'What I'm told, that woman Tamora, the one Titus gave a concession, she's stirring the Mongols. Telling them they can be players.'

Rings: 'It's Mongols alone, Baasie. The old story: turf war. They want the Valley of Plenty.'

Baasie: 'I heard that too.'

Rings: 'How close is your ear, my bru?'

Baasie: 'I hear what I hear. Tamora's name I hear too often.'

Rings: 'You hear what they want you to hear.'

Baasie: 'So tell us, Rings, what's the real scene?'

Rings: 'Baasie, Baasie. Remember who gave you a gap. Remember, remember.'

Baasie: 'I don't forget, Rings. What we all got to remember is the alliance. How we work, tripartite. Us three.'

Titus: 'Baasie, I heard this story about the Mongols moving in.'

Baasie: 'You think they killed Boetie?'

Titus: 'It could've been.'

Baasie: 'Something else I was told, Tamora's son's missing.'

Titus: 'I don't know about that.'

Rings: 'It's true.'

Baasie: 'To me it looks like you and her, Titus.'

Titus: 'Uh uh, I gave her a fishing zone. A bloody good zone for perlemoen. Right there where it's easy. I gave her venture money to buy the boat. She came to me. I said okay, alright. Me, I'm the promo-man here. Why's she want to kill my son? She wants more, we can talk about it. Doesn't have to kill my son. Why's she going to do that? I've been good to her. She wants more business, maybe I can arrange more business. Why's she going to the Mongols?'

Baasie: 'I don't know. Because of the Chinese?'

Titus: 'How's she going to know about the Chinese? Only us know about the Chinese.'

Rings: 'Us and everybody. Our Chinese're on a trade mission here. Meeting government, mining people, political people, estate agents, lawyers all over the country. Chop-chop the Chinese are moving in. You go and look, isn't a dorp there's not a Chinese. Everywhere, they're the new invaders.'

Titus: 'Only we know they're talking to us.'

Rings: 'You think? You think that, you're dreaming, my friend.'

Titus: 'We don't gossip our business.'

Rings: 'We don't have to. This's Chinese. We're talking about two billion mouths. Government has to know we talk to the Chinese. Government probably listening to us now.'

Titus: 'Man, Rings, don't talk bullshit.'

Rings: 'Could be.'

Mart Velaze heard the Voice snort. 'Sharp, sharp, my brothers. What d'you say, chief? You think we should be interested in this meeting with the Chinese?'

'I dunno,' said Mart Velaze. 'These the same Chinese arrived earlier?'

'They are.'

'You know about this Clifton place?'

A sigh. 'No, chief, this is new. They meet there, we're off comms.' The Voice shushing him then.

He heard Luc say: 'It was Black Aron driving.'

Rings: 'What, Luc? What're you saying?'

Luc: 'It was Black Aron driving tonight. Driving the shooter.'

Laughter.

Luc: 'I saw Black Aron.'

Rings: 'Black Aron Chetty? Ag, no, man, Black Aron

is small time. Black Aron wouldn't do that. He'd shit himself.'

Luc: 'It was him.'

Baasie: 'I don't know this guy.'

Luc: 'It was him.'

Rings: 'You're sure?'

Luc: 'Yes, man.'

Rings: 'You didn't see him, Titus?'

Titus: 'I was looking at this whitey waving a gun. Grinning at me. Small-faced whitey. You think I'm checking out who's driving in that situation?'

Rings: 'Hey, okay, okay. I only asked. Okay. You want me to talk to him, to Chetty?'

Titus: 'No, it's alright. We can do that.'

Baasie: 'And now what happens? We all go home to bed?'

Rings: 'Why not?'

Baasie: 'You think they're not going to get me or you?'

Rings: 'Ag, hell, Baasie. This used to happen all the time, man. Ask Titus. Ten, fifteen years ago, you had a drive-by every night. Someone hoping to score a luck. You gotta just be careful. We got a name, we can come down on this.'

Baasie: 'Tamora?'

Rings: 'Tamora too, if you think so. Hey, Titus. You gonna talk to her nicely?'

Silence.

Rings: 'You gonna talk to her?'

Titus: 'Of course, man, ja, I'll talk to her.'

The Voice switched off the feed, said, 'Lots of things for you to work on, chief. All these names: Tamora, Black Aron Chetty, mysterious gunman, Chinese men. You have a life out of a book, Mr Velaze.' She laughed. Ended the laugh with a coughing spell. Said, 'Ah, yes, might be an idea to wire up the security girls.'

Mart Velaze could see Krista and Tami excited about that one.

'Take a break, chief. No need to wait for them to head home. I'll be in touch. Go with the ancestors, chief.'

All the same Mart Velaze sat it out until Baasie Basson in his Lexus pulled away, top down. Ten minutes later Rings Saturen came out with Titus. The men hugged, did the back slap. Mart Velaze wondered if Rings knew he was going home to an empty house. The black Fortuner reversed, drove slowly away. Titus stood there watching Rings out of sight. Stood there till Luc came to the front door, called him in. Twenty minutes later the downstairs lights in the Anders Sunset Beach house went out.

Mart Velaze gave it another ten minutes. He who waiteth is rewarded. Reckoned in the Anders house they'd be taking watches. Only bonus, someone was going to see the sun come up. He checked his cellphone: 2.03. No reward to waiting this time.

Mart Velaze thought about his flat, the unmade bed. Not sure he could face it. Scanned through his contacts. Considered the liebling at the German consulate with the untamed fur, the nipples of the Indian trade attaché, the meaty smell of the American strategic studies researcher. Couldn't see any of them being pleased with a phone call. Tried an Israeli woman, probably Mossad, called herself a travel agent.

She answered on the first ring.

'You want to fuck, Mart?' she said.

'I was thinking about it,' said Mart Velaze.

'Alright,' she said. 'Until three thirty. Then I have to go for a flight.'

'You should make it,' he said.

V

Transcript from the case file of Hardlife MacDonald:

You got imagination, you can work it out as well how it was like for the Pretty Boyz. Me, I got some imagination. In school I won a prize for a composition: my holidays they asked me to write about. Ja, you can work out what my holidays was like. There by the house in Mitchells Plain when I was a lightie they chained me to a pole in the back-yard so I couldn't run away when they went to work. Doesn't matter if it rains, they chain me to the pole. Give me some water in a bottle, maybe sometimes even Coke, and half a bread with jam. Another story, hey? I can say the Pretty Boyz on the roofs saw the lights of the Kadett come into the streets of the Valley of Plenty. The car going fast.

You got to know if you in that car you wanna get the job done. Find the house, throw the bombs, drive fast back to the Mongols before the Pretty Boyz start shooting. In the car they gonna be excited, laughing, shouting, looking for the house the captain told them is ground zero.

Part 2: The Mother City

5

I

Black Aron Chetty woke with the tickle of cigarette smoke in his nostrils. Rubbed his nose. Without opening his eyes, thought, Shit, she knew how the smoke got to him. Nothing he could say about it though.

He opened his eyes, there was Tamora sitting in the chair opposite him, with a Marlboro between her fingers, tapping the head into an ashtray, a pink glass number heavy enough to smash a human skull. Black Aron amazed that anybody smoked Marlboro after what happened to the man. Had wanted to tell Tamora plenty of times, 'What's the packet say? "Smoking kills".'

Tamora exhaled smoke at him.

Black Aron fanned it away, raised himself on his elbows. It was hot in the room. The morning sun full on the windows, not a breeze at the Roman blinds. The city locked down in humidity, the air chemical with traffic exhaust.

He sneezed. Again. Once, twice, three times. His eyes watered.

When they cleared said, 'My sinus.'

Tamora waving him aside like what he had to say was so much smoke.

He watched her walk to the bed, pull down the sheet covering him. Say, 'You screwed up, Mr-meneertjie. You and the Ruskie.' Tamora in some sort of silky gown hanging open, bending down to pinch his nipples. Her tits swinging before his eyes.

'A simple little job you got it all messed up,' she said. 'What's wrong, Ronnie?'

One thing worked sweat into his armpits was her taunting. The sarky Mr-meneertjie. Thing he couldn't do was tell her to quit it. Didn't have the balls for that.

Grinning, watched her blow smoke out the corner of her mouth, crush the cigarette into the ashtray. Felt the painful tweezer of her fingers.

Black Aron grimaced. Went hard. This lady more than he'd ever dreamed of. He had to take her shit.

'How you going to fix it, Aron?'

He wanted to reach up to get a feel of those tits with the big nipples. Raised his arms.

'Don't touch,' she said.

Last night it'd been okay to touch. Last night after he'd called her to say they'd have to make another plan, she'd said, 'Come, Ron, come to Mama.' And had jumped him as he walked in the door. Told him where to put his hands. Told him what to do.

'You and the Ruskie'll have to fix this, Aron,' she said now, stroking a hand across his chest. Black Aron turned on by the milkiness of her skin. The two of them together a double-decker: chocolate and cream.

'This's not what I wanted, this balls-up.' Talking as if they were making chit-chat. Or leaning on the railing along the Sea Point promenade looking at the ocean: big heads of seaweed lolling on the surface, flop-flopping with the swells. The two of them whispering lovers. His fantasy that they were an item. Sweethearts.

Tamora getting intense. A catch in her voice, not a whispering hard case anymore but coming on strong.

'This's not what I wanted, this mess, Aron, you hearing me, Aron, when I say I want this done, I'm saying I want it done right, first time, yes, right the way it should be, no mess-ups, nothing like that, yes, oh, no, move a bit, Aron, you're not bloody dead, yes.'

There she was, mounted on him. Got him underneath her like he was her human dildo. Buzz, buzz.

'You and the Ruskie with his little Uzi got to do the job, yes, Aron, finish what you started without any comeback for me, on me, mmm, no, slowly Aron, just get out there and put Titus and one-eyed Luc and Quint and the lovely Lavinia into boxes that's what I want, okay, and then maybe, yes, maybe, yes, we can think of Baasie next because why not, yes, what has he got that I haven't mmm, if the Chinese want to talk to me, me, Tamora, then this is good, no, good, really good, yes, Aron, stop, Aron, let me do it, mmm, like this, like this, oh yes, no, like this, yes, yes.'

Behind Tamora's moaning, Black Aron could hear her cellphone beeping. No ways he could climax, nothing left to do it with. A chafe on the side of his cock burning like hell. Black Aron relieved when she lifted herself off him, reached for her Samsung. Watched her view the MMS, her jaw gone tight, her face waxy.

She tossed the phone to him. Said, 'Kill Titus. Kill them all.'

Black Aron looked at the screen.

Saw: a teenage boy tied to a chair, looking up at the camera, mouth open.

Heard the cameraman say, 'It's a shit life, bru, any-how.'

Heard off-camera the whine of machinery starting up.

The camera zoomed into the boy's face, fish eyes, blubber mouth. Saliva shine on his teeth. Black Aron heard: 'Please, bru, please. I done nothing. Lemme go, bru, please, my bru. Ag, please.' The focus shifted down the boy's body to his crotch, the boy's pissing himself.

A voice said, 'Bru, we's gonna be quick.'

The camera panned round the room: hooks, racks of knives, stainless steel, to eyepatch Luc dapper in an apron at a bandsaw unit. The camera dollied round the unit, stopped for a shot of Luc. Serious Luc with a gleaming eyepatch pointing at the bandsaw with his short finger.

Luc said, 'We got to move him nearer.'

The image jerked, started again with the boy and the bandsaw in frame. Off-camera Luc said, 'Say good-bye to Mommy.'

The boy sobbed.

'Come'n, bru, say goobyes nicely.'

The camera closed on the boy. The other voice, Quint's voice: 'She can't hear if you cry like that.'

Black Aron heard the boy sob, 'Goobye, Mommy.' He was crying too hard, too much whine from the bandsaw to hear anything else.

'Okay,' said Luc, 'that's gonna have to do.'

Again the image jerked. Re-started with the boy lying on the sluicing tray, looked as if he'd be pushed head-on to the blade. His mouth was now taped, he was trussed legs and arms, he was wriggling like a tuna.

Luc said, 'We'll start small, my bru.' Spoke to the camera. 'You need to help me here, Quint, man.'

The image stopped. Took up with a finger lying on the stainless steel, blood dripping at the raw end. Pulled back to include a hand, a stump where the index finger used to be.

Black Aron wiped a hand over his face. Groaned.

Tamora lighting a cigarette, said, 'Get Miss Beautiful first. Titus's darling. Let the Ruskie do what he wants to her. Then we'll see how Daddy's going to like her. How Daddy's going to live with that shame. You do it the way they did it, okay, on video. You get that Ruskie doing it.'

Black Aron glanced back at the screen: an arm in the drip tray. No fingers on the hand. The camera shifting to the boy's face, the boy still alive.

'First priority, Aron. Lavinia's first priority.'

II

Krista finished her lengths, climbed out of the pool. Changed into a T-shirt and boxers. Both had belonged to her father. On the T-shirt two crossed AKS; *freedom* written on the back. The boxers baggy.

She towelled her hair, left it spiked. Felt the humidity quickly clammy on her skin, the heat pressing down. The day already sluggish, hot. It would get worse.

Inside offered no relief. She stopped in the lounge to listen. Heard neither Lavinia nor Tami stirring. The house quiet, ticking in the early heat. Once there'd been Cat2 to rub against her ankles in the early morning. But Cat2 had disappeared onto the mountain, causing a grief in Krista that had made her howl. Not since her mother's killing had such longing ached in her.

She still saw the movement of Cat2 slipping between rooms, climbing the stairs. Sometimes thought she heard the cat's husky cry. Sometimes called the cat's name. Cat2, Cat2. Ksss, ksss. Nothing.

Krista cut up fruit into a bowl: bananas, mangos, grapes. Her view through the kitchen window of a shimmering city, heat-hazed. On the 567 breakfast show, the drive-by at Lagoon Beach.

Titus Anders saying, 'Me and my family were lucky to escape alive, you know.' A seriousness to his voice like this was a major violation of a code of honour. 'I thought I was finished with this sort of disrespect. Can't a family have a supper in peace anymore?'

The interviewer: 'You're known as one of the Untouchables?'

A laugh from Titus. 'That's just people making jokes.'

'You're a gang lord.'

'No, man, no, you don't understand. That's in the past. Finished. I'm a businessman. Legitimate. You can ask the taxman.'

'So what's this about, Mr Anders?'

'I don't know. Sometimes people get strange ideas in their heads. They don't care what they do.'

'Saul from Mitchells Plain's smsed that you're a perlemoen poacher, Mr Anders? Are you?'

'No, my friend, of course not. I'm in the motor trade. Also I have two florist shops.'

'Mr Anders, I have to bring this up, my condolences on your son's death.'

'Thank you.'

'He died while diving?'

'It was an accident.'

'He was diving?'

'Ja, he was diving.'

'But not for abalone?'

'Please respect my grief.'

'Again, my condolences, Mr Anders. What now? Do you feel under attack?'

'Of course. My daughter is in a safehouse. My sons and myself sleep with guns. This is not good when you have no safety. We don't know if someone's going to shoot us on the street.'

'Have you laid a charge?'

'Against who?'

'You have no idea?'

'Truly no. I don't know who would do this.' The presenter cut to adverts.

Lavinia said, 'He knows who it is.'

Krista glanced round, saw Lavinia standing in the doorway. Lavinia still in her PJs, some silky number that looked expensive to Krista.

'Those guys who followed us?'

'Them and a bitch called Tamora.'

'Yeah, who's she?'

'A bitch.'

'You said that.' Krista pulled out a jar of rolled oats. Set it on a tray. Took a yoghurt from the fridge, bowls from a low cupboard. 'Listen, if we're supposed to protect you, we have to know who from.'

Lavinia came up, touched Krista on the arm, on the white stripes. 'You cut yourself?'

'Who didn't? It was long ago.'

'I didn't. I vomited.'

'Looks like you still do.'

'Sometimes.'

'You going to waste my breakfast?'

Lavinia smiled. 'No, I like it here. Sunset Beach is alright, but here you're up above everything. Like you're flying.'

'Works for me,' said Krista. 'Who's Tamora?'

Lavinia perched on a stool at the breakfast counter, flipped through the novel Krista had left there, Didion's

Democracy, explained. Told her this bitch came up from the streets, probably screwed her father to get an abalone concession out of him. Had made it big time. Like a stellar rise. Even got the Mongols gang eating from her hand.

Krista wondering if daughters all had this thing about their fathers screwing other women. Put it aside. Said, 'Your father runs the abalone poaching?'

'Of course. You didn't know?'

'I lead a sheltered life. Go on.'

Told her Tamora wanted power. Money.

'This woman's going to get rid of your family?' Krista laughed. 'Go against your father? Come on. You've got to be joking.'

'Not only against my daddy.'

'Who else?'

Lavinia explained about Rings Saturen, Baasie Basson. Krista listened while she prepared the coffee. Spooned French roast into a four-cup Bialetti, set it on a gas ring. 'You're telling me this lady's going up against all three of them? By herself? Got to be some woman with balls like that.'

'She's …'

'A bitch,' said Tami. 'I heard that.'

Lavinia almost fell off her stool. Jerked round at the voice behind her, put her hand to her heart. 'You gave me a fright.'

'I do that to people,' said Tami. 'Sorry.'

Krista glanced at her partner, didn't see a trace of sorry in her face. Tami dressed as Tami was always dressed, in uniform: black T-shirt, jeans, black Nike Airs. Formidable. Cute, too, Krista thought. She smiled. Got only a raised eyebrow from Tami.

'You want to take breakfast outside?' said Krista.

They did. Ate at the table beside the pool, in the shade. Sweat soon dampening their armpits.

'Where're you going to take me?' asked Lavinia, heaping nuts, seeds, oats, yoghurt, honey onto the fruit. Mixing it together the way Krista did. For a vomiter she liked her food, Krista thought. But then vomiters did. It was afterwards they behaved badly.

'Nowhere,' said Tami.

'Here's fine,' said Krista.

'They'll find me.'

'Like how?'

'Your car registration.'

'That'll take them to our offices,' said Krista, 'no further.'

Lavinia shrugged. 'I want a gun.'

'Oh, yeah,' said Tami. 'You've got us. Much better than a gun.'

Lavinia looked from Tami to Krista.

'What?' said Krista, chewing her way through a mouthful.

'Nothing.'

'You're thinking, women, what can women do? Some toothless joller from the Cape Flats comes over the wall waving his dick what're we going to do? You're thinking that?'

'Sort of.'

'Here's a story,' said Tami. 'Listen.'

Tami told her about Krista.

It was Krista's friend, her childhood friend, Pumla, who got her into guarding. Well, one of the factors but Tami didn't go into the whole history. Kept it tight, dramatic. The bare facts: Pumla was Pylon's step-daughter. Pumla was raped.

First year of medical school, Pumla's at a party, three guys jackroll her on a nearby rugby field. Knife to the throat, they go at her. Pumla doesn't tell her mother. Her mother knew about this, there'd be cops and arrests and charges and court cases. Pumla couldn't face that. She doesn't tell Pylon either.

Pylon and Mace in those days still running Complete Security. Tami in Johannesburg, Krista signed into the military, running around the bushveld training camps with full-on equipment and FNS.

Krista's come home on an Easter pass when Pumla tells her. They're alone at Mace's home, having a catch-up. Been through a pasta supper, onto their second bottle of bubbly. Pumla gets tearful, breaks down. Lets out the whole story. The two of them close together on the couch, the horror in the room. Filling Krista's head.

She lets Pumla get to the end, sob her way to silence. Asks for their names.

Pumla says, 'I see them. On campus. In the library, at the gym. They're there, like it didn't happen. Like it's nothing. How many others've they done it to?'

Krista gets their names, which residence the jackrollers inhabit. Pumla swears her to secrecy. Nothing to get out to her parents. Ever. She's had counselling. Still in counselling. She's getting over it.

'I'm alright, really. I'll be alright.'

Krista saying nothing to this. Gets her friend through the night.

Sometime later, maybe the next day, Krista's with these individuals in a student pub. The brothers suggest why not go clubbing. Krista's game. Always up for a good time. Pile into their car, a nice Jap SUV, end up on a rugby field in the deep dark night. Krista's sitting in the front.

'Come on guys,' she says, 'what're we doing here?'

The guys laugh. Huge joke, sista, time for fun and games.

Time for some cultural tradition.

The one behind her has a knife at her throat, is telling her what they're intending. All the details.

Krista sits quietly, one hand in the pocket of her jacket. Says, 'No, no, my brothers. Please. You don't want to do this.'

To which more laughter.

'Hey, this crazy sista.'

The driver gets out, opens her door. He's got a knife too in one hand. Other hand rubbing his crotch.

Buti in the back pricks her neck, says, 'Get out, sisi.'

Krista does. Lets the boys come up close with their knives. The boys making kissing noises. Pusssh. Pusssh. Making to grab her breasts.

In her pocket's a gun. Krista doesn't take it out. No.

Angles it to shoot the driver in the leg, he goes down. Shoots his friend in the foot. Takes the weapon out, puts lead into the number three's shoulder. Three boys lying on the rugby field crying. 'Sister, don't shoot us. Sister, don't shoot us.'

Instead Krista photographs the guys with her cellphone. Plays back their threats she's captured on her phone's recorder app. Collects their ID books. Suggests their jackrolling days are over. Leaves in the SUV.

The burnt-out vehicle's found in a squatter camp.

'You want to see the photographs? They're archived,' Tami says.

On other home passes Krista cruised the courts for acquitted rape cases, domestic abuse, did a few more freelance missions.

'That's most of the story,' said Tami.

Lavinia had her eyes on Krista, frowning. 'You should've killed them,' she said. Took a sip of coffee.

Krista not meeting her eyes, looking down into the city. Absent, her thoughts on Pumla. Pumla who'd stayed with the medical course. Become a doctor.

'That's a common consensus,' Tami said.

'I heard about some of those shootings. They thought it was a vigilante. That's what they said.'

'It was.'

'You know, some man.'

'That was useful,' said Krista, snapping back. She stood, stacked their bowls on the tray. 'Now there're things we've got to do. Arrange a babysitter, first off.'

'I'll be okay,' said Lavinia.

'Sure, yeah. But that's not how we like to do it.' Krista smiling at her, headed for the house with the tray.

'She really do those guys?' Lavinia asked.

'I wasn't there,' said Tami. 'But I reckon.'

'She told you this?'

'No. I worked it out. Krista's never said I got it wrong.' She turned for the house, glanced back. 'You want to stay out here, no problem. We've got phone calls to make. Arrange a babysitter for you while we're out.'

She left, didn't wait for Lavinia's response.

Lavinia took her cellphone from the pocket of her PJ shorts. Pressed through to Baasie.

'I'm coming,' he said.

'It's okay,' said Lavinia. 'They're cool. I've talked to them.'

'Last night you were shit scared.'

'Last night we were chased.'

'You think those people won't find where you are?'

'They won't.'

'They will, Lavinia. They will. This's serious. This'll get worse.'

'How do you know?'

She heard Baasie draw in his breath, the way he did when he was losing patience.

'Please, Lavinia. Please, just listen to me. I'm coming to fetch you. My way's better. Better protection.'

'Daddy'll freak.'

'I'll handle Titus.'

'Baasie, please. I'm safe here. Really.'

'No, Lavinia. Listen, please, listen. You're not safe. You're safe with me, that's where you're safe.'

She got up, walked to the edge of the pool, dipped in her right foot. The water felt soft, cool against her hot skin. 'These women're good, they won't let anything happen. They won't let me walk out either.'

'We'll see. Where're you?'

She hesitated.

'Where're you?' he said. 'I can find out, Lavinia. Won't take me long to find out. Tell me, rather. Please.'

She told him highest street on the mountain, the house at the end, furthest away from Devil's Peak. Told him the house had a high wall, a double garage with a black door, a sliding entrance gate.

'You must speak to Daddy,' she said. 'And Rings.'

'I'll sort it. Give me a few hours.'

III

Mart Velaze had kissed Ms Mossad goodbye at three thirty in the a.m. in an empty street. Sleeping blocks of flats all around. No cool to the morning, the air humid.

She'd run a finger down his face, said, 'You're not a bad roll, habibi.'

He'd, grinning, cupped her crotch, said, 'My intombi, compliment returned.'

'What's that?' Ms Mossad smiling at him. 'No, don't tell me.'

Mart Velaze didn't. Didn't want to either, had loaded a certain sarcasm into the word. Virgin being a condition Ms Mossad had long abandoned.

They'd beeped their cars, driven off.

Six hours later Mart Velaze was looking at photographs on his laptop. Thinking technology made zoom-ins so easy. Zooming in to the woman in the doorway.

Mart Velaze squinted at the image, thinking, Thing was, nothing was surprising. You ventured into the land of the Untouchables, you expected some strange connections.

And here was a strange one: this juicy woman, with the come-bang-me body, the lascivious face who went calling on the high and mighty at odd night-time hours. Even letting herself into the cute home of Rings Saturen with her own key.

Rings Saturen supposed to be the fiancé of Lavinia Anders. That'd come as a surprise to the valiant Titus, let alone his daughter. Be interesting to see the old friends work it out. Mart Velaze beginning to sense seismic disturbances.

He'd got a match for the mysterious woman who'd visited Rings chop-chop. Fed his Sunday-night pictures into the system, snap, up popped a mugshot of this woman charged with soliciting, dealing, extortion and intention to inspire fear.

Extortion and intention to inspire fear was the interesting one. An imam had charged her, taken it all the way to court. Little newspaper clipping said the cleric backed down when he heard the evidence was video footage. Out-of-court settlement.

Mart Velaze thought he knew exactly what sort of video footage that would be. Plenty of shots of the imam's naked bum rumpy-pumping between the raised thighs of a woman not the imam's wife. Not the sort of exposure an imam wants in the public domain.

Nothing in the newspaper clipping about the intention to inspire fear but Mart Velaze could imagine that in certain circumstances Tamora would inspire fear. Considerable fear.

He also imagined that probably she'd pulled that fancy number on a range of punters. Chances were Rings Saturen would get similar treatment. Interesting piece of work, Miss Tamora Gool. Interesting too that his informer had mentioned her. From low-grade informers like Hardlife MacDonald you didn't expect much more than background. Sometimes you just couldn't tell who was going to give you diamonds.

Mart Velaze wondered what he should do with this intel. Keep it to himself or tell the Voice? Probably keep it to himself for the moment. See how it played out. Wouldn't be long before Miss Tamora Gool came on the radar. That was a certainty.

He left the picture on his screen, picked up his cellphone, put a call through to Krista Bishop: the Chinese now his morning's priority. Loved the short sharp way Krista answered. 'Who's this?' He came in with a reminder of their last conversation. Ended with, 'I need you to wear a wire.' Stared down at the very pleasant face of Tamora Gool. Could understand why Rings would give her a house key. She opened her legs, he'd be in there too. Stared down at Tamora while Krista gave him lip about the notion of client confidentiality.

He let her explore this topic, let her take on a theme of professionalism: business ethics, business practice, the security industry's code of conduct, personal integrity. 'Are you mad?' were her closing words. 'No. I will not do that. Goodbye, Mr Velaze.'

'Don't hang up,' he said. 'Recall what I told you.' He tried a line intended to inspire fear. 'Hey, sisi, what'd I say about freezing your assets? Wena, my sisi, everything you own goes into the deep freeze. For an ice age. Long, long time, nè. You don't want that, no, no, no. No business, no prospects. Investigations, charges, lawyers, court dates. No, sisi, you don't want that. You don't want Mace's name on an Interpol list. Wanted. No, sisi, you don't want that. Nè. All these things I can do, sisi, my promise.' He paused. Chuckled. 'Okay, sisi, not me but the taxman. The taxman is a lot of trouble. Worse than a debt collector. The taxman comes, he doesn't break your kneecaps. He breaks you. Smashes your life, sisi. Leaves you like a bergie. All you've got left's in plastic bags. No, my sisi, you don't want to mess with the taxman.'

He stopped, waited. 'Sisi?' Then: 'Sisi! Sisi, talk to

me.' Realised Krista had keyed him off. Mart Velaze smiled. One wild child that. He tossed his cellphone onto the desk. Said to the picture of Tamora on his laptop, 'Have to see about her.' Tapped his teeth with the nail of his index finger, the knocking reverberating in his head. You were going to be serious about something, you upped the ante. People appreciated this. People liked being incentivised.

Mart Velaze hibernated the laptop. Picked up his cellphone, checked his gun.

Now was as good a time as any to incentivise Ms Krista Bishop.

IV

Titus Anders, pleased with his radio interview, walked out of his house, leaving the French doors open. Quint on the couch, asleep. Not a worry in the world. Ja, this was his idea of watching out! What'd Luc and Quint know? What'd they know about the olden times of blood? Nothing. Bugger all. They'd come up soft. As boys they might've heard guns and bullets. As boys they might've seen dying and dead but nothing like he'd seen it. Seen it in his youth. Those days'd been war days. Full on, full on. Streets of slaughter, man, streets of slaughter.

Night like they'd just got through, there'd've been no

let up. In the morning corpses. One way or the other, it would have been sorted. One way or the other.

Titus Anders, wearing only swim baggies, walked along the sand path to the beach. The sun hot on his back.

He thought of Tamora. From day one she hadn't given him any trouble. Paid him his cut from the abalone, no hassles. There'd never been any hassles. You had to ask him he'd say she respected him. Alright, she was a lady on the make these days. Ambitious. Making a play for the Mongols? Impossible. Anyhow, so what? Long as she paid him, Titus didn't care. Agreed with Rings. What's a woman going to do? You think some captain'll listen to her? Uh uh. Not a chance. Yet Baasie had told him, watch that one. That one's poison. Titus not listening. Titus reckoning he knew her, knew her mind. He'd grown up in the same place. He was striking fear, he'd do it this way: suddenly, quickly. At her age he'd wanted what she wanted now. The need to be untouchable. In charge. The general. The majesty. He knew her. She was a fighter. A fighter had to fight first, talk afterwards. Now it was time to talk. In their grief they would find words. He'd phone her. The last thing she'd expect was that he'd phone her.

Titus smiled. Stopped at the water's edge. The sea flat, the tide out, a small wave thudding in the shallows. He dropped his towel. Bent to place on it his sunglasses, his cellphone. Straightened, looked up and down the beach.

Up: in the distance a couple walked towards him. Whites, he imagined.

Down: a hundred metres a fisherman sitting, his rod balanced in a forked stick. The man looking at Titus, watching. An older guy. About fifty, fifty-five. Beyond him a woman with a dog. The woman throwing a stick, the dog bouncing into the sea. A white woman.

Titus glanced back at the fisherman, the man digging in a bag. Titus waited. The fisherman hauling out a packet, KFC, white-and-red markings visible.

Titus shifted his eyes to the city, the tall buildings stacked along the Foreshore. Behind them, the mountain rose grey, solid. He waded into the water. Being macho against the cold that clamped his ankles, numbed his thighs. He crouched until he was submerged, let the cold water hold him. Lay there looking at the city. A massive place.

Lying on his back, he turned slowly to face the beach. The couple were closer. The fisherman standing, still watching him, still eating from his KFC packet. The young woman and the dog had disappeared.

He lay at full stretch, his head in the water, listening to the ticking of the ocean, his eyes gazing into the blue. Lay there in the cold as once the European dead had lain in this sea.

Even in that solitude he heard Luc shouting.

'Daddy! Daddy!'

Rose from the water to see his one-eyed son running towards him, shouting. The boy with a gun in his hand.

'Daddy! Daddy!'

Knew it was about Quint.

Saw the approaching couple stop. Saw the fisherman backing away.

Titus ran, ran past Luc, ran along the sand path to his house. Stood panting in the lounge, stared at his son. Quint on the couch bleeding out, a screwdriver in his chest.

V

Transcript from the case file of Hardlife MacDonald:

They got blown up, those three brothers. Sometimes it goes like that. You think it's an easy job, one, two, three: quick in, throw the pipe, quick out. Was supposed to be a job like that. Get them used to the action. Training: satisfaction with the action. Ja, but it wasn't like that. You know you got a problem with a pipe bomb. A pipe bomb's delicate. It's what they call unstable. You got stuff in the pipe that's gonna explode. You got this chlorine, ammonia, even powder off match heads, sometimes powder out of bullets and you got this fuse, maybe which you pull out of a firecracker. A Guy Fawkes cracker. The longer the better. The fuse is slippy. You slide it in and use some glue to keep it tight, nice 'n tight. Sometimes you light the fuse, it burns so fast you must throw quickly. The Chinese fuse is like that. Rubbish Made in China. You see Made in China you know you've got to play fast. You light that, it's gonna burn one time. You got no chance. You gonna see your moer. You want the English word, you can use arsehole. The way I picture it in my head, the brothers got panicked. They light the fuse and the fuse goes whizz into the pipe. The brothers still holding the pipe in the car. They got no chance to get out. No chance to even drop it out the window. When you throw a pipe bomb you gotta be standing in the street. I can tell you there's gonna be big trouble coming.

6

Black Aron Chetty and the Russian sat in Black Aron's white Corolla on Dunkley Square. The windows down. The heat getting intense. Both dudes in shorts: the Russian in a green golf shirt; Black Aron in a tee, neat, white, unpatterned. Their thighs sweating against the cloth seats.

The Russian said, 'This is the place?'

'Of course. The address is that building.' Black Aron pointing at the row of Victorian semis down the north side of the square. 'If my guy gave me the right address.'

'You have other possibilities?'

'No. This's it, most likely.'

'Most likely. You are not sure?'

'I'm sure, okay, I'm sure. Just don't start.'

The Russian sitting sideways in the passenger seat, his door open, smoking. 'I told you they would kill that boy.'

'Yeah, Smirnoff the prophet.'

'Let me see the video one more time.'

'You're sick.' Black Aron bringing it up on his cell-phone anyhow.

The Russian took the phone, pressed play. 'I never seen this happen before,' he said. 'Like *Texas Chainsaw Massacre* but this is clean. Very good. Very professional. In Russia we are more like *Texas Chainsaw*. No one has thought of this idea in a butcher place.'

'You can tell them.' Black Aron squirmed in his seat, flapped his т-shirt to get a movement of air. His back damp, a stickiness in his armpits. 'Introduce some style.'

'Yes, this would be interesting.' The Russian re-turned the cellphone. 'I like it. Very cool.'

'Not cool for his mother.'

'Da, of course. That is why we are here. For the woman's revenge. I know.' The Russian dropped the butt on the tar, ground it out with the toe of his shoe. 'This place is not very busy place. Even at nine o'clock.'

In fact no movement on the square. Too early. Too hot. At Maria's restaurant, a man put out wheelie bins. The other cafés closed. Even the Ikhaya Lodge quiet. Black Aron and the Russian parked on the south side of the square in some tree shade.

The Russian lit another white.

'I heard,' said Black Aron, 'that to kill yourself all you got to do is eat four or five cigarettes. The nicotine takes you out.'

'That is why I smoke them.' The Russian laughed.

'I also heard,' said Black Aron, 'every cigarette costs you eleven minutes of your life. How many you smoke a day? About a packet? What's that, twenty?'

The Russian shrugged. 'Who is counting? Thirty. Forty. Fifty. I dunno. I smoke. That's what I like.'

'Call it thirty, Smirnoff. Thirty times eleven, okay. Eleven minutes.' Black Aron opened the calculator on his cellphone. 'Three hundred and thirty minutes divide by sixty is' – he held up the screen – 'five and a half hours. How's that, my Russian friend. Five and a half hours. In a week that's' – he made the calculation – 'thirty-eight and a half hours. Divide that by twenty-four and you got one and a bit days. Multiply by fifty-two that's eighty-three days each year closer to your death. Shit, man, that's hectic. That's scary.'

'If I die tomorrow, what does it mean?'

Black Aron frowned.

'Nothing.'

Black Aron shook his head. 'Nah, nah, nah. Course it means something. It means … How many years you been smoking?'

The Russian took a drag. 'Since nine years old. Now I am thirty-one.'

Black Aron did the arithmetic on his phone. 'Twenty-two. Twenty-two years you been smoking.'

The Russian exhaled. 'I like it.'

'You times that by eighty-three you get one thousand eight hundred and twenty-six days. Shit man. Divide that by three hundred and sixty-five you have five years. Amazing. Say you were supposed to die tomorrow, Smirnoff, say this was gonna happen, okay. If you'd not been a smoker then you'd die only in five years' time instead. If you didn't smoke.'

'That is nonsense,' said the Russian.

'No. Really.' Black Aron held up his phone. 'See. What's there, five. Five years, my friend. Five years longer instead of dying tomorrow.'

'What happens when there is something like the accident?'

'Such as? A car accident?'

'That is right.'

Black Aron watched a vw Sharan parking outside the Victorian row. 'It's like a moth flapping its wings. When that happens, it starts a storm somewhere else.'

'What moth?'

'It's science. If one thing happens, it has an effect. You know, cause and effect. When you smoke a cigarette, you change your life.' He brought up a pair of binoculars. 'That's the vehicle from last night.' Pointed. 'No Lavinia.'

The Russian looked where Black Aron pointed. 'Yes,' he said. 'Yes, I think so.'

'Hot little fems.' Black Aron handed the glasses to the Russian. Noticed a man get out of a car parked in front of the Sharan. Approach the women. The women turn on him: not happy if you read their body language. The coloured one doing the talking, gesturing. The black one with her arms folded, standing at the gate.

The Russian said, 'Very nice, yes. The same women from last night, yes, I think so.'

Black Aron watched them go into the house, the man following.

They waited. The Russian finished his cigarette, lit

another: 9.10, 9.30, 9.53, the front door opened, out stepped the black woman. Got into the Sharan.

Black Aron started the Corolla. 'You want to wait here?'

The Russian shook his head. 'No, there is no point. What for? Where is the other one going? She has no car.'

'She could walk. Take a taxi.'

'Pah! Who does it in this city? We follow that one. She goes to the woman.'

'You scheme?'

'Spot on.'

Black Aron glanced at the Russian. The Russian deadpan, waving his fingers, Go, go, go.

II

Mart Velaze watched in his rear-view mirror the Sharan turn out of Wandel and come down Barnett Street. Draw up parallel with him, reverse-park two cars back. Good girls, they'd both seen him, checked him out. He smiled at himself in the mirror, went off to meet the gals, called, 'Hey, Krista Bishop.'

Saw the women turn to face him, that no-shit stance they both had. That yeah-arsehole-whaddaya-want? attitude. He liked it. These were wild chicks.

'Krista,' he said, 'we talked just now.' Said to the

other woman in Xhosa, 'You're Tami. Nice to put a face to the name.'

Tami came back, 'What do you want?'

'Go away,' said Krista.

'Nice,' said Mart Velaze in English, 'you speak indigenous, Krista?'

'Go away,' said Krista in Xhosa.

'You don't want me to do that,' said Mart Velaze. 'You need to listen to me, sisi. Both of you. Very carefully, you need to listen.'

Mart Velaze enjoying the way they stared at him. Standing there, full-on confrontational. Fierce. As he'd first thought of them, marvelling at their stride across the airport concourse.

'Why?'

'I told you why on the phone.'

'Like I'm supposed to believe that?'

'You should.'

Tami came in: 'This's our business. We bought it. We got nothing to do with the past. Nothing to do with Mace or Pylon.'

'You think so?' Mart Velaze with his hands in his back pockets, rocking on his Adidas heels. The man: expensive ripped jeans, two buttons of his shirt undone, the shirt white with thin blue lines in it hanging loose, sleeves neatly rolled onto his forearms. Faint aftershave aroma: Dior Homme Sport. For when he wanted his presence to linger.

'I told you, we've got nothing to do with my father,' said Krista. 'His business is his business. It's history. Dead, written off.'

'Oh yes, my sisi, let me tell you that's not so. You heard of William Faulkner?'

'Oh please,' said Krista. 'What're you now, some great literature prof? Going to quote him?'

'I might.' Watched Krista staring at him, nothing but contempt in those brown eyes. Made Mart Velaze think screwing her would be scary. She'd have teeth between her legs. He stopped rocking. 'Can we do this inside?'

'We're not doing it at all,' said Krista.

He glanced at Tami. 'What you think, sisi?'

'I think you're full of shit.'

'Look.' Mart Velaze took his hands out of his pocket, pointed at the house that was their office. 'We can talk about this inside or ...' He let it hang.

'Or what?'

'Or I can do what I said.'

'You can't,' said Krista.

'You can wait and see.'

'Hamba wena, buti,' said Tami. 'Go away.'

Mart Velaze thought, Man, what was it with these sistas? The two women heading for the door of their office, leaving him standing on the pavement. 'You don't want this,' he said, going after them, neither of them stopping him at the door. He followed, closed the door, heard the locks tumble.

He looked up, he was staring at the big O of a s&w .38 special. The six-shot version, called the combat masterpiece. Nice gun.

He smiled at Krista. 'You wouldn't.' Impressed at how she'd magicked it up. So quick, so casual.

She shrugged.

Tami further down the passage said, 'She would. The way we do it, we do the knees first. It's painful.'

Mart Velaze hearing Krista say, 'Off with the ripped jeans, down, on your knees, my brother.' Mart Velaze going, 'Sho, sho, sho.' What was with these sistas? He undid his belt, hopped from one foot to the other getting out of his jeans. Held them at arm's length. Pleased he'd decided on boxers.

'On the floor,' said Krista.

Mart Velaze dropped his jeans. 'You don't have to do this.'

'Knees,' said Krista. 'On them. Toss everything from your pockets. Keys, cellphones, wire, gun, pens, money, wallet. Whatever.'

Out came everything except no wire, no gun. Mart Velaze smug about not carrying a gun, leaving it in the car.

'Now the shirt,' said Krista.

'Ah, come on.'

'The shirt. Let's see the six-pack.'

Mart Velaze unbuttoned his shirt, laid it on his jeans.

'Nice abs,' said Krista, 'for a man your age. Good tone. Check this, Tami.' The two women now shoulder to shoulder in the narrow passageway, looking at him. No give that he could see in their eyes.

'Can I stand up?'

'No.'

Just like that. No. He tried again. 'You don't need the gun.' Watched Krista Bishop drop it into a bag she carried. Some leeway. 'I'm going to stand up.' Put a hand on the wall for balance.

He didn't see it coming. The chick Tami kicked out his hand, sent him sprawling against the wall. The chick Krista had the .38 on his forehead, her knee on his chest.

Mart Velaze said, 'Okay, my sistas, enough.'

They drew back, he waited, got onto his knees again. 'What you want me to say?' Looked at them looking at him. Held up his hands. 'Okay, okay, I'm government.'

'Government what? Hawks? National Intelligence? What d'you call it now: the State Security Agency?'

'Sort of.'

'Sort of's not an answer.'

'It's all there is.' He relaxed as Krista put the gun away again.

'You a cop or a spy?'

'I'm not a cop.'

Ah, what, the two women exclaiming, shaking their heads at him.

Krista said, 'You want us to spy on the Chinese? That's slimy, Mart, even for a spy that's slimy. You blackmail us into guarding them, but really what you want is eyes and ears. Ag, shame, Mart, the spookery short-staffed?'

He shifted his gaze between them. 'We need information, intelligence.' The women staring at him, Krista coaxing with her hands for details. 'More information than we're getting.'

Mart Velaze's eyes locked on Krista. She held up a finger. 'One, you set us up. Two, you threaten us.' Giving him the up-yours sign simultaneously.

'Yes, sisi.' Going for straight confession. Sincerity.

'Not appreciated,' said Tami.

Mart Velaze didn't respond. Knew better than to respond. The women glaring at him like he was dog shit on their carpet.

'What do we get out of this?'

He frowned. 'Sorry?' Saw Tami glance at Krista.

'What do we get out of this?'

Then twigged. The cheeky chickie wanted a kickback. Said, 'Doesn't work like that.'

'Like what?'

'Sisi, listen, listen. We've given you business.'

'Business we didn't want. Business you forced on us.'

'But still business. Money in the bank.'

'Oh wow. Not to mention slimeball businessmen and your heavy shit about revenue and bankruptcy.'

'We want a little return, that's all.'

'So do we.'

'Meaning?' Mart Velaze thinking if he didn't get off his knees they would bust. Said, 'My knees. I need to get up.'

'Don't move,' said Krista.

Mart Velaze grimaced. 'Okay. No more threats.'

'Not good enough. Not believable.'

'What then?'

'The only thing that counts.'

Mart Velaze could hear it coming. It was a sound you heard plenty of these days.

'Money.'

'Chief,' said the Voice, 'I don't believe you. You agreed to this?'

Mart Velaze, dressed, stood in the boardroom of Complete Security gazing at a ceramic vase in a glass case.

'A retainer,' he said.

'Yes, yes, I'm aware of the concept,' said the Voice. 'A visit from revenue would have been cheaper.'

'This is long term. It could be useful.'

A pause, a clink of cup against saucer. 'Chief, you're not balling them? Either of them?'

Mart Velaze smiled at the term. She had some quaint expressions, the Voice.

'No.'

'You have a reputation.' A smirk in her tone that irritated him.

From the passage raised voices. Tami saying, 'You'd better know what you're doing.' Krista saying, 'You've got another way?' The slam of the front door.

'You do whatever,' said the Voice. 'Just remember the bottom line. She's not a civil servant. Or a politician.'

'No problem,' said Mart Velaze.

'Go with the ancestors,' said the Voice.

Mart Velaze thumbed her off, there was Krista in the doorway. 'This your mother's work?' he asked, pointing at the vase.

Krista nodded.

'She was good.'

'She was.' No emotion. Krista Bishop, arms folded across her chest, waiting for him. Mart Velaze letting the moment lengthen. Her phone rang.

'Okay,' he said. 'We can talk.' Looked again at the vase, the smooth curve of its line, heard Krista say, 'The past is never dead. It's not even past.' The Faulkner quote he'd planned to use. She was a piece of work, this one. Bringing it up now. He thought maybe she was remembering her mother. Then heard, 'But it can be negotiated.' Turned to see her, phone to her ear, smiling at him.

III

Titus Anders said to his son Luc, 'You sure this is Tamora doing this?' Titus not holding back the tears, wiping them off his cheeks with a fist. His voice cracked. 'Two of you. I lost two of you now. No, man. What's going on for her to do this?'

'Tamora's doing it,' said Luc. 'You know it's her, Daddy.'

Titus and Luc on the stoep, the sliding doors open to the lounge. Quint in there with a screwdriver in his chest, a blanket thrown over his corpse.

'You didn't hear a thing?'

'Nothing,' said Luc. 'I was upstairs.'

'I went to swim, he was sleeping. Peaceful.'

'Daddy didn't see someone?'

'No, Luc, no. Some people on the beach. That's all. No one else.'

'Must've been someone,' said Luc. 'Someone from Tamora.'

Titus stared at his son. 'I'd've seen someone if there'd been someone.'

Luc kept his eyes on the ships in the bay. Titus facing that way, too, toying with his cellphone.

'This's up to shit.' The tears coming again. He let the sobbing take him. Let it go on until it was over. Stood, inhaled deeply. Blew his nose a nostril at a time into the fynbos. Used both hands to wipe his face. 'We've got to stop this, Luccie. Today. This's up to shit.'

He phoned Lavinia, got her voicemail. Said, 'Phone your daddy.' Said to Luc, 'Where's she?'

He held up his hands. 'I don't know. She sleeps late.'

Titus phoned Krista Bishop, went in with a barrage: Where's Lavinia? She's not answering her phone. What's going on? You supposed to let me know. I must talk to her.

Heard Krista say, 'Maybe she's in the shower.'

'You're not with her? You must be with her. All the time, every second. That's what I'm paying for.'

'My partner's with her.'

'Tell her to phone me.'

'We don't do it this way, Mr Anders. When there's contact there's problems.'

'There's problems, my sister,' said Titus. 'Big bloody

problems. Her brother Quint's dead now.' Pressed the woman off before he could hear her response.

'We should have Lavinia with us, Daddy,' said Luc.

Titus didn't answer. Got onto Rings Saturen. Said, 'Quint is dead.'

Listened to Rings splutter his way out of sleep. 'What, what, what? What you saying, Titus?'

Titus repeated himself.

Rings said, 'You must go, man. Get out of here, out of the city. All of you. Where's Lavinia?'

'She's okay,' said Titus. 'She's safe.'

'So go. You and Luc, go. Baasie and I can carry on.'

'No,' said Titus. 'We're staying right here. I'm going to meet the Chinaman. Then Tamora.'

Left Rings mid-splutter, keyed through to Baasie.

Baasie said, 'Shit.' Left it there. Titus getting traffic noise in the background.

Titus said, 'You hear anything about this, let me know.'

'There's nothing,' said Baasie. 'Nothing I heard that I haven't told you.' More traffic noise. Baasie said, 'Titus, you want me to organise things? The cops? The funeral?'

'Luc can.'

'You want me to be there with you?'

'It's okay. We're okay. I just want to know what's going on, Baasie. What's this about, hey? If Tamora's doing this, why's she doing it?'

'You know why, Daddy,' said Luc. 'I told you. She's on a power trip.'

Titus said, 'It's more than Tamora. This's something else.'

'Like what?' said Baasie in his ear.

'How should I know, man? I don't know. If I did I'd know what to do.'

'You want me to see the Beijing man?'

'That's my scene, that's what I'm doing.'

Heard Baasie say, 'You want any help, you phone me. You want me to come there, you call me. Anything, hey, Titus. Anything. That's what we must do with this. Keep it close. What's Rings say? You've phoned him?'

'Rings says nothing,' said Titus. 'Rings is a politician these days. You know Rings, he's got other stories.'

'We still together, like always. You call and we help.'

'Ja, man,' said Titus. 'I know. I know that.' He sighed. 'I must go now, Baasie. Before Luc calls the cops.'

He placed the cellphone on the table, said to Luc, 'What'd you do with the boy's pieces?'

'Froze them.'

Titus nodded. 'You take them in the veld, burn them. Not all the pieces, okay? Just most of him for her to get the picture. When he's cooked you leave it. Put out the fire. You make a video for Tamora. Give her the GPS spot.' He stood. 'I got to meet the Chinaman.'

Luc said, 'Alright, Daddy. Would've been nice for Quint to help me.'

'Jesus, man, Luc, where's your respect?'

'Was just a joke.'

IV

Krista left Mart Velaze in the boardroom, went upstairs to her office listening to Titus Anders tell her his son was dead. Murdered. The man rang off before she could say anything.

Krista closed the door, opened the window. The room was stifling, stuffy, smelt of old dust. She sighed. Tami wasn't going to like this. Tami didn't like any of it. Thing was, Tami was right.

Bloody Mace had dropped them in it. After all the shit he'd got himself into, running away from it to a life in the Caymans. Typical Mace. Never letting on what other frights were waiting in your sea. You want to swim in the ocean, baby, you got your currents, your waves, your storms, your sharks, your jellyfish. Mace always skimpy on the hardcore details. 'You don't want to let the horror show put you off.' Mace's words. Right, she wouldn't. She'd go with the flow. No ways she'd opt for the Mace manoeuvre. Not going to give up what she and Tami had put together: the business, their life.

Okay, they were in this situation now, like a rip tide. Only way out was to let it take you. No gain in fighting a rip. You keep your head up, you go sideways until you're in still waters.

She phoned Tami. 'You know there's no other way.'

'There's another way.'

'What?' Krista under no illusions about Tami's other way. 'We can't tell them to stick it.'

'We can.'

'And risk everything?'

'They won't take us for everything. What's the point?'

'The point's they've got to show muscle.' Krista used a notepad to fan some air across her face.

'By dumping us on the street? Closing down our business? That's spite.'

'Revenue does spite. They're tough. They're government. They've got laws, secrecy acts, they can shut us up. One way or another.'

'But they won't.'

'You know this?'

No response from Tami.

Krista came in with: 'Look, he says they'll pay.'

'He said it?'

'Uh huh.'

'And you believe him?'

'Why not?'

'He's a spy, Krista. An agent. Lying's what he does. All the time. To everyone. That's how he talks. Paying's like a bribe.'

'Are you driving?'

'Of course I'm driving. I'm going home to look after the woman we shouldn't be looking after. The gangster's daughter. Remember. This's hectic, Krista.'

'We can handle it.' Krista standing at the window, looking at the mountain. The high cliffs radiating heat.

Thing was she was enticed. Being – what'd they call it in the novels? – an asset, a joe, a source, being eyes and ears appealed. Krista thinking, Yeah, why not? For an adrenaline junkie, the way to go.

'Won't be a problem. Be fine.'

'You think so?' Krista heard Tami snort. 'You think so. You don't think babysitting a gangster's daughter is a problem? You don't think some secret agent threatening us, bribing us, is serious shit? You don't think we're out of our play zone?'

'No.'

'Wait, I'm stopping.'

Krista heard the engine die. 'Where are you?'

'Halfway up Molteno.' Then: 'Look, we don't do these sort of people, Krista. We do businesswomen, celebs, movie stars, models, rich girls, women who don't bring Cape Flats skollie wars into our house.'

'We've been through this. We agreed.'

'Agreements aren't stone tablets.'

Krista looked across Dunkley Square, watched a couple holding hands walk away from their car towards the Ikhaya Lodge. Probably headed for breakfast in the air-conditioned cool. Not a problem in the world judging by their attitude. Their lives or mine, she thought. Rather mine.

Said, 'I got a call from Titus Anders. His son was killed. Sounded like in their house.'

Silence from Tami.

Krista heard the car engine start.

'What'd I say about the skollie wars? With gangsters, the only way they solve a problem is they kill you.'

'No one knows where we've got her.'

'You think so?'

Truth? Krista wasn't sure. Tapped her cellphone against her chin. Turned away from the mountain, went downstairs to see what Mart Velaze had in mind.

V

Transcript from the case file of Hardlife MacDonald:

We heard the Pretty Boyz laughed about the pipe bomb. Very funny that three Mongols burnt up in the car. Show you how stupid the Mongols are, they think they can come into the Valley of Plenty and cause shit. My captain he was angry like I never seen him angry. He hit the wifey that there was blood coming out of her eyes. He says we got to show we mean serious business. He says we got to show the Pretty Boyz what's what. We got to have respect. Me myself I heard he was talking to Tamora Gool. I heard she phoned him. If she phoned him before I don't know about it. After he talked with Tamora Gool the captain called one of the other lighties. He gave him a tik lolly. Told him he must take a Pretty Boyz, stick him dead then cut a big M on his chest. On my phone I got pictures of a Pretty Boyz found in the bushes behind the Spar supermarket. I got the pictures of the M that was carved. You can see it. You can hear the one saying to the Pretty Boyz: 'Sorries, my bru. Was yous or me.'

7

I

What Mart Velaze had in mind for Krista was basic: not a wire, not even a voice recorder, but her own cellphone. Switched on the recording app when she went in, kept it running through the meeting. Nobody going to be paying attention to her anyhow.

He sat in the boardroom at the big table, smiling to himself. Heard the murmur of Krista's voice upstairs. The creak of the floorboards as she walked about. Too inaudible to hear what she was saying. Thought about heading up to listen, when his phone rang: the Voice.

'Something you should know, chief,' said the Voice. 'The recording we've got going from the Anders lounge, yes, well it seems the son, Quint, he's dead. Killed. We've got a sound that must've been when it happened then some audio on the other son, Luc, and then Titus. Seems Quint was stabbed. In the heart. By the sounds of it.'

'When?' said Mart Velaze.

'I've just listened to it,' said the Voice. Tetchy quality

to her tone. Mart Velaze understanding the irritability: we've got no budget for constant surveillance. I've got a million jobs to do, I can't be everywhere at once. The Voice not normally strung out. Taking some strain, it would seem.

He said, 'Ummm ...'

She said, 'Time of death was about an hour ago.'

Mart Velaze whistled. 'Daylight. Someone's very serious.'

'So it would seem. You know these gangsters, chief, they mean business. Nasty types. All that mixed blood in them.'

'How?' he said. 'How'd they let this happen? Three of them there. Someone just walks in and does this?'

'Yes. Strange one, yes. I was wondering that myself. Very professional.'

She told him Titus was going to keep his meeting with the Chinamen. 'We need to know what happens there, Mart,' she said, before telling him to go with the ancestors.

Mart Velaze keyed her off, heard Krista coming down the stairs. She walked lightly, reminded him of a cat.

She came in, he was watching. The easy body, the chi-chi boobs in the white т-shirt, the skinny jeans, the black tekkies. The sista was number one. She sat down opposite him.

'So?'

There it was. No bullshit. No niceties. Just: So?

He liked this girl. Not only the shape of her, she had

attitude. 'As I said, what we need is information.' He slid a business card across the table. Watched her pick it up, pocket it in her jeans.

'How much?'

Mart Velaze laughed, shook his head. Looked out the window at the back wall spiked with razor wire. This woman! 'You mean money? Or information?' He brought his gaze back, locked on her eyes. No clues but a glint in them.

'Money.'

Of course, money. Always the hardarse. He could imagine feeling her arse. Running his hand over the curve of her bum. Toned. Firm. Clenching at his touch. 'Depends.'

'No,' said Krista. 'Not depends.'

'It's piecemeal, how we pay. Some stuff is valuable. Some isn't. All depends.'

'Nice one, Mr Velaze. You say what's valuable. You say how much you'll pay. You guys!'

'Today is valuable.'

He named a price. Heard Krista double it. Thought the Voice would hyperventilate, even though using Complete Security had been her idea. Said, 'Alright.' He'd pay in, claim the balance somehow. 'Alright, sisi.' Sat back smiling at her: not a flicker of emotion on her face, no triumph, but that light in her eyes like she was having fun. He shut his face, came forward suddenly. Could smell her deodorant, her shampoo. Something herbal. Noticed she did not flinch at his movement, the finger he brought up to point at her. Didn't back away.

He'd read her army file. Knew what she was capable of. What she'd done. That op in the Congo. A hellfire shit storm that had been. 'You do what I ask.'

'Depends,' she said.

Mart Velaze gave up. Dropped his hand. Put the smile back on his face. 'Sisi. Sisi, sisi, sisi, sisi. You are too much.' Got no response from her. Told her, no wire, no voice recorder, her cellphone would do the job. 'No one'll even question it.'

'You're cheap,' Krista said to Mart Velaze. He heard it, the kidding under the jibe. The flirting. Maybe she wasn't hardarsed all the time.

'Budget issues,' said Mart Velaze, using the same tone.

Got raised eyebrows, a smile that said, Of course.

For a moment he considered telling her about Quint. Then held his tongue. She probably knew anyhow. He reached out a hand. 'Deal.' Felt a cool hand slip into his, tighten hard. He frowned. Saw a twitch at her lips.

II

Black Aron Chetty and the Russian had come up behind the Sharan at the Hatfield Street robots. The Russian hunna-hunnaring to Black Aron about being too close. This was no way to follow someone. She could see them in her rear-view. She'd remember the car.

Black Aron had taken his right hand off the steering wheel, made it into a duck beak quacking. Said, 'Enough, Smirnoff.'

When the Sharan pulled over on the steep climb up Molteno Road, Black Aron had no option but to drive past, the Russian with his head turned away, shielding his face.

'She sees us, what good is that?' he said.

Black Aron thinking, No ways, the woman couldn't have seen them. No ways. He turned right into Garfield, did an awkward five-point turn in the narrow street, pulled over with the engine running. Staring at them was a gardener on a ladder, trimming trees with an electric saw. Had a pile of branches stacked on the pavement.

Black Aron ignored him.

The Russian said, 'He is looking at us.'

'So what?'

'He will remember us.'

'Doesn't matter.'

'In this game everything is a matter, poepiehead.'

'Poepiehead?'

'I heard it. A little girl teasing her friend said it. Shithead is another word.'

'I know what it means.

'I like poepiehead.'

Black Aron raised his hands in supplication. Rolled his eyes. 'Ask him for directions?' – jerking a thumb, indicating the gardener. 'Tell him we're lost. You sound foreign.'

'That is not so funny.'

Black Aron slid down his window, gasped at the heat, said, 'Baba, you speak English?'

The man on the ladder nodded.

'We're lost.'

The man pointed at the intersection, 'That one is Molteno. This one is Garfield.'

'Spot on,' said Black Aron. 'I can see that.'

'Then you are not lost.' The gardener took his saw to a branch.

Black Aron closed the window. 'It is too hot to cut trees.'

The Russian said, 'Maybe she went another way. Go back so we can see her. If she is still there.'

'She has to come past here.'

'Go back. Away from this baba tree cutter. What is baba?'

Black Aron eased the car up to the stop sign. 'Respect. For us it is respect to call an older man baba.'

'Baba is what you call a baby.'

'Yeah, I know. This's confusing for a foreigner.' He looked right. There was the Sharan a block away, pulling out. He let the vehicle pass. 'They've got a safehouse up here? It costs millions up here.'

'Okay, follow,' said the Russian.

'I'm the driver,' said Black Aron. 'Just remember that.'

They followed the Sharan, Black Aron hanging back until it swung right into Glencoe Avenue, then zapping the Corolla into a lower gear and putting foot.

Not that putting foot got them moving much faster. The street was steep. The car was not the Beemer. He should have taken the вм, but that was complicated. Getting out to the factory in Paarden Island, swopping cars, picking up the Russian, getting back to Dunkley Square. Too much travel time. The Corolla was alright but wasn't the вм.

They got to Glencoe, the Sharan was out of sight.

'Shit,' said the Russian.

'No problem,' said Black Aron, 'this road's a dead end.'

'There,' said the Russian, pointing at a flash of white in the distance. 'Catch up.'

They watched the Sharan turn into a driveway.

'Stop,' said the Russian.

'Catch up. Stop. What's your case?' said Black Aron.

'We wait. It is better. We do not know why she is here.'

'Your game, Smirnoff. I'm just the driver.' Black Aron killed the engine.

One, two, three, four, five, six minutes.

The Russian had opened the door, was about to light a cigarette, Black Aron said, 'Hey, what's this?'

There was a new model black Merc, tinted windows, coming out of the drive where the Sharan had gone in.

III

Titus Anders took a call from Luc. Luc said the cops were all over the place, turned the house into a crime scene, wanted to know where Titus was.

Titus was sitting in his standby, a 2009 Jeep Cherokee, outside the Cape Grace, staring across the quay at a Taiwanese fishing trawler. Thinking, You came to a larney place like the Grace and over the water's this hulk. Black, rusty, with washing hanging on a line in the stern.

Working harbour they called it. Supposed to be romantic. Titus didn't think so.

Titus was hurting. Had this pain in his chest called grief. Everything on this day would ache.

First Boetie murdered. Okay, he and Boetie weren't close. Boetie into books, had arty friends probably moffie queers he went camping with. Sometimes Titus had wondered about Boetie, if he needed to talk to him, ask him why there were no girlfriends. Had thought about getting Lavinia to do this. Times like that he longed for Sharmaine. She'd have known what to say. Her passing still a great sadness to him. She'd got him out of the street gangs into management, even found the Sunset Beach house. Many times he'd wanted her quiet words. 'Don't you think, Titus, it would be better if …' 'I don't know, Titus, maybe you should look at …' That way she had of suggesting things. In the end you thought it was your idea. These days he had Lavinia, but Lavinia was not her mother. Lavinia spoke her mind, no subtleties. He liked that too.

Luc said in his ear, 'Daddy, please, man. What do I say?'

Titus stared at the black hulk, mouthing the name Sharmaine. Sharmaine who went off to gym one morning, all bouncy and flying hair, died in the local Virgin Active. Sudden cardiac death. Proof there was no God.

Boetie her soft child. 'That one, Titus,' she'd said so often. 'He's different.' Boetie's death also proof there was no God.

Good thing she couldn't know how he'd died. They hadn't needed to do that to the boy to send a message.

'Daddy!'

'Ja, Luc, I'm here,' said Titus. He rubbed a hand over his face. Boetie shouldn't have taken the hit. Such a soft boy to make such a payment.

And now Quint. This new pain in his chest. This ache that Quint gave him. Quint was a strong boy. No funny shit about him.

Luc said, 'What must I tell them, Daddy?'

'We talked about this,' said Titus. 'Tell them I'm in a business meeting. Tell them my cell's off.'

'I did. They still want to know.'

Titus rubbed at his temples, at a nerve throbbing there. 'Just tell them what we agreed.'

He massaged with his thumb.

'Daddy?'

'Ja?'

'Daddy, one of the medics told me they'd done a bomb blast earlier.'

Titus didn't respond.

'In Mitchells Plain. Three guys in a car. Braaied and fried. A pipe bomb he reckoned.'

Still Titus kept staring at the Taiwanese hulk, rubbing his temple.

'Daddy? You listening, Daddy?'

'Ja,' said Titus.

'In the Valley of Plenty. Pretty Boyz land. Our land.'

'The three were Mongols?'

'I think so, Daddy.'

'Find out, Luc. Okay, find out which one of them's causing this shit, Mongols or Pretty Boyz.'

'Got nothing to do with us, Daddy.'

'Just find out, Luc.'

Titus keyed him off, got out of the Cherokee's cool into the heat, the sweat clammy in his armpits. The ache beating now behind his eyes. Pretty Boyz, Mongols, Chinese, cops, security: he was not into this scene anymore. This was all supposed to have stopped.

He checked the little Kel-Tec strapped to his ankle. A just-in-case. The P-32, seven plus one, that he'd used once only. Did the job that time.

Titus Anders, wearing fawn chinos, a short-sleeved shirt, green with a Nehru collar, a briefcase in his left hand, remote-locked the vehicle. Stood squinting through a headache at his reflection in the side window, the sunglasses, the short hair, the thin moustache above the thin lips, thought, Mr Xing, don't give me grief today. My heart is sore. Headed for the hotel's entrance, a doorman in a tie and blazer beaming at him.

IV

Krista said to Mart Velaze, 'If I'm supposed to do this for you, how about a lift?'

Watched him eyeing her, trying to figure her angle. Not a bad-looking guy, Mart Velaze. Out of her age bracket but that was okay. She liked older. Older were interesting. A daddy complex one of the older ones had told her, a school teacher. That's your problem. Not too much of a problem, Krista felt.

'If?'

'Yeah, if.'

'I thought we had a deal.'

'Almost.'

That way he had of pursing his lips, trying for severe. He'd used it a couple of times already. Then the whole spook thing with the shaven head, the jaunty attitude, the work-out body, very nice. Could imagine him shooting, the perfect posture, the gun held two-handed.

Said, 'Do you shoot?'

Had to like the way his forehead creased, frowning, the puzzle it brought to his face. The roll of his eyes as if he was saying to her: Where did that come from?

'Where did that come from?'

Krista ignored this. Picked up her bag, turned for the door of the boardroom. 'We could go to the quarry sometime, shoot some targets. I've got this Hämmerli.'

Heard Mart Velaze following her out of the room, saying, 'You setting up some kind of date?'

Krista looked over her shoulder, saw the hook to his smile. Cute. 'You wish. I need a shooting partner. Some competition.'

'That can be arranged.'

'But first I need a lift to the Grace.'

His car was a white Audi. Krista said, 'This?'

'I know,' said Mart Velaze. 'Not cool.'

'At all.'

'It's Agency. Mine is a black Golf GTI with tinted windows.'

'Nothing subtle. Nice car though, the GTI.'

'Number-one car.'

'For those car chases.'

'We don't do car chases.'

'Course not.'

'Sort of car fits right in at the One&Only hotel. The hotspot for the high rollers. Know it?'

'Not my style.'

'You should try it.'

He held open the passenger door for her, Krista said, 'Very gentlemanly' – sliding in. Mart Velaze closing the door behind her with a solid thump.

He got in. 'How're you going to drive the Chinese without wheels?'

'Tami'll be joining me. Got to check on the baby and the babysitter first.'

'I could drive you.'

'No, you couldn't,' said Krista.

Five minutes later, stuck in the Adderley Street bumper-to-bumper, Krista said, 'So what's the deal with the Chinese?'

Waited for Mart Velaze to respond, thinking whatever was milling in his head would be worth knowing.

'They're businessmen,' she heard him say. 'Mining interests, mostly. They've got shares in some cement quarries.'

'And?'

'And? What you mean and?'

'And, what else? Spies don't spy on people just for jollies.'

Mart Velaze laughed. 'Sometimes we do. Sometimes it's worth it. Mostly it's a waste of time. Your Mr Lijan and Mr Yan interest us.'

'Because?'

'Because these guys're supposed to be mining. There're no mines in Cape Town. Some cement quarries up the West Coast but they're not headed there. So why're they here? Who're they seeing? What're they talking about? Might be nothing at all except investment opportunities they're seeking out. But.' He shrugged. 'Who knows? That satisfy you?' Krista smiling at his grin. 'Also, a Mr Xing used to be the visitor to Cape Town. Until now. Now we've got two men. Same company but something must've changed. Mr

Xing had major fishing interest, stone chinas with Titus and Rings. Nice to know what's happened there ... for the sake of background.'

Krista was angled to face him, focused on his profile. Not a tic at his mouth, not a tightening in his jaw, not an eye flicker, nothing to say he was telling stories. Thing that puzzled her was the casualness. Like the agency was busking.

'Why not wire up their rooms? That's your specialty.'

'Good question.'

'What's the answer?'

'I dunno.'

Krista laughed, raised her hands in surrender. 'You guys.' She straightened in her seat. Mart Velaze, typical ducker and diver.

'You got it, sisi,' he said. 'Even the agents don't know who the agents are anymore.' He chuckled. Came out of nowhere with, 'Tell me, why'd you change your name?'

'I didn't.'

'The spelling. From Christa with a Ch to Krista with a K.'

'How d'you know that?'

'Old ID documents in Mace's file. You're Christa, Ch.'

'Aai, you guys!'

'So why?'

'It's a kicking K, that's why. More attitude. Satisfied?' Watching Mart Velaze flick a glance at her, a smile on his lips.

'I get it. I bet Mace doesn't.'

'Got nothing to do with him. Or you.'

'Okay, okay.' Mart Velaze holding up a hand in sur-render.

Truth be told Mace'd really been uptight about what she'd done. 'That's not your name. Your mother wanted Christa. That's what's on your birth certificate. Why can't you live with it?' Because Mace, just because. She hadn't told him the kicking-K story. Hadn't given him any explanation. Said nothing about reinventing her-self. Reimagining herself. Wanting to shape her own life. Told him, 'Get used to it, Papa. Please.' The please being her way of asking nicely. Since then Mace had let her have her way. He forgot sometimes but hadn't raised the topic again. Krista liked that about her father: that he did let go of some things, minor things. There'd been an issue with ear studs when she was a girl, he'd got over that too.

On the Foreshore, the traffic eased around the Heerengracht circles, Mart Velaze taking a left into Walter Sisulu Avenue past the conference centre and across the intersections into the Waterfront. Stopped outside the Grace.

Mart Velaze said, 'Call me when you're done. I'll be close.'

'Not that easy, Mr Spook,' said Krista. 'These are my clients, remember. They're paying my time.'

'So are we.'

'Not at the same rate.'

Mart Velaze smiled. 'Just let me know, okay. Wena, sisi, you can be like your father. Bloody difficult.'

Krista thinking she liked his backchat. Liked the look of him. The smell of him. Thinking, Funny this connection to her father. Thinking it would be worth knowing about.

Asked, 'How'd you know Mace? Apart from his file.'

Felt his glance but didn't meet his eyes.

'We go back. Not to struggle times. But, you know, Mace and Pylon were names. Names of legend.'

'But you'd still hurt him?'

'We've worked round it, you and me,' said Mart Velaze. 'Haven't we kept Mace basking on his island?' He laughed. Krista catching some irony. Some untold history.

V

Transcript from the case file of Hardlife MacDonald:

I don't know anything about Tamora Gool, me myself. I heard about her from the captain. I told you you going to hear about her because I heard her name more and more. Me, myself, I haven't seen her. Not for real. The captain has a photo on his cellphone he took on the skelm. You know what I mean – without her knowing. He showed me. You can see her there in the distance on a beach next to a rubber duckie, what they call a Zodiac. You can see she's got the shape. In jeans, sjoe, man, really I can tell you. A fancy lady. The captain says we gotta do what she says. But I can tell you I heard she's from Hanover Park, Bonteheuwel, one of the bad places. She's the same as me. But she's got strong men looking after her. I heard Titus Anders gave her a perlemoen concession. You know Titus Anders? I heard Rings Saturen, they both what we call the Untouchables. You don't want to make trouble with those men. Never. Those men looking after Tamora Gool. She belong to them. They like whiteys. Talk like whiteys. That's all I can tell you about Tamora Gool. I never met her, only the captain goes to her. And we's Mongols. Why's Tamora going with the Mongols? Titus and Rings is Pretty Boyz. You know what I'm saying? Sometimes everything gets fucked up, you don't know what's happening.

But there's something more I got for your information.

Me, I was with my friend Stones. But I didn't know what was going to happen. Strues on my life I didn't know what was going to happen. I would have told you. I would have, but I didn't know. Sometimes everything goes crazy that way. I can say maybe the captain talked to Stones. I can also say Stones did it without a reason. This happens also. You know what's going to happen but something else happens. Takes you by surprise. Maybe not even Stones knew what was going to happen until that moment. We were in Hanover Park on a collection. Nothing serious, every Thursday we make this collection. We walking to the house in the morning there, say eleven o'clock. In the hot sun. All the people got their doors open for a breeze but no Cape Doctor blowing. When the wind blows we moan, when the wind doesn't blow we also moan. You can hear Voice of the Cape radio playing Muslim music in the houses. Outside the house of a Pretty Boyz auntie, we know her family is Pretty Boyz, there is a little girl playing with dolls in the sand. 'W'as your name, girlie?' Stones says. 'Karida,' she tells us. She calls, 'Mommy, Mommy.' Mommy in the house calls back, 'I'm just getting your milk.' Stones takes out a moerse big special. .38. I didn't know this was going to happen. On the Lord's name. I was surprised. Strues. Five in the girl's right leg, one in the left. Sometimes you don't know what's gonna happen. It was Stones did that shooting.

8

What happened to Tami was she came up Molteno with the engine on high revs, pissed off with Krista. Pissed off that Krista was falling for Mart Velaze's crap story. So pissed off she wasn't paying attention, not even noticing the white Corolla that turned out of a side street, followed her up.

At the top she went right into Glencoe, driving fast. At the approach to the house zapped the remote, but, hey, the gate was wide open, rolled back on its tracks. Tami got a hollow sickness in her stomach.

Oh shit!

She stopped, kept the engine running, dialled the babysitter looking after Lavinia. The babysitter one of their freelance contacts: reliable, smart, a boxer with a power left, rode a red Kawasaki Ninja fourth generation. The call went to voicemail.

Not good.

Tami reached down for the pistol holstered under the seat. A Caracal F with an eighteen-round magazine.

Semi-automatic, 9×19mm Parabellum, courtesy of the United Arab Emirates, favoured by various militaries. The sort of firepower Tami liked.

She caught the white Corolla in her rear-view mirror but the car was way back at the intersection with Molteno. Didn't register as anything worth paying attention to. What was important was a new-model black Merc E-class sedan with tinted windows in the driveway. The babysitter's red bike leaning on its stand. No one in sight. The door to the house closed.

Tami stopped beside the Benz, slipped the gear into reverse.

What to do?

Call Krista?

Reverse out, take the reg number, wait down the street?

Go in like Lara Croft?

Playing safe wasn't an option. Nor was phoning Krista. This's you, girl, on your own. On a job you didn't want to be doing anyhow.

Lara Croft then.

Tami switched off the Sharan. Chambered a round. Stayed sitting, listened.

The rumble of the city. Birdsong: prinias in the garden, hadedas higher on the mountain calling. The house quiet.

She looked again at the car.

Black Benz wasn't Cape Flats style. No driver either. Gangsters had drivers. Always someone waiting in the car.

Black Benz spoke of corporate. Businessman. Businesswoman. Someone who'd come alone. Deliberately unchauffeured. Wanted to keep this below the line. Someone Lavinia knew? Someone Lavinia had called? Why'd the babysitter opened the gate, opened the front door? Why the gate hadn't closed, that was strange. An electrical fault? Sometimes the auto-close didn't kick in. Probably nothing more than that. Maybe Lavinia and the visitor were inside talking. Or sitting in the shade at the pool with iced teas. Or maybe this was a lover. Maybe Lavinia was screwing the guy. Except her call to the freelancer had gone to voicemail.

Tami swung out of the car. Number of options: go in the front door, bright and breezy, hi guys, I'm home. Explain away the Caracal afterwards. Or: check over the wall into the pool area. Difficult. Electric wires, razor spikes, not the sort of hardware you want to deal with. Or: creep down the side path to the lower patio, get in through her bedroom's sliding door. Creep upstairs unannounced till she sussed out the scene.

Probably the best.

The path was overgrown. Honeysuckle, lantana, wild dagga, cannas, spindly num-num thorns snagging at her clothing, tearing her skin. Her feet disappearing into vegetation at every step. Could be cobras, puff adders, mole snakes, a host of serpents slithering through the undergrowth.

Tami stepped carefully, moving as fast as she could, the gun held high. Listened at the kitchen window, pinned back against the wall. No voices. No sounds.

From the kitchen window you could see through to the dining room, the lounge, out to the pool deck. Was worth a risk.

She took it.

No one in the kitchen. In the lounge a man on a cellphone, his back to her, facing the pool. Tall, shaven head, black trousers, black jacket on broad shoulders. A big mother. No sign of Lavinia. No sign of the babysitter.

Not good. Could be Lavinia was in her room packing a bag, about to do a runner. Guy could be a lover, friend, go-between. Maybe they'd drugged the babysitter. Except Tami thought not. Miss Kawasaki Ninja not one of your pussy types. Tami was thinking she needed to speak to Lavinia.

She ducked below the kitchen window, keyed through to Lavinia's phone. Heard the phone ring, once, twice. Distinct, close, maybe in the kitchen or dining room. On the third ring it was switched off. Tami tried the landline. Handsets chirped throughout the house: one in the kitchen, another in the lounge, one in Krista's bedroom, one downstairs in hers.

Left unanswered. Lavinia should've picked up. The babysitter should've picked up. Seven rings it went to voicemail. Tami disconnected, switched her phone to silent. The big mother would've seen her number come up twice. He'd be antsy.

Two options: go back, wait at the front door. Or stick to Plan A, get into the house, surprise him. Only problem she'd be coming up the stairs. Not ideal.

But Tami went with it.

Crept bent double beneath the kitchen window, hopped down the path at a clip, no one inside able to see or hear her. Jumped lightly onto her patio, peered through the sliding door. Her room was as she'd left it: the bed made, pillows plumped up, the cupboard doors closed, no shoes lying around, on the bedside table her iPod, the cordless phone handset, a television remote. Everything in its place. Neat and tidy Tami.

She fished out her keys, felt her phone vibrating. On the screen: Lavinia.

For real? Or the big mother dressed in black?

She hesitated. Pressed green. Went upbeat: 'Hi, I'm at the shops, home in ten minutes, anything I can get you?'

Dead air.

No ways anyone inside the house would've heard her.

She inserted the key, unlocked the sliding door, pushed it back. Realised she was sweating, drops running down her back, her fingers slippery on the door handle. Sweat stinging her eyes. She wiped it from her forehead. Carefully unlocked the expander bars, the metal grating on its tracks. She pushed it open, stuck through her head to listen. Noises upstairs. Not talking but movement.

Tami was two storeys down. Spiral staircase from her en-suite up to the bedroom floor: Krista's room, the guest suite where they'd put Lavinia. Wooden treads one flight up again to the living areas. The shitty part. On those stairs you were an open target.

She took the spiral staircase slowly. Step by step, listening, leading with the Caracal. No sound in the house. Could smell the sweetness of a cologne. What was it with the aftershave?

As she came out on the bedroom landing her phone vibrated in her jeans pocket: vriitz vriitz, vriitz vriitz. Might as well have been on full volume in the quiet. She keyed it to voicemail, saw on the log: Lavinia. No ways. Tami licked her lips. Her mouth gone dry, her heart suddenly hammering in her chest.

She pocketed the phone.

Crept round the spiral's rails. Could see the door open to Lavinia's bedroom. Slid back along the wall towards the room, eyes locked on the top of the stairs. No movement.

Inside the room, a damp towel on the floor, the bed unmade. Lavinia's bag missing from the cupboard. No sign bad stuff had happened. More like she'd showered, packed, been intending to leave.

Tami took out her phone, keyed through to Lavinia. Going to give her a piece of what-for. Heard the phone ringing upstairs.

Shouted, 'Lavinia. Lavinia, what's happening?' No response. Shouted for the babysitter. No response. Crept out of the bedroom door towards the staircase, gun in one hand, phone in the other. 'Lavinia, talk to me.'

Went up two steps, sideways, crouching. Caught a movement on her right. Heard the wop of the silencer, the lead smash into the wall behind her head. Swivelled,

bringing the Caracal round and up, squeezing off.
Didn't hear the second wop.

II

Titus Anders grieving for his dead sons thought, No,
no more, enough.

Thought: Revenge.

Knew the death of Tamora's son wasn't enough.

Titus Anders sat alone in the hotel conference room
waiting for the Chinaman, a hurt in his heart. Sat at a
round table with ten chairs, in the middle a bowl of
flowers – daisies, carnations, rosebuds, some long-
stalked purple blooms. On the wall, prints of sailing
ships in Table Bay. Realised he had one or two similar
prints on the walls of his Sunset Beach home.

Newcomers to his house would get the story about
the Portuguese raiding party slaughtered on the
beach, then he'd take you to the pictures, tell you,
'The other side of my ancestors came here on those
boats. Ja, they did.' He'd tap the picture frame with
his knuckle, stab his finger at the non-reflective glass,
leaving a smudge. 'As slaves. Kidnapped from their
homes in wherever, brought here in chains. You understand? Not a very nice situation. One of them was
called Titus van de Caap, that name's come down to
me. What I do, everything I do is for them. Because

they were treated so bad.' He'd eye you when he said this, gauging your reaction. You didn't come in with the right words, Titus the historian would let you know how an earlier Titus had been hanged for killing settlers.

He got up now, stood looking closely at one of the prints, not one he'd seen before. Showed a boatload of people being rowed ashore. Slaves without a doubt, to Titus's way of thinking.

The door opened, in came a Chinaman. A dumpy man with an easy smile. Who bowed. Introduced himself as Mr Yan.

Titus said, 'Where is Mr Xing?'

'Ah, Mr Xing. Ah, Mr Xing,' said Mr Yan. 'We are very sorry for Mr Xing. Mr Xing is not with us anymore. He has gone.'

'Gone.' Titus frowned at the short Chinaman. 'Gone where to?'

'Gone away.' Mr Yan rolled his eyes to the ceiling. 'It was most unfortunate.' He smiled, held out his hand. 'But now I am your man. That's how you say it, yes?'

Titus took his hand, felt hard fingers grip his. Might be a short fat Chinaman but he had an iron fist.

Mr Yan saying, 'How do you do? How do you do?'

Titus said he was fine thank you.

'That is most excellent.' Mr Yan indicated a chair, the two men sat.

Mr Yan went into praise routine number one: great country, great leader, great people, great cities, great hotels, great sights, great food, great doing business.

He smiled when he'd finished. Titus smiled back, thinking, Come on, let's get to it.

Mr Yan cleared his throat, went into praise routine number two: all the wonderful things he'd heard about Titus Anders from Mr Xing. Mr Xing had been very appreciative.

Again the smile exchange.

A pause while Mr Yan stared at his hands clasped on the tabletop. He glanced up at Titus. Said, 'I am pleased to see you are not hurt. This is a dreadful thing that happened to you. Your family are not hurt, too?'

Titus frowned. 'I'm sorry? What's that?'

'The shooting. I see it in the newspaper this morning. They have your photograph. This is most alarming.'

'You can see I'm fine. My family is fine,' said Titus. 'You do not need to worry. We are safe here.'

Mr Yan nodded. 'Please, in the newspaper you are called one of the Untouchables. What is this please?'

Titus laughed. 'A name the press gave us, three of us. Mr Xing didn't tell you?'

'No. It is something he did not say.'

'It's a joke. It's what newspapers call us.'

'You mean you and your partners? It make you sound like gangsters. Mafia.'

'It's nothing.'

'I see.'

'Look, look. It's a name. Journalists give people names. That way they sell more newspapers.'

'But there is always some truth in a name.'

'Not much truth.'

'Now someone wants to show that this is not how it is? That you are not untouchable?'

Titus wished Mr Yan would look at him, Mr Yan with his eyes averted. Even in the eyes of a Chinaman you could see something. Said, 'Maybe.'

After a silence, Mr Yan said, 'We are worried about this matter in the newspaper. It is not good for doing business.'

'Nothing will change. I am here to talk to you. We can do business still.'

'I am afraid, Mr Anders, this is not what we think. We think it is a problem what happened to you. We do not like to have problems. We do not like it when we read of shooting in the newspapers. We do not like our businesspeople to be in the news.' He unknotted his hands, held one out palm down parallel to the table, steady. 'We like our business to be steady. Like this. With no tremble.'

He glanced at Titus, held his eyes. Titus reading there the man's concern. And something else, a question. A doubt. Titus went to it.

'What's your problem, Mr Yan?'

Mr Yan was back with his knotted hands, eyes down. 'I have told you. We do not like people to be in the newspapers.'

'That's all? That's all that's worrying you?'

Again the silence. Then: 'We have a proposition, Mr Anders.'

Titus let this rest. A proposition! The sneaky chinks,

coming with a proposition. 'What sort of proposition?' he said.

Mr Yan responding fast. 'We have a proposition to make changes.'

'Changes? Huh? What d'you mean by these changes?' Titus on the verge of telling the chink to look at him.

'Business changes.' Mr Yan saying, 'In how we do our business.'

'Like what?'

'We do not need for the abalone to be shucked. We have people now for this operation. People in many places in the city for this operation. We do not need your transport. Now we have this sort of business for ourselves. Trucks with refrigeration.'

'You do?' said Titus. 'This's a surprise.'

'There is another proposition,' said Mr Yan.

Titus frowned. 'You call it a proposition, taking away our business. Why didn't you speak to us first?'

Mr Yan ignored this. Said, 'We make a proposition for a lower price, Mr Anders, for the abalone.'

'No, my friend, no.' Titus stood. 'No. This's out of the question. We have costs, input costs: diesel, repayments, maintenance for the boats, risks, insurance. You know what it costs getting abalone? D'you know?'

Mr Yan shook his head.

'No, you know nothing. Let me tell you. Let me tell you it costs many rands and cents. There's sharks in the sea, there's police shooting at us, road blocks, property searches, lawyers billing the hours. Shuckers, drivers, people in the airport, people all along the way.

People giving us information. We pay for this. Thousands of rands. In this business you must have people. People you trust. People with brains.' He knocked a finger against his temple. 'You understand, people with intelligence. People who're your brothers and sisters. People who need us. People need us for their living, mister. You take this away, people'll starve. You want a lower price, there's people won't be able to feed their babies. You know what you're doing here, Mr Yan, you are killing our industry. All the hard work we've done. No, my friend, no, this is bad news, evil news. You people come here and think you can take away our jobs, pay low prices for my heritage. Perlemoen is my heritage. This's my country's treasure. You think we can give it to you? You think this is right?'

Mr Yan said nothing.

Titus wiped a hand over his face. 'There's women I know, this's their only job, only income, what we pay them. Those women lose this work, they have nothing else. These women have children. Children needing food, clothes, to go to school. What's going to happen to them? Huh? You thought about that? Those children become rubbish. Tik addicts. They drink. The women become whores, poesmaids. You …' He pointed at Mr Yan, stood over him. 'You are taking away their lives. Now they have no chance. Because of you, Mr Yan. You are the new invaders.'

Titus spun round in his chair, pointed at the boat bringing slaves to shore. 'That is what you are: slave owners. You bring slaves here to work for you. Forget the locals.' Titus tapped the picture. 'You are never going to stop.'

Mr Yan stood. Now looked at Titus, Titus reading in the man's face no give, no sympathy. 'Perhaps you want to talk with your partners,' Mr Yan said. 'We can wait for two days' time.'

Titus nodded, slowly getting it. 'You're talking to someone else?' He grimaced at the Chinaman, prodded him in the chest. 'Someone else? Who?'

'It does not matter.'

'Who?' Titus spat out names. Mostly small-haul brothers, no one anywhere near capable of matching abalone shell for abalone shell. They got together they might produce a package, but Titus couldn't see them getting together. Too much bad blood. 'Who?' Then: 'Tamora Gool?' That was it. Her.

'It is our business,' said Mr Yan.

'Jesus,' said Titus. 'You people make me gatvol.' He headed for the door. Turned. 'You know what's gatvol? You know what's gatvol?' He drew a line across his neck. 'It means we're up to here with your chinky shit. Up to here.'

Titus wrenched open the door. There was Krista Bishop, arm raised to knock. He blinked, thought, What the hell! Said, 'You?'

'Me,' said Krista, glancing past him into the room. 'Wasn't expecting you in here.'

'What you want? Where's my daughter?'

'She's safe.' Krista angling to slip into the room.

'What you want?'

'Him,' she said.

'Him?'

'Him and his colleague. Where's Mr Lijan?' she said to the Chinese man. 'Hotel security said he went out with some people.'

III

Black Aron and the Russian watched a Benz with tinted windows reverse out of the driveway where Tami had gone in, come along Glencoe, slowing as it passed them, turn down at Molteno Road.

Black Aron whistled. 'Now what's potting? Who's that, hey? In a very larney car.'

The Russian crushed his cigarette butt, swung his legs into the Corolla.

'Come, drive. Now it is our time to visit.'

Black Aron turned the ignition, noticed the Russian had the MP5 on his lap.

They drove slowly to the house with the black entrance gate rolled back, the Sharan parked in front of the garage doors. A big red bike to the side.

'Nice bike,' said the Russian. 'Nice place. These girls' – he rubbed a thumb against two fingers – 'they are rich, yes, they pay big money for a place like this. Very cool. Very interesting. Business is good for them.'

'Girls like these don't buy houses up here,' said Black Aron. 'This's big-bucks territory. You know, bankers, executives, advocates, those types.'

The Russian laughed. 'In my country we call them mafia.'

'You could say,' said Black Aron. He stopped next to the Sharan, switched off. 'And now?'

'We knock on the door like we are visitors.'

'What if the Merc comes back?'

'I not think so. Why? You think is possible?'

'I don't. I'm just saying.'

'No, my friend. This is not a worry.' The Russian raised the MP5. 'Also we have this little dildo.' He pumped it in the air, reached across, pinched Black Aron on the cheek. 'So come. I give my word to finish this. A Russian man lives by his word. You know Ruskies. Honourable people.'

Black Aron rubbed his cheek. 'Don't do that, alright. Don't do that again.'

The Russian was out the car, walking towards the front door. Glancing back at him. Beckoning, 'Come, my friend, come.'

Black Aron wasn't happy. Not happy about the approach, the Russian with the gun in his right hand like it was normal that everyone walked around with a gun in their right hand. Not happy about the car that had driven away. He knew cars with tinted windows. Cars with tinted windows were bad news. Not happy about following the Russian. He powered down the window.

'I'm the driver. I'll wait.'

The Russian came back to the car, pointing the MP5 at him. 'Come. You video on the cellphone. Okay? Proof for my money.' The Russian standing there until Black Aron got out. 'Okay, my friend, that is better. Everything as you say, spot on.'

Black Aron ignored the jibe, took out his cellphone, selected the camera video.

At the front door the Russian said, 'Oo la la, we have a problem.' Pushed at the door, a large door that swung on a pivot. 'It is not locked.'

The Russian went in, Black Aron behind him watching the action on the screen of his cellphone, hanging back to let the Russian get a couple of paces ahead.

The Russian whispered, 'You smell that smell?' Sniffed.

Black Aron smelt it then: cordite. The way the BM had smelt after the Russian had his fun trying to do the job first time round.

The Russian said, 'I see some blood' – whispering still, pointing down at little drops on the tiles. 'Not so much.' A trail of them leading into the lounge.

Black Aron bent down for a close-up, said, 'You see any bodies?' Stood to track the Russian moving into the lounge, moving like he was in a movie, the MP5 in his right hand, right wrist gripped by his left hand. Lots of hot light coming in from the patio.

The Russian went into the dining room, pointed at the ceiling. Black Aron swung the camera up in a blur to a scar in the paintwork. Concrete dust on the dining-room table.

'Maybe a ricochet, yes?' The Russian still sotto voce. 'No more blood drops.'

'You see any bodies?'

The Russian edging towards the staircase, Black Aron staying back.

'Okay,' said the Russian. 'I see one, yes.' He straightened. Spoke normally. 'It is the black woman.'

'You mean the coloured?'

'No, she is black. Black like you.'

'I'm Indian,' said Black Aron.

'You are black.' The Russian pointed down the stairs. 'She is black also.'

Black Aron stepped forward, kept the camera on the Russian, then went left to point down the staircase. On the landing, the body of the woman they'd seen earlier driving the Sharan. A blood patch like a halo round her head.

'That's not the right one. Go down, check the rooms.'

The Russian grabbed Black Aron's arm, brought the camera close until his face filled the screen. 'You are the driver,' he said. 'You do not say orders. Okay? You understand this? No …' He waved the gun backwards and forwards across the screen. 'No orders.'

All the same, the Russian went down the stairs. Not cautious anymore, jigging down like he was right at home. Paused to touch the embedded lead.

'Not such a good shot. The first one miss. The second one hit.' He paused over the body.

'She dead?' Black Aron at the top of the stairs still with his phone on video.

'I am not a doctor,' said the Russian. 'Maybe she is. Maybe she is not.' He stepped over her, looked in the first room. Went on to the room at the end. 'There is no one here.'

'What about downstairs?' said Black Aron.

The Russian wagged a finger at him. 'No orders.' Moved to the spiral staircase. 'Alright. I will see.'

From the room below called up something in Russian.

'What?'

'I say there is nothing. No body.'

'Let's go,' said Black Aron, jittery, pushing open the door to check the guest loo. Tall woman lying propped against the toilet bowl. Syringe still stuck in her neck. A faint pulse beating. He swore, backed out, closing the door. Shouted to the Russian. 'Let's go. Let's go. There's gonna be problems here. I have to make phone calls.'

IV

Mart Velaze left his car outside the Grace, despite the heat, sauntered over to the Waterfront, San Marco's. Not first choice for coffee but a place to watch people. Mart Velaze's specialty.

'My passion,' he would joke about stake-outs.

He took a table in the deep shade, back to the wall. The tourists spread out before him beneath the white umbrellas. Pink-faced Brits, Jap businessmen, Italians showing chest hair, French en famille, German couples with maps, a group of Nigerians on cellphones. The languages lapping at him.

Mart Velaze felt warm and fuzzy. Believed he was picking up a vibe from Krista. The tough little lady had melted. Was flirting with him. Wena, buti, that could lead places. Or one place especially that Mart Velaze had in mind. He shifted on the plastic seat. Had to be almost twenty years between them, he was turning her on. The thought gave him the zippy zappo in the crotch.

'Baba,' said the waiter standing over him. 'What you want?'

He looked up at the man. Young guy, early twenties, probably Krista's age. 'Less of the baba,' he said. 'I look like an old man?'

The waiter apologised. Mart Velaze ordered iced coffee.

Baba! To hell with that!

He settled back in the chair, stretched out his legs.

He liked it here. Good aspect of the Victoria Basin, Mandela Gateway in the background. Nice irony, Mart Velaze always thought, sitting there in tourist heaven among the multitudes. Just an accident of time that fifty years back the Old Man and his cronies were being ferried out from the jetty below for a long spell on the Island. Funny thing, time, the changes it brought.

While he mused philosophical, waited for his iced coffee, the Voice vibrated his phone.

'Chief,' she said, 'listen, I've heard from elsewhere …'

Pausing on the elsewhere. Mart Velaze thinking, Elsewhere? Elsewhere? Sometimes elsewhere was the Voice's doublespeak for somewhere in government, more specifically the other security services post the amalgamation. Specifically, especially the Hawks in their Aviary down the corridor from his office.

In that moment Mart Velaze noticed a table to his right, recognised Rings Saturen sitting there, Tamora Gool, Rings's late-night visitor, the Chinese guy Mr Lijan. The very Mr Lijan supposed to be in Krista's care.

Heard the Voice say, 'Those Chinese, the ones we got the escorts to babysit, listen, there's something else. There's something going on with those Chinese and the Untouchable gents. I don't know what yet. But elsewhere there's some people very nervous. Some people want to increase the security, take it away from our escorts. I don't want that, chief. I want our escorts in there. It's the only way I can know what's going on, nè. But that's my battle, chief. Not an easy battle to fight when you don't even exist. But that's my baby. You know what I call us these days, black black ops.' She sniggered. 'Get it, chief? Black people running black ops.' Again the snigger.

Mart Velaze thought maybe he wouldn't have to

pay Krista out of his own pocket after all. The Voice would back the arrangement. At the same time Mart saw Tamora take out her cellphone, listen. Get up from the table leaving Rings and the Chinese man. He stood, followed her away from the tables, waved off the waiter hurrying towards him. Said, 'I'm coming back.'

The Voice said, 'What was that, chief?'

'Nothing,' said Mart Velaze. 'Just the waiter. I've got to go. Give me five minutes.'

'What?' said the Voice. But Mart Velaze had got rid of her, kept the cellphone to his ear, standing with sexy Tamora Gool some metres off in his side vision. Tamora oozing appeal.

Mart Velaze heard her say, 'This's a cock-up. A black Merc. I don't get who that is. Maybe it's Baasie. Leave. Get out of there. Forget Lavinia. Get Luc instead.' Tamora striding back towards the table.

Mart Velaze kept the play-acting with the cell to his ear, thinking, Black Merc, forget Lavinia, get Luc. Get out of there. Out of where? Had to be wherever it was Krista and Tami had safehoused Lavinia.

He went back to his table, phoned the Voice.

'I know we started this thing watching the bushie coloured gents, the so-called Untouchables,' she said, 'but I don't think they're the main thing anymore. I think we're watching another movie running here, sort of a sideshow, yes? I think getting the escorts was our luck, chief. We scored a luck there.'

Mart Velaze thought, More like I arranged a luck. Given what she'd said not one week back: 'There's two

Chinamen coming down to you from Joburg, chief, I've wangled that I'd arrange security. But not the usual guys. There's two women running a show called Complete Security, them. I want them to do it.'

Mart Velaze had said, 'I know of them.'

'I know,' the Voice had said. 'I read the history in your file. Let's get them on board. Could be useful assets with the work they do. Need to exercise your charms, chief.' The Voice laughing at her own pun. 'Assets. You with me?'

Now she said, 'These two Chinese been doing a lot of investing up here along the Reef.'

The Reef? Huh! Who called it the Reef anymore? Only the Voice with her quaintisms.

'Gone into mining,' she was saying. 'Gone into construction. Made donations to education trusts. Why's that, I ask you?'

'Because it's business,' said Mart Velaze.

'You see,' said the Voice, 'that's the thing with Chinese. Everything's business. When a Chinese gives you money, he's taking it back somewhere else. Taking back lots more than he gave you. That's how they do it, chief. Very smart.' A silence. Then: 'Hang on for me a moment.'

Mart Velaze did. Two minutes ticked by. The threesome were finishing up, shaking hands. Mart Velaze clicked off some photos on his cellphone, signalled the waiter for the bill.

The total just short of thirty bucks. Made Mart Velaze look twice.

'For a short coffee on ice,' he said, pulling out a twenty and a ten. 'Robbery with a smile.'

The waiter smiled.

'Keep the change.'

'Thank you, baba.' The waiter stopped scratching for copper in his purse.

Mart Velaze gave him the baleful eye. Wanted to say, Pas op, my friend, watch it. But didn't. Saw the Chinese man part with Rings and the luscious Tamora.

Heard her say, 'See you this afternoon, Mr Lijan.'

Interesting.

Watched the couple strolling off like lovers without borders.

The way Mart Velaze put it together: the Chinese guy would be heading back to the Grace, the other two for their cars. He took the Chinese option. After all, he needed to hear what Krista had to tell him about Titus, about Lavinia, too.

The Voice said in his ear, 'We've got a conflict of interests opening up here. Just keep on watching the scene, chief. Gather up the scatterings for our files. Never know, do you, when something turns out useful? So often I've seen it happen. Little scatterings of Africa, nè, I thought they were nothing, suddenly they pay out. Insurance, chief. That's our business, insurance. Go with the ancestors.'

She was gone, leaving Mart Velaze walking behind the Chinese man towards the Grace wondering what the Voice had meant. The sun now hellish hot. Sweat making his armpits damp, his face feel oily. What'd she mean by conflict of interests opening up here? Here inside security? Probably. So often he wondered who it was pulled the Voice's strings. Therefore his strings. So often he wondered which side he played.

Up ahead Mr Lijan on his cellphone took his time. Seemed to be unbothered by the sun.

Gave Mart Velaze a moment to think some more. Could be only one reason the Chinese guy met with Rings: abalone. Rings didn't offer any other big-time business. Could maybe open some doors at Customs but the way the Voice spoke, these Chinese were men with influence. Didn't need a gangster-cum-jumped-up-politico like Rings Saturen to hack a path.

His cellphone rang: Krista.

'Another surprise,' he said, 'you phoning me.'

V

Transcript from the case file of Hardlife MacDonald:

Me, I was in the car with Stones. It was a new man driving. We sitting in the car listening to CapeTalk. The woman, what you call them, the presenter, some black woman from Joburg is moaning about gang violence on the Flats.

Then the driver, he says, 'You come down here, my sister, we's got special tricks for you.'

Stones was in the back seat, he laughs at the driver. When Stones laughs you think it's funny.

All the time the presenter on the radio doesn't stop. Over and over the same story: twenty-four dead in six weeks. Seven caught in the crossfire. Six children shot.

'Ag no man,' says the driver. 'Fancy that.'

Me, myself I think the same thing.

Then Stones says his brother's girl got shot through the arm. She's a little girl only four years old.

I don't wanna say anything about how he shot the little Muslim girl six times.

We all blame Pretty Boyz. Blerry gangsters.

On the radio the talk jockey's going on about maybe we should call in the army, that's what the premier wants.

'Call them in,' says the driver like he's talking to the radio. Like the people can hear him. 'Let's teach them about a real war. Give them some practice.'

After that women phone the radio telling how bad the gang war is. We sitting there listening to all this. Stones gets pissed off.

'Nobody says thank you for the money we give,' he says. 'Nobody's grateful.' Strues.

We sitting there in the heat. No breeze. The street quiet, quiet, quiet. Then this old woman comes out to stare at us. Shoo, she tells us. We too hot to even laugh. The driver says, 'Auntie got some cooldrink, please, man, auntie, it's hot.'

'Voetsak,' the auntie says. Waving her arm like she's chasing away dogs. 'You's skollie boys,' she shouts at us. Then she goes inside but we don't move.

We sitting there and sitting there. The driver he says to me, 'How long we's supposed to wait here? It's half the morning already. Some peoples don't go to work early. You become a boss, you can sleep late.' He's talking about Baasie.

So Stones chirps, 'What yous wanna do? Play with your cherrie's titties?' Stones's laughing, snort, snort, snort.

I think maybe the driver's gonna get angry but he says, 'Nice titties. You's never seen such nice titties.'

Then Stones says, 'I seen them.'

I think this could be a problem. With Stones you don't know what's gonna happen next.

But the driver's cool, hey. 'Ja? Never, nooit man,' he says, 'this's my cherrie.'

But Stones just says, 'Sharing is caring.'

And the driver's also laughing, saying, 'Fok yous, my bru, fok yous.' Grinning at me and Stones. Saying, 'Nice titties, hey. Hot onna spot.'

Stones grins at him, points down the street. 'Focus, my bru. There. Check there. Focus.'

I look and I see we got business.

The driver starts the car, a Mazda Étude we jacked. False plates on it. Late-nineties model, one point eight, not much vooma in the engine anymore but enough for this job. I would say nicely kept. Cloth seats clean, no stains, a smell of washing softener, fresh 'n wholesome. You keep the washing softener in the boot, you get this smell in the car. What they call it, a scent. So fresh it makes the driver sneeze, before we get a zol smoking.

We all looking down the road. I hear Stones, 'This's

gonna cause big shit.' I can hear in his voice there's the fear. Like we's all tight on our nerves.

'Ja, man, so what's new?' says the driver.

'Big kak,' says Stones.

I can feel it even now, I'm telling you. 'Just do it nice 'n quick,' I say to Stones.

Stones's got a Taurus 9mm, standard ten plus one clip, with tape where the grips used to be. You can see it's heavy in his hand, the way I know he likes it. He holds it down between his knees.

We watch the Lexus coupé reverse backwards into the street, drive away from us. Top down. The man's mad in the summer sun. Gonna get sunburn. Even for a coloured, you gotta watch the sun.

I tell the driver not too close yet.

We follow the coupé out of Athlone to the highway. The man's supposed to be going to his work, not onto the highway.

'Doesn't matter,' says Stones. 'Doesn't matter where he's going. Where he's going's the same place any direction he takes.'

So we follow the coupé going fast up the hospital hill to De Waal, so fast we getting left behind.

I can see the driver's got the accelerator flat down so I tell him to change the gears. Sometimes people don't know how to drive a car. You got these people never use gears.

'We's in third,' he says.

'We's gonna lose him,' says Stones.

By the time we on De Waal we far back. I can see the

coupé ahead on the lower bends there. When we go downhill we catch up enough short-short to see the coupé take the Jutland ramp left to Mill Street. So at the robots at Breda Street we's just six cars behind.

Stones wants to get out do it there. I tell him no how we gonna get away. I tell him, 'Shit, man, wait.'

So when the robot changes, the coupé goes up the Mill Street shortcut to Upper Orange. At the stop street we pull alongside. The coupé driver looks at me with this frown like we shouldn't be there. You can see he wants to say something, also cos I'm grinning at him.

I know behind me Stones's got his window down, he's raising the niner. I wait for it. Two shots in the man's head. He doesn't even groan. No time. One time he's dead.

'Go,' I scream at the driver. And we go with hot rubber to the robot at Hatfield, back into Mill Street, even through the red at Breda.

I tell the driver slow down cos we don't want a speeding fine.

I can tell you it was Stones did the shooting.

Part 3: False Bay

9

I

Titus Anders had gone.

Had said to Krista on his way out, 'You better look after my girl, understand? You better.'

Had seemed more than upset to Krista. Had seemed angry. Suppressing it. A flush at his neck. A bad smell to his breath. He'd walked out of the room even while the businessman was saying goodbye, Mr Yan's hand reaching towards him.

Banged the door closed.

She'd turned to her client. 'You didn't tell me about this meeting, Mr Yan. We're your security, we're supposed to be here when you meet people.'

The two of them standing either side of the table.

'It was nothing,' said Mr Yan. 'A small business arrangement.' Beaming at her.

'Where's Mr Lijan?' she'd asked then, watching the Chinese man smiling at her.

'He is walking. Tourist walking. This meeting was only necessary for one person.'

'He's not supposed to be alone.'

'Now you are here, we are not alone.' Mr Yan widening his smile to show her his teeth. 'Now we are ready for the sights. Probably he is waiting for us. I will see.'

He'd phoned his colleague, grinning at Krista nonstop. Talking rapidly, not listening. Keying off his phone with a flourish.

'He is coming. He says to tell you this is very beautiful, your Waterfront. Very relaxing. Very safe as houses.'

They'd walked through to the foyer when Krista got the call from Tami. Tami faint, not making sense, saying something about an ambulance. Her voice making Krista's skin crawl with cold fear. Her voice something she'd heard before, the voice of the dying.

Krista had moved away from Mr Yan, was looking out at the yacht basin, at a crew preparing their boat. People laughing, joking with one another. Touching. High fives. Carefree. Her heart suddenly ferocious, thumping in her chest, her breathing shallow.

In the Congo a day like any other: hot, close, the air liquid, pressing down. Six of them patrolling an airfield's outer limits. Walking in single file through discarded wreckage: oil drums, lorries unwheeled, engines, propellers, the carcass of a c17, faded NATO insignia. Not talking. Their weapons heavy, their thoughts on getting through the hours. Dull thoughts of cold beer, cold water. Lying down in shade.

The children rose from the wasteland, shooting.

Afterwards, what Krista felt was her heart heavy, beating, beating, beating. What she heard was the voice of death. Faint, spluttering. 'Help me.' At her feet her bloodied sergeant. 'Help me.'

'Get here. Get here.'

'What? What're you saying? You're freaking me, Tami.'

'Ambulance coming. I've called it.'

Krista snapping into stone-cold focus.

'You're hurt?'

'Shot.'

'Badly?'

'Badly.'

'Lavinia?'

'Gone.'

'Where's ...?'

'Don't know.'

Krista thinking, No, Tami, no. 'Stay with me. Stay with me, okay, just stay with me. Don't disconnect.'

In the marina the yacht cast off, the crew waving at friends on the jetty.

She turned to Mr Yan. 'You wait here. When Mr Lijan comes, you both wait here. You don't leave the hotel until I get back.'

Mr Yan said, 'You have emergency?'

'I do, yes, so wait here.'

'We must stay here and wait? On such a day? For how long?'

'An hour. About an hour.'

Krista left it at that. Rushed out the hotel saying to Tami, 'You're still there?' Heard a faint response. 'Tami?'

Again a groan.

'Speak to me. Say something. Anything.'

'I'm … I'm here.'

'Alright. Listen.' Giving an address to a taxi driver, telling him fast. Get there fast. Back to Tami, 'Listen, I'm going to disconnect. I need to make calls. Can you do that, disconnect? Just a few minutes, then I'll call back. Yes. You can do that?'

Nothing from Tami.

'Can I use your cellphone?' she said to the driver.

'What's wrong with yours.'

'Can I use your phone?' Krista leant forward, extended her arm. 'Come on, please. It's urgent. Please, just help me out.'

'Twenty bucks.'

'Okay, twenty bucks. Whatever you want.' She took the phone he handed over his shoulder, phoned Mart Velaze.

'Another surprise,' he said. 'You phoning me, you'll be giving me ideas. Guess what? Your Mr Lijan's been having secret talks. Thought you were supposed to be their security, mmmm? Be on the inside.' Mart Velaze keeping it light, kidding but also not kidding.

'Listen,' she said, 'I'm not at the hotel. Just listen to me.'

'What's happening?'

'Hectic shit.'

'You want to tell me?'

'No. Just this: Titus Anders was with Yan. When I walked in Anders walked out. So I don't know what they talked about.'

'Okay,' said Mart Velaze.

'The other one, Lijan, he's walking around some-where. But you know that.'

'What's your problem?'

'I can't talk. I've got to go. I told Yan I'd be back in an hour. To wait for me.'

'Not very professional.'

Wanted to tell him, Up yours, spider. Keyed him off instead. She dropped the phone into the taxi driver's lap. 'Faster. Jesus, man, don't you know the back roads?'

'I'm going fast as I can, lady,' he said. 'You wanna go faster, take a helicopter.'

Krista was back with Tami, repeating her name, begging her to say something.

Heard Tami say, 'Can't ...'

Tami.

There was this about Tami.

They'd gone out clubbing. In the early days not long after they'd set up the partnership. A bonding night. Cocktails at Tjing Tjing, then hit the Dragon because Krista knew the owners, the bouncers, everybody.

'My scene,' she'd said to Tami. 'My scene to get out of it.'

They'd danced. For hours and hours.

They'd popped some Ecstasy.

They'd picked up two dudes.

Danced some more, Krista working up the situation with the men.

Chasing a few lines in the loo, Tami had said, 'I'm not sure.'

To which Krista: 'It's a slam, Tami. Nothing wrong with a slam.'

'You do this?'

'Sometimes.'

Tami had said, 'We don't know these guys.'

'That's the thing.'

'So?'

'So they've got cocks. They've also got hotel rooms. They're not locals.'

Tami had looked aghast, eyebrows raised, traces of white at her nostrils. 'You found this out?'

'I don't waste time.'

The upshot was they'd shagged the fellas, bounced, saying slam bam thank you man. At sun-up found themselves back home drinking skinny lattes on the patio beside the pool. Alone. Both of them still ritzed.

Krista had done her swimming thing over a couple of dozen lengths.

Afterwards they'd curled up on her bed to watch an old movie, *Thelma & Louise*. Might be passé, they loved it.

'You see,' Krista had said, 'this's it. The way our lives are. Especially the end.'

'I hope not.' Tami running her fingers through Krista's short hair.

'It's sweet. Nothing wrong with sweet.'

Afterwards fallen asleep. In the grey light of early evening, they'd made out.

Afterwards Krista had said, 'Wouldn't have guessed you did this too.'

Heard Tami sigh. 'I could say the same.'

At the house: armed-response car at the kerb, ambulance reversed into the driveway, emergency response van next to the Sharan. The red Kawasaki on its stand.

Armed-response man with a gun at the front door, said, 'Cops're coming.'

Krista rushed inside.

Found a gurney in the passageway with the baby-sitter flat out. In the lounge, Tami on a gurney being wheeled towards the front door, paramedics holding a drip feed above her.

'Outta the way,' the front medic said, pushing Krista aside.

Krista taking this in, bending to Tami. 'It's going to be—'

Heard Tami's soft, 'My phone. In my phone. Downstairs. Careful. Please go careful …' The rest of the words lost.

The medic shouting, 'Outta the way. Outta the way.'

Krista stood aside. Watched them wheel Tami out.

My phone. In my phone …

Closed her eyes, took deep breaths, went into automatic mode. She'd been here before. Started with the killing of her mother, seeing her mother stabbed, bleeding out. Then her platoon leader on that airfield. Blood spurting from her like she was a sieve. The grip of her fist right to the end. This place of no feelings.

'You can come, lady,' a medic said, his hand on her arm. 'You can be with your friend.'

Krista shook free. Glared at the medic, the medic backing off. 'You can come.'

Krista turned away. 'Go. Just go. Keep her alive.' Saw the blood spots on the dining-room tiles, the chip in the ceiling. Leant over the staircase railings: on the floor below Tami's gun, next to it her cellphone. A blood pool, smeared where Tami'd hauled herself towards the bottom stair. Blood prints on the stairs from the medics' boots.

Krista went down, careful not to step on the prints. Picked up the cellphone, bent low to smell the gun.

Outside, next to the pool, she opened the voice recordings on Tami's phone: 'Black guy. Wearing black. Black Mercedes.' She gave the registration number. 'Didn't see Lavinia.' Tami's voice giving out.

Krista thought: not gangs. A gang would be three or four. Titus Anders had to be involved in something else. Black guy, black Merc. Could be Nigerians. Could be a Joburg syndicate. Israeli even. Could be homegrown secret agents, the friends of Mart Velaze. Too many possibilities. But there was the reg number. At least that.

She would get this guy. She stilled her breathing. Looked at the distant ocean, got quiet inside.

Maybe she should've come back to the house. Not Tami. She had the training. The experience of people trying to kill you. She could've handled it. Saved Tami.

Like, if she'd gone to her mother's studio instead to

fetch the email printout that day, maybe the killer wouldn't have attacked her, a child. Maybe he'd have gone away. Her maman would still be alive.

She'd carried that one for a long time, despite therapy. The what-if reruns. What if I'd dashed ahead of Maman? What if I hadn't been so lazy? What if I'd ignored Maman saying that she'd go? What if, what if, what if?

Replays weren't helpful, she knew that. Stirred up weird guilt that was the guilt of being not hurt, of being alright, alive. Reality was it'd happened. Nothing you could do about it.

There was the thing: nothing you could do about it. Because most of the time you didn't know what was going on. You didn't know when someone'd rise up, shoot at you.

In Mace's words: You never know what shit you're dealing with. You think you've got the job taped. Clients in a safehouse, you've plugged the holes. Days go by, weeks, months. Clients come, go, come again. Never any trouble. Not even a bag snatch in touristy Long Street. You think, Okay, I can handle this. As long as I'm wide awake, I'll see the baddies coming.

Thing is, you don't. Even if you do everything right all the time, even if you don't slip up, some day all hell's going to come out of the wide blue nowhere. Nothing you could do to head it off. You're just in the way. They'll get rid of you like you're dog shit. Scrape you off on the kerb.

That's the problem in this business. There's all this

stuff going on you've got no control over. You don't even know about it. You feel useless. Like someone's pulling your strings. Strings you didn't even know about.

Mace's words.

Papa being Papa. Giving his little girl some advice. Because Papa had been scraped off on the kerb a couple of times.

Wasn't going to happen to her. She would get this guy.

Krista sat out there staring over the city, making her vows. Then worked up a story for the cops.

Story she told was that Tami was home alone. Supposed to be home alone. Thief must've got in somehow, often the patio door was open, panicked when he saw her, shot. Did the visitor.

The detective looked at her, said, 'Bloody lucky shot for him to hit her. Most of these guys can't shoot for toffee.'

Krista said, 'Nice one, detective.'

The cop said, 'Sorry, man. It's a fact. So, okay, that gun on the floor's hers, ja? That's how you found it when you got here?'

Krista nodded.

'She got a licence?'

'Of course. We're security. That's our business. She knows how to shoot.'

The detective looked down into the City Bowl. 'So, well. You want my opinion, you could use some security around here. Tit view though.'

II

Titus Anders heard first about the assassination of Baasie Basson. How he'd been shot in the head, point blank. In full view, middle of the morning, at a busy intersection.

Heard it from Rings Saturen. Rings coming over jittery on the phone, talking full on. Saying, 'That's all I know. I don't know why Baasie was there and not at work. I don't know where he was going. Baasie could've been going anywhere. One of the Kloof Street in-scenes for breakfast. Over to Camps Bay. His larney chommie friends in Camps Bay. Llandudno, Hout Bay even. I dunno. We're not his keeper. The man's got his rich scene. Baasie's with us but what can we do? Can't watch for him all the time.'

Titus said, 'You better watch for yourself.'

Titus was driving back to Sunset Beach, the shit from the Chinaman boiling his brain. Now this drive-by on Baasie.

Baasie dead.

Didn't make sense.

'Hell, man,' said Rings. 'Wasn't a hijack. This was a job. Kill Baasie. Someone said, Kill Baasie. Organised it. Who'll kill Baasie? Baasie was a lover boy. Baasie was a money man. Baasie didn't do like you and me. Baasie had clean hands. No past with the gangs. No Pollsmoor. Hell, man, why kill Baasie? Everybody loved Baasie.'

'Cos he's with us,' said Titus. 'That's enough.'

'Can't be, Titus. Your boys, Quint and Boetie. Baasie. This is out of control. People doing this like it doesn't matter who we are. No, man, we must get a handle here. Bring it under control. Exercise some power.'

'It's Tamora,' said Titus.

'Tamora? Who's Tamora?'

'You know. The one I gave a chance.'

'The little mommy with the pearlies?'

'Ja, her.'

'You think so?'

'Luc does. Luc's been telling me all along. She's coming in. She's got something going. Got the Mongols fighting the Pretty Boyz. She's starting a war. Causing shit for us. What she wants's all the Pretty Boyz business. Everything. Kill us. Smash the Pretty Boyz. She's got the Valley of Plenty.'

'She's a woman.'

'Doesn't matter. You don't think she can do this? Women can be evil.'

'You think? And the kills? You think it's her organised them?'

'Can be.'

'No, man, she's a woman. A woman's not going to do this.'

'Luc's right. I didn't want to think it, but Luc's right.'

'I don't know,' said Rings. 'I don't know.'

Titus turned off the Drive into Sunset Beach. 'Other thing, the Chinese …'

'Say it.'

'They want to cut us down. Don't want shuckers. Don't want fridge trucks. Don't want storage.'

'They laid this out?'

'Also want it cheaper, the perlemoen.'

'Cheaper's for nix. We'll be giving it away.'

'That's what they want.'

'We better have a talk time.'

'We better find another Chinese.'

They left it there. Titus entered his home street, saw the cop cars outside his house. Thought, Shit, how am I supposed to deal with this? As he switched off the Jeep, his phone rang. Complete Security on the display. He killed it.

Went inside, dealt with the scene. Showed his grief and despair to the cops. Made a statement that when he'd gone out to a business meeting, his son was asleep on the couch. Told them Luc had phoned him with the dreadful news.

The detective said, 'What's going on, Mr Anders? Two sons dead. You all get shot at outside a restaurant. Top of a hit list, hey? Popular family.' The detective leering at him.

Titus came across the room in a rush, Luc stopped him.

'Daddy, Daddy. Leave it.'

'Maybe you live in a big house, Mr Anders. But a gangster's always a gangster. Always someone wants to knock him down. It's the truth. Once you're in, you can't get out. No one's untouchable.'

Titus broke free from Luc, got up close to the detective. Cops grabbed him.

'What's it, Mr Anders? There's something you want to add to your statement?'

'Fok you,' said Titus. 'Fok you everyone.' Spitting out the words in white flecks of gob.

'Sorry for your loss,' said the detective, turning away.

'Come, Daddy, I've got tea for Daddy outside.' Luc shuttled him onto the patio, saying, 'You got to make a plan about Tamora. Chop-chop.'

Titus Anders sat there, drinking sweet tea, looking at the bay, the shining sea, with the cops doing their crime-scene stuff in his house.

'We will, Luc,' he said. 'We will.'

Took out his phone, heard a message from Krista Bishop to call him. He did, was told that Lavinia had been snatched.

Sat there looked at the beach, sipped the hot tea, said to his son, 'They've got Lavinia.'

III

Black Aron and the Russian saw the cop cars outside the house of Titus Anders, left the area fast. Went off to the parking spot further down the beach. From there could see the Anders place. All so peaceful from this side: the old man having tea on the patio with his son. No sign of cops anywhere.

Black Aron said, 'What's happening there, you think? All those cops. That's crime-scene stuff. Serious precarious.'

The Russian shrugged, lit a cigarette.

Black Aron phoned Tamora, laid out the scene.

'Yes, I heard,' she said, 'from Rings. Quint's dead, stabbed. Tell the Ruskie boy that's what I like.'

'Wasn't him. He's been with me.'

A quiet from Tamora. 'That so?'

'I'm not lying.'

'O-kay.' Tamora dragging out the word.

Black Aron wondered what she was wearing. She'd been wrapped in a towel when he left. Smoking from one cigarette to the next. Staring over the city. Thing with Tamora, a thing like that with her boy, you never knew what she'd want next. A thing like that would make her vicious. Angry as a snake. Make her dress cool as a Chanel model.

Probably went out in her red capris, white blouse, not a trace of her grief. Black Aron stripped her down till he had her in bra and thong.

Might've screwed earlier, but next time was in the line-up to his way of thinking.

'Interesting, isn't it, Ron?' she said. 'Somebody working hard this morning: puts a screwdriver in Quint, takes Lavinia for a ride. I like it, the dude gets around. Much better than our Ruskie.'

'You think it's the same guy?'

'Could be, Ron. Could be. Just finish the job, okay. Tell the Ruskie, if he wants his bucks, finish the job.'

'Now? There's cops there.'

'Come, Ron, come. Work it out.'

Black Aron hung up, said to the Russian. 'All yours, Smirnoff. The lady says you want your money, just do the job.'

The Russian finished his cigarette, dropped the butt on the gravel, crushed it.

'With the cops in the house?'

'Techies, probably. All in fancy suits with hairnets. They're not cops, Smirnoff. Don't even carry weapons. What's your problem? Easy job.'

The Russian said nothing, kept his focus on the house down the beach.

Said, 'Good. Then this is what you want, then this is what I do. You turn the car. You keep the engine working.' He picked up the MP5, checked the load. 'Good, then I go now.'

'Mazeltov,' said Black Aron.

The Russian looked at him. 'That is Jewish.'

'Jewish, Russian. Sounds Russian. Like the petrol bombs. Molotov, mazeltov.'

The Russian shook his head, got out of the car, took the sand path towards the house.

Black Aron gave him the thumbs up. 'Spot on.'

IV

All morning Mart Velaze wondered about Krista. She'd said an hour. A lot more than an hour had run out. Gone midday now. He'd heard the noon cannon.

All morning said to himself, you've made a mistake, buti. Big mistake. Should have followed the gangster with his squeeza. Maybe there'd have been more action, more entertainment.

Because here were Mr Lijan and Mr Yan hanging, not going anywhere. Not even looking restless. Very relaxed. Slacks, open-necked shirts, loafers. Could be tourists. Could be businessmen with free hours.

Spending some time at the Signal Restaurant yakking over tea.

Now in the hotel library: all leather chairs and wood panelling, very subdued, very cool. Both senses of the word. Wouldn't believe it was 33°c with high humidity outside. The two men sending emails on their Mac-Books, engrossed in their iPhones. Glasses of mineral water perched beside them, lime slices among the rocks.

Not once checking their watches. Not perturbed that their security gals were nowhere in sight.

Funny that, Mart Velaze thought, that they were just so at ease. It was him, he'd be kicking up mayhem, prowling like a zoo leopard. Wanting to be on the move. See stuff. But Mr Lijan and Mr Yan were totally chilled.

Other thing that perturbed Mart Velaze, relaxed in a chair near the door, was how much longer he could sit there. How much longer he could read the newspaper. Before Mr Lijan and Mr Yan got jumpy. Types like Mr Lijan and Mr Yan would notice people who spent too long in one room.

What also played on Mart Velaze's mind was no obvious surveillance. Chinese gents like these two would be watched. Most likely the Agency would have someone in the hotel's CCTV room, eyes on the monitors. Could see stake-out man sitting there, probably wondering who he was, this black guy reading the papers.

Time he moved.

Any other department in the Agency, he'd have a back-up take over. But the Voice wasn't into back-ups. 'Chief, you're a ghost among ghosts,' she'd say. 'We're not on the books, we haven't got a budget. We don't exist. Go with the ancestors.'

Amen.

Truth: Mart Velaze preferred it that not even the Agency spooks knew he was one of them.

He was about to put down his newspaper, in walked a bodyguard, big Zulu in a black suit, wire in his ear. Behind him the deputy minister of fisheries: lady with a spinnaker stomach pulling her forth, hand outstretched like a yardarm. The muscle put himself between the Chinese and Mart Velaze: stood feet apart, arms behind his back.

Mart Velaze thinking, Hey, first the Chinese have

talks with the abalone poachers, next with fisheries. How cosy.

Thinking, Krista Bishop, where the hell are you? Wanting nothing more than a photograph: dep min shaking hands with the Chinese would get the Voice all husky. Would be scoring a luck big time. Would support his theory: sometimes you just needed to wait.

The deputy minister saying, 'Shall we go to lunch, gentlemen?' Leading the way out of the room.

Mart Velaze put down his newspaper. The men had packed up their hardware. As they left, both bowed to him, deadpan faces.

He returned their greeting, as inscrutable, cracking his newspaper to a fresh page.

When they were gone he phoned Krista. Left a voice message: 'Where are you? We have an arrangement. You need to be here.'

V

Transcript from the case file of Hardlife MacDonald:

Me, I can tell you what happened to the woman. The Anders woman. There was no chance to tell you before. I'm telling you this was a thing. Major, major, major kak. First there was the Anders boy they drowned, now the woman. The Mongols are the big boys now. Untouchable.

Like I say, the woman was brought in a big black car. Mer-ce-des-Benz, very larney. A black man driving, very cool man with the woman in the boot. Young man, hey. Not even as old as me. The captain, I can tell you, he knows this man. He even gets his wifey to put a bandage on the man's arm. The captain, he's like very smiley to this man. He call him mister. Me myself I can tell you they musta been talking together before to make this arrangement. Very sharp black man. You gotta be if you drive a car like that.

I can tell you I dunno what he gave her but she's mos away for the day. You got to hold her up. You don hold her up, she drops one time, blah onna ground. The captain tells us take her out the boot.

We got the woman in a old place, maybe it was a shed before. There's wood boards on the windows, a metal door with a lock. You go inside, the walls are black from fires. There's holes in the tin roof. All over the floor is glass, tins, ash, sand, papers, even old newspapers. The floor is concrete with deep cracks. I never been to this place before. If you want I can take you.

The woman's got on jeans, you know they's got what they call designer tears. I can see blood on her T-shirt, dirty marks all over. Omo washing powder never going to wash that T-shirt white again. She lying on a mattress on the floor. That mattress is sponge. Yellow sponge that's got burn marks, piss stains. You know you lie on that, you gonna smell piss.

Me, the captain says to me to watch her. I say captain, no man, let Stones do it. Stones's a good watcher. The captain say Stones got no control. Stones too much like a dog.

When they gone I got to watch her for a long time. I got nothing to do except watch her.

First I watch her through a hole. She's got her eyes open, looking at the shit on the floor. Smelling the stink. You can see her one eye is swollen like a dark brown. There's also blood on her neck where the black man musta stuck her with the needle.

The only thing she can do is lie there. They got plastic ties at her ankles. They got her wrists tight behind her back. I been like that too. One time. You got all this cloth in your mouth so your jaw hurts. The gag. I tell you you think you gonna die cos you can't breathe enough. Your mouth goes dry. You want to swallow but you can't move your tongue. You got to breathe so hard through your nose.

I watch her doing this. She gets the panic. When you get the panic you go mad. You wanna get your feet free, you throw yourself all over. She does this so much she falls off the mattress. Now she lies on the floor. I can hear she breathes like an animal. Then she cries. You make it worse when you cry. It's hard to breathe.

She's tough, this one, I can tell you. The crying stops then she wiggles back onna mattress. She even lies leaning against the wall, facing the door. Like she's gonna challenge us coming inside.

When I hear the car coming I stop watching her. In the car's the captain and Stones. The captain's got this new tattoo on his forehead, just the word: Mongol.

He says to me, 'Ja, Hardlife, you wanna be the first one in the box?'

I laugh at him. But the captain doesn't laugh back. The captain's not a man to laugh. He takes out a key, opens the padlock on the door. We all go inside.

'Hullos, darling,' says the captain. 'Sorry to disturb.' I can tell you that's what the captain said. I can tell you.

10

I

Titus keyed off his phone.

Stupid woman, what sort of bullshit to come with that government had taken Lavinia. Government! Government didn't snatch people. Krista Bishop was full of nonsense. Bad move giving her Lavinia. Bad, bad move. Government? Hell with government. What we're talking, my sister, he should have told her, is animals. Animals don't care about me or you. Don't care for themselves. They live, they die, doesn't matter.

Blood in, blood out.

Boetie dead.

Quint dead.

Baasie dead.

Lavinia!

All the time he'd been talking to Krista, Titus was looking at the parking lot down the beach. From where he sat on the stoep, could see a car there, the sun striking off the windows. Saw a man get out of the car, do some stretches like he might be limbering up for a jog.

In his ear Krista yudder yudder yudder like she was the one being strung out. You should've told me what was going on. You should've told me government was involved. Mouthing off about agents, operatives, muscle men in black cars. Wanting to know what was happening. Jesus, the girlie had a tongue.

Titus held the phone away from his ear. Shook his head. Waited until Krista took a breath, came in with, 'Listen, sister, you fucked up.' Titus keeping his voice low. 'I thought you were good. You're shit. Better you play with your dolly movie stars. Keep outta the real world. Otherwise you're gonna get hurt like your friend.' Disconnected.

In the house behind him Titus could hear the techies finishing their crime-scene work. Next to him, Luc, riding his chair, stared one-eyed at the ocean.

The problem with Luc was he didn't notice things.

Titus watched the car do a U-turn, stop next to the man. The sort of manoeuvre that made no sense.

The man bent into the passenger window for a few moments. Straightened, went down the wooden steps to the path, carrying a small backpack. Quite jaunty. Relaxed.

Titus said, 'Fetch me the binoculars, Luc.'

'What?' Luc jerking back on his chair. 'The binoculars? You want the binoculars?'

'That's what I said. They're inside on the table.'

Luc stood up. 'We got to get that Tamora, Daddy. Only way to make this stop.'

'Alright, Luccie, alright. The binoculars.'

The man had stopped to light a cigarette, stood there facing out to sea, smoking. In the still air, Titus could see his exhale, even at this distance. The backpack rested against his ankles. Funny that he carried it in his hand, didn't have it over his shoulder.

The car was back where it had parked. The driver now outside leaning on the roof, seemed to be gazing down the path, might even have binoculars.

'Won't be difficult finding her,' said Luc, handing the binoculars to Titus. 'Day like today Tamora'll be on the water with her divers. False Bay. We find her, we find Lavinia.'

'You think she's going to do Lavinia like your brother? Drop her down for the fishes?'

'Maybe.'

'Never, Luc. You don't understand bugger all.'

'What you mean?'

Titus adjusted the binoculars, brought the man into focus. Big man, green golf shirt, casual shorts. The man fitted his shirt: thick arms, sloping shoulders. Dress him in black, put him at the door of a club, he's a bouncer. Titus shifted his line of sight to the car.

'They won't do that to Lavinia.'

'You don't think?'

'They'll keep her alive.' He could see now the man at the car had a pair of binoculars. Appeared to be looking at them, but could be looking at anything along Sunset Beach. 'They'll rape her.'

'No ways, Daddy.' Luc straining to see what his father could see.

'For sure. Like you would. Just think of what you'd do, they'll do it. Like you cut up the boy.'

'Ah, man.'

'Fuck her up, Luccie. Ten, fifteen of them. Maybe more. For long hours.'

'Daddy!'

'Make her HIV.'

'Daddy.'

'Bring her back to her daddy with a poes like raw meat. Stinking.'

'Daddy, stop.'

'Damaged goods, Luccie. Damaged goods. How we supposed to deal with that? With the shame?'

'No, man, Daddy, no, man.'

'Yes, man, Daddy, yes, man. Everything you think of, they'll do. Everything. Plus more. More, more, more.'

Titus watched the man take a phone call, look over in their direction. Still too far off to see his face.

'You want to be pleased you're not Lavinia, Luccie. Pleased you're not a girlie. You have to be Quint or Lavinia? You'll want to be Quint.'

The man dropped his cigarette, ground it into the sand. Slipped his cellphone into the pocket of his shorts. Bent to pick up the backpack. All this Titus kept in sharp focus, wondering, If you come to the beach to walk on the beach, why walk on the path?

Because the path didn't go to the beach. The path went parallel to the beach through the sand grass and salvias. Mostly only locals used the path.

Titus also wondering, Why not wear the backpack like you're supposed to?

'You check that man?' he said.

Luc squinted. 'I been looking.'

'Strange, hey? Walking along the path.'

Luc shrugged. 'Suppose.'

'Strange he doesn't put it on his back.'

The man not holding the backpack loosely at his side. Holding it in his left hand, his arm crooked. His right arm also slightly bent, his hand at his waist. Something tense about the man.

Titus said, still looking through the binoculars, 'You got a gun, Luccie? On you?'

'There's police inside the house.'

'Yes or no?'

'No, course not. Only in the safe.'

'Shit,' said Titus. Had the Kel-Tec at his ankle but wanted some weight.

He moved the binoculars away to the man at the car. No change there. Back to the man on the path. Big change. The man on the path walking faster now, not aimless like before.

The man with his right hand on the backpack, un-zipping it. The man's hand coming out with something black. Tugging where it snagged against the bag.

The man about two hundred metres off. Going into a jog, throwing the backpack aside. Clear that he was carrying the sort of submachine gun you didn't want aimed at you.

Titus screaming, 'Get down, Luc. Down.'

Like twice in two days. The snick pah, snick pah, snick pah of single shots. Then fast, snick, snick, snick, pah. The sliding door exploding behind them. So much for bulletproof glass. Inside a cop screaming.

Then the machine gun again. Plaster pocking about.

Titus said, 'Screw this.' Stood up, his little ankle gun in his hand. The man on the path putting the gun to his shoulder, a grin on his face. Had to be more than a hundred metres away.

Titus pulled off all eight, fuck that.

II

'Chief,' said the Voice to Mart Velaze, Mart Velaze in his car outside the Grace, 'Chief, there's things you should know.'

'Listening,' said Mart Velaze.

'You're sounding funny,' said the Voice. 'Pissed off.'

Mart Velaze wiped sweat from his face with the back of his hand. 'No. Everything's cool.'

'I hear it's hot there. High humidity.'

'Very.'

'Here, as well. I'm lucky we got budget for air-conditioning. A perk of the job. Wait.'

Mart Velaze with the phone to his ear listened to nothing, looked at the hulk of the fishing trawler across the basin, no one visible on it. Wondered who the Voice was talking to. How much else happened in her world? This woman sitting there getting the low-down from all over. What she didn't know, like she was a walking archive. What dirt she must have.

'Chief, here's something else from the Anders household: what precisely I can't tell, seems there's been another incident. One of them's dead far as I can gather. Crime-scene people seem to be there. That's what it sounds like. You might take a drive and have a look. Yes? Let me know.'

'Sure.'

'Other thing is that other one in the troika, Baasie Basson, him, he's been shot. Sounds like a hijacking. What do the cops call them, botched hijacking, one of those when the driver gets killed. Coincidence do you think? Coincidence I do not think.'

He heard her drinking something, the clink of crockery: a cup being replaced on a saucer.

'Then I've been told something's going on with the daughter, Lavinia. Corridor chatter only, you get my meaning, something up with the military unit. They may be involved in a situation with her. You know, the military agents, funny guys, those types, very secretive, very cloak and dagger, not integrated, not even thinking of integrating with the rest of us, still doing their own thing when we should be sharing.'

Like you share, flitted through Mart Velaze's mind. The Voice the original need-to-know tactician.

'They've got something going there, chief. What it is, who knows? Nothing I can ask about because ...'

The Voice leaving it unfinished. Mart Velaze finishing in his mind: because officially you have no authority. You're not officially part of the Agency. Meanwhile you're spying on the spies. Black black ops. Very funny.

'If I hear anything more, chief, I'll pass it on. Maybe you can be in touch with your escort gals, ask them what's up.'

Mart Velaze thinking, Well, the cheeky sista, Krista, not exactly playing open cards.

'Then let me know.'

'Will do,' said Mart Velaze.

'And chief?'

'Yes.'

'Chief, what's it you want to tell me? All this morning's activity, you must be hearing lots of cries and whispers. All those little mouths chirping to you. Mr Mart, do you know? Mr Mart, have you heard? Mr Mart, let me tell you. Street talk, chief. What's the buzz?'

'It's quiet,' said Mart Velaze.

'Ah, chief, no rumours, no excitement? Nothing?'

'Nothing.'

A laugh from the Voice. 'You're a one, chief. Silent and secret. But watch out for the mambas, my friend, they can get vicious when you kick them. Remember, surveillance only on this ticket. No funny stuff. Watch, listen, talk to me. Okay, chief, you understand the framework?'

Mart Velaze said he did.

'Then talk to me soon, when you've got lots to tell.

How about it? Don't leave me like a mushroom in the dark. So, chief, go with the ancestors.'

There's a thing, thought Mart Velaze, the Untouchables being touched. Not only touched. Wiped out. Just Rings there sitting pretty so far. Rings the politician.

An sms beep: Where are you?

From the gorgeous Krista. Cheeky chick.

III

At the hospital, the sister told Krista, 'Ag, my lovey, this's not going to do you any good waiting here.' The sister waving her arm towards the people gathered on the chairs and benches.

Krista looked around: numb faces, people could've been extras from a zombie movie.

'Even when she comes out of theatre she's going to be in recovery. We got to keep a watch on her.' The nurse with her hand on Krista's arm. Krista feeling the touch like it was heat. 'Rather wait at home where it's nicer. You can phone me in a couple of hours.'

The sister smiled at her. 'Is she your friend?'

Krista nodded. Unexpected, unlikely friend who'd opened up a whole new life. Business partner who'd helped her into a niche market. Also Tami brought a kind of stability she'd been seeking. Friend was one way of describing her.

'Okay, then. She'll be alright. These doctors're very good. So many bullet wounds come in here. All the time, especially weekends. Don't worry, okay?'

Krista said, 'Thanks. Thank you.' Bringing her focus back to the woman in the white uniform. 'I will. Yes. Alright, in a few hours.' Her cellphone ringing, going to voicemail.

'Have a cup of sweet tea,' said the sister. 'Lots of sugar, okay?' The sister patting her arm. 'You've had a shock. Sugar's good for a shock.'

Krista looked at her phone: Mart Velaze.

'Bye, my lovey. Go now,' said the sister. 'It's better.'

Krista's phone rang again. This time she answered.

Heard: 'It's a government car.' Her contact in the city vehicle-licensing department.

She closed her eyes. Thought, Oh shit.

The sister said, 'Are you alright, my lovey? You want to sit down?'

'I'm fine.' Krista giving the sister a quick smile, moving away.

'Have that sweet tea, okay. For the shock.'

Heard: 'Who's that?'

'No one. Someone I was talking to. So, what department?'

'I can't tell you anything more. It's got a code. Government garage. That's all I know.'

'There's got to be something more.'

'Look, that's it. Far as I go. Sorry.'

Krista thumbed off the call, found herself walking fast towards the Sharan, into the heat. Government?

Government was a bloody big place. Lots of thugs in government: muscle men, cops, spies, dodgy members of parliament. Thing was why would someone in there want a target like Lavinia?

In the car she phoned Titus, put it to him: 'Why would government want your daughter?'

'What're you talking about?'

'About Lavinia, Mr Anders. Why's the government got her?'

'Huh? Nonsense. Bullshit.'

'Why's the government kidnapped Lavinia?'

'They're gangsters have got her. Mongols that've got her.'

'They're government. Probably one man only took her I'd say.'

'Can't be.'

'In a Mercedes-Benz.'

'You know bugger all.'

'Who in government, Mr Anders?'

'Ag, girlie, leave it, alright? I thought you were a good idea. But you're also useless.'

'I know it wasn't Mongols. How'd they know where she was? Nobody knew where she was. Impossible.'

'Someone did. That's how they got her.'

'Nobody could've. Nobody could've known. I'm telling you, nobody.'

'You're still in crèche, meisie girl. This's what happens in the streets. Just thank the holy father you're not Lavinia.' Giving her a run of advice about her professionalism, about playing in the real world, then gone.

Krista stared at her phone: call disconnected. Forced a laugh. Well, up yours too, mister gumbah, hope you find your daughter. Nice enough person, but right now not my problem. Right now, Krista reckoned, her problem was the black dude with the black Benz. And Mart Velaze was a way to come at this one, Mart Velaze being government.

She was about to swing the engine, had the key in the ignition, when Tami filled her head. Tami's perfume. That faint sweet scent of her. Her seriousness: the frown lines, the purse to her gorgeous lips. Her quiet admonishments.

Tami always thinking twice.

The way she would touch: her hand briefly settling, squeezing. Tami's way of saying, You okay? Think again.

Tami on the gurney, covered up, lines into her arms, the paras holding up bags. Her voice weak, blood on her teeth.

Krista closed her eyes, rested her forehead on the steering wheel. Saw the red smear across the wooden floor, could smell it, metallic, rusty. 'You cannot die,' she whispered. 'Do not die.'

Wiped savagely at her face.

Jabbed a finger at the CD player, brought up her obsession with Sigur Rós: the tearing distant wind of the music. Sat there in the car park in the heat under Devil's Peak, filling the Sharan with the strange other-worldly voice calling out. The weird language, the low hum beneath the words until the clash, the sheer electronic fuck-you power took it rolling out. The voice above the avalanche.

Krista switched on the ignition. 'To hell with you, dude,' she said. 'Whoever you are, I'll find you.'

She felt the cool of the air-conditioner slide over her. SMSed Mart Velaze: Where are you?

Next, tried the babysitter's cellphone. Hallelujah, on comes a groggy voice.

'You okay?' Krista asked.

Was told bloody sort of. Massive bloody headache, bloody sore neck where the syringe went in. Bloody arsehole could've bloody killed her. Dropped her in a bloody κ-hole she was bloody lucky to climb out of.

'Bloody ketamine. Know it?'

Krista said she'd heard of it. Said, 'Why'd you let him in?'

Was told. 'Bloody didn't. Turned around from making coffee there he was at the bloody patio door. Huge mother. Shaven head. No jacket, black trousers. You know, like government muscle. Black dude. Cushy lips, bull nostrils. The usual features. Behind him bloody Lavinia's lying on the slabs. Whamo, bloody sticks me in the neck. Strike like a bloody mamba.'

'Huge as in tall?'

'Bloody right, darling. Over two. Well over.'

'Would you recognise him again?'

'Is the president a bigamist?'

Krista allowed herself a quick smile.

'What's happening, Krista? What've you and Tami got into?'

'Good question,' said Krista. Heard something about where's my bike? Replied, 'Speak later.' Ended the call.

The Chinese were waiting for her in the hotel lounge as if she was expected. Both men getting up simultaneously, smiling.

Mr Lijan, said, 'You have missed a most wonderful lunch meal, Ms Bishop. Most wonderful.'

'With the deputy minister of fisheries,' said Mr Yan. 'Very obliging person. A person with far sight.'

'She has only gone now.'

Mr Lijan indicated a chair. They sat. 'This afternoon we have a boat trip arranged, yes. We are invited at this place ...' He checked his phone. 'Miller's Point. At three p.m. You will come with us for the event? And your colleague?'

Krista ignored this last, said, 'This wasn't on your itinerary.'

'No, of course,' said Mr Lijan. 'An arrangement this morning by a very nice lady, Mrs Gool.'

'This morning?'

'Yes, at my meeting with her.'

'Your meeting? There was nothing scheduled with her.'

The Chinese men nodded. 'We must apologise,' said Mr Yan.

'In our business world,' said Mr Lijan, 'there are many things happen on the moment. We must take the opportunity.'

'When people hear we are in the city, they make contact.'

'This Mrs Gool, who's she?'

'Recommended by the trade mission. Very nice person, very knowledgeable on fishing.'

'And she's got a boat?'

'To give us a ride on the sea to Cape Point. This is very interesting to us.'

Krista looked from one man to the other. Strange men. There'd been nothing on their itinerary except a business meeting at eleven that she'd walked into on time to find an angry Titus Anders walking out. Meeting over. Nothing scheduled for a Mrs Gool, no lunch with a cabinet minister.

'Tourist sightseeing,' said Mr Yan. 'It is what we said we would do.' Giving her a smile that showed no teeth.

'I don't know this Mrs Gool. I don't know how safe this is. I should have had information about her earlier. For security purposes.'

'No, no, it is alright,' said Mr Yan. 'The minister says Mrs Gool is honourable.'

'Very nice person indeed. There is nothing to cause concern.'

Krista checked the time on her cellphone. Just after two. Driving to Miller's would take an hour. She needed to speak to Mart Velaze first. She'd seen his car on the hotel approach, seen him sitting in it.

'Ten minutes,' she said. 'Here in the foyer in ten minutes.'

The men beamed. 'Very good,' said Mr Lijan. 'We will be on this spot.'

The sms read: Downstairs in the parking garage.

Which is where Krista found Mart Velaze.

'Very spookish, the underground garage,' she said.

He looked around theatrically. 'Our territory. Also it's cool here.' He leant against a column. 'So where've you been?'

Krista told him most of it. Told him about the car reg, the government connection. Left out the afternoon's tourism. Watched closely for any sign that he knew. Nothing. Might have been talking to a plank the response she got from his face.

'Your friend Tami going to make it?'

'Maybe. Maybe not.'

Krista played the poker face too, gave nothing away. The two of them focused on one another.

'I need your help,' she said.

'That so?' Mart Velaze came away from the column, said, 'My help. Interesting. You want to know who the man is?'

Krista nodded.

'And then?'

'My business,' said Krista.

'The revenge thing, I know. For your friend Tami. No, no, no, my sista. He will kill you.'

'We'll see.'

'He's trained. Experienced. Bigger.'

'He's not expecting it.'

'Those guys expect anything at any time. They're paranoid. Killers.'

'So?'

'So let this go. Do not pursue it.' He stood before her, arms folded across his chest.

Krista didn't move, looked up at him: the hard face, the red veins in his eyes. 'You won't help me?' Thinking, You will, you bastard.

'You are asking me to contract your murder.'

'I am asking you for the name of the man who shot my partner.'

'Same thing.'

'Yes or no?'

Mart Velaze relaxed his arms, took a step back. 'It is not as simple as yes or no.' He walked off. 'There are other things to consider.'

'Like what?'

'Ah ha, that's the question.'

'I will find him. Even without your help.'

Mart Velaze waved a hand. 'Look after your Chinese, Ms Bishop. That is our agreement and your obligation to them.'

Krista watched him walk up the ramp out of the parking garage. A slim, athletic figure that did not look back.

She closed her eyes, frustration pounding at her temples. Saw Tami being wheeled from their home. Heard her, 'Careful. Please go careful …' Her voice fading, not finishing the word.

IV

'Psit, psit, psit, psit. Eight times I can hear it. Where do they go? All those little bullets? You don't even hear them singing.' The Russian drew a line in the air with his hand, dipping downwards. 'They don't reach me. A small stupid gun to shoot with.'

'You didn't hit them, Smirnoff.'

'You cannot say that.'

'I was watching.'

'From so far, what can you see?'

'I got binoculars.'

'No, poepiehead, you are in the car shitting little poepies in your panties. You can see nothing. I see blood. No person can be saved at that closeness.' He held up the kurz. 'The gun is perfect.'

'We'll see, Smirnoff. We'll hear when it's on the news.'

Black Aron and the Russian changed cars in the Paarden Island warehouse, left in the BM with new plates.

'Now you can put me at the Cuban bar,' said the Russian, relaxed, turning up the air-con.

'You don't want to get rid of the gun? Give it back to your Jewish friend? Save yourself some interest?'

'No, I keep it for a few days. The interest is nothing. I talk about the interest with the Jewboy. There are other ways he will understand.' He shrugged. 'Maybe there is extra work I need it for.' He grinned at Black Aron. 'Maybe I need it for you, if you do not pay me.'

'You will get your money.'

'When, my friend? When is that?'

'I told you last time. When it is certain.'

'It is certain by now.'

'Maybe.'

'Ha, maybe. What is this always maybe, maybe, maybe? You have seen it with your eyes. It is, what you say, spot on.'

'Okay,' said Black Aron, 'then later you will be a rich man.'

The Russian laughed. 'Not from this work. You pay mingy, mingy. In Russia it is much better pay.'

'So go back.'

'One day, my friend, but now it is too soon.'

Black Aron dropped the Russian, headed off to his mother for another batch of samoosas. Wished he could chill for the afternoon. Sit in the cool of the Labia, take in a movie. That one: *Drive*. About some guy in the same line of business. But no luck. Tamora was on his case.

'Miller's Point,' she said. 'Three o'clock. We're taking the Chinese for a flip in the rubber ducky.'

Black Aron groaned. 'Ah no.'

'Ah yes. You'll want to be there, afterwards.' A certain seduction in her tone.

Brought up images in Black Aron's mind of screwing Tamora in the rubber ducky. The smell of diesel. Salt on the skin. He licked his lips.

'Spot on,' said Tamora, gave her laugh that made

Black Aron think of red thongs. 'Pick me up. Bird's Nest, St George's Mall.'

V

Transcript from the case file of Hardlife MacDonald:

We call it the Wimbledon. I can tell you me myself I did not do it to her. I can tell you this for the truth. It was the others that did it, the captain 'n Stones. The captain told Stones to. Ja, first we had some vodka, Russian Bear, and some pipes, then the captain said we must show her. Three of us: the captain, Stones 'n me. The captain said this is what we had to do to show that the Mongols were the tops. We taking over now. Everything: tik, pearlies, cars, guns. We give protection. You run a club, you come to us for the guarding service. We gotta send this message that Mongols rule. She going to be the message. We write the message on her body. Hand-delivery. I can tell you I had to do it to her, the hitting. Ja, I hit. I was there. She's mos a brave woman, I can say that. She screamed. Everybody screams when they use the sock. What's in the sock is sand. Then you soak it in a bucket of water. First you got to cut the ties so the person can walk. Afterwards you hit them. Like in tennis. Ja, you understand that's the name of the game. Stones and me on one side, the captain other side then we hit the woman between us. Fifteen love. Fifteen all. Federer to serve. Captain and Stones, they hit everywhere. Head. Titties. Stomach. Shoulders. Everywhere. Just takes twenty minutes, not long. Game. Set. Match. We call it the Wimbledon.

11

I

'Sorry, man,' said Rings Saturen. 'Sorry for your loss.'

Titus nodded. Felt the heat of the hand Rings placed on his shoulder. Said, 'No. No. There is no time for sorry.'

'It hurts in your heart,' said Rings Saturen. 'I know. You are paining. Both of us, you and me. I know.'

'I cannot feel it.' Titus stepped away from Rings, glanced up at the mountain above the university, the back of Devil's Peak hard-lined against the sky.

'I think so. I think you are in pain.'

Titus beep-locked the Jeep. 'Before, in those other years, I didn't feel it. When we were lighties, I didn't feel it. Same now. Now I do not feel it.'

'We cry here.' Rings poked a finger at his own chest. 'By ourselves where no one can see.'

Titus shook his head. 'This time is not for crying.'

'Maybe, maybe not,' said Rings. 'I don't know. This is bad.'

'You got to watch out.'

'I know.' He patted his hip, the pistol holstered there hidden under his shirt.

'We must sort this. One way. Over and done.'

'Sure, sure. Just tell me how, my friend, how?'

Titus put two fingers against Rings's head. 'The only way.'

'You know who's doing this?'

'Of course. This morning again the man tried to shoot me and Luc. I saw his driver, my brother. I saw him: Black Aron.'

'You sure?'

Titus laughed. 'No, man. I'm not only sure, I'm certain positive. One hundred per cent.'

'Let's walk,' said Rings.

They crossed Milner Road, walking onto the spiky grass of the common. Walked towards the trees, stopped when they were still a distance off. Two men, easy targets.

'This thing,' said Rings, 'this thing against us is politics. We cannot fight it. The black people have the power. They are government.'

'They killed Baasie? You're saying they killed Baasie?'

'Maybe.'

'My Quint? My Boetie?'

'It could be.'

'It's my government shooting at me, my family?'

'I cannot say. Maybe, perhaps.'

'Why?'

'It's what I hear, Titus. What people tell me. People with long years being political.'

'No, man, Rings. This is bullshit. No, no. Those blacks in government aren't going to tell us what's what. They're darkies. Just out of the trees. All they want is money. You see them, what they've done? The arms deal? Tenders? They're filling their own pockets. Put all their families in government. Aunties with doeks on their heads; nephews with pointy shoes. Sisters, brothers, it's what you call it, nepo-tis-m?' Titus breaking the sound into three syllables. 'Giving jobs—'

'I know it,' said Rings.

Titus glanced at him. The two men wearing sunglasses, standing in full sun: Titus's shiny bald head, Rings with a floppy golf hat. Sweat prickling over Titus's scalp, soggy in his armpits. Rings's face glistening.

Titus had called the meeting place. 'Where no one can listen to us. In the open. Under the skies.' Rondebosch Common. Only people there'd be mad dogwalkers and joggers. In this heat, a woman with her Jack Russell way off near the trees, a jogger moving along Park Road. The men alone on the tawny expanse.

'Okay. That's what I'm saying,' said Titus. 'This's how we're pushed out. Now the Chinese come along and the blacks give them money, cigars, whisky, nice cars, saying, ah, yes, please, ah, we must all help with developing. What is good for China is good for Africa. And the darkies say yes, please, more money. We have iron, we have mines, we have abalone. Please come here, open your shops, no problem you can have visas, chop-chop. No, man, Rings, this is wrong. I told you, they tell me they going to cut us out. We can do the diving, but the value adding, no, they'll manage that. No, man, no. We can't allow it. They like new settlers.'

'Titus,' said Rings, 'Titus, forget that. We can talk to them.'

'No, Rings, we can't. That's what I tried. That's the problem, we can't talk to them and so they've won then. Then the blacks have won. This's our city. The only place we got. Your people, my people came here in boats. Chained up. Slaves. Not darkie migrant workers going home for Christmas in Eastern Cape. Our people were victims. Here for good and life. Sentenced to life, Rings, in this place. It was human trafficking, hey, human trafficking, against human rights. Now this city's all we got. This's our city because of slave trading in the olden times. We built this city, your people and my people. With our blood, skin and bones. Now the darkies want to take it away. Bring in the Chinese settlers. No. No, man, it's not right. We can't give it up.'

'Baasie's dead,' said Rings. 'Quint's dead. Your young boy Boetie's dead.'

Titus took off his sunglasses, wiped his face with his hand, repositioned the shades. 'They got Lavinia.'

'Hey?'

'They got Lavinia.' He pushed the sunglasses back up his nose.

'What?'

'This morning.'

'Lavinia?'

'Yes, man, Lavinia. My baby girl. They took her.'

'My fiancée.'

The two men stared at one another.

Rings said, 'Only now you tell me this. You stand here and tell me they took her. You standing here telling me all this other stuff. I thought you promised she was safe with the security lesbos. Safe, in a safehouse with the ladies looking after her. Some place nobody knew about. Not even me, her fiancé.'

'They found her.'

'They found her, how's that?'

'I don't know, Rings, I dunno. They found her and they took her.'

'They? They? Come'n man, Titus. Who's they?'

'Government? You say the government's shooting me, maybe it's them. Or Tamora.'

'Tamora?' Rings laughed. 'Nay, no way. What's your problem? Tamora? We been through this.'

'You laugh. It's her. Behind some of this, Rings. Tamora, Black Aron with some whitey doing her orders. Chinese orders, I don't know. Maybe she's with the Chinese. Tamora Gool. The cherrie I thought was okay. She's doing the work.'

Rings turned away. Titus watched him walk off a few paces, come back.

'If they hurt her, Lavinia ...' Wagging a finger at Titus.

Titus reached out to catch Rings by the hand. Grasped him, tightened his grip. 'Help me. I ask you to help me.'

They stood there, each reflected in the other's sunglasses, hand-locked, until Rings broke it. Pulled back. 'Jesus, Titus. What's it you want? What help?'

'Information. Government information.'

'I'm not government.'

'You're in there. Talking with them. You got the contacts. You can find out. You right inside.'

'Find out what?'

'About the Chinese. About what the government wants with the Chinamen. Get me a name. Who's doing this business, who wants to kill me? Kill my family? What government person wants this? Fisheries? Security? Who?' Titus watched Rings, watched his face. 'The rest I can sort. Black Aron, Tamora, the Mongols attacking the Pretty Boyz. I can sort these people.' Saw Rings bring out salve to moisten his lips. Zam-Buk like the blacks used. 'We can't let Baasie go. And Quint and Boetie. We owe them.'

Rings dabbed his finger in the ointment, smoothed it over his lips. 'Nobody said to let them go.'

'We didn't start it, Rings. All of us're the victims here. The innocent. Businessmen doing our own business. Simple as that. Now I got sons dead. My girl taken, kidnapped. A whitey shooting at me. And you tell me government wants to squash me like a blue tick. Uh uh. Time to stop. To stand against them. You going to be next, Rings. Any time.'

He watched Rings replace the lid on the tin, pocket it. 'Maybe. I hear what you say, my friend. Maybe I am on the list.' Rings looking across the common then looking back at him, nodding. 'I hear what you say.'

'We got to tell them enough, stop now.' Titus glanced at his watch. 'I must meet Luc.' He and Rings started back to their cars. 'We didn't want this but now we got it, they can't finish with us. Never, Rings, it's wrong. There's still our names. We still got names.'

Titus sat in his car. Watched Rings drive off in his black Fortuner, turn into Park Road, disappear in the traffic. Something Rings wasn't telling him. Something else Rings was doing.

The problem with Rings, he played the ends. Didn't like dirty hands.

There'd been that time when they were young bloods, when they'd hanged the dog. Their initiation into the Pretty Boyz, to show the captains they had strong bones.

Early evening he and Rings in Newlands Forest. On the paths, joggers, walkers, larneys home from work taking Fluffy walkies.

The scene is: they select a poodle-type, hairy yapper. They come running at man and dog, woman and dog, doesn't matter: in the event man and dog. Man in shirt-sleeves, suit pants, neat combed-back hair like a moffie, shiny brogues.

Rings jumps the whitey, knocks him down; Titus grabs the dog.

The whitey shouting, 'Hey, hey, what the heck! Come back. My dog.' Then he's on his feet, after them. A moffie with balls.

They're running higher into the forest, ducking

branches. The whitey's not far behind, yelling. The dog snapping at Titus's hands, gives him a nip that draws blood.

Back off the paths they've set up a noose in a gum tree. Slip it over the fluffy's head, get the bastard hoisted into the branches. Whitey stumbles up, freaked out. All he can do is scream. Try climbing the tree to save his dog, hanging there, jerking about.

He can't do the climbing, comes then at Titus and Rings, tears in his eyes, lashing with his fists. Titus knifes the man's arm, says, 'Fok, whitey, stay calm.' He and Rings backing off. They turn, split at a run. The whitey still chasing them, but way back, howling.

The plan is: get down to the railway station, make their separate ways back to Mitchells Plain. Which is what Titus does. Later finds out Rings had a car waiting, a brother behind the wheel for a quick getaway.

Typical Rings. In the years ahead always providing other arrangements for himself.

But Titus makes allowances; Rings can pull good deals.

Only thing he wondered now: Does Rings have another deal going?

He phoned Luc. 'You got anything?'

'I know where's Tamora,' said Luc. 'Her and Black Aron.'

'Good. That's good.'

'You wanna know where?'

'Come on, Luc, just tell me.'

'Miller's. Doing some diving for the Chinese.'

'Honest?'

'True.'

'You sure?'

'That's what I heard.'

'From who?'

'I heard, okay. I heard.'

'Alright,' said Titus. 'Alright …' Titus scheming, take the ski-boat out of Simon's Town, catch them somewhere off the Point. Wasn't much in False Bay could outgun two Yamaha 250s. 'Alright,' he said, 'listen, Luccie, get the AKs.'

'For real?'

'Of course, man. For real.' Titus started the Jeep. Drove into the suburb: quiet place, neat houses, neat gardens, no one around, went down Balfour into Arundel along to the stop sign, took a right into Park, eased up at the traffic lights. Telling Luc through the hands-free to bring two clips each. No, make that three. Probably going to need every single bullet.

Luc said, 'Yussis, Daddy.'

Titus turned left at the robots, headed down the peninsula. 'Ja, Luccie,' he said. 'Just like in the olden times.'

He disconnected. Was about to flip the phone onto the passenger seat when it beeped a slew of messages. Titus opened the first multimedia: a video clip.

II

There was Tamora sitting at a café on St George's Mall talking with a black guy. Very relaxed under the trees: cool dudes in the sweltering city drinking white wine. The black guy with his suit jacket over the back of the chair like pickpockets weren't a consideration. A big fella. A fella who pumped iron. His short-sleeved shirt open at the collar, stretched tight across his shoulders. Tamora laughing with him, leaning towards him, almost reaching out to touch him.

Man could be any sort of shaven-head black: politician, BEE arrivista, or muscle. Black Aron favoured muscle. Thing was you couldn't be sure these days, they all had the image. You look at some Armani slicker, he's not a bouncer, he's a Lamborghini millionaire eats sushi off naked women. You had to be careful.

The way they were sitting, the brother had his back to Black Aron, Tamora had him in her line of sight.

Black Aron pulled over against the bollards, raised a hand in greeting, checked his watch. Almost two o'clock. Knew she had seen him, had caught the flick of her eyes away from the man's face. But she wasn't hurrying. Dabbed a serviette at her lips, touched a hand to her hair. Playing with the dude.

Perhaps he should jump out, rush over, say, 'Your car is waiting, ma'am.' She'd love that. Her own driver, her personal chauffeur. Next she'd want him wearing white gloves.

He could see that. Tamora on the kitchen table, dress hiked up, those long milky thighs splayed, saying, 'Fetch the white gloves.'

Like he wanted to feel her up wearing white gloves? Maybe.

Black Aron pictured it: he's coming at her oiled with a full-on hard-on, his hands in white gloves, a bloody coon carnival, Hey mammy, here comes the Alabama. Tamora would go wild. Range of possibilities there.

Spot on.

Black Aron kept the engine running, the air-con turned high, noticed a cop saunter towards him. Large lady moving slowly through the heat. Sort of a waddle, reminded him of a rhino, the bulk. The cop waved him on.

Black Aron buzzed down the window. 'I'm just waiting,' he said, pointed at Tamora.

The cop said, 'You must move.'

'Please,' said Black Aron, 'two minutes.'

'Drive round. Maybe she's finished then.'

The cop had her hands on her hips, her right hand close to her gun.

'Ah, come on,' said Black Aron. 'Please, sisi, two minutes.'

The cop shook her head.

Black Aron looked from the implacable face of the policewoman to Tamora full of laughter. Like she was having a good time with the buti, also especially enjoying the stand-off between him and the lady cop. He gestured at her to hurry up. Tamora not so much as giving him a nod. Ignoring him.

The cop said, 'You must move.'

'Okay, okay,' said Black Aron. 'Give me a break.' Eased the car into the street to cross the brick paving of the mall, had to wait for a group of tourists holding up their hands to tell him stop, their right of way.

He made the circuit, took him five minutes, all the robots against him. When he got back the cop was still there, resting her bum against a bollard. She waved him on. Black Aron pointed at himself, at Tamora, standing now, shaking hands with the suave guy. Gazing up at the tall man. Really big boy with his jacket hooked over his right shoulder. What looked like a bandage under his left sleeve.

The cop tapped on the car window, waved him on with a flick of her hand.

Right then Tamora came up saying something to the cop that made her smile. Black Aron released the door lock, saw the muscleman disappearing towards the cathedral.

Tamora got into the car, breathed wine fumes at him.

Black Aron grimaced, said, 'It's an hour to Miller's. At least. We'll be late.' A pissed-off tone to his voice. Aron taking a liberty because he was pissed off with the cop.

Tamora glanced at him. 'You got a problem there? I hear you taking an attitude.' She straightened herself in the seat, fastened the belt. 'Let's go. Drive. What're you waiting for?' Tamora gesturing with her hand up the street.

Black Aron squirmed. Saw the policewoman smiling at them like this was a real gas, the woman giving her driver lip.

Tamora saying, 'You wearing your costume, Aron? You all ready for this?' Slipped her hand beneath his tee, rubbed his stomach. Slid her fingers under the waist of his shorts into his curlies.

The policewoman had her hand over her mouth, her eyes wide: Yoh, yoh, yoh. Black Aron could hear her glee. He released the clutch, almost stalled, almost crushed tourists.

'Don't overreact,' said Tamora, pulled out her hand. 'Sometimes you men get all worked up.'

Black Aron was worked up, flushed, breaking a sweat, air-con or no air-con. Said, 'Who's he?'

Tamora reached down, took off her shoes. Sighed with relief. 'That's better.' Looked at him. 'Aron, I like you, okay. But you got a job you do for me.'

'I drive you.'

'That's right, exactly. You got privileges too but that's another thing. Alright?'

Black Aron keeping his eyes on the traffic. 'Alright.' Knowing Tamora was playing with him, which got his goat. Raised his body temp even higher.

'The man's name is Mkhulu.'

Black Aron glanced sideways: she was smiling at him, that glint in her eyes like they were diamonds.

'Mkhulu Gumede. That make you feel better? Now

you want to know who this man is?' Tamora's distracted now, playing with her Samsung. 'I'll tell you. He's a contact.'

Short and sweet, got up Black Aron's nose worse than a line cut with rat poison.

'That's all you need to know. A contact.' Tamora looking at him over her sunglasses. 'I'm working this one, Mr Chetty. Now it's my turn to be the boss. You come with me, Ronnie, you got nothing to worry about. You and me, we're riding on the Blue Train. Five-star luxury lifestyle, even for a driver.' Tamora laughing at that snick of sarcasm. Repeating it: 'Even for a driver.'

Black Aron let it go while he took the right into Buitengracht. At the first red light, chanced his luck, said, 'Is Mkhulu government or private sector? A lawyer?'

Tamora held up a hand. 'What'd I say? He's a contact.'

Silence. Black Aron jaw set, eyes unwavering all the way down Buitengracht to the elevated freeway. Aware of Tamora checking her phone, keying off SMSes.

When she'd finished said, 'So your Ruskie boy screwed up. Again. Shit, Aron. Twice he tries, twice he can't get it right. Other people, it's no problem. They do the job, it gets done: Boetie, Quint, Lavinia, poof. Sorted. But your Ruskie waves a big gun around, afterwards everybody's still standing.'

'He told me he shot them,' said Black Aron. 'He said it was a positive.'

'Ah, Ron, I know what goes on. I know what happened. I'm connected, you know that. My people are everywhere. In the cops, government, business, gangs, all over. That's how a girl does it. My people see stuff, they message me.'

Black Aron said, 'I told him, that Smirnoff. I told him. But no, he says, they're dead.'

'They're not, Ron. Believe me. Titus and Luc still walk the earth. But not for long.'

'What d'you mean?'

'They know where we'll be, they'll want to be there too. This's the chance they've been waiting for. Kill me, kill you. The Chinese even.'

'Me?'

'They know you drove the Ruskie.'

'They couldn't.'

'They do. They saw you.'

Black Aron groaned. Shifted in his seat, felt a damp anxiety between his legs.

'It'll be alright, Ron. All over and done with this afternoon.'

'On the sea?'

'Of course.'

'How d'they know?'

Tamora dropped her cellphone into her lap. 'Again the how question. What'd I tell you?'

'You got a message to Anders?'

'Of course. Not that difficult, is it? Luc wanted to know where I was. I helped him find out.'

Black Aron exhaled a long whooo. 'Why?'

'I've told you: so we can finish it, Ron. Wake up.'

'In a shoot-out? With foreign Chinese in our boat?'

Tamora laughed. 'Titus won't have a problem shooting the Chinese.'

'You've got a plan?' Black Aron thinking, Sometimes, most times, you couldn't tell what happened in Tamora's head. She got an idea, most times the idea went off the charts. Went wilder than a tik-cooked crazy. This sounded like one of them.

'It's simple,' she said. 'They chase us. We take them right to where the Borderline Control cops are waiting. The cops shoot them. Problem solved.'

'That's mad.' Black Aron seeing all kinds of room here for problems: top priority, Titus wipes them all one time; second, outruns them; third, the Borderline arseholes aren't where they should be. Then he clicked: Mkhulu Gumede.

Said, 'Mkhulu Gumede.'

'That's so smart,' said Tamora. 'You keep on being smart, Ron, you'll be number one in the new syndicate.'

'Fuck,' said Black Aron. The role Mkhulu Gumede was playing suddenly clear and present.

'You see now.'

'It was him. Both Quint and Lavinia. It was him that did it.'

'They employ good people at the Agency. Keep us all safe and sound.' Tamora held up her phone. 'Check this video.'

Black Aron took the phone, glanced at it. There was

a woman, looked like she was dead, bloodied, something like a scarf or a bra round her neck, naked otherwise. Not much of a bush. Shaved closer than Tamora. Bruises all over her: across her boobs, stomach, thighs. Blood smears, some small cuts. Her face swollen. Her nose broken. Blood leaking from it into the gag in her mouth. The camera moving in to show the woman's eyes swollen closed.

'Shit,' said Black Aron, holding the phone with one hand, toggled between watching the road, watching the video.

'Lavinia,' said Tamora. 'Payback for my boy. About now Titus'll see it as well. Think of that. Going to push his blood pressure to Mars. What a shame. Then no doubts he'll be on the water. So much fun we're all going to have out there. Beautiful time for a little cruise on the sparkling False Bay, show the Chinese tourists the Cape of Good Hope from a different angle.' Tamora giving her laugh that normally tweaked Black Aron's guppie.

Guppie.

Tamora's description of his cock. During foreplay favoured giving it a squeeze to make the mouth gape like a guppie in a fish tank. Very funny. Black Aron'd snigger, going along with it, why not, whatever juices you, baby.

Her laugh not working the magic this time. No ways. Sometimes Black Aron reckoned Tamora should be in Valkenberg with the loonies, then again reckoned without her what'd life be? A dead end. Small-time corner-dealing. Taking kak from kids. With Tamora you got the single-malt lifestyle. Spot on.

He gave her back the phone. 'Gumede didn't do that.'

'You're sharp, Ron. No, that was Mongols.'

She was stoking this war to the max. Mongols against Pretty Boyz. The family of Titus Anders going down. The Untouchables getting it. Tamora making the scene so wild Black Aron couldn't see the end.

He drove up Edinburgh Drive, over Wynberg Hill, down the Blue Route highway. At the mountains took Ou Kaapse Weg, every kilometre the name of Mkhulu Gumede in his mind. They came down the Black Hill Expressway he said, 'You really trust this guy?'

Tamora stretched. Yawned. 'You woke me.'

The blue of False Bay before them, glassy water, not even a lace of foam around the Roman Rock lighthouse.

'What?' she said.

'Gumede. You trust him? He's a spy.'

'That's my problem, Ron. You don't worry about things like that. You drive, Ron, that's your job. You drive. Mkhulu's my man.'

Which kept Black Aron thinking black thoughts through Simon's Town, Seaforth, Froggy Pond to Miller's. They got the Zodiac in the water, changed into wetsuits. Tamora wearing hers to her waist, catching her boobs in a red bikini top. Delicious. Black Aron's thoughts getting lighter looking at her.

Tamora checked her cellphone, said, 'Now where're these people?'

III

Mart Velaze did not drive out to Sunset Beach. Did not check on the whispers the Voice had picked up about the Anders. Instead phoned a cop contact, was told, 'One of the sons got stabbed this morning. Latest thing there's been a shooting. A techie took a bullet.'

Heard the full story: one of the Anders boykies, Quint, was asleep in the lounge, sliding doors open to the world, someone walked in, slammed a screwdriver into his heart, walked out. That was early in the morning, breakfast time.

'What sort of screwdriver?' Mart Velaze wanted to know.

'Ah, shit, man, Mart, what sort of question's that? What's the difference?'

'Detail,' the contact was told. 'What's it the clevers say, devil's always in the detail.'

The cop contact told him he'd get back to him.

'Before that, what about this other thing?' asked Mart Velaze.

'No devils, no details. All I got was there's been a shooting.'

Contact phoned Mart Velaze back a few minutes later with this: 'Still nothing on the shooting except father and son didn't get hurt. That other thing you wanted, the type of screwdriver?'

'Just a joke,' said Mart Velaze.

'Anyhow,' said the contact, 'it was a Phillips, you

know, the star shape, about a hundred mils long with a yellow handle. Everybody's got one.'

'Just not all of us take it to heart.'

He heard his contact gag. Splutter, 'Could say he was star-struck.'

Mart Velaze was about to go with Phillips for heart-burn but didn't.

Instead sat in his car considering the notion of death by screwdriver. On those refresher training camps the instructor always coming at you with a Phillips. The argument being good grip to the handle, strong bit of steel. After you've put it in, didn't need to twist and pull. Could slide it out easily. Assuming you wanted to. Also you could pick up screwdrivers cheap at any Saturday market. Cheaper than knives. Also a fa-voured tool of the gangsters. Which was why the Ops newbies chose it. Queered the pitch, as the Voice would say, that ironic tone to her words. Produced an anonym-ous sort of death. Also Mart Velaze reckoned better to be attacked by a man with a knife than a man with a screwdriver. Getting out of a knife fight way easier. Too many times on those training camps he'd had the instructor put a Phillips in his ear.

The instructor's panted triumph. 'I push this in a little bit further, pellie, you're screwed.'

Always the jokers.

Next Mart Velaze considered the notion of desk time. Major attraction: cooler inside than running around in the fiery afternoon. His line of thinking not so much about obliging Krista but of finding out which of the Hawks in the Aviary were off the perch. The Hawks a cop branch muscling in on Agency work. Mart Velaze could see advantages to knowing who'd kidnapped the daughter of Titus Anders and wounded Krista's partner. Especially if it was an in-house job. The secrets of secret agents. Something to store away.

He went back to the office entered the Merc's reg into the system. Pop: there it was. Simple as that. Government garage special pool. Times out, times in. Drivers' names. Mart Velaze shook his head, incredulous, couldn't believe it. You go out to pull some bad shit, you don't leave a paper trail. You remember the old cliché, cover your tracks, the way they teach you on the training camps. But no, not the newbies. Thing about the newbies, they were arrogant. Cocksure. Believed they were invincible. Untouchables. Invincibles. Brothers full of shit and attitude.

Mart Velaze took a stroll to personnel, pulled rank, got a quick peek at the staff files. Date of birth: 1986. Meant he was eight years old come the great election, no baggage from the old country. Parents deceased. Raised by a granny. Had to be a story in there how he got a private-school education at a larney school in Joburg. A haven for spies, old-boy networks, corporate thugs. Degree in business management, psychology. Recruited at university by National Intelligence. Nothing unusual. Languages: Xhosa, Zulu, English, Afrikaans, Portuguese, French. Quite the post-colonialist. Training: 2006, advanced weaponry, anti-terrorism, personal combat, parachuting, survival, tracking, urban combatives. Interests: iron-man triathlon. Quite the machine. But then also under interests: choral singing, member of the Quarrymen Male Voice Choir. WTF! Postings: short three-month stints: Brazil, Angola, Mozambique, France, Congo. Five months' president's guard 2009. Two-year contract with a Cape Town financial company. Had to be a surveillance job. Some citations for good work. Last page was a mugshot.

Mart Velaze downloaded to a stick, clicked the file closed. On the way out, told the assistant she had lovely hands, delicate fingers. Held her hands lightly in his, stroked the career line in her palm, told her fate was on her side. The young woman blushed, went coy. Mart Velaze thought, Who said blacks don't blush?

Kissed the tips of the woman's fingers, said, 'Thank you, my sisi.'

Went through to the Aviary – a long room, open plan – everyone at their workstations, Mart Velaze found his target: big brother down the far end, jacket hooked over his shoulder, heading for the door. Mart followed. Carefully.

The dude was good. Might stuff up with the internal paperwork but on the street he was something else. Kept his eyes open, knew what was going on. Mart Velaze smiled. Was a change having to be cautious. Most wankers you could walk two paces behind them, they hadn't a clue. Even bump into them, they'd be the ones apologised.

He followed him to a café in the mall, almost laughed out loud when he saw there was Rings's cherrie, Miss

Tamora Gool, waiting at a table with a white wine, lipstick stain on the rim. Watched Tamora guide the chorister in by cellphone. Useful homing device. The two of them shaking hands, disconnecting their call simultaneously. All smiles. Ordered another glass of wine.

Mart Velaze took a table inside Doppio Zero, with a clear view of the mall. The waitress came up said, 'Tata, what can I get you?'

He looked up at the woman. Young, pretty, early twenties, smiling at him.

Tata!

Said, 'I look like an old man? Like your father?'

The waitress put her pen to her lips. 'What father?'

Mart Velaze rolled his eyes. 'Iced coffee.'

'Something to eat, tata?' The waitress with a spark in her eye. The name on the lapel clip: Sibongile. 'Salad with parmesan shavings, perhaps?' The waitress playing with him, grinning.

Mart Velaze felt a heat in his cheeks. This young thing raising a flush? 'Sibongile,' he said, 'just the iced coffee, okay.'

More smile, glistening teeth. 'Alright, tata.' Sibongile the waitress swirled off, gave him a shot of her bum and legs. Pert, round bum, a model's legs.

Mart Velaze sighed. Tata! Baba. What was with this generation?

He took out his cellphone, snapped off a few frames of the patrons under the trees. Not camera quality but good enough.

The couple at the outside table looked relaxed. Clinked glasses when the wine arrived. Tamora doing most of the talking. Maybe Tamora sang in a choir, maybe they were both singing from the same hymn sheet. Mart Velaze grimaced.

'Here you are, tata,' said the waitress, put the long iced coffee on his table. 'You want a straw?' That smile. Not the sort of smile to let go.

'I'll manage,' said Mart Velaze. Asked her in Xhosa where she came from.

'What?' she said, bending slightly, giving him cleavage. 'What're you saying, tata? What language is that?'

'You're cheeky, sisi,' said Mart Velaze.

The young woman laughed. 'That's what they say.' Paused: 'Tata.' Left him to his iced coffee without a straw.

Mart Velaze took a sip, the crushed ice giving him sinus pain. He rubbed at his temples, noticed the BMW stopped at the bollard with the cop gesturing. A wide cop. Could fit a Sibongile into each of her trouser legs.

Saw the driver point at Tamora, the cop taking none of his pleading, waving him on. Five minutes later the BM was back. Now Tamora and the chorister parting. Mart Velaze noted down the car reg, called over the waitress.

'You leaving already, tata?' she said. 'No salad?'

Mart Velaze gave her a fifty, told her to keep the change. 'Pocket money from your tata,' he said, watching over her shoulder Tamora Gool get into the car, imperious, flicking her fingers to order her driver to move on. Very condescending. Wondered how much Rings was involved in the secret life of Tamora Gool.

Mart Velaze headed back to his office, thinking that to keep tabs on all the players was getting to be a really big ask. Wondering if he should petition the Voice for back-up.

So Mart Velaze was distracted. The Indian guy in the Beemer, the sexy Tamora Gool, his own colleague were all clamouring in his mind. So many connections, so many possibilities. So many unknowns. The biggest one being who was Tamora Gool anyhow? Looked a bit tarty. Street prettified. Cute face but a hardness in it like she got her own way. The kind of hardarsed woman appealed to Mart Velaze. All that aggro you needed to lash down. She'd have a mouth: dirty and savage. You put your tongue in, you didn't know if she'd bite it off.

He shook his head to shuck the fantasy. Got back to the real stuff: what was her thing with Rings Saturen? And now the agent? Questions and questions. Diverting him.

Mart Velaze joined the bustle crossing Adderley Street. Figuring to cut down the side of the Slave Lodge, grab a sandwich from the Spin Street café, head out to see how Rings was spending his afternoon mourning.

All this absorbing him which was why he didn't notice the chorister until the man said, 'Haaita, comrade.'

Mart Velaze kept it together, not giving anything away, not showing surprise. Said, 'Yo, my brother.'

The big man nodded, didn't smile, looked down

with that gaze Mart Velaze recognised. The threat: don't fuck with me.

The big man with his jacket slung over his shoulder, the bandage high up his arm, just riding below the sleeve, like some sort of taunt.

He stepped off the pavement ahead of Mart Velaze, Mart Velaze letting him go ahead, watching the broad back, the tight shirt, the shaven head dark as mahogany. The man didn't look back.

Mart Velaze wondering, Where'd he been waiting? When'd the big guy twigged him? Spooky. Very spooky.

Two things occurred to Mart Velaze as he walked down the lane beside the Slave Lodge: even in the shade it was hot, and perhaps there were realities Titus Anders should know.

Only surveillance, the Voice had said. Don't interfere. At all.

Some actions Mart Velaze couldn't resist. Bringing the innocent up to speed being one of them. Especially when the innocent would go ballistic. Especially when others were playing games with him. Whatever the big brother's game was. Whoever was jerking the big brother's strings.

Mart Velaze bought a sandwich, munched it on the hoof back to his office. Resolved a plan of action.

From a stolen phone he kept for such necessities, first sent Titus Anders a photograph of Tamora leaving the cute Pinelands cottage that belonged to Rings Saturen in the deep dark night. Then a picture of the merry threesome shaking hands at the Waterfront café: Tamora, Rings and Mr Lijan. Also a back view of the loving couple walking hand in hand. Very sweet.

From his own phone sent off a multimedia to Krista Bishop: below the photograph the name she wanted: Mkhulu Gumede.

IV

Mkhulu Gumede.

Above the name a head-and-shoulders of a good-looking guy, shaven head, small ears. Even the mugshot couldn't dull the glint in his eyes. Sharp eyes, piercing. No smile on the lips. No creases in his cheeks. Not a man who smiled often. A composed face. A small scar at his temple that could've been from anything: a childhood fall, a stick fight, a pistol-whipping.

Probably not a face Tami even saw in the blur of the moment, Krista reckoned. Would've been just shadows. Shapes. Shooting by instinct.

But she'd see it, that face. She'd get right up in that face. Big time. Watch it change from living to dead.

Forwarded the image to the babysitter. A reply pinged right back: That's him. That's the bloody mother. Bloody hell, who is he?

Krista didn't respond, had the phone in her right hand, balanced against the steering wheel. On the road out of Simon's Town to Miller's Point no traffic ahead or behind her. The views opening up: the mountain rising beside them, False Bay a dazzling blue clear to the open seas.

On the Sharan's middle seat the clients sat paying attention all the drive down the peninsula. Oohing and aahing at the sights.

Asking, 'Where are we now? These are big houses.' Bishopscourt as it happened when that question arose. Krista telling them all the rich people lived there.

'This is very pretty view.'

Down the Blue Route with the mountains at the end. Krista pointing out the shape of an elephant's head on the ridge line as they came off the highway. Telling them it was called the Elephant's Eye.

'Can we stop now, please?' At the shark-spotter's lookout on Boyes Drive. Krista telling them about surfing at Muizenberg, great whites that cruised the backline.

Krista beginning to think she could qualify as a tourist guide.

On the dips through Froggy Pond, Krista took another look at Mkhulu Gumede: wondered how she'd find him. Probably not too difficult. That Gumede was a field agent, she had no doubt. So a couple of hours outside Velaze's office one late afternoon, the game would be on. All she had to do was be careful.

She keyed off the image. Quietly thanked Mart Velaze. But also wondered why he'd done it. She couldn't see Mart Velaze doing anything for no good reason. A reason that wouldn't benefit Mart Velaze. Really, though, not her concern.

Her concern was Tami.

Tami lying in ICU.

'She's critical,' the nurse had said.

Krista on the phone driving down Hospital Bend knowing Tami was inside those buildings. Trying not to imagine her: the wires, the tubes, the bandages.

Had said, 'What d'you mean critical?' Speaking softly, not wanting the Chinese to overhear her. 'Is she ...? Will she ...?'

'She's bad,' the nurse had said.

Which almost made Krista change her mind about the Miller's Point sightseeing. The place she should be was with Tami. To hell with the Chinese.

'There's nothing you can do,' the nurse had said. 'She's out of the op. We're watching her, promise. We're doing everything we can.' There'd been a pause there: Krista fighting the pain in her heart. Indecisive. The nurse had said, 'Look, phone me any time you want. I'll phone you if ...' The nurse hadn't finished the sentence.

Krista disconnected, had to clear her eyes with the back of her hand.

The hell with this life. The shit it caused.

She took deep breaths, got herself settled, caught their eyes in the rear-view mirror.

'You will like it with our associate this afternoon,' said Mr Lijan. 'She a very good person. Pretty like you.' The two men beaming at her. Pleased to be sightseeing.

'That's where we're going,' she said pointing to a spit of land and boulders that spilled into the sea.

'Very nice,' said Mr Yan.

Krista drove into the car park, walked the two men over to the slipway. There was a Zodiac inflatable, a biggie, the size the cops' water wing used, a man and a woman in wetsuits sitting in it. The woman with her wetsuit peeled down, showing off a red bikini top.

The woman waved, got out of the boat to welcome them.

'It'll be bouncy on this,' said Krista. 'Wet.'

'There're life jackets,' said Tamora. 'Oilskins, if they want them.'

Neither of the Chinese men did.

'It is alright to get a little bit wet on this beautiful day,' said Mr Lijan. He sat down to take off his shoes and socks, rolled his trouser legs. Mr Yan joining him.

Krista thought, Great, all I need is wet clothes. 'You got another wetsuit?'

Tamora shook her head. The man introduced as Aron said, 'Only oilskins.' Handed her a khaki-coloured pair, smelt of fish. A life jacket that smelt no better.

Krista stripped out of her jeans, put on the skins.

The man Aron and the woman Tamora watched her, both grinning. He whistled. 'Nice legs.' Didn't stop Krista taking off her top, putting on the life jacket over her bra. Got more appreciation from the man Aron.

The Chinese clients kept their eyes averted, waded to the boat. Tamora said to the man Aron, 'Just start the engines, if you can take your eyes off her for a moment.'

Krista folded her clothes, put them into a plastic bag Tamora gave her. The two women making long eye contact. Heard the woman say, 'You ready now?' Krista ignored her, lifted herself into the inflatable.

They went out slowly along the reef, Tamora telling the two men about endemic sevengill cow sharks in the kelp beds. Right underneath them.

What was it? Krista wondered. You get a couple of Chinese, everyone turns into a tour guide.

'They have nice fins?' said Mr Yan. 'The one on the back?'

'Very small,' said Tamora. 'Not like your white. Your white's got this big fin.'

'No good for eating, if that's what you mean,' said the man Aron, powering the engines as they left the reef, swinging the nose towards Cape Point.

'That is a pity,' said Mr Lijan.

The sea was flat but even calm water has a bounce. The ducky bounced thwack, thwack, thwack, as the man Aron put more juice into the outboards.

Krista sat in the stern behind the man Aron standing at the wheel. Tamora opposite her, the two Chinese up near the bow. No point in talking over the sea thump and engine noise. Krista clutching her cellphone in the pocket of the oilskins.

One of the swims she'd never done was to cross False Bay. Never likely to do either. Few had. Thirty-five kilometres of cold water, white sharks, a swim that would take nine, ten hours on a good day. You needed huge back-up, you had to be mad. Something to think about though. Only one woman had done it. Maybe she needed to convince her father. Get Mace back to give the rah rah. It'd be worthwhile to be far out in these waters between the headlands. Away from all the shit.

Tami.

Tami with tubes, monitors. Tami in a coma.

Tami who could've been full of life if only …

Guilt coursing through Krista like a rip tide.

She shook her head, caught Tamora's eyes. Tamora sizing her up, about to say something but didn't.

What was this joyride for?

Sweetening up the Chinese, special request of the deputy minister? Probably, Krista decided. Fisheries showing the investors the wonders of the Cape of Good Hope.

She looked at the peninsula's mountain spine, the steep slopes that slid into the sea, ending at the arthritic finger of Cape Point. Yeah, like paradise. All the places along this southern reach: Partridge Point, Smits, Venus Pools, Black Rocks. The sea's blue thinning translucent against the sandy shores, could fool you into thinking this place was subtropical.

Yeah, the Fairest Cape.

The guy Aron swung away from the land, gunned towards the open ocean, something like three kays out brought the boat round to face the Point, killed the engine. The sudden quiet, just water lap under the ducky.

'How's this, my friends? Nice on the sea.'

'Ron the poet,' said Tamora, scanning back into the bay with her binoculars.

'You see any ships?' said Aron. 'Any boats?'

An anxiety in his voice, Krista thought.

Tamora ignoring him.

The Chinese had produced small cameras, were clicking at the distant Point, at passing seagulls, at the dazzle of the sea.

They gave their cameras to the man Aron to snap them beaming in the blue expanse.

'Unique,' said Aron. 'Tourists don't come out here.'

'For our families to see,' said Mr Lijan.

'The place of the abalone,' said Mr Yan.

'It's too deep here,' said Aron. 'Closer to the shore, that's where you get the abalone.'

Krista listening but not listening to the run of their burble. Her thoughts on Mkhulu Gumede. She'd get him. Some place he felt safe. Some place he didn't expect to be at risk. Like his home. Invade his home. Whack him without explanation. What use telling him why anyhow? The dead knew no remorse. Thing she could never understand was why you'd need to explain first. As if that would make the guy feel bad for eternity. What eternity? Was only here or not here. No. Put one straight in his chest. Explode his heart. The least she could do for Tami.

She checked her phone, the signal down to one bar.

'You expecting a call?' said Tamora. She'd raised the binoculars again.

'Wanted to know the time.' Krista noticed the smudge

of white that Tamora was watching. 'We can't hang about.'

'You need to get them back so soon?'

'They have a schedule.'

'Okay,' said Tamora. 'That's what you want.' To the man Aron said, 'Let's go.'

Aron mock-saluted, got the engines rumbling. He pointed at the spume of the distant boat. 'Fishermen?'

'Of one sort or another,' said Tamora.

The man Aron headed the Zodiac straight towards them. Opened the power, sending spray cascading.

Krista heard exclamations from her clients, saw them clutching tightly to the running ropes along the sides. In the pocket of the skins, felt her phone vibrate. She took it out: an unknown number. She answered, couldn't hear the caller for the noise, the line breaking up.

'What?' she shouted. 'Come again.'

She caught the word hospital, before the call dropped.

V

Transcript from the case file of Hardlife MacDonald:

I seen the Wimbledon take only ten minutes. Depends what you want. Me, I can tell what we did with her was woes. You know, wild. Quick-quick she was falling like she's drunk. You want to know everything? Okay, we started with the tennis match. Like I told you, me, the captain 'n Stones. Then we cut her clothes off with a knife. Not me. Stones likes doing that. Sometimes he cuts too hard into her skin. That's when she screams again but she's still got all the cloth in her mouth. It's just a numpff sound. When the clothes are off you can see she is a pretty chick. Even after what we done to her. Lots of money gone into her body. I can say I don't think I seen tits like that before, even with the bruises. You just want to stroke them. You just want to feel the nipple. The captain said, ja, it's okay we can do that. He says okay we can feel her poes. The girls I been to got hair over their poes. Thick hair. I like it. This one she's clean. Just a little bit of hair. The captain says it's what they call a landing strip. Like at the airport. You can see there her slit. I tell you in all my years I never seen a slit. You look at it, you want to touch it. She got us standing there ready to go. We stroke her tits, we look at her slit. The captain says to Stones, he can do it first. The captain 'n me watch. Ja, lucky Stones. When he and the captain did Pollsmoor he was the captain's wifey. You know what I'm saying, the captain looks after Stones even now. Stones was quick with the business. He do it from behind, the way you see dogs inna street. After the captain went quick-quick. Me also. I can say on the Lord's name I never done it. Like them I was from the back cos you don wanna look at her eyes. No man. That's kak. So I did it like Stones 'n the captain. Except I got a feel of her poes with my hand, very prickly. Very thin that poes hair. She need a better shave. I rub myself in her bum, that's all

I do. Strues. No judge can say that classed as rape. No ways. So ja, then, we tied her so she's standing up. How we did that is we put a rope over a rafter, then tie her hands over her head. We pull her up like a sack so she stretched. Stones put the ties back round her ankles. The captain fetches a box from the car. A little black box. Inside's a knife like doctors use. Very sharp. All the time she's standing there on her toes, her eyes watching us. The captain says to take the rag outta her mouth. I do that. She screams. But out there at that place no one can hear screams. No one. The captain says to hold her tight. Me 'n Stones do that. Stones got her by the tits. I got her legs. It was the captain did it with that doctor's knife.

12

I

The Aviary was quiet, a few somnolent souls at their workstations, peering at screens. Most with buds in their ears. Probably not listening in to private conversations. Probably listening to Lady Gaga, Kelly Clarkson, Adele, Rihanna.

Better sitting here in the air-conditioning on a hot day than doing real work. Waiting for knock-off time before they hit the beach, the gym, a jog along Sea Point promenade. Like agents operated to a union schedule, like you'd ever have found agents at their desks in the old days, the glorious 1990s. Everyone out there drinking, screwing, doing the real stuff.

Mart Velaze looked round the room, no one there more than twenty-five. Babes in the trenches. Not a clue about the sort of war being fought behind closed doors. The bosses of the old agencies fighting for the top perch.

He sighed. As if doing the job wasn't intrigue enough. To have feathers flying back in the office, that was crap. But maybe not for Mkhulu Gumede, maybe the big brother was deep in it.

No sign of him now though, the guy out and about doing the real stuff. Whatever the real stuff was in Mkhulu Gumede's life.

'You know where Gumede is?' Mart Velaze asked some kid at a computer near Gumede's desk.

The kid took an earphone from his ear, said, 'Sorry, sir, he hasn't been back from lunch.'

Sir? Nice one.

Not far removed from the protocol that got people to their feet when a cabinet minister walked in. Like everyone was still at school, must show respect to arse-holes in suits. Aikona, never, bugger that.

Mart Velaze glanced at his watch. Gone three thirty.

'Shall I tell him to see you, sir?' said the youngster. 'When he comes in.'

If. If he comes in, thought Mart Velaze. Not when.

'No,' he said. 'It's fine.' Headed out of the Aviary, out of the building, out of the city to Sunset Beach. Time to watch over Titus Anders, see what he was making of the photographs. See what he thought of the lovely Tamora and the untouchable Rings.

Mart Velaze first took a walk along the beach, the house closed up. Ambled through the suburb to the street entrance: some crime-scene tape still tied to the gate, but the cops were gone, no cars in the drive. Mart Velaze rang the bell. Had this story he was an estate agent scouting for new properties. No one answered. He hadn't thought anyone would.

Mart Velaze drove to a corner some streets back that Titus Anders would have to pass on his way home. No trees to park under. No shelter from the sun. Just bright blaze on the hot car roof. Have to sit in the tin, sweat soaking his shirt.

Half an hour, he got a call: the Voice.

'Where're you, chief?'

No hullo, howzit, molo, how're you doing. No. Where're you, chief?

Mart Velaze told her.

'Nobody's home,' she said. 'I've listened.'

'I know.'

'Of course you do. You're a good man, chief.'

'A hot, sweaty man.'

'Fieldwork, chief. Perk of the job for you, no paper shuffling, nè?'

'No air-conditioning either.' Mart Velaze wiped sweat from stinging his eyes.

'Tsh, tsh, tsh. You want my job, chief, you can have it. The assegais are flashing.' The Voice sighed. 'Now listen, chief, I've been hearing things ...'

Silence.

Mart Velaze looked at his phone, thumbed it to loudspeaker. He uncapped a bottle of water, took a long pull. If there was a bad time for surveillance it was in the heat. In the cold too, actually. Face it, buti, he thought, his eyes in the rear-view mirror, watching a car approach, there's no good time. A mom's taxi passed with kids in the back staring at him. He stared back. Kids could make you feel out of place.

'Chief,' said the Voice, 'listen …'

Mart Velaze picked up the phone, took it off loud-speaker.

'Listen, I've heard things, okay, I just need your take. What I've heard is mining got hold of fisheries, told them to make things easy for the Chinese. You know, over the abalone, perlemoen, whatever you call it down there. Told them to cut the price, let the Chinese handle more of the process, shucking it, storing it, transporting it, that sort of thing. That's what they like doing, getting jobs for their millions of people. So, chief, that's what I'm hearing. The mining people doing a big raw-material deal with the Chinese, tons and tons, sweetening it with cheap abalone and jobs. As if we have to.'

Mart Velaze thought, Yeah, so far, so likely. Said, 'What'd the cops say? About the abalone poaching?'

'They're cool. Part of the deal's they still get a couple of abalone busts every whenever to fill their budgets. Makes all stakeholders happy. This is what I hear, chief. This's what I'm hearing all over, no matter who I talk to, I hear the same thing. As if … as if they agreed a story for me. So you got to tell me, chief, who's lying to me?'

'There's gang stuff happening here,' said Mart Velaze. 'As a result.'

'I know, chief, I know. Collateral. Everything shifting and sliding. I read the stories about all these gang shootings. Kids too, taking bullets. What's with the coloureds, hey? Completely berserk in Mitchells Plain.

That's the trouble with Cape Town, chief, too much rain, too much crossfire.'

Mart Velaze heard the brisk tapping of computer keys.

'It's not raining now,' he said. 'It's hot. You can't breathe.'

'You know what I mean … in winter. Now listen, chief, I want to know, alright, who's pulling the strings here? Which one of our guys is making this happen? Because there's going to be blood on the floor, you with me? Bodies. One day you wake up, you're buried with the corpses. That's not going to happen. Also I don't like stepping in the blood either, chief, it spoils my shoes. So just find out who and what. No interference. Just find out.'

'Alright,' said Mart Velaze. Considered dropping the name Mkhulu Gumede into the Voice's ear, decided no, everything in its time. Wouldn't do to get the Voice all excited too soon. Bad for her heart. Went with goodbye but realised he was talking to dead air. She hadn't even said go with the ancestors. Matters had to be worrying the Voice. Shame, hey. He tossed the phone onto the passenger seat, said, 'Come on, Titus Anders, time you came home.'

Mart Velaze finished the bottle of water, uncapped another. Wanted desperately an ice-cold beer, golden in the bottle, the bottle icy with condensation. Imagined tilting it to his lips, the strong taste of the beer soothing his throat.

He watched cars come, cars go. More coming than

going. People home early, fleeing the hot city. Wanting the beaches, the cold, cold sea. A cold beer.

A car pulled up behind him. White Chev. Mkhulu Gumede at the wheel.

II

In the car park at the yacht basin, Titus Anders showed his son the photographs on his phone.

'What you going to do, Daddy?'

Luc leant on the bonnet of the Terios, shading the cellphone with his hand, scrolling through the pictures. Squinted at them one-eyed in the hard light.

What you going to do, Daddy?

Titus looked at his son. Looked away, up at the mountain, hazed by the salt heat. Didn't have words for how sick he felt. For the ache in his chest. The hurt of his sons' murders, Lavinia's abduction, rape, shame, everything going wrong. Now Rings betraying him. Betraying his family. Making them fools in the people's eyes. Everybody seeing Titus Anders was a moegoe, a stupid, a foolish old-man moegoe.

Rings working him like a puppet master with a hand stuck up his arse.

Rings supposed to be his partner. Engaged to his daughter. What a lie. Rings, his street brother for all these years. Sneaking behind his back. Let him talk to one Chinese so that he, Mr Rings Saturen, could make plans with the other one. Rings and Tamora scheming. Rings and Tamora screwing. Didn't take the little whore much to get a grip on the balls of the cunning Mr Rings Saturen.

Then all that talk on the Common. Rings spouting bullshit, telling him it was government doings, the killings. Saying, 'If they hurt Lavinia, my bru …'

What was that? Acting. Rings the actor. Rings always the actor. Rings playing to the audience. Rings lying.

'I don't know,' said Titus. 'I don't know, Luccie. We got no options anymore.'

Luc left the photograph of Rings and Tamora holding hands open. 'This's being disrespected, Daddy,' he said. 'You, me, and Lavinia. Rings shouldn't of done this. Rings is like family. Like we used to call him Uncle Rings.' He tapped the image with his finger, the nail clicking against the screen. 'He's brought us shame. Who sent these, Daddy?'

Titus shrugged. 'Private number. No call back.'

'We can still trace it. I got my friend.'

'What for? You going to get nowhere,' said Titus. 'Somebody sends pictures like that, they use a stolen phone, a throwaway. Nobody'll send pictures like that otherwise.'

'We can try.'

'Ja, okay, try then.' He beep-locked his car, started for the boatyard.

Luc hurrying to catch up with him. 'Somebody's helping us, Daddy. Somebody's taking those pictures for a reason. Nobody waits around taking those pictures without a reason. Somebody like a private investigator. Or maybe the Hawks. Maybe even the secret service.'

'No, man.' Titus stopped at their boat, ran his hand over the hull, gritty, salty. The boat up on a trailer, ready for action.

'Really, man, Daddy. Rings is in politics. In politics you gotta watch your back. What Rings is doing with Tamora, somebody's against him. Someone thinks we should know.'

'You think I didn't think of this?'

'So here's a chance. We can sort out Rings. Sort out the chinkies. We got friends in high places.' He gave the phone back to his father.

'You think anything else, Luc?'

'Like what?'

'That maybe someone's pushing us.'

'Pushing us where?'

'To do this. So we're still the stupids doing what someone wants. Someone we don't even know. Someone laughing at us.'

'More like someone giving us a chance, Daddy.'

Titus flipped the Jeep keys at him, said, 'You bring the guns?'

'Of course.'

Titus nodded. 'Alright, get the Jeep here so we can launch.'

He stood in the shadow cast by the boat, watching Luc walk away. The boy all he had left. Not even Lavinia. Beautiful Lavinia. Lavinia was going to come back dead, no question. The hurt in his chest made him groan.

Luc reversed the Jeep up to the trailer, got out leaving the engine running to help his father with the ball hitch.

They got it fastened, Titus said, 'You think this's a good plan?'

'Of course,' said Luc. 'Why not? It's a start, we sort out that dog, Tamora.'

Titus's cellphone beeped an SMS: Luc's finger for Lavinia. The one with one knuckle. He read it again, gripping the phone to stop his hand shaking. Luc's finger for Lavinia. The old code. Blood in, blood out. You give me, I give you. Now Tamora was playing with him again. Shaming him. Disrespecting him. Cutting off his balls. Disrespecting his son.

'No. No, no, no.' Titus groaned, turned away from his son, staggered off a few paces. 'She can't do this. No. I will not ...'

'What?' Luc starting after his father. 'What, Daddy?' He caught his father's sleeve. 'What is the message?'

Titus held up the screen for Luc to read it. Saw the fear in his son's face. Luc clenching his fists, protecting his fingers.

Luc's fear brought Titus back. This was an option. A way to go. Save Lavinia. Bring back his daughter. He looked over his son's head at the sea. Such a calm sea. The everyday sea, the everyday boatyard. He nodded to himself. Ja, he had a chance, he could save Lavinia.

'They can have my finger,' said Titus.

'No ways.' Luc frowning at him. 'They can't have anything.'

Titus clasped his son's shoulder, squeezed. 'This's how it's done, Luc. The old code. We do this, we get Lavinia back. This is how we trade.'

Get Lavinia back. All that mattered to him now. Get her back, then plan revenge. How he would kill them.

'They want my finger,' said Luc.

'They will get mine,' said Titus.

'It's okay, Daddy.' Luc spread his fingers, showing the stump on his right hand.

Titus sighed. 'You're a good son, Luc. A good brother.'

The phone beeped again: Put it at the Smuts statue by the Slave Lodge. Seven o'clock. No finger, no Lavinia. A smiley at the end.

Titus keyed the number, pressed call. Nothing. A dead number. As he'd expected. But worth the try.

'No one.' Titus disconnected.

'What we going to do?' said Luc.

The old code. Would they keep the old code? Would Tamora keep the old code? Titus didn't know, except what other option? Tamora herself was the other option. 'We got other business, Luccie. First we got business with Tamora. Then we'll see.'

III

They powered straight towards the ski boat, Tamora standing beside Black Aron. Krista Bishop behind them. The Chinese up front, enjoying the wind and spray.

Krista shouted, 'What're you doing? We need to get back.'

Tamora half-turned, grinned at her. 'Just people we know. Won't take long.'

They watched the ski boat slow, stop, when they were still a kilometre off.

'And now?' said Black Aron.

'Keep it like this,' Tamora shouted back at him. Tamora bringing up her binoculars, braced against the wheel housing.

Black Aron worried about how this would play out. Tamora's idea on the edge of craziness. He looked round. An empty ocean. It'd be a long run into the arms of the Borderline heroes.

'Is it them?' he said.

'Can't tell with the bouncing.' Tamora lowering her arms. 'Keep it like this, okay?'

He saw Krista tap Tamora's shoulder, Tamora shrug her off. Heard Krista shouting, 'We need to get back.'

Shouted in turn, 'Relax. We're doing that.'

They passed the ski boat close enough to see three fishermen in the stern, baiting up hooks. Black Aron brought the engines down to a throaty idle, felt relief tingling in his legs. He relaxed his grip on the wheel. Saw Tamora had up the binoculars.

The Chinese men waved, the fishermen waved back.

'It's not them,' said Black Aron. 'Even without those things you can tell.'

Tamora didn't respond, kept looking at the fishermen.

'Who'd you think it was going to be?' said Krista.

'Friends.' Tamora put away the binoculars, glanced at Krista. 'Friends. Out here we're all friendly. You got a problem with that?'

Black Aron grinned at her checking out the fem, the aggro in her stance, the tilt of her head. She had her head at an angle like that, Tamora was a ball hair from letting rip.

The woman saying, 'Can we get back now? I've got an emergency.'

Tamora leaning forward. 'We're doing this for the Chinese gentlemen. A special favour for our minister.' Black Aron watching to see what the fem would do now. Tamora up close and dangerous.

The fem not giving up. 'They have to get back to keep their schedule.' Black Aron waiting for the response.

'You're their secretary?'

'Good enough.'

The two women locked in the eyeball challenge, unsmiling. This was nice, he thought. Flashed an image of them wrestling, oiled. Heard Tamora call out to the men. 'Your secretary says we must go back.'

'That is fine,' said Mr Lijan. Mr Yan waved.

'Seems your bosses don't mind, Ms Bishop.' That tone in her voice that Aron feared. Tamora got into that tone, you were boiled. You saw red rage. You could act crazy. Exactly what she wanted. Exactly that moment she took you down.

Only thing, the fem was cool. The fem right up there on Tamora's wavelength. Not rising to her.

Black Aron gave juice, headed for Miller's.

An hour later they were alone in the rubber ducky, drifting near Pyramid Rock where the cow sharks swam. Black Aron uneasy at Tamora's mood. Tamora saying goodbye to the Chinese like she was sorry they hadn't had more time, total insincerity. Tamora not even giving the fem an up-yours which'd made Black Aron snigger. Total sincerity. Fem deserved a snotklap slap in the face. Bit of education would give her a better attitude.

Only when they were gone, Tamora coming over dark. Telling him keep his hands to himself. Saying she wanted to sit on the sea, she needed to think.

'You mean ... out there?'

'Yes, Ron, I mean out there.' That tone to her voice: Don't play games.

Tamora in this mood you kept a distance, like you would from a puff adder. He'd shrugged it off, helped her back into the Zodiac, taken them out along the reef to Pyramid.

Near the rock she'd told him cut the engine. No

ways he wasn't going to obey. They floated there in the quiet. Only sound the slap of the sea against the rock, the suck and pop of seaweed rising with the gentle swells.

Tamora sat up in the bows. Black Aron stood at the wheel housing. Both still in their wetsuits. Tamora now with a T-shirt over her red bikini; Black Aron advertising his pecs and biceps. Ready to rock 'n roll a quickie on the bottom of the Zodiac, if Tamora showed any inclination. Not that she did. Tamora lost in her thoughts.

He sat, watched her. Bloody pretty woman. Body you couldn't get enough of. Only problem, with Tamora in a mood like this, you stayed away. You didn't get your hands anywhere near her. You waited.

'Someone must've warned him,' she said. Black Aron seeing her turn her head to face him. Not a clue what she was on about. 'Warned Anders. Told him we'd arranged a set-up.'

Black Aron went with it. 'It's possible.'

'Someone must've.'

'Probably.'

'Of course. Someone must've. It was all set. Everything. We could've been ...'

Black Aron waited.

'... the Untouchables.'

Even with her sour turn he had to mention Rings Saturen. Remind her. 'There's still Rings.'

Those eyes flashing at him. 'Rings needs me.' Something livid in those eyes.

Black Aron hearing Tamora say, 'You'll have to get the Russian back on it.'

'Ag, no.' He stood up, toyed with the steering wheel.

'Ag, yes. This time he better do it.'

'Smirnoff's useless.'

'So it's up to you.' Tamora glaring at him. Challenging. Defiant.

'Me?' Black Aron let the word out high-pitched.

'You.'

'I'm the driver.'

'So drive him close up, like to the front door. He gets out, knocks. You hoot. When they open, you drive away. Simple, Aron. You drive away, let the Ruskie do his business.'

'You mean leave him there?' Black Aron confused. This woman giving him grief, now sprawled there in the bows with her legs apart.

'Yes.'

'They'll kill him.'

'Depends who gets in first. Should be him but you can't ever tell really.' Tamora stretching, leaning back her head, her neck exposed. Black Aron had to close his eyes.

'Only thing, not tomorrow. On the funeral day. Yes, wait for the funeral day. Spare Titus all that grief of the funeral.' She laughed. 'Come, come, Aron.' Clapped her hands, sat upright. 'Time to go. Got to see what's what.'

Black Aron thought about cow sharks. The cow sharks of Pyramid Rock. Thought you could call them tamoras.

IV

'Her heart stopped.'

That was what the nurse had said, the nurse Krista'd seen earlier. 'But we got her back, my lovey.'

No doctors anywhere to find out anything more. Like was Tami going to make it? How long would she be out? Could she be moved to a private hospital?

Only the ward sister's offhand, 'She's critical. That's why she's here in ICU.'

Krista had wanted to hit her. Lash out an open-hander, across the woman's fat face.

Critical? What's critical mean? That she's going to die?

But she'd kept it together. The nurse reaching out to hold her hand, the one Krista would've used on the ward sister.

After the sister had waddled off, the nurse stood with Krista looking down at Tami wired to monitors, multiple drips feeding gunk into her arms. Tami out of it, in a coma. 'The doctors they do it, induce the coma,' the nurse'd said. 'To help her.' Had also not bullshitted Krista. Had said, 'Say prayers for her, sisi. It's better.'

In the twilight, Krista drove away from the hospital, dreaded the emptiness of home. Put Sigur Rós into the CD player to stop her thoughts. Playing 'Batter' over and over all the way back. Didn't stop her mind working overtime. Bringing up her moments with the dying sergeant among the oil drums.

How at a crouch she'd dragged the sergeant across open ground. Found what cover there was. The children shooting wildly, without pause from clip to clip. Luck, or some design of fate, she'd not taken a hit, she'd thought afterwards. Not wanting to think too deeply about why she'd come through.

Lying there behind the drums with the sergeant, tearing open her gear to staunch the blood. Two chest wounds, the sergeant's right breast shredded. Another puncture low down on her hip. Krista realising no ways the woman was going to live. But telling her, 'Stay with me. Keep looking at me.'

The sergeant one of the few NCOs she had time for. Shared a beer with her sometimes. Had swapped stories of home life. Knew the woman was a single mother. Didn't want to see her die.

The sergeant gripped her hand, squeezed, said something about children.

'What? Don't talk, keep breathing.' Krista bending towards her.

'Shoot,' the sergeant said. 'Shoot them.'

Her last order. Krista had never forgotten that. Been impressed by the sergeant's dying rage.

Anger sometimes all there was against the way of the world.

She parked in the garage beside the Spider, watched in the rear-view the street gate slide closed, the garage door come down. Sat there in the gloom not moving, her head on the steering wheel. Eventually sighed, went in through the unlocked door to the house, paused, listened, as if Tami might be in the kitchen boiling pasta. As if there'd be music, Tami's obsession with Adele floating through the house.

Nothing. She closed the door. Noticed on the tiles the dusty footprints of the cops, the techies, the paramedics.

The house was hot. Airless. Stank still of cordite, blood, antiseptic. She opened windows, the sliding doors to the patio. Took a long look at the pool, thought about swimming, to get the clamminess off her skin. Instead, stripped to her underwear, again winding up Sigur Rós on the sound system. Cleaned off the blood stains. Vacuumed the entrance, the living room, the kitchen. Went downstairs, made Lavinia's bed, bagged sheets and towels for washing. Lavinia. Didn't want to think about Lavinia. Lavinia's life was a sad story. She did think about phoning Titus Anders. Even dialled his number, went through to voicemail. She left a message: 'Let me know about Lavinia.'

Then she swam length after length, her way to get out of the world into a zone without hurt or feelings. Just her body moving through the water. The thrust of her arms, the motion of her legs. The slide of bubbles over her shoulder when she exhaled.

Swim, her father had said. Always Mace's answer to a time of trouble. Swim. You don't think, you don't feel.

Afterwards, wrapped in a kikoi, she brought out a glass of wine, sat on the patio above the city. As she'd done with Tami one evening back, two evenings back, actually done throughout the summer. Looked at the lights. Once, as a child, she'd sat here with her mother and father. Then her mother was killed. Her father went away. Now Tami on life support.

Krista wondering, Shit, had there ever been a time her life was okay? Maybe it was never okay. Maybe it was always about loss. About losing things. How much she'd lost. Her childhood, her maman, then Mace going away. Like she couldn't keep anyone close.

Remembering how she'd been kidnapped by mad Muslims when she was what, eight, nine years old? The fear that'd come. The nightmares, the terror that the time in the dark room had brought with it. Never again feeling safe.

Remembering the attack in the farmhouse: her father shot, bleeding. The dead farmer and his wife. The wife who'd been kind to her. Shown her how to collect eggs in the hen run. Given her home-made toffee. Taken her through the house telling her stories about every room. Till the man came in, shot them all except her. Said he wasn't going to shoot a child. Left her sitting alone in the farmhouse with the dead people, her papa coughing a red splutter. But she hadn't cried, she'd been a brave girl. That's what the cops had called her when they got there. A brave girl. A brave girl who'd lost her childhood.

Remembering her mother's death. The image still stark in her mind: her mother cut, slashed, sliced, bleeding. Lying on the floor, the knife in her back. Mace bent over her, trying to keep her maman from going away. But he couldn't. 'Maman's gone, Christa,' he'd said to her. Both of them weeping.

She took a long swallow of wine, felt the fuzz dull her mind. Didn't stop the pain. Did bring a wry thought, worth toasting: Be a brave girl, Krista. She raised her glass.

Tomorrow the Chinese would be gone, she could start on Mkhulu Gumede. Could start being a player. Could stop being the useless debris in the tideline, washed up by a storm. Her analogy. Time to get with the action. What you got to realise with guarding is you're only ever reacting. Mace's summation. That's hard. Makes you feel like a spare prick. Mace's analogy. So no more hanging about.

She'd downed most of the bottle when her street gate buzzed. Krista went inside, pressed the intercom.

Said, 'Who's it?' as the image came on the screen.

Got a moan. Saw Lavinia on the screen, her face blood-streaked, filthy, bruised, her mouth gaping.

Brought her inside. Lavinia shaking, trembling, whimpering. A wild fear in her eyes. Wouldn't let Krista touch her, sat rocking on a chair, wrapped in a blanket.

Krista phoned Titus. This time the call went through. He didn't let her talk, said, 'I do not know what has happened to Lavinia, okay. Probably she is dead. Do not phone me again.'

'She's here,' said Krista.

A pause. 'Don't play games, my sister.'

'I'm telling you she's here. She needs a doctor.'

'Don't play games, meisie. Just don't play games. Let me talk to her.'

'She needs a doctor. I can take her.'

'Let me talk to her.'

Krista looked at Lavinia.

'You can't. They cut out her tongue.'

V

Transcript from the case file of Hardlife MacDonald:

Stones's got this car, modified Opel with low-profile tyres, a aerofoil on the boot. I can tell you that's a very nice car. We's in it cruising up Adderley Street, eating KFC chicken wings from a big tub, Beyoncé singing to us. Stones's head's dancing to the music even while he's driving. We stop at the robot there at the Slave Lodge, some traffic coming out of Spin going up Wale Street. There's maybe four or five people walking into the Gardens. Everything going slow in the heat.

'Supposed to be there at seven,' Stones says to me. 'You see anything on the statue?' You know the statue of what's name? The guy from the old days. Smuts. Ja, Smuts. I can't see anything on the statue. 'Maybe in a plastic bag,' says Stones.

When the robot changes, Stones drives next to the statue, puts two wheels on the pavement. There's a few people looking at us: bergies 'n tourists. Stones gives the engine some juice to make it growl. The tourists go off, the bergies grin at us.

I say to Stones, 'You sure we supposed to find it here?'

'Ja, man,' he tunes me. 'Go have a look.'

I take a chicken wing from the box before I take a look. Cos I know when I get back Stones's gonna have scoffed too many. So I go all round the statue. 'Fok all.' This bergie says to me can he have the chicken wing when I's finished. So okay, I give it to him.

Stones shouts at me, look on the statue's knee.

Strues. There it is. Blerry lucky a seagull didn't take it. They's stuck it down with Prestik. I gotta climb onto Smuts to get it. A funny finger. Only one knuckle, no nail.

I can tell you I pick up worms, prawns, slugs even. Crickets, too, in the summertime. But no ways I gonna touch a chopped finger. Lucky for me there's rubbish there, plastic bags people have left. I can put it in one of those. You know how you see white people pick up dog shit on the beach with a plastic. They put their hand inside the bag, pick up the shit, turn the bag inside out then yous can hold the bag with the kak down the bottom. Clever Trevor. Like that I did it.

When I show it to Stones he says, 'Only supposed to have one knuckle.'

With some crumbs could be a KFC wing.

Stones drives back slowly up Wale Street. Me, I put the plastic bag with the finger on the floor. Keep it fastened there under my foot. I can tell you that wasn't a nice job.

Part 4: Cape of Good Hope

13

I

In the next days the heat broke. The city woke to a breeze at the windows, the smell of sea and fish.

Black Aron looked at the mountain, at the small streak of cloud against the face, thought, Oh shit, there will be wind. Black Aron hated the wind, the constant thrum of it through the city. The flap of roof sheeting, the whine in overhead wires.

In these early hours at Sunset Beach, bruised Lavinia with a bandage over her mouth made meat pies with thick crust pastry, batches of curried mince samoosas. Used the meat from Tamora Gool's son, stacked the pies and samoosas in the deep freeze.

During the morning, the wind came up from the southeast, brought a cloud down low on the mountain. Roared across the city, put grit in people's eyes. The wind and the glare a blindness by the early afternoon.

In the hospital, Krista sat at Tami's bedside, listened

to the wind moan through the corridors. Tami on life support, still in a coma.

At Truth café on Somerset, Mart Velaze took a cappuccino to a corner table, two tables away from Rings Saturen and Tamora Gool. Couldn't hear a word they said, the two lovebirds whispering.

Didn't matter, Mart Velaze was in the wind. The watcher watching. Hadn't been anywhere near his office in days, been to his flat only to shower, change his clothes. Had spent one night in the Israeli's bed, another at a backpackers, Carnival Court. Mart Velaze was taking precautions. Was in survivor mode.

Had drifted about his days, most of his nights watching Rings or Titus. Not much happening on either score. The Anders locked down, security posted at the door. The Voice nagging for updates: 'What's happening, chief? What's happening? Got to be something happening.' Didn't sound like she believed him anymore. Still he'd not told her of Mkhulu Gumede.

Mart Velaze, his thoughts on Mkhulu Gumede, watched a group of women bent into the wind cross the square towards the railway station. Recalled what Gumede'd said a few days ago. Leant in at his car window, mint mouthwash on his breath, said, 'We see you, comrade. We want to stay your friends.' Nothing more. Said those words without a smile.

The words lingering, We see you, comrade. We want to stay your friends. We?

Mart Velaze had said nothing. Wanted to say, Piss off, choirboy, but hadn't. Had stared into the man's black eyes until Mkhulu Gumede thumped twice on the car roof, returned to his white Chev, drove away.

A threat Mart Velaze took seriously. Didn't change anything, just made his job more difficult.

He sipped his cappuccino foam, a shamrock fashioned there. Halfway down the cup, Rings and Tamora Gool finished up. Went on their separate ways.

Mart Velaze didn't follow. Took his time with his coffee. When he was done, drove to Sunset Beach to watch over Titus Anders.

From where he parked could see the house, the security guard on a chair at the front door. Mart Velaze scrunched into the seat, his back prickly with sweat. Sometimes, he thought, his life wasn't glamorous.

Hadn't been there an hour, his cellphone vibrated: the Voice. He keyed her on.

'Chief,' she said. 'Our business has ended.'

'Yes?' said Mart Velaze.

'Yes. That's what I've been told. We do not need to worry about them anymore. We can leave Mr Anders and Mr Saturen to their own arrangements. Anyhow, all I hear from Mr Anders is music. Louis Armstrong. Frank Sinatra. Big band stuff. That's all he listens to. He's been through a bad time. People come with their condolences. People bring flowers. Cry with Lavinia. He says thank you, serves tea, lets them do all the talking. What's the use of listening to that?'

'There's going to be blood,' said Mart Velaze.

'Of course. But gangster blood. Gangster blood doesn't matter. We have the new arrangements, I've been told. Our Chinese have gone home happy. They have iron ore, platinum, raw material, new businesses, cheap abalone. Our ministers are happy. Everyone has money in the back pocket. The world goes on. We must let it be.'

Mart Velaze heard her sigh.

'But, chief, what do we know? What do we really know?'

Mart Velaze waited for the Voice to answer her own question.

'We know we must be careful.'

A silence but this silence not the Voice attending to other business, this time in the silence Mart Velaze could hear the Voice breathing.

'I think they know about me, chief. I think they know about you.'

'They?'

'The ones from the army. The agents from military intelligence. Our own people. I think they know about us, chief, me and my people, and this makes them nervous. I have to say it also makes me worried. These are dangerous types, these military. They have much to keep secret, much to conceal. They do not like prying eyes. Even when they are our eyes, friendly eyes. They are paranoid, chief. A gang of marabou storks picking through carcasses. Afterwards, chief, afterwards you should take a holiday. An overseas holiday. Maybe on the Dead Sea. You have friends there, nè? Maybe that's the place to go where you can relax with friends.'

'Afterwards?' said Mart Velaze. 'You said we were finished.'

'I did, but not just yet,' the Voice replied. 'We need to stay with this. A little longer, no one's going to know. Just you and me in the know. Then afterwards I think you should vamoose. You should pack a bag, chief. Make the travel arrangements for a month, two months even. You could relax in such a long time.'

'What've you heard? Someone's got a contract on me?'

'No, I don't think so. Nothing like that. Still I don't know, chief, for sure. I hear things but sometimes I don't know what I hear. You know what I mean? No one can say for sure what it means. Operation Protea. Operation Goldstar. Operation Marion. Who knows what it means? It's all code, chief. You know our language, all code. We always mean something else.'

'I see.'

'You do?'

'Yes.'

'Good, chief, good. Go pack a bag. Book a ticket. And, chief, stay quiet, don't tell anyone, afterwards just disappear. No more talking to the little Bishop girl, we don't want … complications.'

Talking to the little Bishop girl?

They'd talked twice on the phone in two days. Once about Tamora Gool, once to fix a meeting. But Krista hadn't pitched.

Complications? What sort of complications?

Mart Velaze heard the Voice say, 'Maybe I must go

pack a bag as well for a little holiday. New York or London, Broadway or the West End, see some nice theatre. But, chief, it's best you go, for the best you go. Nè. Lie in the Dead Sea with your Jewish friends.' She laughed. 'Okay, alright, enough, you have arrangements to make, places to go, people to see. Get everything ready.'

'We're not finished, that's what you're saying?'

'I am. Not finished yet, chief, not yet. Between you and me we're still watching. I'll tell you when we're done.'

After she'd told him to go with the ancestors, Mart Velaze pressed her off, sat toying with his cellphone, wondering why the Voice said one thing when she meant another. Why he hadn't mentioned Mkhulu Gumede. Wondering if he should phone Krista Bishop, warn her.

II

The wind did a drum roll over the roof of the factory in Paarden Island.

The Russian looked up. 'This place is not safe.'

'It's fine,' said Black Aron. 'Don't worry. It makes that noise in the wind.'

The Russian pointed at the corrugated-iron sheeting. 'It's moving.'

'Relax, okay. Forget about it.'

Black Aron pulled the lid off a plastic container: two rows of neatly stacked samoosas inside. The triangles all pointing upwards. He held it out to the Russian.

The man shook his head. Said, 'Tell me again, what we are going to do?'

Black Aron Chetty selected a samoosa from the centre of the box. Examined it. The pastry lightly browned, a bit oily, warm still, the aroma tantalising. He bit into it, chewed, swallowed. 'Listen,' he said. 'Just listen to me.' Popped the rest of the delicacy into his mouth.

The Russian lit a cigarette. 'Talk.'

Black Aron swallowed. 'Hell, they're nice.'

'Tell me,' said the Russian.

'Slowly, okay, slowly. I drop you, you've got this big bouquet of flowers, like a wreath, that you're carrying in your arms.'

'Where you drop me?'

'Outside the house. Listen, listen.' He tapped his own ear, put the box of samoosas on the bonnet of the car. 'We pull up in the вм, this smart car, there's flowers all over the back seat. We pull up and the security looks at us and wants to know about it, we tell them we're boutique flower service. We even wear black suits with white gloves like the funeral men wear. Yes? Really smart-looking delivery boys. Very respectful of the dead and the grieving. Anyhow. You get out, open the car's back door to take out a bunch of flowers. You give it to the security guy. You tell him there're more flowers for this address. Now he's carrying those, you'll carry the others. So he's got his hands full of flowers, no way he can pull a gun in a hurry. You bend into the back, take out more flowers only these're hiding the gun. The security's not gonna see you carrying it cos he wants to put the flowers down inside. Also he's got to open the front door with one hand, balance the flowers with the other. You go in right behind him, say Mr Anders got to sign the book.'

Black Aron smoothed a floor plan on the bonnet of the BM, leaving oily smears from his fingers.

'See here. This's the house. Here's the front door into this big room all open-plan sitting room, dining room, goes that way to the kitchen. From the front door it's this one big room, perfect situation.'

The Russian knocked ash off his cigarette. 'Maybe he's not down there. Maybe he's upstairs.'

'Ahh!' Black Aron raised his hands in surrender. 'He's going to be downstairs. Don't cause problems, Smirnoff. Why're you so negative? Middle of the morning he's going to be downstairs, all of them, sitting on the couch holding hands, tearful and grieving. Just waiting for the angel of mercy. All up to you.'

With a final pull, the Russian dropped the cigarette on the concrete, ground it out. The floor littered with stubs.

'And what about you? You are going to be ready outside?'

'Sure. I'm the driver. Your driver. It's no problem. I'll wait. That's what drivers do. We can get out of there no problem.'

Black Aron looked at the Russian. The Russian staring

back at him until Black Aron glanced away to fold up the floor plan.

'Okay, you think we do it this way, we do it this way.' He rolled his shoulders. 'Where we get all the flowers?'

'Spot on,' said Black Aron. 'I'll organise.'

III

In his house Titus Anders had sat at the dining-room table making arrangements. Phoned a priest, organised a funeral service for his boys. Arranged for the cremation. Placed an announcement in the newspapers. Hired a hall, caterers, waiters. Emailed a funeral notice to his contact list. The name of Tamora Gool on that list.

Luc cradled his bandaged hand, sat on a couch staring at his father.

Lavinia, upstairs on her bed, sore in heart and body, lay watching the wind drive spray across the shallows.

'What?' said Titus.

'Nothing,' said Luc.

'Go check on your sister.'

'What about Tamora? About Rings?'

'Go check on your sister.'

'What we going to do, Daddy?'

'Nothing. Pretend we know nothing. We are grieving, Luccie. Please, go check on your sister.'

'She's okay. Nothing's going to happen here at home. Isn't anything can happen here.'

'You think?' said Titus. 'What about Quint?'

'We got security now.'

'Doesn't matter.' He nodded at the stairs. 'Make sure.'

Luc got up, at the bottom of the staircase called, 'Lavinia. You alright? You want anything?'

'How's she supposed to answer?' said Titus.

'She can SMS,' said Luc.

Titus pointed upwards. 'Go on.' Waited while Luc climbed the stairs. Then phoned Rings Saturen.

'My brother,' he said. 'Can you talk about my boys in the funeral service, Quint and Boetie?'

'How are you?' said Rings.

'Heavy,' said Titus.

'You don't have to do this. You could make it small, the service, family and friends only.'

'They are my boys,' said Titus. 'We must honour them. Show respect. That's why I ask, Rings. Will you say some words?'

Rings cleared his throat. 'Of course. Of course. And ...'

Titus waited.

'What about Lavinia?'

'Not good. She's struggling.'

'I'll come and see her.'

'Any time you can come.'

'I have sent flowers. More flowers.'

'I know,' said Titus. 'There's lots of flowers.' He glanced at the flowers, the bouquets, the wreaths, some in vases, some heaped against a wall still in the shop wrappings.

'Titus,' said Rings, 'what will you do?'

'Do?'

'Come on, man, about what happened?'

'What can I do, Rings? There is only one thing to do.'

'By yourself? Use Pretty Boyz.'

'No. Me and Luc only. They're my boys that're dead. My girl ...' Titus not finishing, his words stuck in his throat. 'They shamed me.'

'There's Baasie,' said Rings. 'Sometime we must think of Baasie as well.'

'I'm thinking of Baasie. What're you thinking of Baasie?'

Titus listened to Rings breathing.

'Afterwards. After all this, alright? Then we can sort out for Baasie,' said Rings.

'I don't want to wait so long. They'll kill Luc, me, you. Mongols killing Pretty Boyz. Pretty Boyz killing Mongols. That's what they want, Rings. That's what they want. For us to fight.'

'Who's they?'

'You told me, government.'

'Leave it, Titus.'

Titus stared at the flowers. So many flowers. So many people thinking of his shame. The shame of Boetie and Quint. The shame of Lavinia. 'I can't. We must be untouchable.'

'Listen to me, Titus, leave it.'

'No, Rings, no. This one we can't leave.' Titus saw Luc coming down the stairs, pause. 'Government's the problem. That's a big problem. Those people taking away our living. How many families live from us?'

'Yes,' said Rings, 'I know.'

The two men went silent. Titus wondering how Rings could lie to him. Betray him. The image of Rings and Tamora, hand in hand. The deceit painful. But he said nothing, tightened his fist, said nothing.

Heard Rings say, 'Till the funeral, my friend. We'll speak later. Strong bones, my brother, strong bones.'

Titus said goodbye, disconnected.

Luc said, 'That was Rings?'

Titus nodded.

'Why're you talking to him?'

'I told you, we know nothing, Luc. We're moegoes here. The stupids, Luc, that's how we fix it. Remember. Nothing, we know niks, nothing' – Titus drawing out the syllables.

Luc shook his head. 'It's not right, Daddy. People think we're weak.' Luc holding up his bandaged hand as evidence.

'Maybe, Luccie. For now doesn't matter what they think.'

Titus went to his son, put an arm round his shoulders. They stood there side by side looking down at the flowers.

The front door opened, the security guard called out, 'Mr Anders?'

'What's it?' said Titus.

Heard the security guard say, 'More flowers, Mr Anders.'

IV

Five ten on the first day Krista staked out the Agency's building, she got to follow Mkhulu Gumede to the train station. He came out of the revolving door, looked up at the sky, looked back towards the mountain, headed downtown along Plein Street. Just another civil servant, no hassles in the world. She had a line of sight on the building's doorway from a café half a block away. Had been there for an hour, drinking lime sodas.

Didn't need the picture on her cellphone to identify him. His features etched in her mind, his attitude what she'd anticipated: cocky man about town. Her only hesitation: could it be this easy? First day right on time? Very convenient. Too convenient.

But she went with it. What other options? Put it off for another day? Wait to see if he had back-up? Play it safe? Nah, she wasn't going to do that. She was going to roll with what came along.

Krista paid up, the last soda half-finished, slipped into the crowd making for the station. At least fifty metres behind him, she could see his bald head bobbing through the pedestrians. An easy follow. Again the nag: was this too easy? At the Shortmarket corner he stopped to window-gaze in a jewellers.

Krista, a block behind, angled across the street, turned into Longmarket. She wore a linen jacket over a white T-shirt, black jeans, a backpack on her shoulders, in her right hand a Woolworths plastic bag. Quickly took off the backpack, folded the jacket into it. Stuffed in the Woolies bag too. Now carried the backpack in her left hand. She scanned the street.

If he had support they might've seen her quick-change act. Back-up could be anyone. Her eyes skipping over the cleaning woman with the head scarf. The young man in shirtsleeves carrying a briefcase. The tourist wearing yellow shorts. The builder in overalls. The office chick poking at her cellphone. Anyone.

But Krista reckoned not. Mr Mkhulu Gumede was too cool by half. He'd deal with his own problems. Assuming he even knew about her mission.

She crossed to the other side of Longmarket, stepped back into Plein Street, jaywalked the intersection with the rest of the city against the traffic lights.

Gumede still stared into the jewellers when she passed on the opposite side of the street. Could be he was monitoring reflections in the windows. She couldn't risk a glance. Had her head tilted down as she scratched in her bag. Preoccupied.

Nothing to be done but walk on by, try to second-guess him. Two possibilities: he was headed for the railway station or the taxi rank on the upper deck.

Krista cut into the pavement stalls, stopped at a mama selling lipsticks, deodorants, nail varnish, perfume. Not a single product Krista was likely to purchase. Pure poison from China or India, she reckoned. The mama smiled at her, wanted to spray Krista's hand with perfume. Krista held out her wrist. Gave her a chance to look back: there was Mkhulu Gumede walking down the side of the post office building. She sniffed at the scent, sweet, cloying. Thanked the mama, said, 'Lovely, just not today.'

'Make you smell like a lady,' said the mama. 'Catch your man.'

Krista laughed, skipped away into the throng, running, dodging between buses, coming out of Castle Street ahead of her man. Car-dodged over Strand Street, a couple of drivers hooting, rushed onto the station concourse like she was going to miss her train. Glimpsed behind her Mkhulu Gumede waiting at the Strand Street pedestrian crossing for the green man. Good law-abiding citizen.

Thing now: train or taxi? Krista gambled on train. Trouble was, which one, which platform? She joined a queue at the ticket office. Watched Mkhulu Gumede stroll in, show a monthly pass to the fat female platform guard at the turnstile. The fat female guard talking to another fat female guard, not even glancing at commuter tickets.

Krista bought a ticket for the south peninsula line. Went through the turnstile: no sign of Mkhulu Gumede. A departing train but she was too late to hop on.

She cursed. One short sharp, 'Shit.' Went home to brood.

Sat on the edge of the pool, staring down at her feet in the water. You know where he works. You know how he gets home. You know more than you did a few hours ago. Her feet ghostly against the black base, moving the way fish fan their tails. Doesn't matter how long it takes. You will find his home.

Looking up at the house empty of Tami, her maman, her papa, Cat2. All gone. A spike of agitation went cold through her veins. She eased herself off the warm tiles, slipped under the water. The distant hum of the filter motor, the harsh kwaak of hadedas coming into the trees. She swam: length on length.

The next day, Krista staked out the station. Sat on the concourse floor, back against a column: a student, bored, waiting for her mates. Wore faded jeans, sexy trainers, silk scarf. Sunglasses in her hair. Buds in her ears wired to an iPod. Patterned canvas college bag beside her. Student Krista intent on SMSing. Her thoughts about getting this over with fast. Find out where he went to bed, deal with it in the dark hours. One day on playing cat and mouse wasn't her style. No ways spying would be a career move.

Ninety minutes she waited, watched shoes and legs traverse the marble hall: the swarm of people heading home, mostly to the Cape Flats war zones. Earnest people hurrying to the place where men cut out a woman's tongue. The woman offered up by Mkhulu Gumede.

Mkhulu Gumede no better than the jackrollers. Worse, because he did it for a higher agency. Get rid of him, another Mkhulu Gumede would step in. Didn't matter, Tami's attacker would be dead. This Mkhulu Gumede would be no more. All she was interested in.

Come half past six, Krista decided Mkhulu Gumede was a no-show.

Irritated, wound up, she went home, swam it off. Afterwards rested her arms on the pool edge, hung in the water, her sightline across the bay to the nuclear power station hunched in the haze. In the thickening twilight her mood tempered, she considered events. Sometimes you got lucky, sometimes you didn't. Couldn't expect a spook to work office hours. Couldn't expect predictability from a spy, from some governmental secret agent. Had to anticipate other possibilities, like maybe he was playing her. Maybe his no-show was deliberate. The thought nagged. A paranoid notion she couldn't shake.

Day three she got lucky. Waited on a concourse bench watching the commuters. Right on time there was Mkhulu Gumede going through the turnstile, flashing his ticket at the platform guard, heading for the south pen line.

Krista peeled off the bench, hiked it after him. This time wearing a spaghetti-strap dress over jeans. The backpack on her shoulders, a bag of Woolies Food meals in her right hand. Going through the turnstile, saw Mkhulu Gumede enter the first door of the second carriage. She walked past, went in the next door.

Surveyed the carriage, most of the seats already taken, Krista having to strap-hang with the latecomers.

She looked down the compartment. Halfway along was Mkhulu Gumede at a window seat. His eyes on her, checking her out the way men often checked her out. Nothing new, to Krista's way of thinking, she turned men's heads. Only thing: being looked at by Mkhulu Gumede was like being looked at by a shark. Dead eyes, no glint of life. Did he recognise her?

She didn't challenge him, let her eyes drift on, tired, commuter eyes. The train filled, the crush jamming her in a corner. Under the arms of two men she could watch Mkhulu Gumede staring out the window. Just another man going home at the end of the day.

At each station the sway and crush of passengers. Woodstock, Salt River, Observatory, Mowbray, Rose-bank. At Rondebosch, he got out. Krista elbowing her way after him. Saw him head down the steps to the underpass as she pulled free, wrenching her backpack from the body press. Waited for him to come out on the other side before she followed. A risk letting him get too far ahead, but no other option. She hurried through the subway, came up, saw him cross the street towards the shops. She needed to catch up. More difficult now without enough people to hide in.

If he stopped, pulled his window-scanning trick, or turned around, came straight towards her, she could only walk on. Would have to drop the trick, get off the street. If Mkhulu Gumede was as good as Mart Velaze put out, he might link her: the woman in the train, the woman from two days back. Would make her job more difficult.

Nothing for it, she walked faster, closed the gap. Kept a handy twenty metres behind the bald head.

Mkhulu Gumede didn't look back, took an easy stroll along Main Road to a townhouse block. Posh townhouses. Turned into a side street, Krista kept on, out the corner of her eye saw there was Mkhulu Gumede talking to a woman, elderly woman with long grey hair. The two of them laughing. He glanced up at her, Krista sensing the movement of his head, but what was she? Another young woman going home? Could even be a student in this place of students, the way she was dressed. Didn't look down, kept her eyes straight ahead, pretended she was self-absorbed.

The paranoid nag re-emerging: did he recognise her? Was he that good?

Krista walked on, kept her pace, wondered if he'd walked up the road to watch her. Couldn't look back, much as she itched to.

That night in the hospital, sitting beside Tami, holding her hand, Krista thought about Mkhulu Gumede. Wondered how'd he afford a townhouse like that in a suburb like that. No ways some agent … What'd they call them? Intelligence strategist. No ways some intelligence strategist could afford property there. Not without a helping hand. Also he was too young to have that kind of money.

She thought too about tracking Mkhulu Gumede.

About his stopping to gaze in the jewellers. About his looking at her in the train. About how he'd walked through Rondebosch to his home without any ducking and diving. Not even once turning round. Like he didn't care. No big deal. He was on home ground. Then that last quick glance while he chatted with a neighbour in the street. No ways he could've been onto her. It was reflex, training, maybe he recognised her from the train but so what? No ways he'd connect her to the woman with the backpack from two days previously. No ways at all.

Except for the niggling doubt. Always worrying at her. He was a professional. He was trained in counter-surveillance. He could be onto her. Could be? How could he be? She brought her focus back to Tami.

Sat there looking at her, thinking how suddenly everything had gone bad. From the good scene they were running, the two of them, to this hell. Tami now in a coma for days, each day pushing away any chance of what they had returning.

Krista shook her head to dislodge the thought. Self-pity not her bag. This was about Tami now, not about what had been. She reached out, laid her hand over Tami's. Felt the warmth on her palm. Tami's hand inert, not responding to her touch. You looked at her she could be asleep. No stress in her face, the shallow rise and fall of her chest. You looked at her without the drip lines, the raised bed, the monitors, you could fool yourself.

Krista didn't.

Later she drove to Rondebosch, parked a block away from where she'd last seen Mkhulu Gumede. Walked to the block of townhouses, found Mkhulu Gumede's name on the board of buzz-boxes at the main gate. Just like that, right there. A spook hiding in plain sight with nothing to hide. Press number five, you could speak to Mkhulu Gumede. Tell him he was going to be dead. Should enjoy his last days.

As she walked away from the gate her phone rang: unknown number.

She pressed on, got into her car.

'Who's this?'

A familiar voice: Mart Velaze. 'Listen,' he said, 'let go of Gumede. He knows about you. He's watching you.'

'Really?' Krista fired the ignition. 'I don't see him.'

'Don't be funny,' said Mart Velaze. 'You know what I mean. Walk away, okay. Just walk away from whatever you're planning.'

Krista hearing the no-bullshit tone to his voice. 'What's happened?'

'Nothing's happened. Just listen to me on this one: drop your stuff about Gumede. How many ways can I say it? Forget him. That story's over, finished.' A pause. 'I can't talk longer, Krista.'

End of conversation. She rang back, there was no answer.

Krista stared up at the townhouse block, Mkhulu Gumede somewhere inside.

V

Me, I didn't know this was gonna happen. Strues. Me, my-self I would have told you. Sometimes there are things that happen, snap, like the click of fingers, suddenly. You know what I'm saying? Sometimes this trouble happens by itself. I can tell you what happened. You want to know how the shooting happened? Alright. So the captain says we must go into the Valley of Plenty and kill the Pretty Boyz. He name six of us. Seven with him. Stones and me's with the captain. Four others going in front. We's got 9mms, police specials, the z88s, .38s, one .45 that's the captain's. We in two cars. Park the cars, walk up the street, the same street where the pipe bombs killed those lighties. There's marks on the tar where the car burnt. We go past this before the Pretty Boyz come out of the houses. The captain says to the Pretty Boyz we don't want to cause shit but now is the time the Pretty Boyz must join with the Mongols. Today is the time we need to talk. He says that their captain must come into the street to talk.

A man comes out I never seen before. Very tall. Very black. Like he's from Africa. Maybe Mozambique. Maybe Angola. He says put down the guns before we going to talk. He's got a funny voice, like he's foreign. The captain asks what the man's name is, he says we can call him Peugeot. Peugeot like the car. Peugeot comes to the street, he walks to the captain. He tells the Pretty Boyz to stay back. The captain tells Stones and me to stay behind. He tells the other Mongols brothers they must come back behind him. The captain, he gives Stones the .45, then he shows the man called Peugeot that he's got no weapon. We stand like that. Everybody still holding their guns. Stones's with the big .45. Peugeot shows there is nothing in his hands. Then he comes closer to the captain for the talk.

I can tell you I don't know which one shot the first bullet, Pretty Boyz or Mongols. If you asked me, myself I would say Pretty Boyz. They got no discipline. With the captain he says no shooting you got to listen to it, that's his order.

The only thing I can tell you is Stones was next to me. It wasn't me 'n it wasn't him shot our guns. Maybe it was one of my brothers from the other group with us but I would say on the Bible it was Pretty Boyz that thought they were clever.

That was the worst shooting I been in. On the other times you hear cluck, cluck, cluck cluck cluck, then it's all over. This time I shot two clips. That's sixteen bullets I can tell you.

The first thing, we got the captain safe behind a wall. By that time the man called Peugeot was probably dead. There was blood on his stomach and his face. I heard it later on the Voice of the Cape he died there on the scene. We got four other Pretty Boyz before the shooting stopped. Stones was hit in the arm, here, the right arm, high up. One of our brothers was killed.

When we listened to the Voice of the Cape we heard a

child was shot in the head, also a girl and a student. I can tell you the girl was in the ankle, the student got two, leg and arm. I can say that we was protected in that fight. Only God can save you when the bullets are wild.

You want to know there will be more fighting? More dead corpses? I can tell you this for sure.

14

I

Middle of the funeral morning Black Aron and the Russian pulled into Sunset Beach. Both in dark suits. Black Aron in a black number he'd hired from Funeral Services, the Russian's was more charcoal grey, borrowed from a Slav friend. They had white gloves lying in the tray behind the gear stick.

'I am not wearing those now,' the Russian had said when they left the flower sellers.

'No problem,' Black Aron replied. 'When we get there, yes?'

'Maybe.' The Russian tapped out a cigarette, pushed in the lighter. 'We do not have to be fools.' The lighter clicked out, he put the coil to his cigarette.

'Blow the smoke out the window,' said Black Aron.

The Russian ignored him, exhaled from the corner of his mouth a thin stream that clouded over Black Aron's face.

Black Aron waved away the smoke. 'Jesus, man.' He sneezed.

The Russian laughed. 'The flowers make you sneeze.'

The back seat was stacked with flowers they'd bought from the sellers at Trafalgar Place. Pulled the car in, loaded up. The flower sellers ripping them off but Black Aron didn't care. Get this done with, top of his mind.

They came into Sunset Beach at a respectable speed. Cruised down the streets to the close where the Anders family lived.

On the back seat beneath the flowers was the kurz, all ready to rock 'n roll.

The Russian flicked his stub out the window, his second since town. 'You will wait.'

'I'm the driver,' said Black Aron, 'that's what I do.'

'No funny tricks.'

Black Aron pulled on his gloves. 'Come on, we gotta do this properly.'

'I know your name. I know your factory. I can find you, poepiehead.'

'Ah, shit. Just put on the bloody gloves.'

'I can find you.' The Russian worked his hands into the gloves. 'I can find you anywhere.'

'You can find me in the car in the street.'

The Russian held up his hands. 'I look like a waiter.'

'It's what funeral people wear, okay, get used to it.'

Black Aron drove into the close, came round the circular street to the Anders house, stopped at the gate. The security guard getting bristly at the door, shifting his hands onto the semi-auto hung round his neck.

Black Aron thinking, you're gonna need that soon, boykie. He braked, kept the engine running.

The Russian stared at him, raised a white-gloved finger. 'Don't move, my friend.'

Then he was out, leaving the passenger door open.

Black Aron watched the security man approach.

'Can you help me?' the Russian said to him. 'We have all these flowers for this address.' He handed a bouquet to the guard, ducked into the car again, passed him another one. 'Please. This will help me.'

The guard said, 'We had flowers delivered yesterday.'

'Yes, these are more,' said the Russian. 'Lots more.'

The security man backed away, clutching the flowers, opened the front door. He called inside, 'More flowers, Mr Anders.'

The Russian scooped up two bunches, the MP5 beneath them. Locked his right-hand fingers round the trigger guard, his left hand on the barrel grip. Didn't exactly disguise the gun but he didn't plan on taking his time about this.

He backed out of the car, said over his shoulder to the security, 'Please, show me where they must go.' The security man leading him into the house.

The Russian came up quickly behind him: saw two men at the dining-room table, the guard to his left saying, 'Mr Anders, I'll put these with the others, if Mr Anders wants.'

II

Titus Anders and his son Luc sat at the dining-room table, Luc cradling his throbbing hand. Daughter Lavinia upstairs on her bed, facing the wall. Earlier she'd written to Titus: 'I can't do this' – using the A4 pad he'd bought her, writing in pencil, her style big, the strokes thin.

'Please, my darling,' he'd said.

'All those people,' she'd written.

'It's your brothers' funeral. We have to show we are a family,' Titus'd said. 'That nobody can shame us.' He'd looked at her swollen face, imagined her pain. The thought tight as anguish in his chest. But he could not glance away.

They had shamed her. In shaming her, shamed him. The weak father. The useless protector. The pitied man.

That Titus had let them kill his boys. Rape his girl.

Shame, man. Shame on him.

You got to feel sorry for him. Every time he look at her, he face disgrace. His own disgrace.

It's a pity, hey. Such a pity. For a proud man like him.

'Please, Daddy,' she'd written.

'We've all got to be there, meisie,' he'd said. 'If you don't stand with me, they're going to think we're beaten. Nobody can do this to us.'

He'd watched his daughter write: 'They have already.'

Sadly shaken his head. 'No they haven't. We are still important people. We still have respect from the community. They look up to us.' He'd gazed at the words on her pad: *They have already*. 'Who do they come to when they need help? Who do they come to for loans?' He'd let the questions hang there. 'Me. Us. The Anders family. We are the ones who can help them.'

'I want to die,' she'd written.

'I know,' Titus'd said. 'We are all hurting. No more shame, my meisie girl, no more shame.'

Downstairs with Luc at the dining-room table, Titus cleaned his ankle gun. Agitated, needing to do something mechanical. Ejected the clip, broke the gun into its parts, the pieces lying there on the polished table. Such a small gun. But the next day, at the funeral, at the gathering afterwards, no ways he would be without it.

Titus wiped down the metal, drew a cord through the barrel, assembled the pieces. He checked the clip: seven rounds.

'You must get one of these, Luc,' he said.

'I don't need one,' said Luc. 'It's like a toy.'

'You think so?' Titus sighed. 'I used to think so once.' He pushed the clip into the pistol grip. 'Nice. Very nice little toy.' Titus sat back. 'Make us some tea, please, Luc.'

Luc got up as the security man opened the front door. 'Mr Anders, more flowers for Mr Anders,' the man said.

'Alright,' said Titus, the gun in his hand.

'Mr Anders, I'll put these with the others if Mr Anders wants?'

'Ja, please,' said Titus.

'Mr Anders, there's lots of people sad for Mr Anders.' The security guard with his weapon slung across his chest, his hands full of flowers, coming into the room followed by a man in a grey suit. This man also with his arms full of flowers.

Titus saw the gun before the man fired. The man giving a shrug to get rid of the flowers, bunches of lilies, carnations, roses fluttering to the floor. Then for that moment standing there, grinning, with the semi in his hands. A grin Titus reckoned he'd seen before, the night of the drive-by.

The man put one round into the back of the security guard, the force of the bullet jacking the guy face-first into the flowers stacked against the wall. Swung onto Titus.

Titus had the Kel-Tec up, squeezed off two, going first for the big target, the chest, raised the barrel slightly for a head shot. A bit chancy with a smaller target but more impact. Both went in, Titus being a mean mister marksman. Always had been. He pointed a gun at you, you were dead.

The man with the shaven head in the grey suit went down on his back, the kurz sliding across the tiles.

Titus heard the car then, pulling away.

III

Mart Velaze started the morning with a couple of hours at Sunset Beach. A cautious couple of hours. Watching not only the Anders house but all comings and goings. Far as he could tell, no one interested in him. No reason why they should be. They, specifically Mkhulu Gumede, knew where he was.

After his talk with the Voice he'd had his car cleaned privately, the guy'd found a tracker screwed tight to the chassis. Nice job, very discreet.

Mart Velaze thought about it. Decided better they knew where he was than he ditched the device. Said to the guy, 'That's fine. Leave it.'

'Really?' the guy'd said, shaking his head. 'You don't mind?'

'Course, yes, I do. But keeping it causes less shit.'

The guy'd laughed. 'Your backside in the fire.'

Too true.

He'd not been near the Aviary. Not even set foot in the street, let alone the building.

If Mkhulu Gumede was monitoring, he could see him trekking about town, sitting long hours in Sunset Beach or Pinelands near Rings Saturen's cute cottage, in the street near Rings's office, chilling in cafés, even know within a hundred metres where he was sleeping. Thing was, no one was doing anything about it. Despite the Voice's warning, everything fine.

So Mart Velaze went with the situation.

What interested him was the calm in the Anders household. Titus rolling out a funeral service, a big community gathering to honour his sons, no sign of vengeance in his actions. Like Titus was in deep grief. Not functioning to cue.

Mart Velaze on this morning sat watching the Anders house when the BM pulled into the close, driving slowly. Two suited gents up front. No business decals on the car doors. Mart Velaze straightened out of his slouch.

Interesting. In a morning when there'd been nothing but a change of security personnel.

Watched the car stop at the gate, the man in the passenger seat unfold, start handing bunches of flowers to the security. Big, tall white dude doing coloured work. An Indian driving.

The big man following the security into the house. From where he watched, Mart Velaze could see the gun.

Surveillance only, the Voice had said. He'd already broken that ground rule.

Considered breaking it again. He started the car, reached into the glove compartment for the Ruger that lay there, already capped. Brought it out, adjusted the silencer.

Before he could move, heard the snick pah of the MP5, a single shot. Two quick snaps from a small-calibre weapon. Then the BM took off, fast but controlled. No rubber screech. As the car approached, Mart Velaze angled his car across the road, blocking it.

The Indian guy didn't even make it out of his car, Mart Velaze was opening the door for him.

'Who're you?' said the Indian.

'Doesn't matter,' said Mart Velaze. 'I'm the guy with the gun.' Waved it in the man's face to get him moving.

They walked back to the Anders house in single file, Mart Velaze a couple of paces in the rear.

'Who're you? Who're you?' the man kept repeating.

'Doesn't matter,' said Mart Velaze. 'Looks like they're not so pleased to see you.'

Titus and Luc now crowding the doorway, grim-faced. Titus with this tiny pistol in his hand. So small you'd hardly notice it.

'Black Aron Chetty,' said Titus. 'You've been causing so much kak.' He pulled the man into the house. 'Who're you?' he said to Mart Velaze.

Mart Velaze gave him the same answer he'd given Black Aron. 'All yours,' he added. 'I'm outta here.' Turned towards his car, walked off.

'He can't go,' he heard the young Anders say.

Heard Titus say, 'Leave it.' Call out, 'We thank you.'

Mart Velaze raised a hand, kept on walking.

He drove to a parking spot off Marine Drive facing the city across the bay. The classic Cape Town photograph, the one all the tourists wanted. A long tablecloth of cloud on the mountain.

He bought an ice cream, sat in his car licking at it, the wind rocking the vehicle. Mart Velaze watched the blowback fraying the tops of the waves, thought one person in the world he didn't envy was the man called Black Aron Chetty.

When he finished the ice cream he rang Krista Bishop, his call going to voicemail. Mart Velaze didn't leave a message.

IV

Her cellphone had rung at three twenty in the morning. Krista had reached for it, heard the voice say, 'My lovey, it's sister at the hospital. I think you better come.'

She didn't remember dressing, getting the car out of the garage, driving through the empty streets above the city. Her thoughts came back to her as she stopped in the hospital's outside parking zone. A couple of other cars there, a man crouched out of the wind behind a 1990s model Cortina, smoking. Krista sat. Fearful. Not yet four o'clock but the faint light of dawn above the mountains. She ran Tami's name through her mind, dreaded what was to come. The wind rocked the car, pulled at the door as she got out.

At ICU the nurse was waiting for her. She took Krista's hands.

'My lovey,' she said, 'this is not good.'

Krista didn't reply, her gaze down the ward at the unit were Tami lay. Activity there, doctors, other nurses.

'Come.' The nurse took her by the hand.

They stood inside the room, two doctors bent over Tami, a nurse adjusting IV flows.

'What happened?' said Krista, her voice scratchy. She cleared her throat, said again, 'What's wrong?'

One of the doctors glanced back at her, said something she didn't understand.

'I'm sorry?'

'She was in a stable condition, she's not anymore.'

'She stopped breathing,' said the nurse. 'The doctors got her back.'

'She keeps doing it,' said the other doctor. 'Just stops breathing.'

They stood around the bed watching Tami. Ten minutes. Fifteen minutes. Again her breathing stopped.

The doctors struggled with her, shook her, pumped her chest. The one muttering, 'Breathe, dammit, breathe.'

Krista watched, her eyes tearing up. Couldn't stand to see Tami being pummelled like that. 'Stop,' she said, reaching out to the doctor nearest her, clutching at his arm. 'Stop. Let her go. Please let her go.'

'We can't,' he said. 'We can't do that.' Turned back to his job. The two doctors almost wrestling with their patient. Tami as floppy as a doll.

'It's okay,' said the nurse, 'she's breathing.'

They laid Tami back, her head turned sideways on the pillow, no trace of anxiety in her face. To Krista, the way she looked when she slept.

The doctors went away, the nurse left Krista in a chair beside the bed.

'What if she stops breathing?' Krista said.

'Then we'll come, my lovey,' said the nurse. 'All you got to do is pick her up, squeeze her chest.'

All you've got to do.

It happened fifteen minutes later. Krista was staring at her, watching Tami's chest move slightly beneath the sheet: up, down, up, down. Then nothing. A perfect stillness.

Krista jumped up, hugged her, felt the slightness of Tami's body, the soft squash of her breasts. Hissed at her, 'Don't do this to me. Just breathe, please breathe.'

The nurse came in, the two of them struggled.

'How many minutes?' The nurse panting with the effort.

'I don't know. One, two.' It felt like longer. Krista ready to say again, Just let her go. It was what Tami wanted. If she wasn't breathing, she didn't want to breathe.

But then Tami shuddered, a long intake of breath that she exhaled in a sigh.

'Okay,' said the nurse. 'We've got her again.' Lay Tami back on the pillows. 'You okay?' she said to Krista.

'No,' said Krista. 'No, I'm not. I hate this. She wants to die.'

'Ja, my lovey, she does. Sometimes hospitals aren't the best place for people, you know what I mean? Sometimes we get it wrong. We supposed to care for people, and we do. But sometimes what you supposed to do is …' She shook her head. 'Sometimes it's not the right thing.' She looked at Krista. 'You want some sweet tea?'

Krista nodded. Sat again in the chair beside the bed watching the rise and fall of Tami's chest.

The nurse returned with the tea. 'You don't have to sit here.'

'You called me,' said Krista, took the mug of tea.

The nurse dampened a cloth, wiped Tami's face. 'I thought she was going.'

'You're not letting her.' Krista sipped the sweet tea, scalding her tongue. She blew at the steam.

'I know. I know.' The nurse fussed about Tami, straightening the sheets. 'I seen this before,' she said, 'people get tired.' She looked at Krista, Krista looking back at her saw fatigue in the nurse's eyes.

For an hour Tami breathed easily. Krista dozed in the chair, her head lolling. At every jerk she woke, saw Tami peaceful.

Close to six o'clock, a green daylight in the ward, Tami stopped breathing. This time Krista didn't move to grab her. Rose from the chair, held Tami's hand, waited for the rush of nurses. They came. The pushing, squeezing, pumping started. They called for the heart kickstarter, for oxygen. Nothing helped.

'She's gone,' said Krista. The words a whisper in her throat.

The nurse heard her, said, 'Ja, my lovey. This time.'

When it was over they let Krista sit there. She leant forward from the chair, her arms on the bed, her head resting on them. The door to the unit was closed but she could hear the noises of the ward. The hum of the air-conditioning, the squeak of trolley wheels, the whisper of nurses' shoes across the floor. Voices, soft voices discussing heart rates, blood pressure, the conditions of the critical. Somewhere, behind it all, the rattle of wind.

She must have slept. She woke with her arms lame, the arms of a dead person. Sat up, letting her blood uncrinkle the vessels, the release of a thousand pins and needles.

She said goodbye to Tami then. Quickly kissed her lips, and left, pausing in the doorway, not looking back.

Outside the wind rushed her to the Sharan, the bright day making her squint. Krista drove home as she had driven to the hospital, not thinking, stuck in the slow bumper-to-bumper grind of the morning traffic along De Waal Drive. Below, the city, white in the wind haze. Above, the cloud heavy on the mountain.

At home, in the house without Tami, that was also the house without her mother, the house without her father, the house without, Krista changed into a swimming costume. For an hour swam lengths in the pool where she had no thoughts, no memories, only the rush of the water at her ears, the steady propulsion of her body.

Eventually she stopped, rested against the side. Considered where she would kill Mkhulu Gumede.

V

Transcript from the case file of Hardlife MacDonald:

The captain says we must all go to the Valley of Plenty. There's gonna be a meeting for Mongols and Pretty Boyz with the top man Rings Saturen, the one they call Untouchable. He also a politician. The captain told us stories about him, you can't believe it's the same man. He was wild. In those other times before I was even a lightie he was wild. People have respect for him. Today more than ever before, people respect Rings Saturen. In the afternoon we go to the street where there's been all this trouble. They's already there, Rings Saturen and Tamora Gool. This the first time I seen Tamora Gool. Very beautiful lady. I heard all the stories about her. That she is wild. That she from our streets. That she got a heart of stone. I heard how she killed people. But I can tell you she a beautiful lady. When she smile. Then you can't believe she done any of those things. She so pretty she could be a model for fashion. Be in the magazines. We see her standing there next to Rings, I can tell you we think this is a smart lady. In a suit, as well. Like she's a banker or a major businesswoman. Both she and Rings speak to us. They stand in the street like us and tell us now new days is dawning. A new time when we going to make more money. They say we now in business with the Chinese. Ja, I tell you that's what they say.

15

Black Aron needed water, his mouth was dry, his tongue sticking to his palate.

'Some water, Uncle Titus,' he said. 'I can't move my tongue.'

'You lucky you got a tongue,' said Luc.

'Shush, Luc.' Titus raising his hands to calm his son.

Black Aron watching Titus watching him. Giving Titus his sad eyes, Please don't do this. No twitch of compassion in the face of Titus Anders.

Black Aron sweated. He could smell the stink of his own sweat, it was that bad. He wanted to pee too.

'Tell me again,' Titus was saying to him, tapping him on the knee with a long-handled wooden spoon he'd had Luc fetch from the kitchen. 'This time slowly.'

'I told you yesterday.' Black Aron watched the spoon softly smacking his knee. 'What you want that for?' he said. 'That spoon?'

'You never know,' said Titus, keeping up the jig. 'Now tell us.'

Black Aron sucked in his cheeks, trying to stimulate saliva. 'Again?'

'Ja,' said Titus. 'Why not? Don't you like the story?'

Black Aron sitting on a straight-backed chair in his dark suit, hands behind his back fastened together with a plastic tie. Plastic ties at his ankles binding them to the chair legs. Some crimson marks on his white shirt, blood drops from a gash at his mouth where Luc'd hit him. The only time he'd been hit. He squirmed from the heat, sweat stinging his eyes. Black Aron still wore his white gloves, his hands feeling like they were on fire.

'Give me some water,' he said, trying for bravery, trying to speak his mind. 'It's hot.'

'Please. Say please. You have manners?'

'Huh!' He stared at Titus.

Titus sitting opposite him straddling a chair, leaning forward against the chair back tap-tapping him on the knee with that wooden spoon. 'Please.'

He blinked to get the sweat out of his eyes. 'Please, Uncle Titus.'

'Alright,' he heard Titus say, 'drink some water. Luc, get him some water.' Relief going through him as if he was already swallowing the water. Titus and Luc way out there on the scary edges, the way he saw it. So calm, capable of anything.

'Thank you.' Black Aron squirmed. 'Please, Uncle Titus, man, undo me. It's too hot, man. I've told you everything. On my heart, there's nothing else.'

'Surely,' said Titus. 'Probably you're right. But just once more, okay?'

Black Aron slumped, watched Luc coming back with the water in a tall glass, the glass clouded with condensation. Felt the coldness against his cheek when Luc held the glass there. Ice-cold fridge water. Luc playing the glass over his face, bringing the glass to his lips, teasing him.

'Please,' said Black Aron, 'please, man, please.' He opened his mouth, felt the icy edge of the glass against his lower lip, felt it knock against his teeth. Anticipated the wet relief.

Then it was gone. Luc had put the glass on the table. Luc with that blind grey eye, like a glob of mucus.

Black Aron wanted to cry. 'No,' he said, his voice a sob, 'please let me drink some. Please.'

Heard Titus say, 'Tell us again first.'

Black Aron let his head fall forward: felt the strain this put on his arms, the pain in his knees from the awkward position. The tap of the wooden spoon, unceasing.

Said in a whisper, 'They want to kill you.'

'They?'

'I told you already.' His voice still a whisper.

'Their names.' Titus shouting at him, smacking the spoon against his knee. 'Say their names.'

Black Aron snicked in a breath. 'Rings and Tamora.'

'Not so bad,' he heard Titus say, felt the spoon under his chin, Titus putting pressure to make him raise his head. He lifted his head, looked at Titus. 'Now the story,' Titus said.

Again Black Aron told it. Dreaded each word but he

told it. That Rings wanted to be alone, the main man. No Baasie, no Titus Anders. Mr Clean Politician without gangster connections. Tamora helping him sort it. Rings promised her the perlemoen business, all of it. She could run it, deal with the Chinese. She got the Mongols to kill Baasie. Hired the Russian too. Even Rings was going to have to watch out for Tamora.

'I was the driver,' said Black Aron. 'Just the driver.'

'What about my boys? My Lavinia?' Titus's voice sounding like it came from a long way away. 'Why're they dead? Why's Lavinia raped?'

'I don't know, I don't know, I don't know.' Black Aron let deep sobs shake his body. 'I don't know about them. I don't know what's going on. I'm just the driver, Uncle Titus. Truly.'

'Ja, ja, Aron,' said Titus. 'What'll we do with you, hey?'

'I'm outta here,' said Black Aron. 'You let me go I'm outta here. Outta the city, outta the country. Far away.' Black Aron shook more sweat from his face. 'Please, let me have some water, uncle.' He looked from Titus to Luc.

Luc said, 'We could cut him up.'

Black Aron shut his eyes. Heard Titus say, 'I've got another idea.'

II

In the afternoon, there they sat at the funeral, the Anders family, Titus, Lavinia, Luc, alone in the front row: Lavinia with a black veil over her head covering her face, Luc with his bandaged hand. Titus straight back, head erect.

Up at the lectern, Rings Saturen praising the dead Anders boys, Boetie and Quint, praising the Anders family. Talking about their standing, what they'd done for the community. Said how he and Titus Anders were like family. Rings holding up two fingers of his right hand close together.

Titus tried to focus. Keep his mind on what Rings said. All the time could feel the gun strapped to his ankle.

Rings saying something about Baasie Basson. A good man down. About the power of the gangs. Rings saying something about the violence on the streets. The deaths of innocents.

Rings going politician: 'I promise you, my brothers and sisters, it will end. We are hurting ourselves. We cannot bear the pain.'

Titus aware that behind him the church was packed with mourners: people they knew, more people they didn't. In a pew at the back sat Tamora Gool. He'd seen her come in, seen her slide along the bench to the end near a door. Her quick-exit plan.

Titus felt her there, her eyes never leaving his head.

Challenging. But he did not look round. Kept his gaze on the coffins of his boys. Felt beside him the shame of his daughter and his son.

Walking out of the church behind the coffins, didn't acknowledge anyone. Knew Lavinia was weeping. Luc stone-eyed. Felt hands reach out to touch him, pat his shoulder, briefly grip his arm. He walked robotic.

Then in the cortège to the community hall, sat in the black Benz, wearing sunglasses, grim.

At the hall, Titus spoke to those gathered, said his boys had been too young to die. His Lavinia too young to know such violence. His Luc mutilated for no reason but necessity.

His voice stopped. Rings helped him to a chair.

Luc stood behind his father, Lavinia beside him, the veil still covering her face.

'You don't have to stay,' said Rings.

Titus said, 'You don't know what's in my heart.'

Lavinia pointed at the door, reached for his hand, her eyes telling him, Please, Daddy, I don't want to be here. Titus saw her tears.

'It's okay. Everything's okay now,' he said.

She frowned.

'What's Daddy saying?' said Luc.

'Daddy's got a plan.' Titus squeezed his daughter's hand. 'Daddy's got a plan.' He stood up, beckoned to Tamora Gool.

'Tamora,' he said to her, 'come, eat with me.' Titus breaking a savoury pie, handing Tamora a piece. He bit into the crust.

'Why?' said Tamora Gool, but took the piece of meat pie.

'Please eat. In settlement.'

'You want me to play nice. I don't think so. Never. After what you did.'

He shrugged. 'We can eat together.'

'Okay. Okay. We draw a line.' She bit into the food. Chewed, swallowed.

Titus leant forward to whisper in her ear.

III

Mart Velaze noted a police presence in the side streets. Couple of vans, the cops looking tense. Not the sort of scene they fancied.

At the gathering, kept at the back. Held a cup of tea, a plate with two small sausage rolls. He wore a suit and tie, stood with some people as if part of their circle. Surveyed the crowd: picked out Tamora Gool edging towards the Anders family where Titus sat.

He went nearer. Saw Titus rise, call over the Gool woman, offer her food. The two of them eating together.

Wondered, What's this? Titus making a peace offering? A kiss and make up? Couldn't be. Not with those photographs.

Mart Velaze bit into a sausage roll, nice porkish flavour.

Watched the tension in the group: Luc staring at the woman, his jaw clenched; Lavinia with her head down; to the side Rings, worried, shifting from foot to foot like a boxer. Only Titus with a slight smile while the woman ate. The woman nodded her head, approving of the food.

Mart Velaze finished, swallowed the remains of his sausage roll.

Saw Titus put his head close to Tamora Gool.

The Gool woman drawing back, her hand coming up to her mouth. Her eyes on Titus. She screamed. Hawked, spat out a mouthful, bent over, retching up her food. People pulled away from her.

Luc laughing.

Lavinia with her face turned to the gagging woman.

Mart Velaze seeing it in slow motion.

Rings kept up his dance, supported his lover, his hands gripping her shoulders. Tamora shaking him off. Vomiting a spew of meat pie on his shoes. Rings hopping away.

Mart Velaze saw Titus reach down, draw a pistol from an ankle holster.

The small gun in his right hand, that hand bringing the gun round to Lavinia's temple. The shot. Lavinia staggering back against the wall, sliding to the floor.

Mart Velaze jerked with surprise, slopped tea, dropped the cup and saucer.

Saw Titus sweep his arm round to point at Tamora Gool. A quick movement, decisive, the gun hardly kicking. Tamora looking up at Titus, vomit on her chin, hate in her eyes. She took the bullet in the fore-head.

Then saw Rings come in at Titus, grabbing at the weapon, the two of them struggling. Luc getting into the action, lashing a fist at Rings's head.

Bushie gangsters, thought Mart Velaze. Once and always. Heard the gun fire twice, saw Titus and Rings separating. Luc going to his father. Rings with the gun.

People screamed. Some pushed to get out, some pushed forward to see what was happening. Mart Velaze went with the exiting crowd, walked quickly to his car. Replaying the order of events. Titus went down, Rings had the gun.

He'd parked a block away. As he reached his car could hear sirens.

He ripped off his tie, sat in the driver's seat: the man had shot his own daughter. Mart Velaze phoned it in.

'Amazing, chief,' the Voice said. 'So typical of our citizens. Very tragic, shooting your own child. Like a real tragedy.' She went into one of her silent pauses. Mart Velaze drove off while he waited her out.

'You on a hands-free?' she said.

Made him shake his head. You tell her of mayhem, she asks if you're on a hands-free. 'Loudspeaker,' he said.

'Good, chief, good. Don't want the cops pulling you over. Now, listen, you've got that bag packed?'

'Like you said.'

'Excellent. Probably we're getting to the end here, chief. Just have to see what the night brings, nè?'

'You want me to do something?'

'No, nothing. Nothing to be done. Go see a movie. What's it the English say about waiting? They also serve.' She laughed. 'English people say some funny things. No, chief, nothing to be done that the night can't do for us. Tomorrow's another day, nè? Tomorrow you can check on everybody.'

IV

Krista was in the café with the line of sight to the building's entrance across the street. Perched on a stool at the long window table. The moment Mkhulu Gumede stepped out, she'd see him.

Same time as before, five ten, there he was. She didn't move, sat watching him, her head resting on her hand as she read a book. Just enough angle to keep him in view.

Mkhulu Gumede went through his routine: looked up at the sky, looked back towards the mountain, took a couple of paces along Plein Street then crossed towards the café.

Krista slid her hand further over her face. She had a beret pushed back at an angle on her head, sunglasses stuck in her hair, was wearing a T-shirt patterned in pale blue stripes, dark cargo pants, her black tekkies, nothing she'd had on before. Had ditched the backpack too, replaced it with a Book Lounge bag.

He entered the shop. If he glanced at her she couldn't see but expected he would. Mkhulu Gumede would look at every young woman. Krista tensed. She was unarmed. The gun in the car. She hadn't expected this. Had expected he'd walk down Plein to the station, catch his train home.

Did he know she was there? The words of Mart Velaze returning, Let go of Gumede. He knows about you. He's watching you. Walk away, okay. Just walk away from whatever you're planning.

Like she was going to do that.

Hearing Mace, If you start something, finish it or it comes back to bite your bum. I know.

All this advice.

When here he was, a metre from her, she could smell him: the cigarette smoke in his clothes, the faint sweetness of a deodorant. Also something minty.

Her pulse picked up, her muscles tensed.

He asked the barista for an apple Danish, a short macchiato.

'With wings?'

'Nah,' said Mkhulu Gumede, 'I got time.'

Krista thought, Oh shit. The only chair vacant the one next to hers. He moved in there, he'd talk to her.

The man slid onto the stool, placed his pastry and coffee on the long table. Ignored her. She brought her book closer to give him more space.

'It's okay,' he said.

The lead-in. She waited for the chat-up. What's that you're reading?

Wondered should she respond, You killed my friend. I'm going to kill you.

He ignored her, bit into his Danish, bringing a hand up to stop the leak of apple filling. She sensed every move he made. Every slurp at the coffee, every bite and chew.

Mkhulu Gumede, Tami's killer, sitting beside her. A detail she hadn't anticipated. Didn't alter anything as far as she could see.

The way she'd pictured it was at his townhouse. She'd ring his intercom. When he answered she'd mention the name Tami Mogale. Tell him he'd killed her. Curious, he'd buzz her up or tell her to wait there. Either way was good. If she went up, the moment he opened the door she'd put one in his eye, push his falling body backwards, close the door, walk away. Quick. Simple. A silenced .22 was like that. If he came down, same scenario except he'd end up dead on the path.

Her cellphone vibrated in her pocket. There'd been calls from Mart Velaze all day. She'd ignored his voicemails. Ignored his SMSes. Hadn't even read them. Nothing Mart Velaze had to say that she wanted to hear.

Glancing sideways she saw Mkhulu Gumede wipe his mouth with a paper serviette, take a last swallow of his macchiato. He swivelled on the stool, said cheers to the barista. Then was gone, striding out the café, crossing the street through the traffic. Not so much as a backward glance.

Krista noticed a business card next to his cup. She

picked it up: the name Mkhulu Gumede, a contact number, an email address. On the back two words in black ink: *Forget it*.

That quickened the blood to her heart.

Forget it.

She slid the card into her pocket. Didn't change anything though. But it meant he knew. A tick for Mart Velaze. A tick for her paranoid sixth sense. Wasn't going to change anything, just convinced Krista of some hidden agenda. Something sinister operating in the background. Time she had her say. Let them know there were consequences to what they did. Them: the malicious manipulators. Didn't matter how Mkhulu Gumede had figured out her plans. That he'd led her to his home. Shit. That he'd played with her like she was an amateur. Also meant he'd have no hesitation in buzzing her up. The man was all ego.

She looked into the street, down the way he'd gone: Mkhulu Gumede was nowhere to be seen.

Five minutes later, Krista left the café, walked to her car parked in the back street. Didn't matter that there were hours of light remaining, she was on the hunt. Took De Waal Drive out of the city, a slow crawl in the evening traffic. Kept Sigur Rós at high volume. Came off at Rondebosch, parked down Gumede's street with a clear view of the entrance to the townhouse complex. All she had to do was wait.

Mkhulu Gumede did not come home. Day turned to twilight turned to night.

Krista sat there. Okay, maybe he had a tracker on

her car, knew where she was. Was spinning out the game. Testing her patience. He'd pitch, though. If he knew where she was, he'd pitch. Trouble was, her advantage of surprise was gone.

Also this wasn't a scenario she'd expected. She wasn't prepared. Had some bottled water but no coffee, nothing to eat. Couldn't duck down to the Woolies Foodmarket in case she missed him. Had to sit there waiting.

At gone one she buzzed his box, hoping maybe there'd been a moment she hadn't seen him arrive. An act of frustration mostly. Mkhulu Gumede wouldn't slip quietly into his house. He'd tap on her car window. Frighten her. Her buzz going unanswered.

She went back to her car. One thing at least, the wind had died down.

Passed time listening to her messages. Among them one from Mart Velaze. 'I'm sorry about Tami.'

News got around. Nothing the spooks didn't know. She thought about Mart Velaze. A nice guy. She could talk to him. Maybe she'd even take it further. Get him out to the quarry for that shooting date. Suggest dinner afterwards, see how he reacted. She stopped herself: Jesus, what was she thinking?

Krista didn't message back.

Two o'clock she was still there.

She got out of the car. Did stretching exercises, got her blood moving. Walked fast up and down the short street. The agitation getting to her. She didn't do sitting and waiting.

In the Congo that had been her problem, day after day it felt like they were waiting. Waiting for what? A rebel attack? A rain of mortars? Another posting? Day after day nothing happened. Except she could feel a tension building. More planes flying in. More soldiers at the base. The officers telling them, Sharp eyes. The tension had given her a bad taste in her mouth.

She'd had it the day the kids rose out of the ground. Children in rags with guns. Massive automatic weapons: Kalashnikovs, French combat rifles, Russian Saigas, South African FNs. The kids standing there firing. Not running even when the patrol shot back. Even when they were cut down, the ones alive didn't run. Six kids, boys and girls, standing there shooting until they died. Krista knowing she'd exploded a girl's head. Seen another kid punched back by their bullets. Still the bastard got up to have a full go. Through the lead spray, she'd dragged the sergeant behind the drums. The sergeant telling her, Shoot them. Shoot them. Shoot them.

Which they'd done. Children not children when they're killing you.

The bad taste in her mouth. Before and afterwards.

The taste she had waiting for Mkhulu Gumede.

She returned to the Sharan, squirmed down in the seat. None too soon. A car turned into the street, stopped in the middle of the road thirty metres away, bright lights blinding her. With her right hand she shaded her eyes. Her left hand sliding across the passenger seat to grip the pistol. The car came forward, swung across the street into a driveway, an automatic gate closing. Krista steadied her breathing. Wished she had water to swill the foul taste from her mouth.

Four o'clock she thought back twenty-four hours. Twenty-four hours ago she'd been at the hospital watching Tami die. Holding her unresponsive hand to the final moment. How quickly everything had changed afterwards. How long ago it seemed. She blanked the pain of Tami's death from her mind. No point now in waiting, if Gumede returned to his townhouse at all it would be daylight. She drove home through the city streets, crisp and quiet.

The darkness was fading when Krista stood in her kitchen boiling the Bialetti. The sour taste still in her mouth. She looked through the glass doors to the patio, realised that sitting there was a figure: a big man with a bald head watching her. Mkhulu Gumede. She took the gun from her bag, screwed on the silencer. The man kept watching her. When the coffee boiled she poured herself a demitasse, drank off a scalding mouthful. Racked a load into the pistol.

It was now light enough to see his face. The black eyes watching her.

V

Transcript from the case file of Hardlife MacDonald:

I can tell you, me, I was there at the funeral for the Anders boys. I see you. I see the lady Tamora Gool. Where I stand was not close in, I stand on the edge. I know with funerals sometimes it can be funny. Not funny when you laugh, funny when people go mad. People do things. So I stand where it's easy to make a break. Me myself I didn't see what happened, not actually. From the edge there's too many people in the way. I's short. I can't see over those heads. When there was gunshots, then I went away quickly. I didn't run, I walked quietly. I had my escape plan. The cops see a running man then they gonna chase you. Back at the house I heard that three people was shot. On Voice of the Cape they say one person has connections to the Mongols. I don't know who this person is. They also say police are looking for drugs and perlemoen smuggling in connection with the shooting. When they talk about gangs on the radio they always say that. They even got the premier on the radio asking for the army to come in to stop the fighting. She says there is warfare in the streets. That's nonsense. I don't know what she means. We okay. The Mongols and the Pretty Boyz we one. Now we got Rings.

16

I

'Who're you?' said Luc.

'I'm your security, Mr Anders.'

'Sitting in here, inside?'

'They told me to.' The man rising from the sofa where he'd been flipping through a magazine. 'I'm sorry, Mr Anders,' he said. 'I heard about what happened.'

Luc rubbed under his eyepatch with his good hand. Said, 'Look, you must guard outside. That's what we agreed.'

'They told me I must check all the rooms before you sleep.'

'Okay,' said Luc. 'Do it, okay.'

'I did it.' The security man not moving.

Luc said, 'You want to make some coffee, take it outside?'

'Thank you, Mr Anders.'

Luc collapsed onto the couch. Sat with his head in his hands, his elbows on his knees. Some blood-seep in the bandage where his finger'd been taken.

II

'You mustn't come here. Why're you here?'

'Checking up, Mr Saturen. Checking everything is okay.'

'Someone could be watching.'

'No one's watching.'

'You said …'

'I said?'

'You said there was a man watching.'

'Before. But not now. Right now, he's going phata-phata with Miss Israeli.'

The two men in the lounge of Rings Saturen's Pinelands cottage. Three in the morning.

'What's it you want? Why're you here at this time?'

'Like I said, just checking. After what happened.'

'I'm fine, okay. Fine. Go, now.'

'Sorry for your loss.'

'What?'

'Your girlfriend. Tamora Gool. She was very sexy. I liked her.'

'Fuck's sake, Gumede. Fuck's sake. That animal cooked her son. Baked him in a pie.'

Mkhulu Gumede nodded. 'We didn't know that.'

'You don't know nothing. Fuck all. Tamora …'

Mkhulu Gumede stepped in close. 'She would've stuck you with a knife one day. Stuck it right in your heart.' Mkhulu Gumede stabbing his finger against the chest of Rings Saturen. Rings knocked away the hand.

'Don't …'

'I have a message to give.'

'A message.'

'Yes, a message.'

'From who?'

'Doesn't matter. From people.'

'What message?'

'We've helped you, Mr Saturen. You're the man now.'

'That's the message? What you want, Gumede?'

Mkhulu Gumede dug under his arm, pulled out a stub-nose revolver. Rings Saturen laughed.

'That's the message? You threatening me? You need me, Gumede. Without me you're in shit. No abalone. No Chinese. Do me a favour, pellie. Fuck off out of my house. Tell those people, your bosses, this's Cape Town. You don't fuck with strong bones.'

III

'What's it you want?' said Mkhulu Gumede.

'To kill you,' said Krista.

A long pause.

'Why?'

'You know why. She's dead, the woman you shot. The woman you shot here in my house. My partner, Tami Mogale, is dead.'

'I'm sorry.'

'Oh yes, sure, of course. It couldn't be helped. Could it?'

'No.'

'A necessary kill.'

'Something like that.'

'You bastard.'

'No. I am like your gun. A mechanism.'

'You will bleed.'

'Yes. But that will not be the solution, killing me. Others will come.'

'Let them.'

'You do not want that.'

'I want you dead.'

'A stupid solution. Very stupid.'

'Not for me.'

A silence between them.

'I've heard about your father,' he said.

'Everyone's heard about my father.'

'He was a hero of the struggle.'

'Maybe. He did what he did.'

'No. You're wrong. He was a hero.'

'So what?'

'So, it is important.'

She stared at him, about nine metres separating them.

'You don't want to kill me,' said Mkhulu Gumede.

'I do.'

'Like I said, it'll cause you shit for the rest of your life.'

'I'll live with it.'

'We don't like it when one of ours is killed.'

'To hell with that.'

'No.' He stood up. 'I can help you.'

She raised her gun. 'Stay there.'

'I'm armed,' he said, a silenced pistol in his right hand, dangling down.

She shrugged.

'I said I can help you.'

'Oh, sure. That's what you all say. We can help you.'

'I can.'

'Help me what?'

'Help your business.'

'You shot her.'

'She would've shot me.'

'Of course. She was protecting someone. You broke in.'

'I had to.'

'Following orders.'

'Of course.'

'Doesn't work that way anymore.'

He stood there, with the gun in his hand. Krista held her pistol on him.

'D'you know what they did to her, Lavinia?'

'I can imagine it.'

'Because of you.'

'Not because of me. Because of many other things. Her father is a gangster. Abalone poacher. It was because of that. Because of gang things and government things. And industry things.'

'The Chinese?'

'Yes, the Chinese. We do what they want. They've got the money. We've got what they want. It's called trade.'

'Doesn't matter if people get hurt? People die?'

'It does.'

'But you still do it.'

'Us. Or someone else. Better if the trade is ours.'

'I didn't mean that.'

'I know. I'm just saying.' He took a step towards her. 'Please. Please lower the gun.'

'It doesn't work that way.' Krista kept the pistol level. 'Step back.'

He didn't.

'Step back. Sit down.'

Mkhulu Gumede didn't move. Except the grip on his gun tightened.

'We have a proposal for you.'

'We?'

'My office. I am the messenger boy.'

'You come with a gun. That's a message.'

'Please. Can we talk?'

'That's what we're doing.'

'Inside.' He motioned with his free hand towards the lounge. 'Some coffee perhaps?'

'No.'

He stepped towards her.

IV

'Chief, what's the story?'

'You don't know?'

'I'm asking you, chief.'

'Luc Anders is passed, bullet in the back of the head. Shot in his lounge.'

'No place is safe.'

'Maybe there's something recorded.'

'I'm sure there is. What else?'

'I checked on Rings Saturen.'

'And?'

'He was watering his garden.'

'Watering his garden.' She laughed. 'You mean with a hose pipe. Standing there in the morning sun doing the watering? Before he has his breakfast.'

'Yes.'

'Like a good citizen. Standing there watering the flowers. That's wonderful. Amazing. Everyone's dead around him, he waters the flowers. Untouchable Rings.'

Mart Velaze listened to silence. Then: 'They need him, chief, they must need him badly to keep the Chinese happy. Yes, to keep the Chinese happy. Rings is a lucky man.'

'For now.'

'I suppose, chief. I suppose everything is for now. That's all we can say. Tomorrow we can be in deep trouble.' She paused. 'Story's over for now. Holiday time, chief. Time to relax, get a bit of R&R.'

'There's something else,' said Mart Velaze.

'What's that?'

Mart Velaze in a crouch, straightened.

'Where are you, right this moment, exactly?'

'Don't you know?'

'Somewhere on the mountain it looks like.'

Mart Velaze smiled. Not only Gumede tracking him, the Voice too. 'In a garden overlooking the city.'

'Ah, a nice view from there.'

'I'm looking at two people,' he said.

A pause before the Voice said, 'Who?'

'The one is Krista Bishop.'

No response from the Voice.

Mart Velaze looked at Krista Bishop, the single bullet wound in her chest. Her T-shirt bright with blood.

Mkhulu Gumede had taken two bullets. One in his right arm. Another in his head. The gun was in his left hand.

The way Mart Velaze read it, she'd fired first. Why had she given him an opportunity? Why hadn't she done the job with the first shot?

'Why're you there?' said the Voice.

'She was working for us, remember.'

'I told you, keep away.'

'I did.'

'This is not our scene.'

'It is. The other person works for the service.'

'Do you know this person?'

'Mkhulu Gumede,' said Mart Velaze.

'I don't know him.'

'He knew I was watching him.'

'You were?'

'He came up.'

'Wena, chief, you didn't tell me.'

'No.'

'That is wrong. Why not? That is wrong. I must know everything, chief. Everything. Who was Mkhulu Gumede? Who did he do jobs for?'

'The Hawks. Fisheries. Maybe Rings Saturen. Maybe other gangsters.'

'Shooo. You say he was with us?'

'In the local Aviary.'

Mart Velaze waited.

'No reports, chief, only verbal with me, that's best. Ai, those gangs. Those gangs are wild. I don't like the coloured gangs. They make everything messy fighting each other.'

'And here?'

'Leave the house. It is a job for the police now. Fly to your friends, chief, fly to your friends at the Dead Sea. And chief?'

'Yes,' said Mart Velaze.

'Go with the ancestors. Hamba kahle, my friend, go well.'

Mart Velaze keyed her off, knelt again, put his fingers to the soft neck of Krista Bishop. Brought up his phone, dialled an ambulance.

V

Transcript from the case file of Hardlife MacDonald:

Ja, I heard about that man found by the children in the Atlantis sand dunes. I heard he was standing up, what they call buried upright with his head out of the sand. I heard on Voice of the Cape the police say it is a gang-related killing. That is what the police always say. I can tell you I don't know about this man. I can tell you I know nothing. I know about the things I told you, the pipe bomb, the shootings, the business with the woman, also about the finger, the shooting where those people died, those things I know. Myself, I only seen this man one time. Maybe. Maybe when Rings and Tamora talk to us in the street, maybe he was there. What this business is with this man I don't know. Maybe I seen him around, maybe he was the driver for Tamora. I can say for sure I don't know for sure. There's always things happening we don't know about. You got to think of it as business. We in the gangs just trying to make a living. I can tell you that is not easy in these days.

The v&a Waterfront. Cocktail hour at the One&Only, the Sol Kerzner wonderland hotel. Approached through palm trees, it stood golden, glamorous, glitzy, the Versace look and feel. On the forecourt the high and mighty parked their Mercs, their Porsches, their Audi TTs, their Golf GTIs, headed through the columns past the smiling doormen for the Vista Bar.

Nothing to beat the view from the Vista Bar. Full-framed Table Mountain in the window. Looked out at the pool, the beautiful on their loungers, honeymooners in white towelling gowns. Around the bar celebs, CEOS, DGS, politicians, the city's movers, the city's shakers, the ganglords scrubbed up.

Titus Anders came here in his time. Baasie Basson, too, frequently. Even now Rings Saturen over there surrounded by his people, smart government congregants.

A place for business, for deals, for liaisons. The place to be seen.

Outside, at a table beneath a wide umbrella, three people easy in their chairs. Long glasses of mineral water close to hand.

Mr Yan beaming. 'We are very glad to see you again. Most grateful for your service. It is an honour to be in your hands.'

'We give our condolences for your colleague.' Mr Lijan, reaching across to take nuts from a bowl. 'And so sorry to hear of your misfortune. This was most regrettable. We were concerned for you. We are pleased to see you are healed with no problem.'

Mr Yan leant forward, placed his hands on the table. 'You

are better now? You are recovered? It is so dangerous in your job for a young woman.'

'I'm fine,' said Krista Bishop. 'Thank you.'

After months of being at what Mace called death's door. Mace having flown in from the Caymans on the turn. His daughter suddenly his only concern.

In the beginning, in the ICU weeks, her father there whenever the pain brought her round. Beside her bed reading aloud. Her father who never read.

'Actually,' he'd said when she was home convalescing, 'I get this thing you have with books. You get hooked into a story, you don't want to leave it. It becomes real. Know what I'm saying?'

Mace the doting father, a new role for him. He seemed to enjoy it from what Krista could tell. Certainly wasn't going to stop him progressing into full carer mode: cooking pretty good meals, bringing her tea, coffee, smoothies on demand.

Fussing.

'You must rest, C.' The old endearment back. 'I can't call you K, can I? Sounds like that writer you fancy. Kwetzee.' Mace hamming how foreigners pronounced Coetzee.

'Kafka.'

'Either one. Get some rest, okay? I've been through gunshot wounds. I know about them. They can be tricky, getting over them. Remember that time in the farmhouse? That guy came in and shot us all. Well, not you, thank God.'

How could she forget. Her father drowning in his own blood.

Now Krista smiled at her clients. The concern on their faces. They smiled back, relaxed as she sipped her mineral water. The businessmen on an annual pilgrimage to inspect their assets.

'We are in your complete security?' said Mr Lijan.

'You are.' Krista slid a schedule of security arrangements for their meetings across the table. 'Mostly I'm your contact,' she said. 'I'll fetch you each morning, take you to your appointments. Two of the evening runs my colleague will be driving you. That's okay?'

It was.

She could see Rings Saturen glancing their way. Repeatedly. Irritated. Eager to get the men introduced to his people. Finally, broke away from his group, headed towards them.

'Here comes your first client.' Krista gestured at Rings Saturen bowing at her clients, greeting them effusively. Ingratiating.

The thing about Rings Saturen that had changed in the last year was the smoothness. Not only to his voice, to his mannerisms. Nowadays he was leafy-suburbs hoity. He was … Krista thought, hesitating, watching the droop of his wrist as he bent to shake hands with the shorter men, oily. What Mace would call a slimeball.

'Come,' he was saying, 'come, Mr Lijan, Mr Yan, you must meet my colleagues.' Ushering them away as if Krista didn't exist. The businessmen embarrassed, raised their hands in gestures of helplessness. Krista smiled, shook her head, amused.

Watched them gather at the Vista Bar, Rings Saturen solicitous.

Krista finished her water, gathered her time sheets, slipped them into a briefcase. Was about to stand, was thinking what Tami would say, her absolute disdain for the hotel, for the people, for having to babysit men, Chinese men. A firm hand pressed on her shoulder, a voice in her ear.

'Our Mr Saturen at his best, nè, sisi.'

'Hummf. You could say so.' She snapped closed the brief-case. Said without looking up, 'That work for you, did it, Mr Velaze? Give your techies enough time?'

'No need for sarcasm, Ms Bishop. As ever we thank you.' Mart Velaze pulled back her chair, she stood. 'Nothing they say, or do, we won't hear it.'

'So much for privacy.'

'In a transparent world, no one needs secrets.' He put a hand under her elbow. 'Let's go somewhere more tasteful.'

Krista hesitated. 'Should we be seen together?' Saw Mart Velaze glance at the patrons of the Vista Bar, shrug. Smile at her.

'Why not? Just another black dude hitting on a pretty coloured chick.'